Curse of the Midnight Dragon

Book 2: The Moonlight Dragon Duology

Dorothy McFalls

Barking Dog Press

Wings.

Fire.

Magic.

That–that isn't
me. Is it?

Interior Artwork: Dorothy McFalls and Canva Pro

Cover Artwork: The Book Brander

Editor: Nicki Richards

Page edge design by Painted Wings Publishing Services

Trigger Warnings: Violence, Kidnapping, Death, Forced Proximity, Open Door Spice, Betrayals

Dedication

To those who are grieving.

Let this tale be a moment of lightness in the long
journey you're taking.

🌙⋆

Jayden Continent

Prologue

Amaya

"A malevolent magic is blowing this way."

The old woman who'd made that terrible prediction tugged at her tattered shawl until it lay snug against her bony shoulders and arms. Her movements reminded me of an automaton as she rocked in a chair by the fireplace. Her joints creaked with the movement like gears in need of oiling. She'd arrived a fortnight ago from the north during a blinding storm. No one this high up in the Andalotian Plateau knew her. And despite our urgings, she refused to offer up her name.

But since Beithir society required us to give hospitality to travelers, I'd opened my family home to her when she'd appeared at my doorstep and kept her well-fed and sheltered within the ancient manor house's walls.

Anther, my adoptive brother, wanted to turn her out after the first night. He'd said he didn't like the smell of her. As if we could smell intentions on humans. He'd started telling me that she'd already overstayed her welcome as soon as the skies had turned sunny again.

Usually, I would have heeded his advice. He had, after all, lived twenty years longer than I had. At twenty-three, I was still considered an infant. It chafed how the others treated me sometimes. Still, my adoptive parents had left the running of the family manor to me, not Anther. They should have returned months ago.

To say I was worried about their prolonged absence would understate the turmoil of my emotions, which was why the old woman's warning had sent an extra chill down my spine.

I picked up a few logs and tossed them into the fireplace. Without considering the human in the room with me, I opened my mouth and sent a stream of fire to set the new logs blazing.

The old woman's eyes widened.

"You're one of them," she whispered, tightening her shawl even more. Like that thin cloth would protect her from the heat of my flame.

I snorted, and a tiny whisp of smoke spiraled from my nose. I wasn't supposed to show who I really was in front of *humans*. But our kind had been living apart from the rest of the Jayden Continent for so long that I hadn't stopped to think about how many of my everyday actions might be considered magical.

"I've been told that dragons were nothing more than myths." The old woman coughed.

"Dragons?" I raised my brows as if to suggest I had no idea what craziness she was talking about.

She didn't seem concerned that she'd somehow found herself in the middle of a dragon's lair. *Foolish human.* "Glad to see the storytellers are wrong, child. Still, your powers don't change my words. Wickedness is blowing this way. You did me a kindness by taking me in when my old bones could go no farther. I feel a debt needs to be paid, no matter what you are." She leaned forward. "Be on alert. I fear you'll find yourself standing alone and broken before the dark times have passed."

Eight Days Later

I tied back my long, black hair with a strip of leather cording and peered over the side of the cliff. The old woman's ramblings about wicked magic must have been rubbing off on me. I couldn't shake the feeling that someone (or rather some*thing*) was lurking out in the wilderness watching…waiting. I no longer felt safe on our own land.

My fellow dragons would scold me for my hesitation. They raised me to be fearless. *I am fearless.* Creatures living in the forest below this plateau trembled at the sight of my shadow whenever I'd soar above their heads.

I shed my clothes and shifted to my true self. Stretching my long, black wings, letting them soak up the warmth from the midday sun, helped me push aside the old woman's warning.

I dove off the side of the cliff. For a moment, I felt the rush of falling. And then with a snap, my wings caught against a current of air, and I soared. I spiraled up, up, up with the sheer joy of flying.

It was my turn to hunt for the household, but the prey could wait. The deep blue of the sky called to me. The sun heated my midnight black scales as I swooped down and let the tips of my wings skim over the tops of the pine trees. I couldn't understand why anyone in Beithir would ever want to leave this village…or why my parents had not yet returned. This place, our home on the top of the plateau, was paradise.

A healthy herd of deer lived in our forest that surrounded the plateau. They belonged to our lair. I could smell them as I flew toward the Farreau River. I swooped lower, readying for the kill. A young buck would feed us well. I sniffed again.

Wait…

No…

The scent. It was wrong. Twisted.

Blood. The rancid metallic stench of blood and rotting flesh hit me like a punch to the gut. I threw my wings back and shot like an arrow out of the sky, diving toward that disgusting odor.

No. No. No. The entire herd of deer lay dead, scattered on the banks of the slow-moving Farreau.

How could this happen? Our carefully tended food source. Gone.

And under my watch.

Should I have taken extra patrols? Should I have sent scouts out to search the woods surrounding our lands after the old woman gave her warning?

But why would I have believed the ramblings of an old human? What did humans know about anything?

My fault. My fault. I was going to have to confess my failings to my parents when they returned...*if* they returned. It felt as if my entire world was ripping apart.

And the rest of the dragons. How could I face them? They always expected me to bring destruction to any task I'd been given. Hell, they were right to believe that of me since I failed every time I tried to prove the clan wrong.

I spiraled in the air, putting a halt to my sharp drop from the sky. No need to land. Dead was dead. Gone was gone. By the bitter scent assaulting my senses, the deer had been dead for more than a few days. The meat already taken by rot.

I roared my fury. The ground shook from the shock of it. I roared again, sending birds scattering into the sky for miles around. Whoever had done this to our land would die a painful death. A *slow*, painful death.

My wings beat an angry tattoo, causing me to jerk in the air, which made for a messy ascent as I turned back toward the plateau, back toward home. While I dreaded facing the others in the village with this news, waiting would help nothing. The old woman had warned this would happen. Our lands had been invaded. I hadn't smelled magic in the air, but since the kill was days old, the stench of evil castings probably would have dissipated by now.

Human hunters who occasionally wandered into our territory would kill one or two of our herd for their own bellies. They'd never slaughter an entire herd, never leave the dead to rot.

There had to be magic involved.

But why? What was the purpose of killing our deer? *All* our deer?

A blood sacrifice?

Vampires used blood in their black magics.

Our kind had escaped the vampires ages ago, fleeing our lands, abandoning our kingdom. Only the tales survived, making it feel as if the age of the fifth kingdom were a fantastical dream—a time when dragons had ruled over the Jayden Continent. History books would report that our numbers on the continent had been so great that flights of dragons would darken the sky when they had passed overhead. But the human authors of those histories were careful to note that this must be a myth, a falsehood created by superstitious humans before they developed a rational mind.

But it wasn't a myth. Dragons did once rule...didn't they? They'd ruled the continent until the vampires found a magical weapon that could kill us all. A weapon that fed on blood.

What this weapon was and how exactly it worked had been lost in the mists of time.

And yet there wasn't a dragon alive who didn't fear it. Myself included.

I needed to get back home to warn the others.

If the vampires were hunting us again—

If that happened, we were all doomed.

The plateau was speeding toward me when something foreign and fiery tore through my side. I cried out in pain and crumpled in on myself. My wings collapsed. And suddenly, I was falling, tumbling out of the air like a boulder breaking off the side of a cliff. The pine trees cruelly ripped at my scales, tore at my wings as I crashed through their canopy. I then slammed into the straw-covered ground with a bone-bruising jolt.

Each breath hurt. Poison. I must have been shot by a poisoned arrow. One tinged with that cursed blood magic. A mere arrow wouldn't have taken me from the sky. It felt like the poisoned fire that had blasted into my side was spreading, consuming me from the inside out.

"Well, well, well," a deep voice rumbled.

I peeled open one eye halfway. My fuzzy vision could barely make out a tall, shiny black boot and the end of a black cape. I blinked several times, as I struggled and failed to bring the blurred face of my attacker into focus.

A gloved hand pressed on the side of my face. "You're a young one, aren't you? But strong." He stroked the shimmering scales beneath my eye with the tips of his fingers. "Pretty, too. You'll do nicely."

I tried to pull away from him.

"Ah-ah-ah," he murmured. "Don't fight me." There was a clank of metal before a heavy cuff—imbued with so much of that blood magic that its power tunneled deep into my scales—closed around my leg. And then another. And another. And another until all my limbs were shackled. "You're mine now. You move only when I tell you to move."

"You can't do this," I tried to protest. But the world went dark as my

body shifted. Without my consent and with a fiery explosion of pain, I shifted from the sleek shape of a midnight dragon back to my soft human form.

"I can do this. And I have," he said as he wrapped his thick cloak around my naked body. He lifted me into his arms as if I weighed nothing. With a sigh, he started the long trek out of the forest.

Chapter 1

Celestina

"Vampires are conniving creatures. They'll charm you. They'll lure you with their honeyed words. You'll feel safe with them when what they are really doing is cleverly springing a trap," I would tell the four lively young princes under my care when I was a Queen's Lady in the Kingdom of Earst. Ronald, Rupert, Ryan, and Robert loved to listen to tales of the cunning vampires that had reportedly hunted throughout the Jayden Continent. Only the princes' mother, Queen Beatrice, could protect us from their bloodlust.

My days spent looking after the royal tots felt like a lifetime ago, instead of only a few weeks. Little did the queen know that when she'd enslaved me to the fearsome Beast of Fein, she'd inadvertently enslaved me to a warrior who was also a vampire prince.

Or perhaps she had known...

The queen had, after all, intended to use me as a weapon to destroy the mysterious Kingdom of Fein's army.

I used to be a Queen's Lady, and now I was a slave...and I was also a princess. A living contradiction. One in search of answers.

I hoped to find answers in an enemy kingdom located in the southern part of the continent. A dangerous undertaking, but traveling to that perilous land would be worth the risk if it meant I could stop a prediction given to me by an old seer—a vision warning me that all my newfound friends would suffer a fiery death. I would do anything, risk anything, to keep that horror from coming true, including doing something that felt rather reckless.

As the ship we were sailing in rocked on the swaying waves, I knelt on the bed in the vampire prince's cabin and, as instructed, obediently held out my hands.

"Soren?" My voice squeaked as worry tingled the base of my spine. Allowing myself to be restrained didn't seem wise. Not while alone with a vampire. Sure, I trusted him. *Mostly.* But still, it was impossible to completely erase a lifetime of being taught how conniving and dangerous vampires could be.

The corners of Soren's green eyes crinkled. The gold flecks in them sparkled. He gave me a wicked look while his battle-roughened fingers moved quickly, looping a smooth rope around my wrists several times, binding them tightly together.

"Soren?" I repeated, a breathy whisper. My heart started to race when he tied a Tiburnian hitch knot that looked as if it would be impossible to undo. "I'm not sure about this."

"Protests won't help you. Not even that adorable frown that puts those tiny creases between your pretty brows won't sway me," his deep voice rumbled. "If you want to escape, you'll need to do what I taught you." He tugged at the rope to make sure the knots were secure before stretching my arms above my head. With a sinfully playful grin, he pushed me down onto my back on the shipboard bunk we'd been sharing. He followed, laying practically on top of me.

"You have five minutes to free yourself, Princess," he purred against my lips as he fastened the ropes to a metal loop on the headboard. "If you fail, you'll be at the mercy of my teeth and tongue until you're screaming for me to stop."

His sharp fangs scraped against my neck's tender skin. I shivered and squirmed beneath him. Suddenly, I wasn't sure I wanted to win his game.

"This-this isn't fair, Soren. You're distracting me."

"If you're being held prisoner behind enemy lines, do you expect your captors to play fair?" He nibbled on my earlobe, making me squirm even more. "Do you think they'll put you in a 'distraction-free' space so you can concentrate on nothing but escaping?"

Ever since we'd boarded his brother's sleek spy schooner, sailing toward the Tiburnian Kingdom—the same kingdom that had attacked my homeland of Earst and had lured my parents into committing treason—Soren had made it his mission to instruct me on methods of defending myself.

Although he never voiced it, I could tell—in the careful way he watched my movements when he trained me in defense maneuvers and how he obsessively gave me advice—that he was deeply concerned about what might happen when we arrived in Tiburnia. *Never offer information. Never let them see fear. Show your magic only if there is no other option.*

My magic.

I still had a difficult time believing I possessed any kind of magic. In the Kingdom of Earst, only the female members of the royal family had access to magic. It was because of their biology. One had to be born into magic to be able to use it.

And yet, dragons used to live in the valley below Earst's castle. And didn't the storytellers always go on and on about how dragons were essentially the continent's earliest and purest forms of magic?

So maybe what I'd been taught about life and magic in Earst had been wr—

Soren shifted lower on the bed. His tongue grazed the swell of one of my breasts. And even though I wore a thick, black tunic that was the standard uniform for his army, the pressure of his hot mouth had my back arching off the bed.

"So not fair," I repeated, more breathless than annoyed. I tugged at the ropes binding my wrists. They were impossibly tight. There was no way I could twist out of them.

"I'm beginning to suspect I didn't think this scenario through well enough. Goddess, Sky Girl, I want you to run out of time. I want to pleasure you while you're helpless under me." His voice sounded gruff. Obviously, he was feeling as affected by this game as I was. His fingers worked the knot on my legging's ties. "And still"—his teeth pulled at my tunic's fabric, giving my nipple a tug—"another part of me needs you to win."

Liking the direction his lips were heading, I lifted my hips to make it easier for him to slide the leggings down to my ankles. My legs naturally dropped open.

"Why do I get the feeling you're not taking this training session seriously?" Soren scolded.

"Oh, I'm taking what's about to happen very seriously…as I always do, my cruel prince."

His grim expression lightened. He shook his head. "Sky Girl, your eagerness to have me explore your body is one of the reasons why I love you so much. But"—he playfully slapped my thigh—"I want you to focus on getting that knot loose. I need to know that you'll be able to keep yourself safe when I'm not around."

"I will focus. But maybe you should return your attention to distracting me, yeah?" I said, not stopping to wonder too hard why he thought he wouldn't be around to protect me. What did he think was going to happen in Tiburnia?

Thankfully, the sight of Soren's warrior body was enough to distract me from thinking too much about the future. Just running my gaze down the hard planes of his chest made my heart beat faster. His dark hair, slightly too long, hung loose around his face. And his eyes seemed to glow with desire. Desire for me. Being the sole focus of his intense concentration made tiny dragons flutter in my belly.

Gracious, I love him.

And I loved that he was steadily working that delicious mouth of his lower and lower on my body as he taunted and teased my sensitive skin with his lips. I needed…I needed…more.

I dug my fingers into his thick wavy hair.

He stilled.

Slowly, his head lifted, and his sultry gaze locked on to mine.

"You escaped," his deep voice rumbled.

"Whoops." I tried to slip my hands back into the ropes. But there wasn't enough give in them to get both my hands secured again. "I'm still your captive."

His gaze flipped to the impossible knot and back to me. "How?" His brows knitted. "How did you get loose so quickly? And without undoing the knot?"

I shrugged. "I didn't really pay attention to what I was doing with my hands. My mind was on"—I sighed—"other parts of my body. I—I'll try to get the knot undone, like you showed me, if you'll keep up with the distractions."

I wiggled my hips, attempting to draw his attention back down to where he had been heading.

"Magic?" he asked. "Did you use magic to free yourself?"

"I don't have that kind of magic," I reminded him. "My hands must be slippery from helping Patty in the kitchen."

"It's a galley," he said, his eyebrows still knitted.

"What?" I wiggled my hips again, not ready to give up playing our game.

"The kitchen on a ship is called a galley," he clarified.

"Whatever." I wiggled more forcefully. Banging my hips against his chest. "I thought we were having a knot-untying lesson, not a lecture on nautical terms." I'd lived my entire life within the walls of Earst's castle. This was the first time I'd ever seen the sea or sailed on a ship. And as interesting as all that was, it wasn't nearly as interesting as what he was about to do with those talented lips and teeth and tongue. "Sor-en," I whined.

"Right." His eyes darkened. "I do owe you a reward for getting your hands free, even if you didn't untie the knot." The timbre of his voice dipped nearly to a growl as he moved down toward the apex of my legs.

"Yesss," I breathed with anticipation.

But before his tongue could get anywhere near where I wanted it to go, a loud knock sounded at the door.

"Go the fuck away!" Soren roared to the unlucky person on the other side of that door. Or vampire. It could have been a vampire who'd knocked.

"Can't!" Gray shouted from the other side of the door. A human, then. Gray had been one of the King's Guards assigned to protect Soren. He'd given up his post to follow Soren on this quest to find my parents.

A quest being undertaken without the king's permission. In fact, the King's Guards and Soren's army had clashed as we'd escaped from

Soren's kingdom. Guilt over the deep rift I'd created between Soren and his father had threaded itself like a thorny vine into my soul. I owed Soren a great deal for helping me in my search for answers.

Gray banged on the door again. "Two ravens have arrived with letters for you. One of them is from the king."

"He's not going to go away," I said, letting my head fall back onto the pillow.

"Sorry, Princess," Soren whispered as Gray continued to bang his fist against the door. "He's as tenacious as a burrowing worm."

"Gah, I've heard of those. Don't they burrow into your—?"

"They do." Soren shuddered before pushing up to his knees. "Do you want to stay here? I could come right back to reward you for slipping out of those bindings."

"I'll come with you." I slipped back into my leggings. I was curious about what the king—who had tried to use force to keep us from leaving—would have to say to his two wayward sons.

Gray led the way from the front of the ship to its aft. (I did sometimes listen to Soren's nautical lectures.) As we stepped out onto the deck, the first thing I noticed was the icy shoreline that was now visible in the not-that-far distance.

"That's your kingdom. That's Earst, Princess," Soren said as if he'd read my thoughts.

"Somewhere, much farther inland, would be Queen Beatrice's castle, then." I wondered about her young boys. I hoped they were safe. I also wondered about the queen and what she might be plotting now.

Would she still try to use me as a weapon against the Fein? She could. No matter how much I wished for the circumstances to be different, she still held power over me.

I headed toward the railing with my gaze fixed on that shoreline. Five days ago, Soren's younger brother, Cullen, had taken two of his men in a small boat. They'd rowed through a storm toward Earst. And still hadn't returned. The rest of Cullen's crew had lowered the sails and slowed the ship's progress south as they waited for Cullen and his men to rejoin us. How would such a tiny boat find us in the middle of such a large ocean?

"Caw! Caw!"

I whirled toward the bird's angry cry to find a pair of ravens perched on the railing.

"Terrifying, aren't they?" Gray said. Seeing him cower away from the birds struck me as funny coming from a hulking warrior who was just as tall as Soren, and a bit bulkier.

Granted, the ravens did appear to be larger than usual. One tilted its head left and right as it turned its gaze toward me. Trained ravens were the favorite method within the elite of society to send mail. The shiny black birds were also rumored to be used as spies. Of course, the owners of the ravens would have to possess some kind of magic that allowed them to communicate with the birds if they wanted to use them as spies. I wondered if Soren's father had that ability. Had he sent the note as an excuse to see what his sons were up to?

Probably.

Raya, another one of the King's Guards who had defected when we'd fled the Kingdom of Fein, sat perched on a barrel at the back of the ship. She jumped to her feet when she spotted Soren.

"I told Gray not to disturb your training session. I can't imagine there's anything so urgent in either letter that an hour or so delay would make a difference." She glared at Gray.

The warrior gestured toward the large black birds. "The ravens looked like they would start pecking at us if we didn't take the letters to him. It was an act of self-preservation, Soren. I swear it!"

The vampire prince gave a half-smile that revealed one of his fangs as he shook his head. Even though Gray and Raya had once been tasked with protecting Soren, the three of them had formed a close friendship over the years. Boundaries and lines of propriety that should have been followed between a crown prince and his underlings didn't exist with these three.

Coming from Earst, where stepping a toe out of line meant having that toe literally chopped off, I found Raya and Gray's behavior along with Soren's response to them both terrifying and…well…well…wonderful. If someone had banged on Queen Beatrice's door demanding she read a message, the queen would have immediately assembled her court to make a bloody spectacle out of them. And she'd have done it by slowly chopping off body parts.

Because she was fun like that.

Yikes. I used to think that kind of behavior was normal? The queen would tell us that her actions were necessary, that her brutality proved how strong a ruler she was.

The Fein—purportedly the most violent society in all the four kingdoms—however, viewed the queen's actions as the behavior of an immature sovereign. From what I'd witnessed, the Fein treated their people fairly. And Soren, who was supposedly the most brutal Fein of them all, tolerated his friends' teasing without ripping off anyone's body parts and seemed to be genuinely loved by everyone who knew him.

Including me.

Raya scoffed before handing both letters to her commander. Soren frowned at the one from his father before shoving it into his pants pocket. The other letter, the one from his brother, he tore open. He arched an eyebrow as he read. It took a while for him to reach the end. We were all hovering, anxious to hear what his brother had been up to. From what I could see, his brother had used tight, tiny handwriting to cram as many words as possible onto the pages. Once Soren got to the bottom of the third piece of paper, he looked up at us.

"And?" Gray asked before I could.

"Cullen says he'll meet us at the dock in Tiburnia." He crumbled the pages of the letter and, still frowning, tossed the wadded ball over the railing and into the churning waters of the Winter Sea.

"What else did he say?" I asked. An uneasy feeling sank into my stomach as I watched the letter disappear beneath the waves. Why would he toss his brother's letter into the water? And what did the letter say that had him looking upset?

"Nothing worth repeating." Soren's answer came with a shrug. "Cullen loves talking about his books and research."

The clenching in my stomach eased...a bit. "I suppose," I agreed.

"That boy is an even bigger bookworm than you are, Sky Girl," Gray said, giving me a nudge.

A member of Cullen's crew, who happened to be walking by at that moment, slowed his step. Besides being a scholar, Prince Cullen also ran his father's spy network. All the members of this ship's crew worked for Cullen. The crew, unlike Soren's band of warrior friends, kept to themselves and only spoke with us when absolutely necessary.

To say they made me uneasy would be an understatement. Spending time in the company of those silent shipmen, with their ever-watching eyes, chilled me more than the frigid wind blowing off the icy waters.

The collar at my throat started to burn as the man continued to glare at Gray. Something bad was going to happen. Something the collar Queen Beatrice had secured around my neck seemed to blame me for.

"He was joking," I said quietly to the collar, not nearly loud enough for anyone to hear me.

But even so, the crewman's angry eyes jerked my direction. His lips tightened as he looked me over from head to toe.

I shivered even harder, before mentally giving myself a stern shake. I couldn't let the crewmen intimidate me.

I was a princess now. *Their* princess.

With that in mind, I drew a slow, steady breath, lifted my chin, and glared right back at him.

"Is there something wrong?" Soren asked. He'd moved closer to me. His hand already on the hilt of the dagger he'd taken to wearing on his hip. We'd had too many close calls with Soren's own warriors trying to break *the unnatural hold* they thought I held over Soren.

"I don't know," I answered, keeping my gaze locked on to the crewman. "Is there?"

"Driscoll?" Soren stepped in front of me. I didn't mind his overprotectiveness. I had no desire to be the victim of another attack or spill any more of my blood. "*Is* there a problem here?"

"No, General Kitmun." Driscoll's voice sounded oily. When we weren't on Fein soil, everyone dropped Soren's title of prince. Even when we were out to sea with no one within shouting distance, he was General Kitmun or simply Soren. "We should reach Tiburnia in two days. You may want to prepare your...bonded one...on what she might expect."

"What might I expect?" I demanded of Driscoll as I brushed away a lizard that had been trying to crawl up my boot. Hordes of the little, green creatures had somehow sneaked on to the ship with us.

"We shouldn't expect anything different than what we've encountered anywhere else we've been," Soren was quick to answer.

"Violence and deceit, then." *Oh, goodie.*

Still, something didn't sit right. Why would Driscoll think I needed to know something specific about the Tiburnians? A sinking feeling of dread returned. Soren was keeping secrets from me.

He'd done it before. More than once.

I fisted my hands on my hips and put myself in front of my stubborn vampire prince, which meant I stood with my back to Driscoll. Not the smartest move. But I admit I don't always make the best decisions when I'm about to lose my shit.

The collar around my neck sent a punishing pain down my spine. "Dammit." I gritted through the pain. "What. *Exactly*. Should. I. Expect?" I managed to get out the words despite the metal collar threatening to cut off my air supply.

Soren put his hand on my shoulder. "Be calm, Celestina."

His order struck like a thunderbolt. I jerked from its impact. My lips pressed together, and my gaze turned submissively down. At the same time, a large wave hit the side of the ship, sending me stumbling. My knees were on the verge of slamming against the ship's wooden decking when Soren caught me around the waist.

"I didn't mean that as an order!" Soren lifted me and made sure I had my feet under me. And even though I was no longer in danger of falling on my face, he kept his arms protectively wrapped around me as I reeled from the aftereffects of the collar's agony. "Fuck!"

Driscoll, I noticed, had moved closer. He prodded the metal collar I wore with his slender forefinger. "So, this is Queen Beatrice's magical slave collar? It appears quite effective at controlling your dr—"

"Celestina is not my slave nor mine to control through magical means. Queen Beatrice shouldn't have punished her for crimes her parents committed. She's my bonded partner. She's my forever, and I'll thank you not to go poking at her like she's a thing," Soren growled at the crewman.

Driscoll held up his hands. "I meant no disrespect. I was merely curious about the royal magic coming out of Earst."

"You can assuage your curiosity without putting your hands on what's mine." Soren tightened his arms around me until my face was pressed up against his chest. His warm, solid chest. A splendid place to be.

Driscoll didn't appear put off by Soren's warnings, though he did keep his hands to himself. Wise man. "How much control do you think Queen Beatrice has over her actions? Can she send commands from afar?"

"We don't know," Gray said, easing himself between Driscoll and me. "All we know is that the damned collar sometimes acts on its own to punish our Sky Girl."

"And there's really no way of removing it?" Driscoll seemed determined to peer at me like I was an exhibit in a traveling menagerie. "Good god, the metal appears embedded in her skin."

Raya, I noticed, had joined Gray. She crossed her arms over her chest and glared at the nosy crewman. "Anything involving the princess is on a need-to-know basis. And you, little man, do not need to know any of this. So, shoo."

Raya, with her high cheekbones, dark skin, toned body, and long braided hair was equal parts stunningly beautiful and terrifying. Even so, Driscoll didn't immediately leave. He seemed transfixed by the slave collar the queen had placed on me as a punishment. Raya took a menacing step toward him.

"I'm going," Driscoll muttered before turning around and hurrying back the way he'd come.

Soren rubbed his hand up and down my back. "Forgive me?" he whispered.

"Always," I said. I knew he hadn't meant to trigger the collar. He hadn't meant to command me to be calm. As the general of the entire Fein forces, giving orders was what came naturally to him. Thankfully, the effects of the collar's punishment had already started to subside. My spine no longer felt like it needed to bow. And I could take a breath without my lungs burning as if they'd been stuffed with broken glass.

I wiggled out of the cradle of his arms. The cold sea air instantly chilled me. I hugged myself, while the rough waters drew me toward the ship's railing. This was the Winter Sea. Thanks to strange currents swirling around the shore—currents that may have been influenced by magic—ice floated in the water beside our boat.

"There will be no reply to either letter," Soren informed the ravens still perched on the opposite railing. I turned and watched as the large black birds seemed to nod in understanding. The larger of the two then glared at me with its eerie yellow eyes for several more moments before launching itself into the air. With its wings beating a quick tattoo and circling the ship, it gained enough height that it was not much more than a dark speck against the bright blue sky and then headed off toward the coast, toward Earst. I could see why Gray was wary around those winged beasts. They were creepy.

"Now, princess, should we get back to that reward I owe you?" Soren asked. He'd wrapped his arms around my shoulders and started walking back toward the cabins.

Part of me wanted to say no, wanted to deny him, wanted to stand my ground and urge my prince to talk about what else Cullen had written in his long letter and to also demand he tell me about what Driscoll thought I needed to know before we reached Tiburnia. I was tired of pretending that the secrets he kept placing between us didn't matter.

But, heavens, denying him would also mean denying myself. And Soren knew how to tease pleasure from my body in a way that made my toes curl and my eyes roll back into my head. He nuzzled my neck.

Hmm...I liked that. I liked how he softened around me, how he snuggled against my body, reminding me of the furry little nennix monkeys huddling together in their cages at the traveling menagerie that would visit Earst every spring.

At the same time, Soren was still my dark, scary vampire that sent shivers down my spine. A vampire with fangs. Sure, being tied up and at a vampire's mercy had terrified me. And yet, a twisted part of me liked the fear. Liked it perhaps too much.

"I wouldn't mind feeling your fangs on my neck," I murmured my confession.

He lifted his lips from where he'd been nuzzling me. His sultry green eyes searched mine for a moment. "Really?"

Ever since I'd learned that I'd been attacked and had nearly died because of a deceit he'd orchestrated, he'd stopped taking my blood. He hadn't meant for me to be harmed. And he felt terribly guilty for it. So much so, he denied himself the power of my blood. "I've kind of missed it," I wasn't too proud to admit.

By the way he looked at me, you would have thought I'd just presented him with all the treasures on the continent. "I—" He framed my face with his strong hands and kissed me with enough passion that it took my breath away. "You, Sky Girl, make me want to slay wild beasts for you." He gave me another long, drugging kiss. "I thank all the bad circumstances that sent me to Earst. Because without them, you would have never ended up in my life."

He scooped me up into his arms and started running toward our cabin. Laughing, I let him.

Still, no matter how well his skills in the bedroom distracted me, I knew I'd no longer let him keep his secrets. Not anymore. There were too many now. Like termites in wood, they were starting to break down our relationship.

But…

After…

I'd ask him all the hard questions *after* he fulfilled his part of the bargain. For now, though, I simply wanted him hard.

Chapter 2

Amaya

I traveled for three days with the human who'd wrapped me in nothing but his dark cloak. After carrying me out of the forest, he'd dropped me onto the floorboards of a closed carriage with the windows tightly shuddered from the outside. He'd ridden with the driver, leaving me alone in the tomb-like darkness that had bumped and jolted me around on the human's rough road. He'd let me out of the carriage twice a day, once in the morning and once in the evening to feed me, let me drink a little water, and take care of my business.

Talk about the humiliation of doing *that* in front of him. For he never left me alone. What did he think I would do? Run? I could barely walk in the heavy chains he'd refused to remove from my ankles and wrists. And he hadn't provided me with clothes. All I had to cover myself was his black cloak which was too long and was starting to give off a foul smell.

"I need clothes," I told him that evening after he'd handed me a hunk of dried bread.

"That would require I remove your chains so you could put the clothes on. And if I did that, you'd transform back into your dragon and fly away. You'd likely kill me before flying back to whatever cave you call home."

I don't live in a cave, you stupid barbarian. Instead of giving away any vital dragon secrets—like where we lived—I hissed at him. Fire should have flowed from my mouth and singed off his eyebrows and maybe even some of that black hair of his. But the blood magic embedded in the metal kept me from accessing any of my powers.

It felt as if someone had hacked off my wings or an arm or—

"Please," he said as he sat on a large boulder. He pulled off a hunk of dried bread from the loaf he kept wrapped in a cloth. After taking a bite of the bread, he motioned to the space on the boulder next to him. "Sit. Eat. I don't wish you harm."

I glanced over at the carriage driver, who was taking his late afternoon meal with the horses. My captor usually ate with the driver.

"I wish *you* harm," I snarled, letting my lip curl.

"I imagine you do." He pointed to the chain and shackles on my ankles. "Hence the need for those. I wish to look at the wound on your side before we resume our travel."

I wrapped the cloak tighter around my body and glared at him. "You will not touch me."

He sighed. "I need to assess its condition. You've been moving as if it pains you. I've been told that dragons have incredible healing abilities, but I'm worried that being cut off from your magic has blocked your ability to heal. If it's festering, I have a salve that—"

"You will not touch me," I said, my voice firmer.

"If a wound like that becomes infected, you could die," he warned. "I don't wish for you to die, dragon."

That's what he called me—*dragon*.

He'd never asked if I had a name. Not that I would have given it to him. He treated me with the same care his driver gave to the horses. I was nothing more than an animal to him. A clever animal, one who could speak, but an animal, nonetheless.

I dropped the bread he'd handed me to the hardpacked ground and turned away from him. "Then I shall die."

The wound in my side did burn as if a poker from a fireplace were constantly pressed against it. I'd figured the burn was from the aftereffects of the poison he'd painted on the arrow that had pierced me. The poison had felt like the same fire. But what if what he said was true?

"I'd rather die than let you put your hands anywhere near my body."

"Very well." He shook his head before breaking off another piece of that awful bread. "At least eat, dragon."

I took the bread he offered and tossed it next to the other piece I'd dropped.

"Cling to that stubbornness all you want. We'll soon be meeting up with someone who'll make you as obedient as my carriage horses. After he gets done with you, you'll be eating out of my hand and begging for my praise. But perhaps I'll remember how you're acting now, and make you work extra hard before I give you even a crumb of kindness. What do you think of that, dragon?"

"Oh, just take a knife to my throat now, you overgrown mushroom. I'll never bend to your will." I tried to march away from him, but I'd misjudged the length of the chain linking my ankles together and tripped. I landed face-first in the pile of crumbly bread and dirt. Ohhh! The sudden movement must have ripped open the wound just below my ribcage. My side hurt so fiercely, I curled into a tight ball to escape the pain.

The man chuckled. He yanked me up by the chain that connected my wrists and pressed the tip of his long nose to mine. "We'll see how you act after my friend works his way into your mind. I wager you'll do anything for me just to get him to stop. But by then, my pretty dragon, it'll be too late. Hell, it's already too late for you. It's time you start accepting what has happened to you. I own you. I will own you until the day you die." He gripped my chin, pinching the skin between his fingers. "I worked too hard to capture a dragon to let my prize die before it serves its purpose. So, eat the damned bread off the ground like the beast you are, or I'll take Henry's carriage whip and teach you a lesson you'll not soon forget."

He shoved me, and I landed back in the dirt with a hard thud. I groaned and curled back into a ball of agony. That wound must be doing what he said it was doing…*festering*…whatever that meant. I'd never experienced such sharp pains. And since I didn't care to add more pain to my already miserable existence, I picked up one of the now soil-encrusted breads and made sure he watched as I took a bite of my gritty dinner. I ate every crumb while picturing ways I would kill the worm as soon as I managed to work my way free of these cursed bindings.

Like I suffered now, the human would suffer later. Yes, he'd die a slow, painful death. So painful he'd be crying for a release that just wouldn't come. Not until I was ready. Not until his pain erased the shame I felt for being this helpless. *Oh, yes, you despicable, ugly excuse for a human, I vow to personally see you hurt until your pitiful end.*

Chapter 3

Amaya

I woke up shivering and hot. And confused. So confused.

"She has a fever." I didn't recognize the voice who'd spoken. And I found what he'd said hard to believe. I had a fever? Me? I'd heard of those. Humans fell ill with fevers. Dragons didn't. How could I, a superior creature to humans, fall prey to a fever? "How did this happen?"

"The dragon has been unable to heal the wound she received when I shot her out of the sky. It's festering." That was *the man*. When I escaped, I planned to roast him alive and suck the marrow from his bones.

I was no longer in the carriage, though it still felt like the world was swaying around me. There was a mattress beneath me and a blanket over me. It took quite a bit of effort, but I managed to peel open my crusty eyelids. Although my eyesight was blurred, I could make out the shape of a tall black-haired man. He was dressed in dark colors and wore gold-rimmed glasses. The frames glinted in the sunlight coming through the narrow window. He must have noticed that I was watching him. His gaze locked with mine. He stepped toward me.

"She's naked, why?"

"Because I had to act quickly to secure her. The dragon's system quickly dispels the poison I used to capture her. The first dragon I shot escaped and killed the man I'd sent to carry out the task of securing it. I needed to get those bindings on her immediately. And I can't very well take them off. As soon as I remove them, she'll shift back to her dragon form and kill me."

The new man continued to stare at me. "I doubt she'd have the strength to do anything other than growl at the moment."

"With your help, Prince Cullen, I plan to nurse her back to health and get her back into her dragon form as quickly as possible."

So, this is the friend who would scramble my mind? I'll use his ribs as toothpicks. I took a sniff. He wasn't—

The room swam in and out of focus. *What was I thinking about? Toothpicks?*

"I don't know." The prince's gaze felt like it penetrated deep inside me. Like he could see all my secrets. Like he now knew everything there was to know about my family and my home. But that couldn't be right. No magic could do that, could it? "With her so weakened, I might damage—"

"You agreed," the man snapped. "I'm taking a great risk getting your brother and his dragon into Tiburnia without alerting those in the army who would wish to seek revenge against him for how he decimated our forces. And in exchange, you agreed to—"

"Yes. Yes. Very well," the prince angrily interrupted. "I'll do what needs to be done." With a sigh, he crouched next to the bed. After a silent moment, he adjusted his glasses. His brows furrowed. "What's your name?" he asked, his voice as soft and gentle as a warm summer breeze.

"Amaya." My voice cracked.

Why did I tell him that? He was the enemy, the one who'd been brought here to break my mind.

My mind is already broken. The fever seemed to have done that.

A smile creased the corners of the prince's mouth. "Amaya." I liked how my name sounded on his tongue. "A beautiful name. Doesn't it mean the journey's end or homecoming?"

"Heavenly valley." I had to work to get the words out.

"What's that?" He leaned closer.

"It means heavenly valley in the Eirid tongue." Again, why would I offer that? It must have been this fever that was weakening me, causing me to make these awful mistakes. Causing me to speak too much. At least I hadn't told him that I was named after the spring green valley not far from my family's home.

"Beautiful," he repeated. "Let me see if we can do something to help you feel better, Amaya. I'm going to lift this blanket to have a look at the wound. I won't touch you other than to care for your injury. And I will find clothes for you to wear. Do I have your permission to do this?"

"Permission?" *the man* scoffed. "She's my possession. You do what needs to be done to keep her alive whether she wants you to or not. Why don't you just burrow your way into her head now while she's weak and crack her open like an egg?"

Prince Cullen closed his dark brown eyes and drew in a couple of deep breaths before rising. Though he was a slender man, he was tall, taller than the stranger who had captured me.

"You need a weapon—*her*—for the coming war, is that not correct?"

"You know that I—"

"If I take away her thoughts, you'll have nothing. On a battlefield, she will serve as a warrior in the air. You need both her dragon's instincts and her ability to think for herself."

"I don't need that. I will be riding her."

Excuse me? He'll be doing what?

"True, but you still can't do all the thinking. Even a warhorse in the thick of battle makes many of its own decisions. And you'll be riding not a horse on the ground, but a dragon in the air, which is a thousand times more complicated. What you don't need is a useless shell. I can soften her to you, but you're going to have to do your part to convince her to help you, to work with you."

"How can I do that? All she does is plot ways to kill me."

That's the truth. And I'm going to do those deliciously gruesome things to him, too.

Prince Cullen nodded. "Perhaps that's your own fault."

"I captured her. How I've treated her afterward wouldn't change how she thinks of me. She hates me for stealing her freedom. I tried being kind and got nothing but venom."

The prince made a chuffing sound in the back of his throat before he crouched back down beside the bed again. "Do I have your permission to help you, Amaya?" Again, his voice washed through me.

"*Please*," I rasped, hating my helplessness. Hating myself for letting myself become this hurt and helpless. "*Please, help me.*"

He gave a curt nod and lifted the blanket. I closed my eyes, not wanting to see the prince's eyes take on the same leering look *the man* had given me when he'd tended to my wound. Prince Cullen almost immediately sucked in such a sharp breath that it had my eyes fluttering open. "I thought you said you'd been taking care of the wound?"

"I have! I've been putting this salve on it." *The man* held up a brown jar. He seemed to enjoy pressing the acrid paste into my wound until I cried out for him to stop. When I escaped, I was going to rip his arms from his body while *he* cried for *me* to stop.

"With an infection this deep," the prince pointed out, "a simple salve is likely doing more harm than good. I'm not even sure taking off the shackles will help her. The infection has her so weakened I suspect she wouldn't be able to tap into her magical reserves."

The man swore viciously. "I'll start a fire. We're going to have to cauterize it then, which means she'll be no use to us until the burnt flesh heals."

The prince started to say something—perhaps to agree to let *the man* make my wound worse by burning it—but after glancing at me, he stopped. "You know, I can make a tea my family cook used to make to heal my brother and me when we hurt ourselves as kids. It tastes awful. I do apologize for that, Amaya. But if you drink it, you'll feel better almost immediately. I'll need to go fetch my haversack for the ingredients. But I'll be right back."

I liked how he spoke to me instead of to my captor, whose pale skin I planned to turn into leather boots.

The prince wasn't gone long, but I missed him. How strange was that? That I missed someone I'd met only a few minutes ago. That I missed someone who'd promised to scramble my brain. Maybe he'd already started that brain scrambling. Yes, that must have been what was happening. He was already using his magic on me to soften my anger toward them.

When he returned with his bag, he set up the ingredients on a bedside table. He worked with his back to *the man*, taking his time as he prepared this special tea of his. I tilted my head so I could watch him work.

The prince had a slender nose, deep brown eyes, and a wide mouth that even now curled up with amusement.

"What are you putting in the healing tea?" *the man* asked while trying to get a look at what Prince Cullen was doing.

"Sorry, friend, it's a family secret. Mary, the cook who taught it to me, would beat me bloody with her oversized wooden spoon if I dared speak a word of what went into it." While he hid his work from the man, he didn't do the same with me. I watched with growing curiosity as the prince took a small blade and sliced it across the palm of his left hand. He squeezed his hand into a fist and held it over the pewter goblet he'd been using to mix his concoction. A steady flow of blood dropped into the goblet. He'd done all of this without letting *the man* see any of it.

"Okay," Prince Cullen said. He tucked a cloth into his hand to stop the bleeding before turning. "It's ready." He picked up the pewter goblet and, kneeling next to the bed, brought the tea to my lips. I was too weak to hold the cup or even raise my head, so he had to do both for me.

I snarled at him when he cupped the back of my head and lifted.

"Shhh," the prince said gently. "I'm going to save you, Amaya. I promise."

I coughed and sputtered, trying to expel the foul drink he was forcing down my throat. It was poison. He was trying to kill me with that thick potion. I coughed some more. The dark liquid dribbled down my chin and puddled on my neck. The stench of it was awful. I gagged and coughed some more, desperate to get it all out.

"I know it's putrid. But I need you to *drink*," he said.

The full timbre of his voice seemed to vibrate deep within my bones. *Yes, I should drink this. He's trying to help me.* My throat relaxed. And I stopped struggling against him. I swallowed a mouthful of the disgusting tea. And then swallowed some more. Once I'd finished the goblet, or what I hadn't spit out, he carefully lowered my head back to the mattress. I was panting from the effort.

"Did she get enough?" *the man* demanded.

"If she doesn't improve, I'll make another batch. But let's just give it a few hours and see if this works," Prince Cullen said. He grazed his cool knuckle across my achy forehead. "While she rests, we can find her some proper clothes. Certainly, someone at this inn can direct us to where we might purchase a dress. Dragons are proud creatures. You must treat them with dignity. Hauling her around naked was a mistake."

"She would have killed me if I'd removed those bindings. She's dangerous."

The prince looked down at me. Our eyes met, and he smiled. "Yes, I imagine she could tear us apart without exerting much effort if given the chance. That's why you wanted her, isn't it?"

"That's why I need her leashed," *the man* corrected. That was all he talked about—getting me under his control. He wanted me to fight for him.

Well, cretin, that isn't going to happen. Dragons didn't fight alongside other creatures, especially not with humans. Humans made their own messes—messes that had nothing to do with us. If they wanted to kill themselves off, well, good. We'd happily watch as they—

Wait. Wait. Wait. Wait a damned minute. What he'd said earlier had suddenly worked its way through my sluggish thoughts to a part of my mind that was actually working.

The man had said that the prince's brother had control of a dragon?

Was this crime against dragon-kind Prince Cullen's doing? Was he going around the continent enslaving dragons to fight for humans? Was this evil prince the reason my family had failed to return home? I drew in a long breath fully prepared to roast the men in the room with me.

But, of course, I couldn't. The chains and bindings kept me from doing anything other than seethe. And yet, that deep breath brought the scent of the prince, flooding my senses.

Citrus and juniper and leather and something slightly metallic.

No. No. No. Dammit. It can't be. The prince isn't human?

The man was human. Like the sausages my brother liked to make, he stank of briny water and pig. While Prince Cullen carried a scent I'd only caught on the air once before.

"Keep away from those kind," my father had warned as we'd watched a small troop of the creatures cross our land many, many years ago. *"They are mortal enemies of the dragons. It's been this way since the dawn of time."*

Prince Cullen, unlike the stupid man who'd captured me, was a vampire.

Every magical creature on the Jayden Continent could trace the origin of their magic to a mating—or multiple matings—between some non-magical creature and a dragon. Every. Single. Magical. Creature.

Except the vampires.

Their magic came from the taking of blood. A dragon's magic was a beautiful dance between the natural world and the unseen forces that flowed through everything. Blood magic was the opposite. Blood magic tore power from nature's veins. Theirs took without offering anything in return.

Goddess help me, this Prince Cullen is a dragon's mortal enemy. And I'd just allowed him to feed me his blood so he could work his perverted magic on me from the inside? I couldn't stay here. I couldn't let him infect me further. I struggled, trying to gather enough energy to fight him and *the man*, to get away. *Damn my weak human form.* My arms flailed as I tried to roll out of the bed.

Prince Cullen moved swiftly to the side of the bed. "What has upset you, Amaya? You're going to hurt yourself," he said more to himself than to me or to *the man*—the man whose eyeballs I planned to pluck out and feed to the first vultures I could find. But before I could do that, I needed to get out of this room, out of this inn.

"*Be calm.*" The prince pressed his hand on my shoulder and pushed me back onto the lumpy mattress. "*Sleep.*" His voice seemed to echo inside my head. No, not in my head, but through my entire body. *Sleep.* That one word made me feel as if a heavy weight had been pressed on top of me, and the only escape from it was to close my eyes and…start…to…drift…

"What color dragon is she?" I heard the prince ask as I sailed toward a place where I felt like I might float. It sounded as if he were suddenly speaking from the end of a very long tunnel.

"Black," *the man* answered. He, too, sounded as if he'd left the room and were miles away. But that didn't make sense, if he were miles from here, I wouldn't be able to hear him.

"Black? As in the color of the sky at midnight? That's…not…poss— er—that's interesting."

"You might not know this, living so far away from the plateau. But like dogs and horses, dragons come in different colors."

What a fool, but I already knew that about *the man*. Our colors were part of who we were, a part of what formed our powers. And I was the first midnight dragon to hatch in our lands since the Vampiric Wars.

"She could be purple with pink polka dots for all I care. What I need is your help to make my dragon into a ridable weapon."

I'm not his dragon.

"Yes," the prince said, his voice lulling me back to that calm floaty place he'd initially sent me to. "I can see how you'd want to make her that. Now, *sleep*, my unique Amaya. When you wake, you'll be healthy enough to show me those pretty scales of yours. I bet they sparkle like stars in the moonlight."

Chapter 4

Celestina

"Try to keep the tip up!" Soren shouted three days after the letters from his brother and father had arrived. A wave had smacked into the side of the sailing ship, sending me shuffle-stepping to the right in my struggle to keep from landing on my backside.

"I'm much more concerned about not tumbling over the side of the ship than the position of my sword tip," I complained while rubbing my already bruised bottom. A rude reminder of the number of times I'd already fallen.

Soren lightly tapped my neck with the wooden practice sword he wielded like an extension of his arm. "Keeping your sword tip up could mean keeping your head attached to that lovely neck of yours."

The rolling waves didn't seem to affect him. He stood there smiling at me as if the ship were sitting in calm waters while I struggled to get back into a fighting stance. *Show-off.*

The sleek, black sailing ship had resumed its swift speed now that we were no longer waiting for Cullen's return. As we neared the Tiburnian Kingdom on the southernmost tip of the Jayden Continent, Soren's training sessions had turned more serious.

Something was waiting for us in Tiburnia, something dangerous. Something Soren still refused to talk to me about. I'd begged him to tell me. I'd pouted (not my finest hour). I'd threatened, which only earned me a painful punishment from Queen Beatrice's collar. I'd even withheld my body from him, which had proved torturous to myself and hadn't lasted more than one night.

According to Cullen's spies, my mother and father weren't bad people. They'd turned against Earst because they thought they were trying to help me escape from the cruel Queen Beatrice.

I still didn't fully understand why they'd decided to act against the queen in such a dramatic fashion. Both Cullen and Soren believed I was a—

The slave collar wouldn't let me even think the word without punishing me.

Wings.

Fire.

Magic.

That-that wasn't me. Was it?

I'd been an overlooked and unpopular Queen's Lady, a handmaid who had done the queen's bidding. I'd mainly acted as a nanny for the queen's four sons. That was before I'd been given to Soren, the Beast of Fein, as a reward for him and a punishment for me. The magic both Cullen and Soren sensed on me had to be the magic Queen Beatrice had imbued in the cursed slave collar that was now fused to the skin of my neck. Only the female royals in Earst possessed magic. And while my parents held court positions, neither they nor I had any claim to royalty.

But Soren wasn't simply the Beast of Fein. He was also the crown prince of Fein and a vampire. (He should have told me those last two bits of information about himself before letting me fall deep, deep, deep in love with his warrior ass.) He believed I was a magical creature that had the ability to destroy the vampiric Kingdom of Fein...or at least powerful enough to start a war.

The King of Fein (Soren's father) considered me Queen Beatrice's "blade of death." And perhaps he was right. I could fully believe that Queen Beatrice had gifted me to Fein's battle-hardened general because she feared the strength of their army and wanted to weaken it. Or perhaps she'd discovered that Fein's ruling class and most of their population were all secretly vampires. She did like to preach to us how she used her magic to find and destroy nests of vampires.

Whatever the reason, I knew that as long as I wore Queen Beatrice's slave collar, I couldn't stay in Fein. I couldn't put innocent citizens at risk.

I hoped my mother or father could help explain my magic—*do I really have magic?*—and help stop Queen Beatrice's destructive plans.

"Sky Girl!" Patty shouted as she came running on to the deck.

The teenager wasn't supposed to be on the ship with us, but when we were sneaking away, she'd joined us, insisting we needed her to serve as our cook. And before anyone could tell her that she wasn't old enough to embark on such a dangerous quest (not that I would have been the one to tell her that and crush her teenage pride) the King's Guards had attacked. Gray had scooped her up in his arms and had run with her over his shoulder all the way to the ship.

Thanks to the huge crush she had on Gray, Patty had loved every heart-pounding second of our escape.

Gray, on the other hand—

"Sky Girl!" Patty called. "Sky Girl!"

With my sword tip held up, I twirled around in search of the danger. The ship lurched. She slammed into me, sending both of us careening dangerously toward the side of the boat. The railing wasn't nearly high enough to keep us onboard.

Patty screamed. I wrapped my arms around my friend, hoping I'd be able to grab on to something…anything before we plunged into the frosty Winter Sea.

Soren cursed, tossed aside his wooden sword, and moved with mind-blurring vampire speed. Raya also moved faster than my eyes could track. Soren's strong arm encircled my waist with such force, my feet went flying into the air. He whirled in a graceful arc that shifted our momentum and kept me on the ship. Raya snatched Patty by the arms, catching the poor girl just as she tripped over the railing. The two of them fell backwards landing on the deck.

"What the hell, Patty?" Gray shouted as he caught up to the rest of us. He yanked the girl from Raya's grasp and shook her shoulders. "You could have been killed!"

Patty, her entire body shaking, pointed into the sky.

As we all looked up, Soren's arms tightened around me.

Dragons.

I pressed a hand to my mouth.

Dragons.

Two of them.

Their leathery wings seemed to spread across the sky as they glided like clouds above the ship. A red one. And—tears sprang to my eyes—was that...was that my green dragon?

The sun glinted like gold off the green dragon's scales.

It is him! It is him! My heart sang. The echoes of the child who used to watch the dragons and dream of running away with them ached to dance around on the deck with unfettered joy at the sight of my green dragon tracking our ship.

He used to sun himself in the valley next to Earst's castle. I'd watch him and dream that he'd one day rescue me from the tower Queen Beatrice had stuck me in. And then, just recently, he'd returned to save me.

But he couldn't carry me away. The magic in my slave collar had repelled him like two magnets trying to touch their north poles together.

What is he doing here? Why is he following me?

It wasn't as if he were truly *my* dragon. Pretending he'd been mine had been a girlish daydream—a wish—not reality.

Still.

Look at him!

A smile sprang to my face.

My dragon.

He hadn't abandoned me because of this vile collar I wore.

I grinned at Soren. "He's magnificent, isn't he?"

Soren didn't smile back. All the color had drained from his face. "We need to get you inside."

Prince Cullen's creepy crewmen were flooding the deck with crossbows in their hands.

"What's happening?" I cried.

"They'll protect you." Soren grabbed my hand and tugged. I pulled back, resisting his efforts to get me off the deck.

"I don't need protection. Not from them." I gestured toward the sky. "They're *mine*. They're my dragons."

Soren was shaking his head. "What if they try to take you?" He held both of my wrists now and was pulling me toward the door that led to the cabins. "What if they try to carry you away? The collar will—"

"No!" With the same kind of slippery move I must have used to free myself from his ropes, I twisted away from Soren. I couldn't let him take me away when Cullen's men were threatening my dragons. I charged over to Driscoll, who had already raised his crossbow and seemed to be taking aim at the green dragon.

"*No!*" I used my growly voice. It was a voice I'd once used as a playful voice to scare the young princes under my care. It was the same voice I'd later learned carried a strange magic that compelled magical creatures to obey me.

Driscoll, being a vampire, was a creature susceptible to the power of this voice. He immediately lowered the crossbow.

"*Don't shoot them!*" I growled to the entire crew. "Leave them alone! Leave them alone!" At the thought that any one of those three dragons might be harmed, my growls turned to sobbing hysteria, which apparently carried no magic. The more I shouted and cried, the less control I had over the crewmen. One by one, the men started taking aim with those awful crossbows again. "Stop! Stop! Leave them alone!" How could anyone wish to harm such beautiful creatures? It was a miracle that there were such things as dragons in the world, and Cullen's crewmen wanted to destroy them? "Stop it! Stop it now!"

"Stand down," Soren called to his brother's men.

Driscoll glared at Soren, his crossbow once again pointing toward my green dragon. "I have orders to protect—"

"Stand down," Soren repeated, "or I'll take that crossbow along with the arm holding it."

For several tense moments, Driscoll kept his gaze and his aim on the dragons above us. Finally, with a muttered curse, he let the crossbow drop. It clattered as it fell on to the ship's deck.

The other crewmen, watching this, lowered their weapons.

The red dragon above us opened its mouth and roared. Fire poured from its mouth. The flames were so intense the air all around us heated up. I threw out my arms, closed my eyes, and reveled in its warmth. The heat danced like pinpricks of lightning on my skin.

Oh, if only I could join those dragons in the sky. If only I could soar with them like giant sailing ships.

"They're going to roast us!" Patty shouted.

I opened my eyes to find Patty huddled on the deck with her hands over her head. The crewmen were raising their crossbows again. Soren wrapped his arms protectively around my shoulders and pulled me snug to his side.

"We've got to get you to safety." He looked more worried than I'd ever seen him. Gray and Raya were at his side with their swords in hand.

Fire licked the sides of the ship.

"They're going to sink us!" Raya warned, her muscles tensing as if preparing to battle the dragons singlehanded. "There's nothing we can do to stop them."

Everyone on the ship seemed to be in a panic.

But me.

I didn't know why I felt this calm. It wasn't as if I had any control of the situation.

Wait. I did have a way to control magical creatures, creatures like vampires and dragons. Well, I hoped my powers worked on dragons.

"Stop." My voice sounded hoarse, nervous even. If I couldn't summon my only magical power—and fast—someone, or some dragon, might die. Not willing to let either happen, I clenched my fists and steadied my nerves. *"Stop,"* I repeated, louder this time. I used my growly voice, trusting there would be magic in the sound. Even if I didn't understand how it worked, I needed to trust that my voice would have power. *"Stop antagonizing each other."* I looked up to the sky and shouted to the dragons. *"You have to go. You're scaring my friends."*

My heart shattered when my green dragon and his companion obeyed me. Almost immediately, they altered course, turning away from the ship, away from me.

Come back.

Come back.

My heart cried at losing them for the third time. How many more chances would I have with my dragons? How many opportunities would I get to see them?

Even though they were flying away, we weren't out of danger. Fire raged on the deck all around us. It was too late. The ship would sink. And we'd all die.

The green dragon circled back around, diving low. As he approached the ship, he dipped the tip of his giant wing into the sea. With a great swish, he sent a wave crashing over the side of the boat, soaking all of us. I stood shivering in the drenching cold as the long shadow his green wings had cast over our ship lifted. The sudden return of the bright sunlight felt unwelcome and wrong. I didn't want to feel the warmth of the sun if that meant my dragons were gone.

Soren, his arms still wrapped protectively around me, muttered words in a language I didn't recognize. He was likely cursing in ancient Eirid, a forgotten language Soren's army spoke when they didn't want the enemy to understand them. He then pressed a rough kiss to my lips before hurrying off with Raya and Gray to help the crewmen bail out the water the giant wave had left behind and battle what was left of the fire that the wave hadn't managed to douse.

I started to go along with them, but then I spotted Patty still huddled in the middle of the deck, her hands covering her head. Her shoulders were shaking. Damn, she was crying.

"Patty?" I knelt next to her. I gently touched my hand to her back. "Patty? It's okay. They're gone." When her shoulders continued to tremble, I rubbed up and down her spine. "I promise. They're gone." I swallowed the sob that rose to my throat. My grief wouldn't help soothe my friend. Nor would it bring back the dragons. "They—they won't be coming back."

She lifted her head. Her face was shiny from being washed in tears. Her eyes were red and puffy. Even her twin braids were coming undone. "Truly?" she whispered. "They're not coming back?"

Knowing I wouldn't be able to answer her without starting to cry myself, I shook my head. My green dragon was gone. I'd sent him away. And because of it, I might never see him again.

She threw herself at me, wrapping her arms around my chest so tightly I could barely breathe. "Thank you. Thank you for saving us. Those dragons. They're awful. I was sure we were all going to die when they flew up to us." She looked up at me with her big, innocent eyes. "They were coming for you, weren't they? Of course they were. They want you. They want to use you. And they wouldn't care who they killed as long as they could get their talons on you."

"I'm not sure that's true. I am after all—" The collar struck. I wasn't allowed to talk about or even think about what I was. I hissed a strangled breath.

"You're not like them!" Patty hugged me even tighter. "You're—" She opened and closed her mouth as if unsure about how to explain it. "You weren't raised with them. You don't destroy on a whim like that. You're not *evil*." She whispered the last word.

Not evil.

I'd been taught my entire life that vampires were evil beasts who lived in darkness and spent all their time luring unsuspecting victims into their nests. None of that was true.

It had to be the same for Patty—what she'd been taught about dragons her entire life couldn't be true. Not my gentle dragons.

I peered around. Black scorch marks marred the deck. The sails hung in burnt tatters. And what hadn't been burned was now soaked. Perhaps the dragons had acted without thought, without caring that they might be leaving us stranded in the middle of an icy sea. Perhaps they were creatures of destruction.

"The red dragon wasn't trying to destroy us on a whim." I didn't know how I knew this. But I felt it in my bones that this was true. "He was angry about a wrong done to him. Very angry. And for some reason, he blamed us for it."

"You don't understand," Patty cried. "Dragons and vampires are mortal enemies. They always have been. Always will be."

"I'm sure that's an exaggeration. I'm sure there are instances where—"

"No!" She was adamant. "Everything is incompatible. The magic. The culture. The everything! Dragons and vampires can't be together. They always destroy each other. Everyone knows that."

I didn't.

I suddenly felt the frigid cold air that was slowly causing my soaked tunic and leggings to freeze. Everything seemed to be turning to ice. Especially my head and my heart.

Dragons and vampires couldn't be together? Was that true? The storytellers that had visited Earst rarely combined stories with both dragons and vampires. Sure, there were tales of the old War of the Magics where the vampires and dragons had nearly wiped each other out. But those stories were vague. And one always expected two warring sides to always be at odds. The humans were part of that war, and despite that, they were mating and having offspring with the dragons, creating mages and magical royalty.

Did the vampires, like the dragons, create magical creatures? Could they?

Vampires and humans lived together in Fein. Did they fall in love and bond? Was that even allowed?

"What are you two doing out here in the cold?" Gray scolded as he came back on the deck. "With those wet clothes still on, you're going to turn into icicles that we'll have to scrape off the deck." He stomped over to us, picked up Patty, and tossed her over his shoulder. "Come on, brat, let's get you inside and dried off."

Raya followed behind him with a couple of towels draped over an arm. She handed one to me and then tossed the other over Patty, who looked pleased as anything to be carried away by the grumpy warrior. Gray, on the other hand, simply looked annoyed.

Patty smiled and finger waved at me as he carried her off, presumably toward her cabin. But with Gray, one never knew. He could have been carrying her to the kitchen—*galley*—to warm herself over the oven.

"I'll help with dinner prep after I put on fresh clothes," I told her.

"In that case, I'll heat up some water for you to use to clean off the sea water and thaw out those blue fingers of yours," Raya said.

But when I went to follow them, Soren appeared at my side. He placed a hand on my arm. "I heard what Patty said to you."

"Is it true?" I asked him, suddenly desperate for him to tell me that our incompatibility was as made up as the stories I'd learned about vampires.

"Can vampires only be with other vampires? Fein is a country of vampires and humans. Do they never bond? Never mate?"

"It's not preferred, but there are joinings between the two species. For the most part, their offspring don't possess magic."

I nodded. I didn't really want to ask the next question. But seeing how I wanted him to be honest with me, the flipside would be that I needed to ask questions.

I hadn't forgotten how frightened he'd looked when the dragons had started flying overhead. They'd clearly terrified him, which meant I probably already knew the answer this time.

"Patty was right about dragons and vampires, wasn't she?" I asked. "The two are mortal enemies."

A muscle in his jaw tensed. "Yes, that part is true."

"Then what part of what she was telling me isn't true?" I asked, feeling more than a little anxious. Was our relationship doomed? He'd bonded with me, for goddess's sake. It was an unbreakable bond. If I died, he died. There was no undoing that.

"What wasn't true was the part where she said we couldn't be together." He hooked his finger under my chin. "Celestina, there's nothing in this world that will break us apart. I'll rewrite the fucking laws of nature to make sure you stay with me. I need you."

I leaned into him, and his warm, strong arms went around me. This felt natural, like I belonged nowhere else but here in his arms.

"I need you, too."

Chapter 5

Amaya

When I woke up again, I was feeling much healthier. And yet, the world was still swaying. Did I still have a fever?

I lifted my head, blinking in the nearly nonexistent light. Gradually, I realized where I was. I was back in the dark carriage, lying on the narrow bench with that putrid cloak still wrapped around me.

Had I dreamed up the fever, the room at the inn, and the vampire prince?

I growled. When I escaped, I would chop off the human's dangly bits, roast them, and force him to eat them.

"Are you still coming up with creative ways to kill those who have done you wrong, Amaya?"

Startled by the amused, deep voice that rose from a shadowy corner on the opposite bench, I lurched upright. And then immediately tightened the cloak around me.

"You." If I hadn't been holding the cloak closed with the grip of a choking vine, I would have swiped my claws at him. Only…I didn't have claws. Not on these useless human hands. I was so used to parts of my dragon form emerging whenever I needed them, that it felt as if someone had hacked my body to bits. If I needed fire, I could breathe fire. If I needed to climb, my claws would be there. If I needed to fly, I had wings. I didn't need to be in full dragon form to access my magic.

Not being able to access any of it made me feel as if someone had emptied my soul. Being locked naked in a closed carriage with a vampire who wished to do me harm left me wanting to strike out and hurt the smooth-talking vampire prince before he could put his hands on me. Before he managed to suck me dry.

If I moved fast enough and surprised him, maybe I could get the chain connecting my wrists wrapped around his neck. If I pulled with all my strength, I bet I could sever that head from his body. I seemed to remember being told once—perhaps by my brother—that the only way to kill a vampire was to remove its head. I was more than happy to try it out.

With a battle yell worthy of my fierce warring ancestors, I launched myself at the shadowy prince reclining in the corner.

Of course, the chains connecting the shackles on my ankles got in the way. I went flying across the small space. My head smashed against the carriage door, and I fell into a tangled heap.

"Is this how you thank someone for saving your life?" Prince Cullen said as he reached around my waist and dragged me up. "By doing more damage to yourself?"

I struggled like an eel. "Get your hands off me."

He set me on the bench and made a show of raising his hands in the air. "My hands are off."

I growled.

He chuckled as he settled back into his dark corner, which only made me growl more.

"I like how feral you are."

I bared my teeth, wishing they were the needle-sharp teeth from my dragon form. "Let's see how much you like it when I eat you alive."

"Oh?" He leaned toward me. "You'd do that for me?" It took me a moment to realize that he'd taken what I'd said to mean sexually.

I pulled the cloak tighter to myself. "You won't like it."

"You'd be surprised by what I like." He chuckled again, which made me want to feel the spray of his hot blood when I ripped out his throat. But since I couldn't access the necessary teeth to do the job, I turned my head toward the sliver of light coming through a crack in the shutters.

"You promised to find me clothes," I grumbled.

"And I did."

I looked down at the cloak. And then sniffed. Okay, the cloak tucked around me wasn't the human's old stinky cloak. This one was thicker and crafted from a finer material. Silk? I ran my hand over it. The heavy stitching felt intricate. I wished more light shone through the slivers where the shutters met so I could see the design.

"Being wrapped like a loaf of bread in some stray cloak you likely found in someone's rag bag isn't what I'd consider being provided with clothes."

"That cloak is mine. And I merely draped it over you while you slept because you looked cold. I expect it back."

I rolled my eyes. But it was so dark in the carriage, I doubted he could appreciate how unimpressed I was with him.

"Roll your eyes all you want, I'm not gifting you my cloak. And I did find you a dress. Had to buy it from a seamstress down the street from the inn who took one look at me and doubled her prices. So, you're welcome."

I stared down at my bare legs.

"A dress?"

He nodded.

Turning away from him, I took a quick peek under the cloak. Sure enough, I was now wearing a lightweight dress that cinched just under my breasts and flowed nearly to my knees.

"A nice one," he said. "Too bad you can't fully see how well the blue of the dress compliments your olive skin tone."

I'd never worn a dress a day in my life. "How very…human. Wouldn't have expected a vampire to pick out such a common garment."

"The human seamstress wasn't offering much in the way of choices. But I promise you, this one looks much prettier on you than the gown she'd made from a printed cloth sporting large pink and purple flowers." He leaned even further forward, propping his elbows on his knees. "Besides, the dress I purchased isn't much different from something my sister would buy."

The monster has a sister?

No matter. A sister to a monster must also be a monster.

"Dresses are for the weak." I didn't know if I really believed that or not. The old woman who was staying with us at the manor house wore a patched gown. And I didn't consider her weak. She had, after all, survived the long hike up onto the Andalotian Plateau. How had she gotten up there? And why? Was she the reason the herd had been slaughtered and I was captured? Had she been sent as a harmless-looking scout to find us?

I should have killed her.

This is what hospitality had gotten me—me and my people.

When I escaped, I planned to scorch the human's and vampire's lands. I'd turn the ground so black with cinders, nothing would ever grow there again.

Ugh! I wish I could do that now.

"I don't wear dresses," I grumbled, keeping my head turned away from the prince.

"Pants might be warmer and more comfortable, but pants would cause trouble when you had to, you know, answer the call of nature. With your wrists and ankles…" He pressed his wrists together, miming how mine were shackled.

Although he might have had a point, I wasn't going to agree with him.

"I'm told you are a—" He stopped.

I looked over at him.

"It seems impossible. Well, two impossibilities occurring at the same time seem even more impossible." He shook his head as if trying to clear away the thought. "Is it true, Amaya? Are you a midnight dragon?"

"How could I be? There haven't been midnight dragons on the continent since the Vampiric Wars. They were annihilated. The eggs smashed. The babies torched. By the vampires. By your kind."

His soft brown eyes looked large behind his glasses. "Yes, Amaya, how could this be true? How do you exist?"

"I don't. Not like you and your delusional friend out there believe," I said, leaning forward now, too. "Dragons are myths, bedtime stories created to entertain children. I'm a simple village girl from the plateau caught up in a deranged man's fantasy. Abused." I rattled the chain connecting my wrists. "Trapped."

Prince Cullen chuckled. "If only that were the truth."

"My brother will come looking for me," I warned.

Anther must be tearing apart the plateau searching for me. He would have found the slaughtered deer and scented my blood on the ground. And my wound had been bleeding and festering (like I was a human) for days. It would be easy enough for him to follow the scent trail.

It should have been easy to follow me.

"He should have found me by now," I said aloud.

"I am sorry," Prince Cullen said softly.

"Sorry?" I jolted off the bench. "Sorry?"

Did that stupid human kill my brother? Did he kill the dragons that had stayed behind in our village? Were they all dead because I'd let myself be captured? No, that buffoon couldn't have managed to do something like that. Not without a vampire's help.

Dammit. The human did have a vampire's help.

"I'll kill you!" I threw myself at the prince for a second time and managed to drag my nails through his face before he grabbed my wrists. He gave my wrists a painful twist before he roughly shoved me down to the carriage's hard floor.

With the efficiency of a highly trained fighter, he released my wrists and pressed a knee against my side, pinning me against the dirty, rough boards.

"Damn, that hurt," he grumbled.

I glared up at him, wishing I could tear his heart out of his heaving chest. Even in the gloom of the closed carriage, I could see the score marks I'd made across his cheek. Blood beaded from the four of them. I might not have been able to produce my claws, but I supposed these frail human nails weren't as useless as I had thought.

"I hope you bleed to death."

"You'll have to dig in a lot deeper than that to cause any serious damage, my pretty menace." He pulled a black handkerchief from his jacket's interior pocket and pressed it to the side of his face. "As I'm sure you're already aware, vampires are notoriously difficult to kill."

"Then I'll eat you alive."

"Ah." He lifted the handkerchief and studied the blood there. "Haven't you already promised to do that for me?"

I snarled at him.

And the bastard chuckled.

The way my captor had looked at me had made my skin crawl. But Prince Cullen didn't leer at me in the same way. Instead, he stared as if I were a puzzle he wanted to figure out. He spoke to me as if he were somewhat in awe of what I was. But that didn't mean I wasn't going to kill him.

"The reason your brother won't be able to find you is because of those." He pointed to the shackles around my wrists. "They not only deaden your magic, but they also render you untraceable."

Driven by instinct, I reached out to my clan. It was one of the powers I had that the other dragons lacked. It was a power that felt as natural as breathing. I could connect with anyone who was talking about me or thinking about me. But like all my magic, my access to this ability had been so solidly blocked, that it felt as if I'd never possessed it in the first place. "Blood magic." I curled my lip in disgust.

The cost of using blood magic was high for the user. I hoped *the man* ended up with boils on his bottom and decades off his life for what he'd done to me.

"That's right. Blood magic crafted the shackles." Prince Cullen lifted his knee. He reached down and, grabbing hold of my wrists, helped me maneuver on to the bench across from him. "Your shackles have been imbued with one of the most powerful blood magic spells in existence. And that spell is what made it possible for you to be stolen."

It didn't matter if I couldn't be traced. "My brother will be tearing up the sky, searching for me."

"I'm sure he will be. And, if he's lucky, he'll learn where you're being taken."

"Good." My clan would burn down the world to rescue me. "I look forward to the destruction that will befall you and your people for stealing me."

"My people are not stealing you."

How could Prince Cullen claim that? He was the vampire. He was the one with access to blood magic.

"Don't lie to me. You gave the human the blood magic he used to trap me, which makes you responsible."

"No. We don't—"

"Then how would a human get it? How would a human even be able to use it? I don't smell even the smallest trace of draco power on him, so he's not *from the line*."

"From the line?" Prince Cullen asked. His voice was so smooth, like silk gliding over glass. "What does that mean?"

"Those that are *from the line* can trace their roots to foolish, and unfortunately promiscuous, dragon ancestors. That's where the root of all human magic comes from. If they have magic, they're *from the line*. Related to a dragon, but not fully related."

Prince Cullen sat back and steepled his fingers below his full lips. "If dragons are no more than myths, how could this be?"

Dammit. Why was I talking so much? "What's the use? You and I both know the truth."

"The truth?"

"Oh, I'm going to enjoy picking the meat from your irritating bones. Stop pretending."

"I'm not pretending, Amaya. Yes, I'll concede that I know of the clan of dragons living somewhere on the Andalotian Plateau. It's *your* existence that confounds me. As you said, the midnight dragon line was killed off during what you call the Vampiric Wars. We call it the War of the Magics." He locked his gaze with mine. His voice deepened. "Stories have existed for centuries telling of a moonlight dragon hidden away somewhere, that this moonlight dragon would one day return to the world. But there are no such tales about midnight dragons. So, if centuries ago all of your kind died, how do you exist?"

This was a secret only a handful of dragons within the clan knew. "Not all the eggs were smashed in the war." Why did I tell him that? "Two eggs were hidden away. One egg contained a midnight dragon. The other egg held a moonlight dragon, the kind of dragon that the world likes to tell stories about. Two powerful magics—one light and one dark—kept in stasis as a failsafe if war should happen to break out again. The two dragons, when hatched, were supposed to work together to safeguard our secrets, to protect the last of our kind. And to eventually produce a new line of warring dragons, if necessary." I'd carried this knowledge all my life like a heavy cloak. At times, as a child, it felt like I would collapse under its weight. How could I be the savior of a nearly decimated race? I didn't even have the aid of the moonlight dragon. She'd been stolen away when we were only a few days old. It wasn't until I'd grown older that I learned how to trust myself, and that I wasn't alone. While the responsibility to protect my kind sat squarely on my shoulders, I had all the dragons in the clan to aid me.

Save for one.

She'd been forever lost to us. Perhaps, by now, she was dead.

"But there is no war." Prince Cullen's soothing voice reminded me of waves on the sea. "Why did the eggs hatch?"

"No one knows. It's considered a—"

I tore my gaze from his. The spell he held over me seemed to snap. *Dammit! I shouldn't have told him any of that!*

"A bad omen?" he guessed.

Yeah, that's what it was. But I wasn't going to let him know he'd guessed right.

"You used your compulsion against me. How. Dare. You."

"You wouldn't have told me otherwise. And"—he shrugged—"I was curious. I won't tell Proctor if that's what you're worried about."

"Who?"

"The human who captured you. You're telling me that you traveled with Proctor for days, and he didn't give you his name?"

"Why would he? I'm an animal to him. Do you go around introducing yourself to your horse or your dog or your dinner?"

"As a matter of fact, I do. Seems like good manners, no?"

I snorted.

"Don't pretend to be friendly to me. You could have used compulsion on the human and helped me escape. But you didn't. You're as guilty as he is."

The prince was quiet for such a long time I thought he might not respond to that. But then, in a quiet voice, he said, "You're right. I am."

Chapter 6

Celestina

Patty nudged my shoulder and giggled. We were dressed in the army's standard black tunic and matching black leggings (thankfully dry) and both standing side-by-side chopping vegetables in the ship's long, narrow galley. It was hard to believe that barely a month ago, I had no clue how to dice an onion or chop a potato or julienne a carrot. Now, my paring knife moved with an almost musical rhythm in time with Patty's as we worked our way through the small pile of vegetables that we planned to use as the base for a savory fish stew. I liked the work. It calmed my mind.

"Did you see how Gray picked me up off the deck after the dragons left?" Patty giggled again. "He's changing. He doesn't think of me as a little kid anymore."

"Do you think so?" I didn't see it. Gray treated Patty like a younger sister.

"Oh, yes. Gray finally experienced a little of the crushing worry I feel for him every time he goes into battle. Those dragons could have easily destroyed me, and it woke him up. He knows he loves me now. He must! Did you know he told me that I should never have come on to the deck with the dragons flying above us? He's so dreamy when he gets bossy like that!" Patty had a habit of speaking in exclamations. It was equal parts endearing and painful to my ears.

"I've never seen any of them frightened like that." Especially Soren.

"Like I said, dragons and vampires…" Patty shivered. "Dragons want to kill all the vampires!"

"But you're human," I gently reminded her.

"When a dragon breaths fire, a human living in a vampire-run country and traveling on a vampire-owned ship is the same as being a full-blooded vampire!"

"You do have a point there." I dumped the peppers I'd finished chopping into a large pot and started on the carrots. I'd just gotten halfway through the first carrot when a tingling on the skin of my neck had me turning my head.

Driscoll had entered the galley. He stood in the doorway with his arms crossed, watching us. His too-aware eyes reminded me of Krisp, the royal guard who used to watch me and, whenever he had found me alone, had tried to put his hands on me. I hated the feeling of helplessness that man had instilled in me. I was determined not to let another man make me feel that way ever again.

I glanced down and found that I'd completely decimated the carrot I'd been chopping. I drew a long breath and set the knife down. "What do you want?"

"We travel with extra sails," he said. "The men are hoisting them now. Despite the dragons' efforts to harm us, we won't lose much time in getting to Tiburnia."

"And you're telling me this, why?" I asked.

"What are you doing here!" Patty added. "Standing there without saying a word is creepy! You're weirding us out!" She shook her knife at him in the same way her grandmother would shake her oversized spoon to threaten people who made her unhappy. "Look around you! You're the only one not working! We're busy here! We have a ship to feed!"

"Wow," I said. "You sounded just like your grandmother."

Patty swung toward me. I had to duck to keep from being stabbed by the knife she still clutched. "Thanks!" She giggled. "She's the best, isn't she?"

"She is," I agreed. I missed Mary. And I realized Mary, cranky as she could be, wouldn't tolerate our idleness. I was about to return to chopping carrots when I noticed that Driscoll hadn't moved. "Obviously, this guy has never met Mary, or else he'd be running."

"Look. We don't trust each other," Driscoll's low voice rumbled. "But Soren's life is now tied to yours, and that's a problem."

"Only if my life is ever in danger."

He rolled his eyes in a way that seemed to suggest he thought I was stupid. "I've overheard you asking Soren about what you need to know when you get to Tiburnia. And I've overheard him not giving you an answer."

"You've been spying on us?" I fought an urge to shake my paring knife at him. I doubted a paring knife would be considered much of a threat to a nearly indestructible vampire. But the collar might think otherwise and punish me for my aggression.

"This is a spy ship," Driscoll said without any remorse. "What did you expect?"

"I expect you to treat the prince and princess of your country with respect and not listen in on private conversations." What was hard about that?

"Here's the thing, *princess*." He said "princess" with a sneer. "Prince Cullen seems to care about what happens to you. So much so, he asked me to keep an eye out for your safety. And I've been hearing things, things that will threaten that safety."

"We've been on a ship for over a week and a half. Where have you been hearing things?" I demanded.

He raised his eyebrows but didn't give me an answer. "You need to watch yourself when you visit your parents. There's a reason Tiburnia risked an entire army to attack Earst. And it wasn't simply because your parents wanted to get you away from the capricious Queen Beatrice. It was because the Tiburnians wanted to get their hands on you. They desperately want to use you."

"Use me?"

"As a weapon."

"I'm not a weapon."

"Ah, princess, but you are. I'm told you're well-versed in the continent's ancient lore. Think about it. What did those tales say about the dragons and their role in the War of the Magics? Which dragons posed the greatest threats?" Without waiting for me to respond or even react, he stepped out the door like an eel slipping free of its net.

Often when I talked about, and sometimes when I *even thought* about the dragons, the collar would punish me. But if Driscoll were telling the truth—something I wasn't convinced of—it was worth risking the collar's pain to try and figure out the puzzle he'd given me.

I'm not a weapon.

Sure, I could compel other magical creatures…vampires included. But I'd never use that magic to harm—

Oh, but that power could be used as a weapon.

I unlocked the door to the cabin I shared with Soren and let myself in. Soren was still on the deck talking with Gray, Raya, Patty, and the crewmen. While he hated court life, he loved spending time with others in the military service. Very unprincely to associate so freely with the hoi polloi. And yet, this everyman manner he'd developed was probably the main reason he was so popular among his people. It was one of the reasons I loved him. He accepted me as I was. He didn't care that I'd come to him as a slave, gifted like a trinket from Queen Beatrice's vast storerooms of junk she liked to offer visiting dignitaries.

No, even from the beginning, he'd treated me like I mattered. *Me.* Not as if I were a prize he'd won. Or a plaything for his bedroll. I was a person, just like any of the others under his command. And he treated me in the same friendly, accepting manner as he treated his warriors and friends.

Coming from Earst society, where lines of hierarchy might have well been etched in stone, and friends had to come from the same level as yourself, the thought of a general—much less a prince—acting in such a pleasant way had been confusing at first. I'd kept waiting for him to explode whenever one of his friends disagreed with him.

He never had.

That was why when I'd discovered Soren had lied to me and that lie had almost gotten me killed, it had cut me like a knife to my soul.

And now, according to Driscoll, Soren was hiding from me what we were going to face in Tiburnia. I mean, he didn't have to tell me that he was worried about going into enemy territory. I knew that by the way he insisted I train for so many hours a day in ways to defend myself and ways to elude and escape capture.

But if it was my magical abilities—and Tiburnia's lust to use it—that had him so worried, why wouldn't he tell me? In the past, we'd talked about my magical abilities without causing the collar to punish me.

But, if not for my power of compulsion, how else did the Tiburnians believe I could be used as a weapon? The power to compel others was my only magic. Not that I'd use that power to harm someone.

Of course, the Tiburnians didn't know me. Heck, my parents didn't know me very well. This had to be the troubles that Driscoll had wanted to warn me about. But if that were the case, why was Soren refusing to talk to me about it?

Was it because I'm a drago—?

The collar struck like a punch to my chest. Gasping, I dropped to my knees.

Driscoll had told me to remember the old tales. *The old tales. Those tales have nothing to do with me. Those were safe.* I pressed my head to the wooden floor planks and breathed deeply. I remembered a story about how the moonlight dragon had been stolen. The other dragons had left their cave to go hunting, leaving a hellhound to watch over their precious baby dragon. When they'd returned, they had found the dog had turned wild, vicious. And the baby dragon was gone. *But how does that story help me?*

The pain had started to recede. My head started to clear.

No, not that story. Although, it was my favorite. So heartbreaking. So filled with hope for a lonely girl. I used to pretend that the dragons who liked to sun themselves in the valley were there because they were missing me. Never did I believe that it could be—

No, don't let your thoughts go that way. I didn't want to give the collar another reason to hurt me. My body was already going to ache for at least a day from that last hit.

Focus on the stories, the ancient ones that date back to the War of the Magics.

With my forehead still pressed to the floorboards, I tried to remember the tales of the War of the Magics. Not all dragons were equal in their ability to fight. The race of midnight dragons was like Soren's warriors— fierce and deadly. The moonlight dragons were just as deadly. But, according to the stories, they weren't warriors. They were protectors.

And according to the storytellers, the moonlight dragons were the only dragons that could defeat the vampires back during the War of the Magics. That had remained true until the vampires discovered an enchanted object that helped them defeat the moonlight dragons. This mysterious object allowed the vampires to take over the lands the dragons had called home, the lands of the lost fifth kingdom.

According to some of the myths, the last moonlight dragon, with her magic of the air and night, would return from the Great Beyond. When that happened, this powerful dragon would rebuild her fifth kingdom and destroy the race of vampires.

If the vampires believed that, then they had every right to fear the dragons, especially the moonlight dragon.

An *unbeatable* moonlight dragon.

Driscoll's warning must be related to that.

Honestly, I'd never paid that much attention to the stories recounting the War of the Magics. I much preferred listening to the beautiful tales of the dragons, especially the ones that told of a moonlight dragon that glowed in the night as it flew large loops in the dark sky. She was a peaceful creature. Unless threatened, she tended to keep to herself.

The Tiburnians, after hearing these stories about how the moonlight dragon could destroy the vampires, could logically be interested in gaining control over such a creature…if my parents had told them about me. *Not that I'm thinking about that. Nope. I'm not. I'm not risking another punishment.*

I lifted my head—and holding my breath—waited for the collar to react. After several stuttering heartbeats where nothing bad happened, I released my breath. My gaze landed on the locked top drawer on the small desk in the cabin. Soren had put his father's letter in that drawer.

I wondered if he'd read it yet. I wondered if it contained a clue as to why Soren and Driscoll were so worried about my safety.

I rubbed my aching chest as I pushed up to my feet. After pressing my ear to the door to listen for footsteps in the hallway to make sure Soren wasn't returning, I hurried over to the locked drawer. Like teaching me how to untie knots, Soren had also trained me to pick locks. As soon as I mastered the skill, the two of us had then sewn lock picks into the hems of every tunic I owned.

He'd done it because he thought I was going to run into danger in Tiburnia, and it was going to be a problem…for me, for Soren, for everyone.

I pulled two metal rods free from my tunic's fabric, stuck them into the lock.

And froze.

I couldn't seem to get my hands to cooperate and unlock the drawer.

It wasn't the collar that was compelling me to stop doing what I was about to do. I would have felt searing pain down my back if it had been. It wasn't even Soren's own magic—his ability to compel others to do his will—stopping me.

It was me.

I didn't want to do this. I didn't want to breach Soren's trust. And dammit, I didn't want to risk losing *my* trust in *him*. What if I learned something about Soren that I didn't want to know?

He'd lied to me once. *More* than once. What if…?

No. Not opening that drawer was a coward's way out. That letter might hold vital information, information I needed to know. And if that were the case, I shouldn't rest until I had read what his father had written.

The letter might hold personal information about Soren's relationship with his father. What if the king had disowned his sons? What if he was sending troops after us? Those were things Soren might be reluctant to tell me. I couldn't support him with matters I knew nothing about.

Drawing in a long, slow breath, I finally managed to convince my hand to use the lock picks. With a few careful maneuvers, the drawer's simple lock clicked open. As expected, I found the letter in the drawer on top of several other official-looking papers.

I'm not here to snoop, I reminded myself as I picked up and unfolded the letter.

Unlike Cullen's three pages filled with cramped writing, the king's missive contained only one sentence:

As you predicted, Queen Beatrice is leading her army to our border in preparation for an invasion.

No animosity.

No demands that his sons return home. No mention of the near coup that had occurred when we escaped, with Soren directing Fein's army to raise their weapons against the King's Guard. No warnings about what the Tiburnians might do if we were discovered sneaking into their kingdom.

Just a statement about what Soren had predicted?

The backs of my legs hit the bunk, and, still holding the letter tight between my fingers, I sank to sit on the edge. I couldn't seem to pry my eyes off that one sentence.

No, not the complete sentence. I just stared at the first part: *As you predicted...*

The door to our cabin opened. I didn't need to lift my gaze away from the letter to know who was entering. I could tell by the cadence of his footfalls and by his delicious scent of pine and snow and caramel. The essence of him wrapped around me like one of his warm embraces. I wanted to lean into it. I wanted to let being near him be enough for me.

Don't ask questions. Don't make waves. That was how I'd survived as long as I had in Queen Beatrice's court. It went against every piece of me to speak up.

But I had to.

"It was all a ruse," I stated. There was no need to parse it as a question, no need to give him the opportunity to lie. *As you'd predicted...* The letter in my hand, although only one short sentence, had said enough. "Us fleeing the palace on this ship. Your father knew of and approved of your plans to leave Fein." I finally looked up at him. "Perhaps it was even his idea?"

Soren looked at me and then at the letter I still held in my hands. He sighed. "It was my idea."

"And the battle that raged as we ran to Cullen's ship? That was what? A show for—?"

"For you," he finished for me.

My heart sank at his words. "It wasn't a show for Queen Beatrice?" If it had been for Queen Beatrice, I could understand it. We didn't know how much Queen Beatrice could glean about the Fein through the collar. Could she see through my eyes or hear through my ears?

"It was a show for you. Why would I even think about Queen Beatrice?"

The letter in my hand trembled. "But you'd been talking to your father about this, about what your absence might mean. You clearly knew—"

"Celestina." A muscle in his jaw tightened. He'd spoken my name softly, and yet it still sounded like a warning, like I was treading into territory he didn't want me to enter.

He'd never put barriers up between us like this before. At least, none that I'd noticed.

"You made it look like we were instigating a coup," I said, still not willing to believe that the show hadn't been for Queen Beatrice. "You did it to show that Fein's power structure was crumbling. That—"

"No, that's not what happened." He heaved another sigh. "Look. I had to do something dramatic because I didn't think you would have gone through with our plan to leave the kingdom. You would have sacrificed your opportunity to question your parents if you'd thought my leaving Fein would endanger the line of succession. That's why I had my father's men chase us out."

"But this trip endangers you and everything!" I tossed the letter at him. "You should be back in Fein. You should be protecting what is yours instead of risking our lives by traveling into an enemy country. Especially if Queen Beatrice is looking to invade."

He scoffed. "My army is well trained. My officers are more than capable of thinking for themselves. They don't need me standing with them to tell them how to defend our lands against a weak country grasping for power."

"Is Queen Beatrice invading because you didn't fulfill your promise to kill me? Is this her retribution?"

"No." He seemed surprised by my jump in logic. "No," he repeated. "Remember how my father scolded me when I returned to the palace because I'd left Earst before completing the real reason my father had sent me and his army to Queen Beatrice?"

I nodded. "Your father wanted to keep Tiburnia from making a land grab and also from becoming a threat to the remaining two kingdoms. That's why he sent you and his army to assist the Kingdom of Earst. Weren't you at least honest with me about that part of the plan?"

"I haven't lied about—" He fisted his hands and closed his eyes as he drew in another long breath. "It was true, Celestina. I swear it. Plus, you were there. You saw that I accomplished that part of the plan. I'm my father's sword. And a damned good one. But I was also in Earst on a diplomatic mission. While the Kingdom of Tiburnia was anxious to push out their borders, Queen Beatrice has also been showing signs of wanting to do the same. For three years, Cullen's spy network has been reporting on her preparations for an assault on one of the other three kingdoms. But we didn't know which kingdom she was targeting. I was sent to charm her into telling us her plans. And to convince her to keep her damned self away from the Fein borderlands. But I couldn't bring myself to be charming around her, not when I was feeling furious over how she had treated you. You'd saved her fucking sons' lives and the thanks she gave was making you a slave?"

"But my parents—"

"I don't care that your parents had tried to help the Tiburnian forces. She punished you. You! Even after you put your own safety on the line to protect the royal lineage. Even after you proved to her that you stand with her. Even now, you're opening your mouth to defend Queen Beatrice, aren't you?"

I closed my mouth and pinched my lips together because he was right. Defending the queen had been so ingrained in my upbringing that it came as naturally to me as walking or breathing. It felt wrong to even listen to Soren criticize my queen.

She's not your queen anymore. You belong to Soren now. You belong to the Fein.

It wasn't that long ago when the thought of belonging to a vampire would have sent me screaming through the corridors in horror. But now, thinking about how I belonged to Soren (thanks to the collar) and how he belonged to me (thanks to his bonding his life with mine in a very public ceremony) made me feel happy. Protected. I'd found a family with Soren and his friends. I felt safe with them—a feeling I never experienced in Queen Beatrice's court.

"So, yeah, I failed in that mission, Celestina, because when I went to that damned ball of hers, all I could think of was how she'd ordered you to be tortured and then put to death and how angry I felt about that on your behalf." His green eyes sparked with anger from just talking about it.

"When she rubbed up against me and acted like I should be pleased by what she'd done to you, I had two choices. I could speak my mind and start a war with Earst or I could leave the ball. As you see, neither of those options would accomplish my father's mission."

I looked down at the letter I still held and reread the warning of an impending war. If only I'd gone looking for the princes earlier. If only I'd stopped them from putting themselves in danger in that bailey yard in the first place, none of this would have happened. Soren would have been able to charm Queen Beatrice and work out a peace agreement. And he'd be home with his family now. He'd be helping run his country.

"I'm sorry," I whispered.

"That. That right there is why I felt like I needed to lie to you. I know you, Celestina." He knelt in front of me and took my hands in his. "I know how you've been taught to put yourself last. It's so ingrained, I doubt you even realize you're doing it. Finding your parents—if they are indeed your parents—finding who you are and *what* you are is important. You're important, more important than you can ever realize."

I don't know why those words hurt me, but they felt like tiny daggers in my chest.

You're important.

Tears prickled the backs of my eyes. I desperately tried to shake them away.

You're more important than you can ever realize.

Soren tightened his hold on my hands as if I'd been trying to pull them away. Had I been trying to pull away from him?

"I love you, Celestina. I love all the parts of you, even the sneaky parts that make you pick locks and snoop through my papers." Those words hurt, too. But not nearly as much as the others.

"It's your fault, you know. You taught me how to pick that lock," I reminded him.

He smiled and shook his head ruefully. "So I did."

Chapter 7

Celestina

"It's not too late to turn back," I said, despite Soren's promises that I was important to him and that this journey was important.

Soren was important to me, too. I didn't want to put him or any of my friends at risk. I didn't need to know about my past, or if I was magical, or why my parents had aided the Kingdom of Tiburnia. I didn't need to know any of that. I could live out my days being who I've always been. Simply Celestina.

Heck, I wasn't simply anything anymore. I was a princess now. And Soren loved me. Why would I need anything else?

"Really, Sky Girl? You're going to make me repeat myself? Not that I mind. I'll say this until you finally believe that it's true. And not just because I'm saying it. But because you should feel these words and the truth of them here." He placed the palm of his battle-scarred hand on the center of my chest. "You. Are. Important." He repeated it, slower this time, "You. Are. Important. And finding out about your background, about your magic, about anything that can help us get that damned collar off you is important. Do you hear me?"

Tears clogged my throat and stung my eyes as I nodded.

He kissed my forehead. "I'll repeat it again first thing tomorrow morning if you think it'll help you remember. I'll repeat it every morning of every day of our lives if I need to."

"That might be excessive," I said.

"We'll see." He kissed my forehead again before standing. He then slipped a dagger from his boot, putting it in its proper place where he stored his other weapons. He then slipped his tunic off over his head. "Damn, it's been a long day," he said scrubbing a hand over his face. "Those dragons nearly sunk this ship. And we have no idea why."

"I'm sorry about that."

"It wasn't your fault."

"It feels like it is."

He grunted. "You know we can't talk about it. Not as it relates to you. Not without risking—" He pointed to the collar. "But we don't know if that attack had anything to do with you. It could be because of something else. Probably is because of something else, seeing how they put your life at risk."

"Are you going to tell me what that something else is?" I jumped to my feet. He'd distracted me with that pretty talk about how important I am. Then he'd taken off his shirt, which was an even bigger distraction. And it had almost worked.

Under Queen Beatrice's cruel regime, asking questions, asserting myself came with punishments and, for the unlucky ones in the court, gruesome deaths. But while speaking up always felt like a risk—even away from her court—I wasn't ready to forget Driscoll's warning. "And let's also talk about why you're so worried about taking me to Tiburnia. Creepy Driscoll came to talk to me about it while Patty and I were prepping for dinner. He gave me a hint about why I should be concerned about the Tiburnians and why they're a danger to me."

Soren stepped toward me. "He did what?"

"He told me to remember the stories about the War of the Magics and which creatures played the biggest role in defeating the vampires."

"And?" Soren asked, his eyebrows raised.

"And I did as he suggested. I thought about those stories." I crossed my arms and met him chest-to-chest. And pretended that the collar wasn't already starting to punish me for talking about the dragons. "I thought about how a certain mythical creature of the moon was a fierce protector of her fellow creatures. Now, if the Kingdom of Tiburnia, as you just said, has been looking to push out their borders, wouldn't the possession of such a fierce warrior creature help them accomplish that? With such a creature clearing the path into the other three kingdoms, couldn't they conquer the continent? Is that why they convinced my parents to help them? I bet the Tiburnians promised my parents jewels. They've always been attracted to precious stones. With a"—I gasped at the pain the collar was causing, but I was determined to keep talking about it even if I couldn't say the word "dragon"—"*mythical creature* to use as a weapon, they'd be unstoppable."

"Nearly unstoppable," Soren corrected. He wrapped his arms around me in a protective embrace. One hand rubbed up and down my back, unerringly going to the spot where the pain was the worst. And yet, he didn't scold me for insisting we talk about it. He didn't demand we stop. "But you're somewhat off the mark with your theory. The Tiburnians aren't as picky as you're suggesting. According to Cullen, the leaders of their armed forces don't understand the differences between the dragons. Any dragon will do. That they'd nearly won themselves a moonlight dragon would have been dumb luck on their part."

"Do they know the difference now?" I asked as I leaned into his warm chest.

"No. The books that talk about such things are locked away in the Palladian Central Library in our capital. And this is one reason why we don't allow outsiders access to our stacks."

"I still disagree with you hiding your vast collection of knowledge away like that. But in this case, I suppose I'm glad."

"The Fein have their reasons for not wanting to share."

"And those reasons are…?" I wondered if he'd tell me.

His arms around me tightened just a bit. He sighed. "You know the stories of vampires. How we're heartless killers. How we live in nests. How we can't walk in daylight. And how we kill everyone we feed from."

"But none of that's true." I had initially believed all those stories because I'd grown up hearing them and being afraid of what was lurking outside in the dark. And even though I'd been traveling with the Fein army, many of whom were vampires, I hadn't realized who they were because I'd been taught that vampires were heartless and that they couldn't walk in daylight. Except for feeding from the blood of other creatures—it didn't have to be from humans—the Fein did none of those things the stories had said about them.

"There's a reason those stories exist. They were created centuries ago by our enemies to make sure humans continued to fear and hunt our kind. This happened after we had fought back, after we'd created our kingdom's walls and closed ourselves off from the rest of the continent, not so we could hunt humans in secret, but to keep our own kind safe from the human hunters."

"Your enemies made the stories?" I lifted my head to peer up at him.

He was looking off into the distance, frowning. "They're gone now."

"Dragons?" I whispered. The collar sent the worst kind of stabbing pain into my lower back.

Soren swept me off my feet and into his arms. He held me tightly. "Dammit, this is why we can't talk about these things. I won't have the collar hurt you. I won't." He placed gentle kisses on my forehead, my cheeks. "I need you whole and healthy, my princess."

"But...but this is important." The pain, thankfully, started to recede. The aftereffects would linger, but it wasn't as bad as some of the collar's previous punishments. Sometimes Soren had the ability to curtail what the collar did to me, like this time. Other times, the collar seemed to take over and hurt me until I wished for it to finally end me.

"Yes." His warm lips brushed against mine. "But you are even more important. Goddess, I love how you feel in my arms." His lips closed over mine again. When his mouth lifted, we were both breathing harder. My fingers were gripping his biceps with what had to be bruising strength, not that Soren would ever complain. Or bruise. I'd never seen a vampire with bruises.

"But the danger?" I asked rather breathlessly, sounding just like a heroine in the romances I would read with my friends in Earst. "When we get to Tiburnia?"

"The danger is real, I'm afraid. Because of what your parents must have told the Tiburnians to convince them to attack Earst, it seemed to have whetted their desire to get their hands on you. We don't know exactly what your parents said, though Cullen is trying to find out. But we do know that if it's discovered you've entered their kingdom, they will do everything in their power to keep you from ever leaving. And if that happens, my options will be severely limited. If I attack or order Raya and Gray to defend you, the Tiburnians might kill you. And that…" He kissed me again with a passion that heated me from the inside out. "That would be intolerable."

"Because my death is yours, too." I hated that he'd bonded his life with mine. And I loved him for it. He'd done it to protect me and to show his parents and all the people of Fein that I was important to him.

Important.

Why was it so hard to accept that my life could be important?

"Princess, there's no world good enough that would even tempt me to want to live in it without you."

I swatted his shoulder. "Stop saying things like that."

"Why? Because you're afraid you might start to believe them?" He tossed me onto the bunk we shared, making me bounce on the thin but springy mattress. "Well, Sky Girl, that's my goal here. To keep you safe while convincing you to believe in me. To convince you that you own my soul."

His green eyes had darkened so much they were nearly black. "Since my words aren't working"—*they are totally working*—"I feel like you need some physical convincing of my feelings."

He climbed on to the bunk with me. His lips met mine. His touch was gentle. Moving slowly as if in reverence of me. *"Celestina,"* he whispered between sweet kisses. *"Celestina."*

While a gentle Soren was something wondrous, I liked it when he played rough with me. I liked it when my lips were a little swollen and bruised and my thighs ached enough to make walking and sitting a chore. I liked feeling his marks on me the next day when every movement would serve as a reminder of what we'd done, when I might sit in a chair and remember his teeth and tongue tugging on my clit. It was like getting to enjoy the sex all over again. I dug my teeth into his earlobe to encourage him not to hold back.

He groaned. *"Celestina."* While he'd never come out and admit it, I suspected he enjoyed a little pain with his lovemaking…just like I did. He bared his fangs as he smiled down at me. "Goddess, but you tempt me."

"I want you," I growled. "I want all of you tonight."

Tomorrow, we would be walking into danger. Tonight might be all we had left for us.

"I would never deny you." He lifted his wrist to his mouth and ripped at his skin with his sharp fangs. Thick red blood oozed at the wound. "Drink." His voice was a husky invitation.

"I'm not injured," I said, confused by what he was doing. I only drank his blood when I was hurt and in dire need of healing. Vampire blood had magical healing properties. When we were together like this, he drank my blood. And the effect would make me go wild with lust.

"I want you to drink for two reasons. First, my blood will heighten everything you feel. And secondly, after I get done with you, you will need the healing help my blood gives you."

I squirmed at the thought of Soren taking me so close to the edge that I'd need his blood.

"So, will you drink?" He held up his bloody wrist.

"Uh-huh," I squeaked. I wrapped my hands around his thick forearm and brought his wrist to my mouth. I licked the wound and then sucked. He groaned. It sounded deep and guttural and wild. I sucked some more of his rich blood into my mouth. It tasted metallic and sweet and like pure power. It made me feel like I might be able to glow in the dark.

"That's it, Sky Girl, take some more," he ground out.

As I drank in his blood, my own blood started to race through my veins like fire racing through dried kindling. I wrapped my legs around his thigh and bucked against him until I was wild with need.

"*Enough,*" he breathed as he lifted his wrist. No, I wanted more. I needed more. My mouth followed, my teeth biting into his skin, unwilling to let go. "This is just the beginning, I promise," he whispered before replacing his wrist with his own mouth. Like a feral animal, I bit down on his lower lip. He groaned and shifted so that he was lying on top of me. He sucked my lower lip between his with bruising strength.

I wrapped my legs tightly around his middle, still bucking my hips. I was desperate to get to the part where he was inside me. His blood had put me into a mindless frenzy. And I fucking loved it.

"Not yet, Sky Girl," he said unwrapping my legs from his middle. "We need to get our clothes off. And then I want you to take me in your mouth."

Oh, yes. My mouth watered at the thought. I wanted to taste him. I *needed* to taste him.

"But before that—" He pressed my shoulders into the mattress. He then sweetly nuzzled my cheek, easing my head to one side, exposing my throat. My core clenched knowing what would come next. He struck hard and fast. The pain of his fangs piercing my neck had my entire body jerking. He took one long pull that I felt from the tips of my toes all the way to the edges of my ears.

He lifted his head. His pupils had grown so large, they'd completely obscured the green irises. "Princess, we're just getting started." He sounded as unhinged as I felt.

While my legs were no longer wrapped around his middle and I was barely touching him, having his heated blood coursing through me and hearing the need in his voice tipped me over the edge, I came hard and fast clenching against empty air.

"We need to get our clothes off," Soren said as he pushed off the bed.

Unable to trust my voice, I nodded and followed him. I stood there, my legs shaky, as I tried not to fall over. But then again, we were on a ship. It could simply be that it was rocking in the waves.

Soren, with his absurdly steady balance, had his boots and leggings off before I could pull my tunic over my head. He helped me with my leggings, putting his hands everywhere I wanted them to be, while kissing me silly.

Soon we were both naked. But still standing.

Soren cradled my head between his rough hands as he peered intently into my eyes. "Princess, if you need me to stop anytime, if this becomes too much, just tap my arm or leg or say 'stop,' yeah?"

I swallowed hard. Would this be too much? He'd never given me blood prior to sex before. What was he planning to do to me that he thought he'd needed to do so now? My heart pounded hard against my chest in anticipation. I pressed the palm of my hands against his bare chest, not to push him away, but because I wanted to feel his light dusting of hair, and the movement of his muscles under his warm skin.

"Celestina?" He crouched down slightly so his eyes were exactly on my level. "Are you okay with me showing you how fucking much I want you right now?"

"*Goddess, yes,*" I whispered, while nodding like a ninny. I cleared my throat, but it did nothing to get rid of the raspy sound of my lust-addled voice. "*Please.*"

Soren groaned. With his eyes still trained on mine, he eased me down onto my knees in front of him. "Open your mouth," he growled.

As I parted my lips, he took his erection in his hand and stroked it several times before feeding me the entire length. It filled my mouth and started to push down my throat. I gagged and sputtered.

"You're doing so good, Princess. Breathe through your nose and take me deeper."

Tears sprang to my eyes as his cock pushed into my throat again. I gagged, but not as harshly as before. His movements were slow at first, gentle, as if teaching me how he liked me to take him. I leaned into the soothing rhythm of the in and out. It took several thrusts for me to relax my throat's muscles enough that I rarely gagged as he pressed even deeper into my throat.

He groaned and his hands fisted in my hair.

"Celestina. What you do to me. You make me…"

He pulled out and then slammed into my mouth. His hips moved faster. I had trouble keeping up with the demanding movements. But he kept pounding into me.

This. This is what I needed. His thighs rubbed against my sensitive breasts with every thrust, making my nipples pebble. Heat gathered between my legs. I wanted to rub myself against him. Against anything. But he held himself away from that part of my body as he continued to work my mouth and tease my breasts.

It was almost too much. I was going to have to tap his hip to get him to stop. Because I needed…I needed…

He jerked his cock out of my mouth. His breathing was as ragged as mine. His eyes lost to lust. He pulled me by the arms and helped me get my shaky legs back under me.

"Goddess, you make me want to explode." He ran his hands up and down my thighs, pausing at my upper thigh as if waiting for me to stop him. I sighed and leaned against his chest. Even if I did feel wary by how hard he'd worked my mouth and that he'd stopped himself before finding satisfaction—meaning he'd be just as rough with my other parts—I didn't want him to stop.

His lips touched my swollen lips, tentatively at first, and then he savored the taste of my mouth with the hunger of a man who'd been starved of affection. The intensity of his kiss threatened to overwhelm me.

"I want all your hard edges tonight," I confessed when he peeled his lips from mine long enough for both of us to get a few good breaths of air. "I *need* all your hard edges. Don't hold back any of it." I kissed him, tasting his fresh scent. He rocked his tight groin against mine while running a hand through my hair, hair that now ached from where he'd held on so tightly.

With a quick move, he hooked his hands on my thighs and lifted me off my feet. I wrapped my legs around his waist as he sank his fangs into my neck. I gasped at the sudden sting. But he swiftly withdrew from the bite. My blood dripped from his fangs as he smiled at me. "Delicious. But not what I'm hungry for."

He dropped me onto the mattress, and then buried his face between my legs. He hummed with pleasure and did a swirly thing with his tongue that had my hips lifting off the mattress. *Sweet goddess, that feels good.*

His fangs scraped me down there.

He wouldn't…

He wasn't going to…

He dug his fingers into my hips, holding me tight against his mouth as he kissed me oh, so gently. He thrust his tongue as deep as it would go. All my muscles relaxed. This…this was the best kind of torture. I could feel my core tightening as it inched ever so much closer to the edge.

His grip tightened some more. A heartbeat later, his fangs sank into my tender flesh. "Soren!" I cried out as I arched against the sudden jolt of pain. The pain was immediately replaced with an orgasm that pulsed in time with the beat of my racing heart as my blood rushed to the area.

My heart was beating erratically by the time he finally released me. He looked up and smiled so hard the corners of his eyes crinkled and the gold in his eyes glittered. "Now, that, Princess, was the fucking treat I've been craving."

I nodded, unable to catch my breath or utter any words.

"Brace yourself." He flipped me over onto my stomach. "We're not done yet. Not even close."

He settled his body behind me on the bed, using his thighs to spread my legs wider. He lined up his cock to my opening and slammed in all the way to the hilt. That was when the real fun began. His body battered mine for so long, I lost all sense of time and space. I became nothing more than a tingly sensation. And I loved every second.

"We'll be docking in Tiburnia, tomorrow," Soren said as I drifted in a cloud of orgasmic bliss on the bed. He pulled a warm blanket over both of us. "If you stay close to me and try to not fall on any swords, we should be able to get in and out safely." He gently brushed a kiss against my still swollen lips. "I…I won't let anything happen to you. I won't. I can't give you up. Not for anything, Sky Girl."

His determination to keep me safe warmed me nearly as much as the blanket. But the way he held me close to him on our bunk, like he was afraid to let me go, made me wonder if he was telling me these things because he needed to convince himself that he'd be able to protect me from a city crawling with our enemies.

Oh, goddess. We were going to be anything *but safe* when we went to visit my parents. I prayed we'd be able to get in and out of the capital city without anyone dying.

Chapter 8

Celestina

All the large cities on the Jayden Continent had built sturdy walls around them during the War of the Magics. I'd heard about them from storytellers and travel books. Some of the cities had let their walls crumble in the centuries that followed the war. Other cities had knocked the walls down as their settlements expanded beyond their ancient borders. In Earst, the castle was a veritable fortress. The village surrounding it was too small to be considered a city. And their only protection from invading forces—as recently experienced when the Tiburnian's had attacked—was to bring the citizens into the castle before the castle warden closed and sealed the portcullis. Anyone left outside the castle walls had to fend for themselves. There was no protection for the villagers' livestock, houses, businesses, or deeply loved belongings.

In Fein's capital city of Sukoon, the city walls were meticulously maintained as if the kingdom expected invaders to try and breach the thick, tall walls at any moment. And perhaps they did expect that. I didn't exactly know since Soren never talked about such things with me. And yeah, even though we'd had an important conversation last night (among doing other things), I still couldn't shake the feeling of doom that was hanging over me, making me think there might be something big I was missing, something Soren wasn't telling me that could destroy our relationship.

I stood on the deck of the ship shortly after we'd docked on the outskirts of Tiburnian's capital city. I kept trying to swallow down the dread that refused to go away. *Don't borrow tomorrow's troubles,* I scolded myself. If everything in my relationship with Soren came tumbling down tomorrow, I wouldn't regret a moment of our time together.

The rising sun glinted off the pair of golden raven statues perched on the tops of the plinths that flanked two massive iron gates. The gates were open, letting people pass in and out of the City of Ganfrid. Not freely, though. Just like in Sukoon, guards manned the gates, taking the time to speak with everyone entering or leaving.

I frowned at that. *How are we going to get inside the city without alerting the entire army that we've arrived?*

Gracious, the walls and the gates surrounding the city seemed to soar up into the sky. Palm trees that were as tall as the walls lined the perimeter. The palms were so tall and skinny, they provided little shade from the southern coast's punishing-hot sun. The spiky green fronds made loud shush-shush sounds whenever the humid breeze stirred.

A man with medium-length dark hair that had been slicked back with some kind of oil waved as he approached the ship. I glanced around me. Besides the little green lizards, which had traveled with us from Earst and then from Fein, I was the only one on the ship's deck. The man wore lightweight silks that flowed as he walked quickly toward the gangplank that the crewmembers had lowered not long after securing the ship to the dock with several thick ropes.

"Hello!" he called out, smiling broadly. *Too broadly?*

"Soren!" I called. I wasn't armed. And even if I were, I wasn't planning on taking unnecessary risks. "Anyone?" I whistled. "We have company!"

Soren popped his head out of the doorway that led to a nearby storeroom. "Be right there!"

Driscoll sauntered on to the deck. He wore no swords or any visible weapons. He'd changed out of the Fein's military uniform of a black tunic and leggings and into a lightweight white sleeveless shirt and tan linen pants that had a loose fit. On his feet he wore sandals.

I'd never seen sandals in person before, but I'd read about them in books. And those strappy things tied to his feet had to be sandals...not that I was going to ask Driscoll.

The spy nodded at me as he made his way to the gangplank.

"Oy!" he called to the man approaching our ship. "You're early."

A lizard leaped from the side of the ship onto the dock. Another followed. The man heading our way didn't seem to notice them, I was glad to see. I didn't want to be blamed for causing yet another outbreak of lizards in yet another kingdom. Not that it was my fault that the lizards had followed the Fein's army out of Earst. But knowing that didn't stop me from feeling guilty.

"If we're going to sneak inside, we need to get moving," said the man as he jogged up the gangplank. He was wearing a curved sword at his hip and had a purple paper-wrapped package tucked under his arm.

He bumped elbows with Driscoll, a form of greeting I'd never seen before. "Well met, old friend," the stranger said to the spy. "I hope the waters were good to you."

"We had a little run-in with some dragons." He gestured toward the damaged hull. "The ship is singed but otherwise unscathed."

"That must have been terrifying." As the man said this, his gaze darted in my direction. His lips formed the shape of a smile, although there was nothing friendly about the expression as he inched toward me. It was much too predatory. *Too much like Krisp's.* Never again would I let anyone get close enough to treat me that way.

So, when he moved even closer, I backed up. Quickly.

And hit a wall. Wait. There shouldn't be a wall in the middle of the deck. I pressed my palm to the wall I was leaning against and discovered that it was not a wall, but a chest.

"I've got you, Princess," Soren whispered against my hair, igniting memories of the things we had done last night. My cheeks suddenly felt like they'd been blasted by dragon fire. Just thinking of the way he'd made my body burn had my body craving more.

He placed his hand on my shoulder and gave me a gentle squeeze.

I smiled up at him, and my smile froze. "What are you wearing?" He was dressed nearly identically to Driscoll, with a sleeveless white tunic and loose-fitting tan linen pants. Only, on Soren, with his corded arm muscles on display like that, the outfit looked yummy. My heart beat double time. "You look—"

"Ridiculous," Soren said. "I know." He tugged at the tunic as if it were strangling him despite the loose fit.

"I don't know. I like it nearly enough to rip it off you," I said, my mouth starting to water at the sight of all that skin.

"Really?" Soren sounded honestly surprised. The corner of his mouth tilted up like it did when he was truly pleased by something I said or did. "Really?" he repeated.

I swallowed over a lump of lust and nodded. With the memories of last night's passion still so freshly marked on my skin, I found myself wanting to pull him back to our cabin and spend the day there with him instead of undertaking this risky trip into an enemy city to talk to my traitor parents.

"Well then," he said, standing even straighter. "I suppose the Tiburnian fashions do serve a purpose." He waggled his eyebrows.

"We're wearing these clothes," Gray said as he emerged from that little storeroom dressed identically to Soren, "because we need to blend in with the locals."

The man who'd come aboard the ship cleared his throat. "General Kitmun," he said and thrust out his hand to Soren. "I'm so pleased to finally meet a warrior as accomplished as you are. Your brother has spoken about you. I'm Captain Proctor."

Soren glanced at the man's outstretched hand but didn't take it. I almost kicked Soren in the shin for insulting the captain by refusing to shake his hand. I *would have* kicked him if I didn't think doing so would make Soren look weak in front of our enemy. Soren often lamented how he never knew how to handle situations that required any sort of diplomacy. He'd much rather swing his sword than chit-chat with politicians. And this man, despite his status as "captain" held himself with an arrogant cock of his head and overly decorated clothing, reminding me of the arrogant courtiers that filled Queen Beatrice's court—the ones who would sell their own children if it meant gaining more influence.

I started to speak up for Soren—I'd had enough experience as a Queen's Lady to know how to play the political game of words—but Captain Proctor spoke before I could.

"My goodness," he said as he lowered his outstretched hand and closed it into a fist at his side. His gaze had returned to stare at me as if I were a treat for his taking. "Your dragon is as tame as a kitten, isn't she? She lets you touch her and…more, I see." I blushed as I felt his gaze zero in on the bruises and bites lining my neck. "I envy you of that."

Soren's fingers tightened where they gripped my shoulder, but he didn't rebuke the man. I supposed he had to hold back because Captain Proctor was the one tasked with getting Soren, Gray, Raya, and me past the guards, into the city, and to where my parents now lived.

Patty had fumed earlier, but both Gray and Soren had insisted the teen stay onboard the ship with Cullen's spooky—and quite probably deadly—spy crewmen.

The captain licked his lips. "Here." He handed Soren the package that had been tucked under his arm. "Have the dragon put this on. It's standard wear for a woman of high status. And you said another woman is accompanying us?" He looked around as if he might find Raya lurking behind one of the singed masts. "I included a second dress for your other companion."

Soren's eyes narrowed. "Where's my brother? He was supposed to meet us here at the docks."

The captain tilted his head to one side. "Was he?" He shook his head. "He got tied up with that side project he's doing for me in exchange for my help here. It's been a real challenge. He said he'd try to meet up with you at the Vacker's home." He attempted again to hand Soren the package. "We need to get through the gates before the guards' shift changes. Which means we need to hurry."

This time Soren accepted the paper-wrapped package. "We'll be ready in ten minutes."

Soren accompanied me to the small storeroom, with Gray covering our flank. "I don't like him," I said. "How can we trust him? He'll sell us to the first royal he finds."

I wanted to stop this mad scheme. The more I thought about it, the more convinced I became that this was a terrible idea. The risk was simply too great.

"Both Cullen and Driscoll have used Captain Proctor for this purpose several times before," Soren said. "And Cullen is doing the captain a huge favor right now, which means the captain owes us."

"Is that what Cullen wrote about in his letter?" I asked. The letter that was probably in the belly of a large fish.

"Partly," he answered. "You know Cullen. He goes on and on about so many things."

Raya was waiting for us in the storeroom. Soren handed her the package.

"Your clothes," he said as he stopped before stepping through the doorway. "Gray and I will be waiting outside the door. Don't take too long. The Tiburnian man says we have a schedule to keep."

"We'll try our best," Raya said. "But, sometimes, beauty can't be rushed." She flicked her long braid over her shoulder.

"Rush it today," Soren snapped and closed the door.

"Testy." Raya tsked. "You'd think he'd be in a better mood after the workout the two of you had last night."

My face heated. "I don't know what you mean."

Raya nudged my shoulder with hers and laughed. "Liar. You know exactly what I mean. The two of you weren't even trying to be quiet. Even with the noise of the wind and the sea, I could hear you…um…enjoying yourselves."

I buried my face in my hands and groaned. "Goddess. Your cabin isn't anywhere near ours. Everyone must have heard. Including that awful Driscoll."

"Even him." Raya laughed again. "Don't worry about it. You're with the prince. No one will dare question your unbridled lust for him."

"You're not helping!"

"I know." She gave me a smile that showed off her vampire fangs before ripping open the paper package. "Now, let's see what we have to wear."

The fabric that slithered out of the package couldn't be right. For one thing, there wasn't enough of it to make one dress, much less two. And for another, the pale pink fabric was so thin, it looked like it would tear in a stiff breeze.

"Oh no," Raya said, pushing the fabric at me. "I'm not wearing that."

"But the captain said this was what women in Tiburnia wear," I countered, not yet able to figure out how the slippery fabric bundle formed a full dress. I held one of the pieces of fabric up and gave it a little shake. "This can't be right. It's not long enough to cover…anything."

"Luckily, I came prepared." Raya grabbed her leather travel bag and dug around in it until she pulled out a silky, light blue dress with a swirling design in various shades of blue. "This came from a trader who said he picked up the dress in a port near here. It'll be close enough."

I peered into her leather bag. "You don't happen to have another one of those dresses in there, do you?" While the fabric was the same lightweight quality and lacked any covering for the arms, at least hers covered her legs.

"Sorry, Sky Girl. I just have the one dress. You're going to have to wear one of those."

"Maybe I can wear both at the same time?" I held the two flimsy dresses up against my body as if they were patches from a patchwork quilt. "One to cover my legs and another for my torso?"

There was a sharp knock on the door. "Are you almost done in there?" Gray shouted. "You've been taking forever."

"We've only been but a minute!" Raya shouted back. She then lowered her voice. "We do need to blend in with the locals if we're going to get in and out of Ganfrid unnoticed. Here, let me help you with the dress. I've seen women wearing clothing cut like this before. And it can be a lovely look…even if there's not nearly enough of it."

Raya and I both managed to get dressed and braid our hair in the style Raya said she'd seen Tiburnian women wearing. The braids circled around into a pair of big hoops that ultimately formed crowns on the tops of our heads. It felt odd but wasn't unattractive when I peered into the mirror Raya had found in that leather travel bag of hers.

The dress, on the other hand, was another story. It was too sheer! And too short! I kept tugging on the hem to make certain my bottom wasn't on display for anyone walking behind me.

When we exited the storeroom, Soren took a hasty step toward me. He stopped himself and swallowed hard.

"Sky Girl…that dress…" His voice sounded rough.

"It's ridiculous," I finished for him, echoing what he'd said earlier about his outfit. "And indecent." Certainly, he wouldn't want his bonded partner walking through a city dressed this way. Surely, he'd help me find something better to wear.

"It's…" He shook his head. His eyes darkened. "Goddess, that dress makes me want to toss you over my shoulder and take you back to our cabin."

"Not again." Gray groaned. "We already lost a night of sleep because you can't keep your hands off our princess."

"What can I say?" Soren didn't sound or look the least bit embarrassed. "She's addictive."

Gray tossed his arm around Soren's shoulder. "Never thought I'd see the day you'd fall so hard for someone." He slapped Soren's chest and backed off. "It's disgusting."

Soren chuckled. "We can't wear swords when walking through the streets. But are we adequately armed?"

Raya tapped her thigh. "That's why I had to bring my own summer dress."

"I have a short sword and a couple of daggers," Gray said.

"Really? Where?" Raya eyed Gray up and down.

"A guy's gotta keep his secrets." Gray winked at Raya. She punched his arm. And the two of them headed over to where Captain Proctor was chatting with Driscoll while waiting for us.

When Gray walked away, I squinted at him. As a human in a vampire army, he tended to carry more weapons than his preternaturally stronger counterparts. But I couldn't discern an outline of a dagger or a sword anywhere beneath his lightweight clothes.

Soren hooked his arm with mine. "His sword collapses into the size of a dagger," he said, answering my unasked question.

"Are you sure you can't read minds?" I asked, not for the first time.

"Wouldn't that be useful?" he said. "Now, let's get this reunion with your parents over with, so I can enjoy that dress of yours in private."

I shivered at the thought. "Quietly, though."

"But I like it when you scream for me, Sky Girl."

Chapter 9

Amaya

Magic is a strange and beautiful power. Like the air around us, it flows through every living being, providing one of the necessary substances for life. Dragons were the first to be gifted with magic. Others, like vampires, wrenched control of the world's magical currents in an unnatural way.

Through blood.

Blood magic taints and corrupts all it touches. Thanks to the blood-enchanted shackles digging into my wrists and ankles, I could feel its corruption burrowing into my soul. I needed to get them off before the damage became irreparable. *The man* had taken me to his southern lands. Tiburnia, he'd called it. The dragons had a different name for the land below our Andalotian Plateau—the Torrere, or burnt sands, Desert.

I supposed I should have been grateful that *the man* had stashed me in a dungeon beneath his ugly palace. At least the air felt cool this far down in the ground.

He'd attached a long chain to the shackles binding my wrists after I'd attacked him when he'd entered the dungeon one afternoon. I'd managed to tear a piece of flesh from his shoulder with these worthless human teeth. The long chain he'd added connected to a hook on the ceiling grate far above my head.

Because of that chain, I couldn't walk the entire length of my cell. I couldn't sit on the wooden platform that served as a bed without the chain holding my arms in the air. I couldn't lay down at all. I could barely eat, could barely take care of myself without that chain getting in my way. I yanked on the damned thing—not for the first time, or the second, or the hundredth. It refused to break. In a pique of frustration, I threw my head back and screamed and screamed and screamed.

The metal door to my cell flew open with such force that it crashed against the stone wall with a loud clang.

"What'yer caterwauling for again, creature?" A burly guard came thundering into my cell. He pulled back his arm to hit me. My face already bore bruises from past encounters with his fists. I pinched my eyes closed and tensed in preparation for a world of hurt. If I was lucky, I would pass out quickly like I had the last time.

"Don't." A familiar, grumbly voice warned.

"She's screamin' again. Disturbs the others down here."

"Don't touch her." Cullen's voice carried the full strength of his vampiric compulsion. *"Ever."*

I opened one eye in time to watch that ugly guard drop his arm and, like a zombie, walk out of my cell. Even before he was gone, Cullen moved as quickly as a striking viper. He grabbed the side of my face and tilted it to one side.

"Did he put those bruises on you? Did he?" he demanded.

"Why do you care?" I jerked my head away from his grip. "The guards treat me with the same respect you and *the man* do."

"So, the guard hit you." Cullen stepped back and crossed his arms over his chest. A muscle in his jaw tightened. "If you call Captain Proctor 'the man,' I suppose you call me 'the vampire.' I have a name, you know."

I sniffed and turned my head away from him. I didn't want to let Cullen see how vulnerable I felt around him. He could melt my thoughts, turn my mind inside out, and there was nothing I could do to stop him. That he hadn't done it yet didn't give me comfort. But he was wrong. *The man* was 'the man.' I couldn't be troubled to remember the inconsequential slug's name. Why would I need to know his name when I pulled his bones from his still living body? But Prince Cullen? For some reason, *his* name had stuck with me. His handsome face stuck with me. His likeness visited me in my dreams—dreams where he rescued me from this hell. *Stupid dreams.*

"Look. While I don't agree with the captain's methods, I do understand his reasoning for why he thinks he needs your help on the battlefield. And there *is* a battle coming. Maybe that's why yours and the moonlight dragon's eggs hatched when they did. You have a part to play in the coming conflict."

I stared at the wall as if the bare stones were the most interesting view in the place. It wasn't. That honor belonged to the dashing Prince Cullen, curse his pretty brown eyes.

"No matter what I say, what I do, you're not going to help us, are you?" he asked.

Those stones were stacked quite neatly to form the dungeon's wall. But over toward the corner, the stones looked as if they were haphazardly laid. *Two different workmen? Two different time periods?* I wondered how handsome Prince Cullen would look after I bit his nose clean off his stupid handsome face.

"Look at me, Amaya," he said in that deep, voice that was thick with magic.

My head snapped toward him, not because I wanted to, but because of the power of his compulsion. But as soon as my gaze landed on his, I was able to shake off the magic.

"You have a strong will. Stronger than most," he said. "My compulsion won't last on you. And there's nothing I can do or say to convince you to help us, is there?"

"Why should I help a vampire, or even a kingdom of vampires? If you and the humans wish to go to war to kill each other to extinction, this continent will be a better place."

Cullen sighed deeply. "What if our war threatens your kind as well?"

"Why should it? We no longer live within your reality. We keep to ourselves, away from your settlements. Most in the four kingdoms believe the dragons all died out centuries ago. Others question if we ever existed."

"And yet, here you are, Amaya. A mythical dragon chained in a human's dungeon. So, not as separate and forgotten as you'd hoped, perhaps?"

I snarled at him. The inhuman sound that came out of my mouth seemed to startle him. He backed away to put more distance between us but stopped himself. He stiffened and then leaned in closer.

"Amaya," he said softly. "I hate this for you."

"Soon, none of it will matter." I dropped to sit on the wooden platform I was supposed to use as a bed. The chain yanked my hands above my head. "I'm dying."

"No. Proctor won't allow you to die. You're much too valuable to him."

"Doesn't matter what that creature wants," I spat. I thrust my chin in the air as if proud of what I was going to say next. "Dragons and vampires are mortal enemies for a reason. Our magics are incompatible. Your blood magic is corroding my insides."

"It's not my—" he tried to explain, but I didn't let him.

"Every day I'm forced to wear these shackles is a day closer to my death. Soon, nothing you do will be able to save me…not even removing the shackles." His blood, *the man's* blood. It really didn't matter where the blood came from. The magic was poison to me.

He sat on the platform next to me, hooked his thumb under my chin, and turned my head so he could stare at me from behind his thick glasses for a long breathless moment. "You're telling the truth," he said slowly. A note of awe blended with worry as if that lone fact surprised him. "You are dying."

"Why should I lie about this?" I rattled the chain connected to the ceiling, making it bang loudly against the thick bars on the ceiling grate.

"To trick me into releasing you."

"What would it matter?" I hated how defeated I sounded. "If you were going to help me, you would have already done it." I needed to accept my fate. The two dragons born into a world they were supposed to save were destined to be killed by it. Maybe that meant the world wasn't worth saving. Maybe that was why fate had chosen this path for me and the moonlight dragon. Because it was too late. The world had already been so corrupted by blood magic that there was nothing left to save. And the only meaning left in my life was my death.

"If you promise not to fight us, not to escape, I could convince

Captain Proctor to remove the shackles. All you have to do is promise to work with him instead of against him. Can you do that? Can you take that small step toward helping save yourself and, well, maybe all of us?"

"You release me from these bonds, and I'll grind your bones and drink it like tea," I said holding his gaze with mine.

He smiled at that, but there was no humor in the expression. Only sadness. He patted my knee. "Still so creative with the violence."

He stood and, without a backward glance, walked out of my prison cell. He didn't even bother to close the door behind him. Why should he? The chains alone kept me from escaping.

I stared at my bruised wrists and sighed. I was going to die here. Like this. With my hands suspended above my head.

Goddess—I stifled a sob—*I don't want to die.*

Chapter 10

Celestina

While I felt rather ridiculous dressed in the sheer pink dress as we left the ship, the style of dress—lightweight and without any sleeves—was what most young Tiburnian women my age indeed wore in the city. Soren kept his arm draped over my shoulder and me tucked against his side as we headed through the busy maze of streets.

"How do you manage her so well?" Proctor asked Soren after we'd walked for several blocks. "Is it the collar? Or do you use compulsion as well? What did you do to her to make her so tame?"

"I don't know what you're talking about." The muscles in Soren's arm tightened.

"Come now," Proctor said with a chuckle. "You don't have to pretend with us. Your brother told me all about how you acquired *her* and how you plan to use her."

"Use me?" I cried at the same time Soren started to say, "It's not—"

"I have recently acquired one, too," Proctor blurted. It sounded as if he couldn't hold in the news a moment longer.

"Cullen mentioned that in his letter," Soren angrily replied.

I opened and closed my mouth, not sure what to address first. The fact that this man thought Soren planned to use me as his personal dragon. *Is that true?* Or the fact that this man had captured a dragon. And Soren knew about it. *Urgh!*

I couldn't really tell Captain Proctor what I thought about him (I never had liked a braggart) or my thoughts on the fact that he was holding someone like me a prisoner. (He deserved to be punched in the nuts.) Not while we were out here on the street. Not where someone might be listening. We were in enemy territory, which meant we needed to guard our tongues. Captain Proctor had apparently forgotten that.

"Mine is as vicious as a crystal cobra." He was speaking too loudly. Was he trying to get us caught? "No matter what I do, no matter how harshly I punish her, I can't seem to break her. Cullen has been trying to help, but he's been unsuccessful as well. She seems immune to all but the simplest compulsions. I was hoping you could lend a hand, that you could use your…um…beast to—"

"No." Soren bit off the word.

"Beast?" *Did he just call me a beast?*

"But that's why you have her. To—"

"No," Soren repeated. His jaw muscles tensed. "Not here," Soren added quietly when the captain seemed eager to persist with his questions.

"Right. Right." The captain gave Soren a sheepish look. "It's just…I've been so frustrated by my…and my general is pushing for results…but…I understand. Later."

With that said, Captain Proctor led us to the door of a three-story house with a wide front porch. Unlike many of the houses on the street, this one detached from the neighboring homes. Instead, it was ringed by a tidy flower garden that was bursting with large pink blooms. It wasn't a wooden house, like those in the village surrounding the castle in Earst. This house had been crafted from what looked like clay. Pale, pink clay that was nearly the same shade as the flowers.

"My parents live here?" I asked.

Proctor barely glanced at me before he knocked. A gray-bearded man in a crisp linen suit and white tie opened the door almost immediately.

My heart fell. That wasn't my father. Proctor had led us to a trap.

The man at the door took one look at the five of us and opened the door wider. "The Vackers are waiting in the sitting room, Captain," he said to Proctor with a slight bow.

"What is this place?" I asked, refusing to pass through a door that might lead to a room filled with enemy soldiers.

"Your parents' home," Proctor answered smoothly.

"No. This can't be their home. They'd brought no riches with them. They'd fled with only the clothes they were wearing."

"They brought us something better than riches. They brought information. And here in Tiburnia, information is worth more than gold. Prince Soren, please, her parents are waiting." Proctor made a gesture, indicating I should be the first to enter the home. That wasn't going to happen. Even if I were foolish enough to do such a thing, Gray, Raya, and Soren would never allow it.

Gray, with his hand on his hip—presumably where he'd stashed his collapsible sword—made a cautious entrance into the home. "I don't like this," he grumbled to Soren as he passed by us.

Gray continued into the sitting room, taking a quick look around before stepping back out to nod to Soren. Soren, with his arm still wrapped around my shoulder, led me toward the room where my parents were supposedly waiting. My heart beat wildly as we entered the large space. Silky drapes billowed at the tall windows that looked out onto the street. There were three sitting areas in the room where an array of luxuriously upholstered sofas and chairs were arranged with small intricately carved tables interspersed between the chairs. Golden trays piled with pastries sat on a few of the tables. On some of the other tables, finely cut glasses filled with a deep red drink sat on silver trays. I swallowed hard and hoped my parents weren't serving us blood.

"Darling!" my mother crooned as she ran across the room to greet me. She pulled me away from Soren and into her arms in a hug that took me completely by surprise. My mother had never been the hugging type. She kept hold of my shoulders even after letting me out of her tight grasp. "Look at you." She tsked as she ran her long, graceful fingers over the slave collar. Her hand stilled when it reached the faint bruise on my upper neck, one that even drinking Soren's blood preventatively hadn't been able to completely erase. Her gaze flew to where Soren stood behind me. Her entire body stiffened as she looked him over from head to toe. Her cool, blue eyes narrowed.

Despite the scowl she was now wearing, my mother was as lovely as I remembered her. Her pale blonde hair matched her perfect pale skin. She wore her hair in an elaborate coronet of braids. Little blue sapphires threaded through the braids sparkled in the sunlight streaming through the open windows like tiny stars. She was about a head shorter than me, and as slender as a rail. She wore a white sleeveless gown that swept the carpeted floor as she moved. "If you had let us help you escape, Celestina, you wouldn't be wearing that awful thing. Queen Beatrice has always been jealous of you and looking for excuses to harm you." She gave Soren another hard look. "Clearly, you've been quite roughly used. We wanted to prevent something like this from happening. That was why we acted as we had." Mother waved her hand toward my bruised neck. "If only you had obeyed us."

"The princes' lives were in danger. I couldn't have left them, even if I'd wanted to. They are too young to be left vulnerable like that."

My mother tsked again. "You saved her sons, and this is the thanks Queen Beatrice gave you. She made you a slave. Gave you to our enemy. You know she doesn't care about her children. They're nothing but annoyances to her." My mother spoke quickly, as if she'd been waiting to see me again just so she could scold me for disobeying her and Father.

I lifted my chin. "Someone needs to care for those boys. Whether their mother dotes on them or not, they're innocent children. I'm not ashamed that I did what I did to protect them." I knew what it was like to be raised by indifferent parents. From my earliest memories, my parents had often ignored me and left me either alone or, if I was lucky, with castle servants to watch after me. The only rule they enforced, with the assistance of the Royal Guards, was that I could never wander beyond the castle walls. Such a cruel rule to make for a curious and lively child. "But this isn't the time to point fingers. What is done is done." I kept my hand fisted at my hip to keep from reaching up and touching the slave collar. "There's much we need to discuss."

My father cleared his throat. "Perhaps we should sit." He gestured to the closest seating area. Like my mother, my father looked well. He wore his dark, brown hair a little shorter than he had in Earst. But he still sported a close-cropped beard that was speckled with a few gray hairs. He was dressed in a light tan sleeveless suit that was very similar in style to the white ones both Soren and Gray were wearing. "Please, take this chair, Daughter. We should discuss why you have sought us out. And why you have brought an enemy general with you."

Soren eased his arm around my shoulder again and leaned into me until I was once again tucked against his side. "Celestina is my bonded partner."

My father's deep green eyes widened with surprise. "I've heard gossip through the years about the Fein system of taking bonded partners. Those are lifetime bonds, are they not?" He frowned at me before returning his gaze back to Soren. "Unbreakable?"

"That's correct. Not even death can break this bond," Soren said, his voice a deep warning. "She is mine."

"I see," my father said after exchanging a long glance with Captain Proctor. "We have much to discuss, then. Please, let's sit."

Soren didn't move. "My brother? I was told he'd meet us at the dock. He was not there. I was then told he would meet us here. He is not here. And I do find it tedious to have to repeat myself, but here we are. Where is my brother?"

Captain Proctor raised his hands as if in surrender. "It appears the young prince is running late. If you feel it necessary, I could send someone to find out why he's been delayed. In the meantime, we could—"

"Do that," Soren said, interrupting the captain. The man had been gesturing toward the same grouping of sofas that my father had wanted us to take. They both seemed determined that we sit down and eat their food and drink that— *What is that deep red drink?* "Find my brother. We'll wait."

Captain Proctor frowned. Clearly, he hadn't expected to be taken up on his offer to send a scout to search for Cullen. After a tense moment, he left the sitting room.

Soren remained rooted where we stood. "Is it really necessary to literally stand our ground?" I whispered.

"Yes," he whispered back.

Gray had taken a position at the one entrance to the room, his hand still resting on his hip. His eyes were constantly roving, as if searching for a reason to fight. Raya stood on the opposite side of the room near the windows. She had taken an equally tense stance, like a cat prepared to leap into a fight.

But this was my parents' home. Nothing would happen to any of us here. My parents were flighty and vain, but generally harmless. Save for that time that they had helped the Tiburnians attack the castle...and so many soldiers had died as a result.

"Tell me, Father," I said, as we stood awkwardly in the middle of the room. "Why did you ask the Tiburnians to protect me? Why them?"

My father looked around him. He then smiled at my mother. She smiled sweetly back. "See all this, darling? They gave us all the luxury we could ever wish for—more than we had expected—and that was after we failed to deliver you to their care. They are a fair people. Their rulers are elected by the citizens, not by blood. They don't limit who can do magic to just their royals. Quite frankly, this is a better place than Earst."

"That's not a high bar," Soren muttered.

I started to defend my home country but stopped myself. Soren and my father weren't wrong. Life in the Kingdom of Earst had been oppressive, not just for me...but for everyone. We couldn't speak freely. The queen dictated how we dressed, how we wore our hair, how we lived. The consequence for not conforming was often death.

Even under the rule of Queen Frieda, who had been decidedly less capricious than her daughter, death was still a common punishment for both major and minor crimes.

"And what would the Tiburnians have expected of me if I came with you?" I asked instead.

"Why, they would have asked you to help with protecting their borders from invading forces," my father was quick to answer.

"They wanted me to join their military?"

My father chuckled. "Come now, Daughter. Everyone in this room knows what you are, what you're capable of."

"We have to approach this subject with care," Soren warned. "The collar doesn't allow Celestina to talk about her true form. But that is why we are here. We want to get information about how she came to be in your care and—"

"The Fein wish to use you? I knew it." My father's eyes lit up. "And what, may I ask, are you willing to pay us for this information regarding my daughter? As you see, we are being well compensated and taken care of here in the warm embrace of our southernmost kingdom. It would have to be an impressive deal to get us to want to make a move to the continent's northernmost, most closed-off, and presumably most dangerous kingdom."

"Celestina is no longer yours to use to barter for a richer future," Soren pointed out. He bared his fangs. "She's mine."

"Ah." My father didn't appear at all flustered by Soren's claim over me. In fact, he seemed to relish the challenge. He smiled even more broadly. "But you are here, in my home. And—"

"Father. Mother." I wasn't anyone's property, nor did I want to be treated as if I were. And this grandstanding was wasting our time. We needed to find out what my parents knew, gather up Cullen, and get ourselves the hell out of this country before one of us got hurt. Or worse. "Please." I stepped out of Soren's embrace and held out my hands to my mother. "Please, I'm here because I need to know how I came into your care. I'm not your natural daughter, isn't that true?" It hurt to ask that.

Even if they hadn't been the best parents or the most loving, they were the only parents I'd ever known. It pained me to say aloud that I didn't truly belong to them. It felt as if I were severing a line to my past. What if my parents agreed that I wasn't their child? What if the outcome of my stating that I, too, knew the truth of my adoption meant that they would no longer love me? No longer claim me?

"We should tell her," my mother said at the same time my father said, "What are you willing to pay for this information, General Kitmun?"

My mother pressed a gauzy handkerchief to her lips with a trembly hand. "I couldn't have a child of my own. We tried many times, but my body proved to be too frail to successfully carry an heir. The repeated losses were…quite painful. Queen Frieda, she watched us struggle to try and continue your father's lineage. She felt our pain. Your father could have disposed of me and taken a new lover." Her eyes grew dewy. "But he loved me. The queen saw that as well. And since your father had always been a fierce supporter of the crown, she wanted to reward him for his unwavering loyalty."

My father closed the distance between him and my mother. He kissed her gently on the temple. "Queen Frieda brought you to our chamber in the middle of the night, Celestina. You were so small. Helpless. The queen is the one who told us your name." As he spoke, he held my mother's gaze. "The queen also told us that she was entrusting us with the greatest weapon the world would ever know. She had plans for you. Great plans. You were to be one of the most powerful subjects under Queen Frieda. But that was all taken away when Queen Beatrice poisoned our beloved ruler."

"What were Queen Frieda's plans for Celestina exactly?" Soren asked.

My father waved away the question. "What does it matter? She is dead now. And Queen Beatrice has plans of her own, plans that never required Celestina or our assistance. That's why we had to get Celestina away from Earst. What Queen Beatrice is capable of is terrible. We realized that to have any hope of stopping her from destroying the entire continent, we would also have to save Celestina."

Chapter 11

Celestina

I needed to sit down. I understood that Gray and Raya had taken up defensive positions near the exits, and that Soren wanted to keep me within arm's reach and on my feet in case we needed to run. But after hearing how my parents had risked their lives to selflessly save me—even though I wasn't their natural child—my legs wobbled. I hurried over to the seats my father had been trying to usher us toward ever since we'd entered the room and plopped down on a plump peach-colored brocade chair with a high back.

Soren followed. "Celestina?" he asked, looking concerned.

"I feel…" Dammit, tears filled my eyes. I blinked madly trying to get them to go away. "I don't know how I feel," I admitted. "It's all too raw. Too…" I shook my head.

Captain Proctor returned with Prince Cullen. Behind them, a bevy of servants carrying trays holding more of that dark red drink that I hoped wasn't blood entered the room.

"Sorry I'm late," Cullen said as he punched his brother's arm. "I was delayed when picking up a case of Tiburnian plum wine. After one sip, though, you're going to agree with me that it was worth the wait. This drink is considered quite a rare treat."

With the influx of so many new players, Gray and Raya moved to flank Soren and me.

"Oh! It is indeed rare to get your hands on our country's plum wine. Let's freshen those drinks," Proctor said jovially. It felt odd that he was playing host. This wasn't his house. So why was he making these kinds of decisions? But I supposed I couldn't be entirely certain of what freedoms my parents had given up in exchange for such an opulent home.

No one seemed to question Captain Proctor's ordering around my father's servants as they swept up the trays that were already on the table and replaced them with the trays they were carrying.

"It looks as if you can use one of these, princess." Prince Cullen picked up one of the goblets and handed it to me. "One sip should cure whatever is causing you to scowl so."

I stared at the dark liquid swirling around in the goblet.

"Plum wine?" I sniffed the drink.

"Yeah. What did you think it was?" Cullen asked.

"Nothing. It just looked so... Nothing." I took a sip. It was sweet. But I didn't mind the taste. I took another sip, hoping the subtle alcohol would help settle my jumpy nerves.

"Here." He handed a goblet to his brother. "Let's celebrate. We're finally all in Tiburnia. I hope you're getting the information you need." He lifted his eyebrows in question.

Soren took the goblet but just stared at his brother. "You're acting strange."

"Am I?" Cullen shrugged. "Perhaps. It's been a strange day. Raya? Gray? Join us, why don't you?" Neither of my friends moved a muscle.

Soren set down the goblet and turned to his brother. "What's going on?"

Cullen held up his hands and stepped closer to Soren. When he spoke, he'd lowered his voice to whisper. "Sharing a drink is an important part of Tiburnian culture. I've gone through a heap of trouble to bring this wine to impress Captain Proctor, who has the patience of a man being eaten by a swarm of flesh beetles. Don't forget that we're in enemy territory, under his protection. He will be gravely offended if you refuse to have a drink with him, especially considering that we're drinking his country's best wine."

"I won't drink alcohol, not in a situation where I need all my wits. Nor will my seconds," Soren whispered back.

"Just smile and make a show of drinking it," Cullen said with a false smile. "And get Gray and Raya to do the same or else Captain Proctor might decide to improve his position in Tiburnian society by handing over the fabled Beast of Fein instead of helping us."

"I'd like to see him try to do that," Soren growled. But he picked up the goblet and took a small sip. He looked over at his friends. "This is the best plum wine I've ever tasted. Raya, Gray, you should try it."

Raya gave a sharp nod and reached for a goblet as a smiling Captain Proctor launched into an explanation of how farmers pick the plums at their height of ripeness, and how the wine is then left sitting in barrels crafted from fragrant cedar trees for more than fifty years.

Raya took a small sip of the wine, her eyes widened with pleasure. She elbowed Gray in the side. "Drink the damn wine, nimrod," she whispered.

Gray, scowling, did as he was told. But like the others, only took a tiny sip.

My father rubbed his hands together with delight as he and my mother took a seat on the sofa that was adjacent to the chair I'd selected. "It is indeed a treat. This plum wine is as rare as a flower blooming in winter. I'm impressed you were able to get your hands on a case of it." He picked up a goblet and took a long, deep drink. He smacked his lips and smiled. "So good."

My mother sipped daintily. But, I noticed, her glass quickly emptied. She set down her goblet and swiped at a lizard that had crawled on the sofa. "Ugh. I thought we'd seen the last of these when we left Queen Beatrice's court. Disgusting, slimy things."

I fought an urge to apologize for the lizards that must have somehow followed us to my parents' house. It wasn't my fault that they crawled into every pack they could find.

So instead of taking responsibility for them, I yawned into my hand. Gracious, I shouldn't have let Soren keep me up most of the night last night. "Father," I said while fighting off another yawn. "Do you know how Queen Beatrice's magic works?"

We'd come to Tiburnia in search of two main pieces of information:

Where I came from, and how to remove Queen Beatrice's collar.

We may have struck out on the first one, since my parents didn't know how Queen Frieda had managed to get her hands on a baby dragon in human form. But that didn't mean that they couldn't be helpful in ridding me of Queen Beatrice's awful collar.

"We need to know more about her magic so we can get the collar off her," Soren explained.

"Really?" Captain Proctor tilted his head to one side. "I would have thought, you'd want to keep it, use it."

"She's not a slave," came Soren's automatic reply. "She doesn't deserve to be treated like one."

"What a heartwarming sentiment," my mother said over a yawn. "If I'd never heard of you or your exploits, General Kitmun—the Beast of Fein—I'd almost believe that was what you sincerely wished."

Soren merely shrugged. "There is magic upon magic wrapped around my Celestina. I wish to untangle all of it."

"Some of it is old," Cullen added. "Presumably cast by Queen Frieda. Our mages are guessing that those spells are meant to bind Celestina to her human form?"

My father shook his head. "If that's true, Queen Frieda didn't tell us about it."

"And Queen Beatrice's magic? Is there a way to unlock this slave collar?" I pressed.

My father glanced at Soren before answering. "Queen Beatrice is as impulsive as she is powerful. She rarely thinks things through to the end before she acts. And now she's surrounded herself with lackeys who will go along with whatever ill-conceived whim she conjures. I daresay she created that collar in a fit of anger, casting a spell that has no reversal. That's how her magic usually works." He looked at me. "Remember her best friend, Lady Shirely? Remember how angry Queen Beatrice got when Lady Shirely won a card game they were playing?"

Thinking about that spectacle made my stomach churn. I took another sip of the sweet wine. "Queen Beatrice hates to lose," I said.

"And when Lady Shirely placed the winning card on the table," my father continued, enjoying his role as storyteller, "Queen Beatrice exploded in a burst of magical anger and turned her dearest friend into a pile of flesh. Flesh that was still living, still suffering." My father shuddered.

"Gods," Gray breathed.

"Yes," my father agreed, leaning forward. He lowered his voice for dramatic effect. "Queen Beatrice kept the quivering bloody flesh bedside her bed for days, cursing her friend, kicking it. And then one morning she woke up and, as was often the case with the queen, discovered she was no longer angry with Lady Shirely. In fact, she missed her best friend. She missed giggling with her, going riding with her. Queen Beatrice, you must understand, grew up having few friends who were truly hers. Most of the lords and ladies in the court pretended to be Queen Beatrice's friend because they enjoyed the power and prestige being close to royalty could bring them. Only Lady Shirely, a friend from birth, had truly loved Queen Beatrice. They'd shared secrets, men, clothing."

"And now that friend was a pile of flesh," Soren said.

My father nodded. "Bloody, *living* flesh. It was a gruesome sight. One the queen truly regretted. And this is a queen who regrets very little. Queen Beatrice tried for weeks to reverse the spell she'd cast in anger. But unless she puts a great deal of thought into her magic-work, her spells can only go one way. There's no undoing what has been done, even if she wishes to undo it with all her heart."

This wasn't the news I wanted to hear. I clutched the metal around my neck. Would this collar control my life forever?

"What happened to the lump of flesh?" Captain Procter asked.

"Oh, after the queen realized she'd never succeed in bringing her friend back, she couldn't stand to look at the physical evidence of her failure. She screamed and raged and killed four of her servants before tossing what was left of Lady Shirely into her bedroom's fire grate. She then gave the order to keep the fire burning until nothing remained but ashes. Some believe the ashes never died but continue to suffer to this day."

"There must be another way," Soren muttered, more to himself than to anyone else in the room. He then looked at me. "Magic moves like the wind. But it also ebbs and flows like the ocean's tide. And like the tide, the moon tugs at it, making the magic seem stronger at certain times of the year. If we picked one of the moon's cycles when the magic is at its peak to direct the magic at the collar, we might break its spell."

"Possible," Cullen said. "But the amount of magic needed would be risky. It could just as easily kill Celestina, the mage wielding the spell, or both."

While Cullen explained the mechanics of such an unbinding spell, I yawned. That was when something disturbing dawned on me. Everyone in the room had sipped from a goblet of plum wine. Except for Prince Cullen and Captain Proctor.

I yawned again.

My thoughts felt muzzy.

I shook my head, trying to chase away my growing drowsiness. Why had Captain Proctor and Prince Cullen skipped drinking the wine? Especially Cullen. He'd demanded his brother and Gray and Raya drink it. He'd insisted drinking the wine was a display of diplomacy. But he hadn't even picked up a goblet. He hadn't even *pretended* to drink. If diplomacy were that important, shouldn't he have had the wine too?

Something was wrong about this, *very* wrong.

"Soren?" I grabbed his wrist as I tried to rise. "We need to—"

Soren's brother spun so quickly I barely saw the movement. Cullen slammed his fist into the side of Soren's head. My fierce warrior stumbled. It was just enough of an opening for the men posing as servants in the room to spring to action.

Gray had his sword in his hand almost immediately, but Cullen whirled from Soren to Gray, knocking him out with a two-fisted slam to the side of his head.

I tried to cry, "Stop!" in my loudest, most magical growly voice. But a hand slapped over my face before I got out much more than a "st—"

"Cullen warned me about the power of your voice, dragon. I look forward to using it," Captain Proctor's oily voice dripped into my ear. "But right now, I need your silence."

"Get your hands off her!" Soren shouted. A growing pile of injured and possibly dead men was forming around his feet. More men kept streaming into the room. There were at least five men attacking Soren. His hands were shackled behind his back, but that didn't stop him from using his legs, his feet, or his bound arms to fight off the men who kept coming and coming.

Gray was out of commission on the floor with his wrists and ankles bound in shackles. His eyes were barely open, and he looked dazed.

Raya must have snagged Gray's sword as he fell. She held the short sword in her right hand and a dagger in her left. And goddess, she moved with such speed, whirling in broad circles, holding back the men who were trying to subdue her. Her eyes looked clearer than either Soren's or Gray's, which made me wonder if she'd only pretended to drink the wine.

My parents were slumped down on the sofa, my mother's head dropped into my father's lap.

Soren would have been able to maintain the upper hand against all those men if his brother hadn't sucker-punched him. And drugged him.

"Raya, go! Get help!" Soren shouted, clearly realizing that despite their advantage as highly trained warriors and vampires, the number of men and the effects of the poisoned wine had put them in a no-win situation. He took several more blows to his head and stumbled to his knees.

I tried to cry out. But the captain's hand remained plastered across my face. I tossed my head from side to side to no avail.

Raya hesitated. Our eyes met, and she nearly lost her advantage. But she quickly recovered, slashing the sword across one of her attackers' chests, slicing him open. She gave Soren an unhappy nod before backflipping over the men who were trying to creep up behind her. She disappeared like a wraith through the open window.

"Let her go," Cullen called out to the men who had rushed to pursue her. "We'll be long gone before she returns."

"What have you done?" Soren roared at his brother as he continued to fight the three men on top of him and the bindings that held him.

"He made a bargain," the captain answered for him.

"It had to be done, Soren," Cullen said as whatever drug he'd put in our drinks started to pull me under. Captain Proctor lifted his hand from my mouth. Without him holding me in place, I slid out of the chair and sunk to the floor, spilling the drink I still held in my hand all down my ridiculously flimsy dress.

"I'll kill you for this," Soren growled, still fighting the men. But by this point, with him so bound up, it really was a losing battle.

"Take my brother and his man to the ship," Cullen ordered. "And for goddess's sake, don't hurt him any more than necessary. You should have finished the goblet of wine, big brother. This would have gone much more smoothly if you'd just drunk the full goblet."

"Don't hurt them," I cried from the floor at the foot of the chair as those horrid men dragged Soren and Gray out of the room. Well, those were the words I'd tried to cry. It came out more like, "Dnnnahuurrrlhum."

Captain Proctor bent down and poked me in the cheek. "She's so docile." He poked my other cheek.

"Useless, really." Cullen scoffed. "Maybe it's because she was raised with humans instead of her own kind. She's not a fighter like your dragon. She'll never be a fighter. She'll never be powerful enough to change the outcome of a battle, not like your dragon. This one is too submissive, too soft." His words stung. Not that I ever wanted to be a warrior like Soren. I didn't. But the words still stung because I'd thought Cullen liked me. I never would have guessed he thought I was useless. I thought we were family. How could he do this to me? How could he betray his brother? By handing me over to the enemy, Cullen was putting his brother's life at great risk. Did this mean that Cullen wanted to take Soren's place as crown prince? Did he lust after his father's crown?

"Yes, I can see that now," Proctor said. "So…why are we stealing her from your brother?"

"Because your dragon needs to be given something she'll find valuable. She needs to be given something she'll want to protect. Something we can take from her if she doesn't cooperate."

"And you think this weak dragon will be important enough to my dragon to do that?"

"I know she will be," Cullen said coldly. He stepped in front of Captain Proctor. "Since she belongs to my brother, let me be the one to take her to the dungeon."

"Very well," the captain said. "I don't have the patience to fight my dragon right now anyhow. She's always telling me of all the ways she plans to kill me. If you can stop her from doing that, I would be grateful."

"I'm sure this will do the trick." Cullen lifted me into his arms.

"I am sorry about this, Celestina," he whispered for my ears only. "But I could think of no other way to save her."

Her? Who was he talking about? And why had he traded my life for hers?

Chapter 12

Amaya

"Oh, no. No, don't you bring that-that human in here." I tried to block the entrance to my grimy cell, but the damned chain connecting me to the ceiling grate jerked me back from the doorway. Prince Cullen gave me a smirk. He was carrying what looked like a damsel in distress draped across his arms. Her head flopped with every step. "She's not dead, is she? You're not putting a dead body in here with me, are you? I mean, if I was in my dragon form it'd be a treat. I could eat her. But honestly, do you know nothing about dragons? We don't like to eat our meat raw." I rattled the chains loud enough that it should have woken little Miss Sleeping Beauty up. She didn't stir. "She looks dead to me," I grumbled.

"She'll come around within the hour." He settled the little piece of feminine fluff onto my pallet.

"And now you're putting her on my bed? Nice. Nice. Why don't you bring in more prisoners? There's plenty of room for more on my one insanely narrow bed. Not that it's a bed, is it? It's a board. But it's all I have in here. And you're giving it to that thing?"

I couldn't even lay on it thanks to this damned chain. But that wasn't the point.

I snapped my teeth as I watched Cullen carefully arrange the skirt of the woman's short dress, to make sure she was as decently covered as possible. He pushed back a bit of her hair and then whispered something only she could hear, which was ridiculous.

"She's unconscious. She can't hear you," I spat.

"Maybe telling her what needs to be said makes me feel better," he explained not looking up from his task of making the obscenely pretty woman as comfortable as an unconscious person could be on a narrow wooden board. When he was done, he straightened and turned to me. "I'd appreciate it if you didn't try to roast her. Give her a chance. I think the two of you will become close friends."

Friends with that? I snorted. "Is she your sidepiece?" She had to be. He wouldn't be so doting on her otherwise. Ohhhh, I hated how the thought of him having romantic feelings for this dewy-faced woman—*did she have to look so pretty?*—made me want to rip her face off that pretty head of hers and then rip his pretty face off, too. Was that a gold necklace she was wearing? Looked snug. But expensive. *I bet he gifted that to her.* I growled. "Did she do something to hurt your fragile ego, so you decided to banish her? Or did you find someone younger and prettier and didn't want to bother with the fuss she'd make when you set her aside?"

"None of that, actually," Cullen said. He crossed his arms and tilted his head as he watched me. One of his dark eyebrows quirked up. "Careful, Amaya, you sound jealous."

"Jealous?" I snorted.

He looked like a hero guarding his beloved lady from the dragon instead of the villain he actually was.

"I think the two of you will become friends," he repeated.

"I'm not going to befriend your cast-off lover."

"She's not my lover, Amaya. Current. Former. Or otherwise." He sighed. "If you must know, she's my brother's bonded partner."

"So, he's casting her off? And making you do the dirty? What a guy. Villainy must run in the family. I'm sure your parents are beside themselves with pride."

"Truthfully, I'm sure my brother is going to try and kill me for tearing her away from him and imprisoning her down here with you."

I knew I shouldn't care about anything he did. But at the same time, I couldn't stop myself from asking, "Then why did you do it?"

"I followed what my instincts were telling me to do." He snapped out the words, sounding angry about them. Was Cullen honestly worried about facing his brother? Maybe his brother, after murdering Cullen—*wait, I* want *to do that!*—would come looking for his "bonded partner" and free me, too.

"Do your instincts often tell you to kidnap women and toss them into cells so nasty even the rats avoid?"

He raised his eyebrows and gave me a look as if he thought I should already know the answer.

"What's wrong with her?" I still thought she looked dead lying there with her wavy brown hair framing her delicate face and her hands resting one over the other on her bosom. Part of me wanted to go over to her and give her a sharp pinch just to see if she would react.

"I drugged her."

Oh. "Classy."

"I can't stay." His voice took on that calming quality that made me think of wind currents and ocean waves and swaying trees. "I need you to promise me that you won't hurt her. Her name is Celestina. And she's…she's special."

"So special you've given her the best accommodations in the place."

He stared intently at me. *"Don't. Harm. Her."*

I easily shrugged off the compulsion he was trying to weave around me. But I decided to willingly agree to what he was asking of me. For one, I didn't need or want to prolong my time with Cullen—the vile bastard who was too handsome for his own good. "I already told you that I don't eat my meat raw. And in case you forgot, I don't have access to my fire." While killing her might be a way to hurt Cullen, I suspected that the unconscious woman being thrust on me was simply another innocent, another victim. And I didn't have the stomach to harm an innocent. "I'm not a mindless beast. I do have standards, especially when it comes to what I put in my mouth."

"I'll have to trust…" He stared at me for several moments before giving a sharp nod. "Yes, I trust you'll give her a chance. If you're still here by sun fall, I'll return with two plates of dinner."

With that, he walked out of the cell. This time, he closed the door behind him and made sure to lock it.

As soon as he was gone, I did what I always did after spending any amount of frustrating time with Prince I'm-too-handsome-for-my-own-good Cullen. I stomped my feet and growled.

It accomplished nothing...but felt good.

Wait...he said if I was still here. What did he mean by that? Where would I go with shackles that make it impossible to cross the entire space of this cramped cell? It wasn't as if I had the means to get them off me. If I had, I would have escaped immediately. I would have then roasted the man's balls and force-fed them to Cullen's decapitated head. *Maybe I'll keep Cullen's pretty head on a shelf in my bedroom to look at.*

Why did Cullen think I'd be gone by dinnertime?

My gaze darted over to the sleeping woman.

Does he think she might—

No. She looked incapable of harming anything. Not even a lacewing fly needed to tremble in her presence. Cullen couldn't be concerned that she might kill me.

He must have said that to tease me...or to trick me into treating his brother's bonded partner with a level of respect I didn't usually give to humans.

I moved closer to her.

Her eyelids twitched and fluttered as if she were desperately trying to escape her drugged sleep.

I wasn't sure if I wanted her to wake up or not. As long as she didn't prattle on like an empty-headed ninnyhammer, I supposed I wouldn't mind the company. And it was creepy sharing a cell with someone who looked like a corpse. Besides, if she woke up, we could join forces and plot devious ways to torture and kill Cullen and *the man.*

But what if she were an actual danger to me?

Well, that didn't really matter either, seeing how I was already slowly dying. Maybe Cullen had brought this mysterious Celestina woman into my cell as a twisted sort of kindness. Of course, he could have simply removed these shackles if he'd wanted to help me.

The damn vampire hadn't done that.

I leaned down to peer more closely at the woman, which wasn't easy to do with the chain that had me tethered to the ceiling. My wrists throbbed every time they were jerked above my head. Bending down like this also made my shoulders twist to an awkward angle as my arms were pulled in the opposite direction to the wooden pallet.

"You're in my bed," I grumbled as I studied her perfect olive skin.

As if responding to my voice, her eyelids started to move more frantically.

"You should wake up and entertain me." I rattled the chains, hoping the noise would rouse her. "Come on. Watching you sleep is soo fucking boring."

She moaned.

"That's it. Wake up! You don't get to sleep when I'm forced to stand here and stare at you. Wake up and entertain me!"

"Urrrgggg…" she groaned. It sounded slurred. I think she might have been trying to talk. "Soooorrr…"

"Sorry? Yeah, you should be sorry," I said. "There's barely room in here for me. And you're hogging the one place where I can sit down."

Her eyelids fluttered and then opened. Her one green eye and one brown eye stared directly at me in such an intense way, I immediately straightened and backed away. My heart thumped wildly in my chest.

"Soren!" she shouted as she sat up with a jerk. If I'd still been leaning over her, we would have knocked heads. She spun on the wooden pallet until her feet were on the floor. She tried to stand but wobbled and plopped back down. "Soren?"

"Sheesh! You don't have to shout. I'm the only one here. And the guards out there don't like the prisoners to scream. They'll come in and use their fists to shut us up."

She blinked her large, odd-colored eyes several times and then, groaning, let her head drop into her hands. "Cullen betrayed us. Why?"

"Why wouldn't he? He's ruthless. Cruel. Brutal. Hard-hearted. Callous. And he forced me to wear this dress." I kicked out the skirt and then watched it flutter back into place. "I despise dresses."

The woman looked up at me. "That was quite a thesaurus of hatred there. Cullen is my…" She wrinkled her brow. "He's Soren's brother. And he'd promised to help me." She shook her head. "But then he said he had to do this to save—" She gasped. "*You.*" She tried to stand again. And this time she succeeded. "You must be the one he was trying to save."

I laughed bitterly. "How is locking you in a prison cell with me saving anyone? Cullen is only looking out for himself."

"No. For Soren's sake, I can't believe that." She stepped toward me. "Who are you? What are you to Cullen?"

"I'm his captive." I wasn't going to give her my fucking name. It was bad enough that Cullen knew it.

She looked human. But if she were a vampire's bonded partner, she might be a vampire. "You're not here to drink my blood, are you?" Had Cullen sent her in here because she was better at the powers of compulsion than he was? Likely any vampire with half a brain was better at compulsion than him. It took very little effort to shake off the magic he tried to weave around me.

"Drink your—? Why would I want to—?" Her eyes widened.

"You do know they are vampires, right? Cullen and his brother—your bonded partner? They're vampires."

"I know." She blushed as she said it. "Of course, I know. How could someone not know when they come face-to-face with a vampire?"

I spotted that lie too easily. "So, you know what they are *now*, even if you hadn't known right away. You must totally be hating them. Is that why they have you locked away? Because you discovered your vampire's dirty secret after you bonded with him? I bet you hate him for that. You could help me come up with ways to torture them when we finally escape from this hell."

"I don't hate him. Soren saved me. More than once. I love—"

"No! Don't say it. Don't be that vapid heroine in those horrid romances who loves the villain even as he destroys her."

She crossed her arms over her lovely chest and turned away from me. "I'm not vapid," she muttered. "The stories about vampires…they're wrong. So wrong. It wasn't my fault I didn't know what he was." She paced the cell a bit, studied the heavy door, the grate at the ceiling that served as our only window and source of light, poked at a puddle in a corner I couldn't reach with the toe of her shoe, and then turned back to me. "There's no getting out of here. Why are you so heavily chained?"

I bared my teeth like I would if I could conjure my dragon's long pointy canines. "Because I'd kill them if I wasn't."

She nodded but didn't look suitably worried that, even with these chains, I could still harm her. Her lack of caution made me growl.

She held up her hands and smiled. "I'm not the enemy here."

I hissed. "Everyone here is my enemy."

"I'm not." Instead of backing away from me, like I hoped she would, she came closer. "I know what it's like to be a captive." She touched the golden necklace that was cinched so tightly around her neck it appeared to be partially embedded into her skin. "I know what it's like to lose your free will."

"And yet, you still fell in love with your captor. Pitiful." I sniffed. I'd always heard humans were weak.

"Soren never wanted to be my captor," she said. "He took me to save me."

I heard her deluded words, but the scent I'd caught on the air with my haughty sniff had so caught me by surprise that I didn't pay that much attention to anything else she had to say about the vampires. Because the aroma I'd sensed coming from her wasn't a vampire's spicy scent. Or a human's piggie one. It was a scent I knew well. Too well.

"You're a dragon." *Dammit.* "You allowed yourself to be bonded with a vampire?" That was beyond foolish. A dragon would know better than to fall into such a trap. We're superior to all the other creatures. Smarter. Wiser. Stronger. "Dragons and vampires are mortal enemies."

"He didn't ask before bonding himself to me." She rolled her eyes.

"Figures." I scoffed. "Those damn brothers."

"Soren meant well. This collar bonds me to him. He was only trying to even the playing field."

"Meant well, my ass. Vampires are our enemies. They know it. We know it. Their blood magic is poison to us." I rattled the chains while despair clawed at my throat. This delusional dragon was doomed to die like I was. "They put their tainted magic on these shackles. And it's killing me. It hurts to keep fighting Cullen's compulsions. Hurts to feel their blood magic spiraling deeper and deeper into my tissues, into my bones. It hurts as their magic takes my life force away from me." I slumped, letting the chains pull at my bloody and raw wrists. "It even hurts to take a breath."

She shook her head as if trying to deny it.

"You're a dragon, just like I am! How can you do this to your own kind? How can you defend what wants to destroy us? How can you betray the dragons like this?"

She cried out as if I'd struck her. "The collar...I can't..." Her knees smashed against the rough stone floor. She grabbed at the necklace that couldn't be comfortable, scratching her neck in her desperation. "I can't...talk...about...this..."

"I don't care." I wanted her to hurt as much as I was hurting. "You can't hide from the truth. Vampires are the reason we're suffering. We are dragons. And this is our time to make our stand and fight."

This was the reason I was born. This was the reason midnight dragons existed in the first place. We were fighters, warriors, killers. I'd been told my entire life that there would come a time when I'd have to lead my fellow dragons into war. "The time has come," I said, "for dragons to step out of the shadows and take back what is ours."

"Please," she whimpered and reached out her arm as if her movement could block my words.

"No!" I grabbed her wrist and squeezed. "You must face this!"

Magic sparked and danced like a lightning storm in the air between us. Was this her magic? No, the sharp sting of power felt distinctly like mine. But how could that be? The shackles blocked all access to my magic. And yet, my skin burned from the intensity of the power gathering where my hand was touching her skin.

Touching this other dragon had unleashed my magic. Which would have been great if I had the ability to control it.

"Who are you?" I cried.

Celestina

"Who are you?" the other...the other...*dragon*...had demanded. Gah! I couldn't think about what that creature clasped on to my wrist like a lamprey was...or what I was, for that matter. Doing so would surely kill me. The collar was already punishing me for her mentioning that I was—a thing—not to mention how it'd been sending steady beads of pain down my spine just for being so far away from Soren.

Soren. I prayed he was safe. He had to be safe. Cullen wouldn't kill his own brother. He wouldn't!

And now, I had to figure out how to stop this…*urgh!*… *Can't say what the creature is.* But I had to figure out how to stop it from triggering the collar so much that it ended up killing me. I had to stay alive. If I fell, Soren fell. I would not be the cause of Soren's destruction. I would not let that happen.

Oh, how I wished he hadn't bound himself to me in such a fatal way.

The shackled woman tightened her hold on my wrist. Her magic pinging off my skin hurt almost as much as the collar. "I know all the dragons in my clan," she growled as her grip on my hand tightened more and more. "And the dragons outside of the clan are few and old. So, who are you?" Her eyes sharpened with a pained look. "How are you doing that? How are you…? You're pulling my magic to the surface. How?"

"I am?" The collar sent a sharp warning down my spine, and I suddenly couldn't breathe. I couldn't breathe. She needed to let go of me. She needed to break the connection or else I would die, and Soren would die. And despite learning from Proctor that Soren was planning to use me as a weapon for his army, I didn't want my prince to die.

The lightning storm brewing in the dungeon cell started to expand. The sparks landed on my skin like hot embers. They sizzled and burned.

"What are you doing?" the shackled woman growled in a voice that no longer sounded human. Her eyes, like the hand wrapped still around my wrist, were now glowing as bright as the sun. It hurt to look in them. And her skin seemed to have become black as if the sparks had burnt her to a crisp. She threw back her head and screamed.

Suddenly it was no longer a hand that held my wrist, but talons. Their sharp points dug into my flesh. Tears streamed down my face from the pain. I was going to lose my hand. But perhaps that wouldn't matter since the collar kept growing tighter. The collar was going to break my neck, and there was nothing I could do to stop it.

I'm sorry, Soren. Maybe we'll get another lifetime. Another chance. Another world.

Vampires and dragons. Two incompatible fates. How could our story's ending be anything but tragic? My biggest regret was that Soren wasn't here with me. I would have liked to have held his hand one more time. Looked into his expressive green eyes. Whispered to him how much I loved him and thanked him for how safe he'd made me feel in a world that could never be safe. Not safe for him. Not safe for me.

And I regretted that fate hadn't allowed us more time.

The dank cell seemed to tilt toward darkness as the last reserves of air in my lungs were used up. I hadn't been able to breathe for a while now. And honestly, I no longer wished for air. I welcomed the thought of being released from this endless cycle of pain. Free. I would finally be set free. It would be a relief.

Was this Cullen's plan all along? He couldn't save the abused woman in this dungeon, but he knew bringing us together would cause a violent magical reaction that would free us both from our bonds…forever.

I could think of no other way to save her, he'd told me.

Perhaps he somehow knew what would happen in the same way that he could see past a person's artifice by simply looking at them. I prayed he'd be able to live with himself…in the after. He'd make a good king as long as he was able to forgive himself and move beyond his grief after losing a brother he clearly adored.

I hoped for peace for him and for his kingdom—a kingdom I'd once envisioned making my home—as my heart thudded…

One.

Final.

Time.

A sea of black silence washed over me.

Chapter 13

Celestina

"*Celestina.*"

A deep voice called my name. The sound pulled me back from the darkness.

"*Celestina!*"

The world exploded.

"*What's happening?*"

Hot metal rained down on me, sizzling as it hit my skin.

"*Get back!*"

How could there be there pain after death? And whose voice was it that I kept hearing? It sounded familiar…and yet, my mind didn't seem to be working right.

"*It's too bright! I can't… I can't…*"

The talon digging into my flesh had never loosened its grip. Goddess, my wrist hurt.

"*Celestina! No!*"

My eyes fluttered open as if compelled by an outside force. I squinted through the unnaturally bright, piercing light. The cell's walls tumbled down around me like a child's wooden block tower.

Wings, the color of the blackest of nights, unfurled and seemed to soak up the unearthly light. Was this the goddess Perth coming for me? They said she rode into battlefields on leathery wings. With a violent tug on my wrist, the talon gripping me yanked me into the air. I gave a pained shout as the sharp movement dislodged my arm from my shoulder. Was this the goddess of death pulling me from this world so violently while the voice calling for me to stay grew fainter?

An inhuman clawed arm wrapped around my middle and pulled me snug against midnight black scales. The talons digging into my wrist released me. Battered and confused, I cradled my bloody hand to my chest and watched in horror and wonderment as the beast holding me rose jerkily out of the ruins of a rough-hewn stone building.

This wasn't the goddess of death pulling me from the wreckage of war. No, this wasn't death. Not when...not when I could still breathe. I drew in a deep breath, filling my lungs with the hot, dry air of Tiburnia's desert.

A beautiful black dragon had rescued me. I tentatively touched my neck. My fingers came back wet and sticky. The skin of my neck had been reduced to painful ribbons of raw wounds, which should have been worrying. But there was no metal.

Tears filled my eyes again. But this time they were born from joy.

The collar was gone.

I'd survived its removal. I was alive, which meant Soren had to be alive. I cried out with relief. I was safe—for the moment—and in the arms of one of my beloved dragons.

And, finally, I was free.

Amaya

I flew toward home. While my first instinct was to reduce my captor's stinking city to ashes while enacting my slow, painful torturous promises on *the man* and that stupidly smug Cullen, the heavy scent of blood on the dragon I'd dragged out of the dungeon cell with me was concerning enough to convince me to set aside my glorious plans for revenge.

Why hadn't she shifted? Touching her had pulled my bound-up magic to the surface. The sudden burst of magic had forced me to shift back to my dragon form. This dragon had to be powerful to pull off a stunt like that. No dragon I knew could control the flow of magic within another.

No dragon *should* be able to control another dragon's magic like that. It was unnatural. And a violation. The magic she'd pulled to the surface was mine and mine alone to call.

More of her blood dripped on to my taloned arm. It was warm and sticky and there was absolutely too much of it. In our fragile, human forms, a dragon could easily bleed to death. She needed her dragon form.

"Why don't you shift?" I asked her.

She didn't reply. Was she still alive? I gave her a little shake. She squeaked. Or screamed. I wasn't quite sure what to make of the sound she made, other than to think it sounded like something a prey animal would make, not a noise a fierce top predator would claim.

"Why don't you shift?" I repeated.

Again, silence.

"Why do you refuse to answer me? Are you angry with me?" She didn't have any right to be angry. She was the one who'd reached inside me and pulled at the magic. She shouldn't have done that.

Except…the burst of power had blasted off the shackles and shifted me into my true form. I stretched my long neck to the left and then to the right, moving muscles stiff from disuse. *The man* had kept me in that human form for too long. I usually shifted at least once a day. Only rarely would I go more than a few days stuck in that limiting human shape. How could a dragon accept being stuck in such a weak form when the air and wind called to her? The pull to fly alone should cause her to shift.

No matter. I would take this human-bound dragon back to our clan. Someone there should be able to tend to her wounds. I reached out with my mind, trying to connect with my parents or my brother to let them know I'd escaped and that I was coming home with an injured dragon.

My powers allowed me to connect with anyone who was thinking of me, no matter the distance. It allowed me to see into their thoughts, to see what they were doing, and to slip thoughts into their minds. It was a talent only midnight dragons possessed. At least, that's what I'd been told. Since I was the only midnight dragon in eons, I wasn't sure if my powers were unique to me or to my dragon lineage. Unlike the moonlight dragons, with a rich history of stories and lore, the midnight dragons' history had been kept in a shroud of darkness. They were known for their fierce fighting skills, but beyond that, little was known about them, even within the clan elders who seemed to know everything about everything.

"Anther?" Surely, my older brother would be thinking...*worrying* about me. I reached out with my mind to make a connection with him.

"Like I already told you, she was dying, Soren. Short of starting a war, I didn't know what else I could do to save her."

Prince Cullen? Ugh! Why would I connect with that smooth-tongued vampire? Even the thought of him talking about me made me want to rip out his tongue and eat it.

I shook my head and tried again to reach out to Anther...or anyone who wasn't a stupid vampire. But my connection to Cullen only grew stronger, clearer.

"We'll get Celestina back, I promise." I could see through Prince Cullen's eyes that he was standing in the dank dungeon. Bright sunlight streamed in through the gaping hole in the roof that my blast of magic had created. Cullen looked up at the ruined dungeon and frowned. He wasn't the only one standing in the ruins of the cell. A beefy vampire with shoulder-length black hair and startling green eyes stood next to him. Cullen's companion picked up the shattered remains of the tight golden necklace the dragon I now held had been wearing.

"It's covered in blood." The beefy vampire sounded anguished.

"But that damned thing is off her. It worked. The collar is broken," Cullen said.

"There's so much blood." The vampire wasn't wrong. I could see through Cullen's eyes the startlingly big puddle of blood in the middle of the cell. It was worrying.

"Are you still with me, dragon-girl?" I asked my companion.

She didn't answer, so I shook her again. She whimpered.

Which meant she must still be alive, although not as active as before. I flew higher in search of a stronger current of air. I needed to get her to help as soon as possible. I didn't relish the thought of carrying a dead dragon back to the clan with me. Our numbers were small enough as it was. Every dragon's life was important.

"They needed to be together," Cullen was telling this other vampire. Was this his brother? The brother Cullen had been worried would kill him for tossing his bonded partner into a dungeon? It looked as if the vampire could take out Cullen with a swipe of his hand. I hoped he didn't. Cullen's life was *mine*. I planned to chop off his stupid ears and stuff them up his stupid nostrils. "I know it's painful for you, Soren, but this had to happen."

"The blood." The other vampire looked like he might be sick at the sight of the puddled blood. Who would have guessed someone with a warrior's physique would be so squeamish?

"You're alive, which means she's alive."

For now, I thought.

Cullen flinched. He looked around as if searching for something. He shook his head and muttered, "She'd said she could do it, and she has."

"Do what?" Soren asked.

"She'd told me she could make contact with anyone who was thinking about her. Amaya has Celestina. Celestina is hurt, but Amaya is flying Celestina to her clan to get help. *Isn't that right?*"

"How should I know?" Soren asked.

"I wasn't asking you. I was asking Amaya. She's listening in on our conversation."

"I have his dragon," I said. It felt only fair that I answered him. *"I'm taking her far, far away from you slaving bastards. But as soon as she's safe, I'm coming back, and I'm going to roast your ass."*

"Don't forget you promised to eat me alive first," he said with a smile in his stupid voice. *"You promised me that more than once."*

I screamed and cut off the connection. I didn't dare try to find Anther or anyone else in my family for fear of ending up in Cullen's head again. I didn't want to risk having the conceited jerk get the idea that I wanted to be sitting with him in his thoughts.

Although…his head was a calm place. Like the forest below the plateau on a quiet spring morning. His thoughts flowed like the serene waters traveling down the slow stream where Anther used to take me to go wading on hot summer days when I was just a little hatchling. It was so different from the firestorm of anxious thoughts that usually engulfed my head.

"Hang in there, Celestina," I said to my silent rider. *"The Andalotian Plateau lies just beyond that horizon."*

Chapter 14

Celestina

The dragon carried me for what felt like forever. I passed out several times, only to be jolted back awake when the dragon would shake me. What a relief to be able to think about dragons again!

A storyteller once told the royal court about a dragon thief who would sneak into royal bedchambers and fly away with sparkly jewels to carry back to her hoard. One day, the dragon snuck into a chamber only to find a pretty young maiden, a lady favored by the queen of the kingdom, sleeping in her bed. The dragon had never seen such a beautiful woman. Instead of taking the lady's cache of emeralds and diamonds, she stood transfixed. She instantly loved the fair maiden and couldn't imagine ever leaving her side. Not even when the maiden woke up and started screaming. Not even when the Royal Guards came marching into the chamber. Not even when an axe was swung at her neck, she never moved from her spot where she could gaze upon the most beautiful creature the dragon had ever seen. Because she'd loved so recklessly, she lost her life that day.

When I first heard that story, I felt sorry for the dragon. And angry.

Why would the dragon let herself become entrapped by love? Didn't she recognize the danger? I'd never fall for such a trap. And wasn't it a wonder that I could remember that tale without having a collar punish me for thinking it?

The sun was starting to disappear beneath the horizon—streaks of red clawed like a dragon's talons through the sky—when the dragon carrying me slowed and lowered us to a clearing on a flat-topped mountain.

Dozens of men of various ages and an older woman carrying a large wicker basket raced out from the shadowy forest to meet us. The dragon carrying me landed near them. She then placed me on the soft, mossy ground with surprising gentleness. Even so, I hugged my ruined wrist and curled in on myself to escape the pain that made me feel as if my body was tearing apart. I felt too weak from blood loss to do anything else other than to hug myself, even too weak to be curious about what kind of people would come to greet a dragon.

"Where the hell have you been?" a tall blond-haired man dressed all in black shouted at the dragon. "We've been searching everywhere for you! There was no trace to follow! Nothing! I thought you had died!"

"Anther, cease," the older woman said. She knelt next to me and pushed a clump of my tangled and blood-matted hair out of my face. "By the stars," she gasped. "It-it's you! And blessed be, you're hurt. Don't worry, dear one. We'll take care of you."

"Soren," I whispered his name since it hurt like the devil to speak or breathe or move. *"He…heal."* His blood would make all the pain go away. He'd done it before, given me his blood to heal me. And it had worked miracles. *"Soren."*

"You're in good hands, child." She laid a cool hand against my cheek. "You've come home." She looked up at a shadow standing behind her. "Trace, do you see? It's her! It's her! After I get bandages on her injuries and stop the bleeding, I'll need you to carry her up to your house. It's only right that you be the one to watch over our precious one."

The shadow stepped forward and gradually took the shape of a man. He wore deep green trousers and a natural wool sweater that had been knitted with an intricate basketweave design. His slightly too long brown hair was mussed. And he had a fierce scowl on his lips. But his crystal blue eyes warmed when they landed on me, and then the corners of his eyes crinkled. "She no longer wears the collar, but she's not yet free of the binding spell. We can't—"

"She is here now. We should feel blessed for that. And she needs our help," the woman cut him off.

The man snapped his mouth closed and jammed his hands into his trousers' pockets. "Yes, ma'am."

The woman had already taken my arm in her hands and was wrapping a damp, herbed gauze around my injured wrist. The herbal wrap dulled the pain almost instantly. She worked quickly and efficiently, murmuring apologies when she caused me pain. Another woman came running into the clearing. Like the men, she too was wearing trousers and a woolen sweater. "Is it true? Is it her?"

The older woman looked up and nodded.

"Bless us. What a day." But then she saw me and gasped. She pressed her paint-stained hands to her mouth. "Is she...is she going to live?"

By the way she'd paled several shades, I figured I looked as bad as I felt. I held my breath waiting to hear what the healer thought.

She seemed to sense I was listening intently and patted my good hand. "We're a hardy lot. She'll heal up in no time."

"Don't know why you left her with those horrid people. Look at her. And from the stories I've been hearing, she's had one brush with death after another. They don't know how to care for one of our kind," the woman with the paint on her hands complained.

"She was fine until those vampires got involved, Mother," Trace said.

The black dragon who'd brought me here had wandered off with the man who'd scolded her. When Trace mentioned vampires, the dragon turned her head back toward us and hissed.

"Don't wander off too far, Daughter," the healer called to the dragon. "I want a full accounting of what happened as soon as I get Celestina's wounds cared for and her settled." She looked down at me again. "How does a nice healing tea sound, dear?"

At the thought of tea, tears sprang to my eyes. Soren had hidden that he'd been feeding me his blood by mixing it in with Mary's horrid healing tea.

The woman patted my hand again. "Don't worry, dear. You'll get stronger, and things will work out for the best. You'll see." She looked up.

"Trace, I'm ready for you to take her."

Trace gave a grim nod and then squatted next to me. "I'm going to pick you up, Celestina. It might hurt. And if it does, I apologize."

Although being moved did hurt, having him whisper a pained, *"sorry,"* several times as if he were suffering along with me seemed to make the pain ease a little.

He carried me into a thick forest that blotted out the fading sun. It felt cold in the shadows. And when I shivered, Trace held me closer to his chest where I could snuggle into the warmth of his thick, wool sweater.

"It's not far," he said as his long stride swiftly ate up the distance.

At the end of the trail, which was covered in juniper needles, the trees thinned out and a tidy village came into view.

"Welcome to Beithiria," Trace said, with a nod toward the beginning of a stone path that led to a small downtown where one and two-story stone buildings lined both sides of the street. As Trace walked through the middle of the village, people came out to gawk.

"Is it her?"

"She looks awful?"

"What happened to her?"

"Was it the vampires or the humans that hurt her?"

"She's finally home."

"Look at them together already. They will make a handsome couple."

"I'd given up hope of this ever happening. But here she is. And in his arms."

"Sorry about that," Trace said, his cheeks darkening. "To most in our clan, your existence has become more of a myth than reality. You've been gone that long. They hear the tales, especially the old ones. And that's all they know of you." He sighed. "When you're stronger you'll be able to meet the clan. And they'll get to know you for who you are instead of what you represent." He looked down at me. The corner of his tight mouth loosened just enough to form a ghost of a smile. "We all will."

"What do they think I am?" I asked, my voice raspy and rough.

"Our future."

Amaya

"*What* happened?" Anther jumped up from the armchair he'd taken before I could snag it. That was my favorite armchair, which he knew. He'd taken it just to vex me. As he paced the living room, I slipped behind him and settled into the armchair. After pulling my legs up under me, I wrapped myself in a wool blanket my mother had knit last season.

"I already told you what happened," I said wiggling until every bit of me was enclosed in the cocoon of the soft blanket. "Although, I'm just as surprised as you seem to be that the girl dragon I dragged out of that dungeon cell is *our* moonlight dragon. Like, wow. I'd assumed she'd died at the hands of the vampires."

My parents, who'd been away when *the man* had captured me, had returned as soon as they'd heard I'd gone missing. They sat side-by-side on the sofa near the manor house's huge fireplace with their hands clasped. The old human woman, oddly enough, was still in residence and had somehow talked her way into joining us in the room. She huddled in a small chair that she'd pulled so close to the fire, she was practically sitting in the flames.

"We knew the moonlight dragon wasn't dead, dear," my mother, Juniper, said in that soothing voice of hers. "Trace has been keeping watch over her. At least, until you disappeared. We were all so worried at the possibility that we'd lose both of you that all of us—Trace included—rushed back to join the search. Are you sure you're unharmed? None of those nasty blood spells left any lasting damage, did they?"

"Can't believe you let yourself get caught by a human. What happened to all those safety lessons I taught you over the years? Did they go in one ear and out the other?" Anther nagged.

"I'm fine. Honest," I answered my mother, while ignoring my brother. Poking at me was his way of letting me know my abduction had scared him.

"The Tiburnians shouldn't have shackles that can bind *and* hide dragons. Where did they get them?" Anther demanded. "And why didn't we know they had them?"

"That's something we'll be investigating," my father, who was the leader of the clan, answered gravely.

"Whatever the moonlight dragon did," I said, "it broke the shackles and allowed me to use my powers again. I've never felt such a burst of power. I feel stronger now than I've ever felt."

My mother nodded. "Our stories tell us that moonlight dragons are the most powerful magic wielders in our world. Clearly, we're fortunate to live in a time to see that power at work. Thank the goddess. Although, I must admit it hurts to see her so injured." My mother was the village healer, a talent rarely needed in a village filled with dragons who only needed to shift forms to heal.

"But that's the thing," I said. "You say she's powerful, but she didn't use her magical abilities. She pulled *mine*. Even though the vampire shackles had blocked access to my ability to wield magic, the moonlight dragon pulled at my magic as if the shackles meant nothing. My magic exploded out of me in a way I've never experienced before. Stronger. More out of control. One moment, I was in human form, glowing like a star, and then the next I was in my dragon form. I didn't know how she did it. Or why she didn't then shift to her dragon form." I looked over to my mother. "Why doesn't she shift? She lost so much blood. And those burns and deep cuts on her neck and wrist look painful. Why doesn't she shift and heal herself?"

"She can't, honey. The human queen who stole her trapped Celestina in her human form. She's been that way since she was a baby."

"From what Trace has told us, I don't think she has access to any of the magical currents," my father Drix chimed in.

"She sure had access to my magic." I didn't like it. I wasn't sure I even liked her.

"If her queen had Celestina living as a human with no wielding abilities, does she even know what she is or what she means to us?" Anther asked.

Mother shook her head. "I don't know."

Anther stopped pacing long enough to playfully punch me in the arm. "You're no longer the only special one, squirt. How does it feel?"

I growled and sank lower into the chair and into the cocoon of the blanket. The moonlight dragon was the light to my darkness. She'd always been the clan's symbol of hope for a new life and a new country. The clan called midnight dragons death-bringers and war-enders. Stories about my kind involved gruesome violence.

Growing up with the knowledge that I was the only remaining half of a power duo, I was okay that others feared me. In time, I became the strong warrior the clan had expected of me. Now that the moonlight dragon had returned and I'd tasted the giddiness of the clan's hope in the air, I no longer felt comfortable with the role of death-bringer that I'd been assigned.

I didn't want to be the brute force to the moonlight dragon's beautiful peace. I didn't want to be the moonlight dragon's puppet like I'd been back in the dungeon.

Without her, I wouldn't have escaped. Without her, I wouldn't have survived those shackles. Yeah, I should feel grateful.

But I didn't.

I sneered every time my mother, father, or brother mentioned the moonlight dragon. And now that my family was satisfied that I wasn't injured, her miraculous return was all any of them wanted to talk about.

This was Cullen's fault. If only he'd done the decent thing and helped me escape right away, I wouldn't be sitting here now, while wallowing in this puddle of stinking self-pity. *Stupid vampire.*

Chapter 15

Celestina

"I brought you fresh clothes," Trace said as he entered the bedroom. He had to duck to not hit his head on the doorframe. Keeping his eyes diverted from where I was convalescing in the bed, he placed the small bundle on a table near the door and started to back out. "I cooked dinner if you're hungry. I can bring a plate up. Or, if you'd prefer, you can come down to the kitchen to eat there."

"I'll…" I shifted uneasily in the bed. I hadn't been awake long enough to assess the state of my injuries. But at the same time, I didn't want to stay cooped up in this room for any longer than necessary. "I'll try to come down."

He glanced over at me. He was tall and broad, and his presence seemed to fill the entire space. "If you don't feel up to it, don't push yourself. If you don't come down within the half hour, I'll bring up the plate and more healing tea." He stepped out of the room and started to close the door.

"How long?" I called to him. I hugged the blanket to my chest and wiggled to sit up.

He waited until I stopped flopping around like a fish before asking, "Pardon?"

"How long have I been here?" I felt so disoriented. The healing tea was strong. And while it tasted so much better than Mary's pungent tea, it had made me sleep for I-don't-know-how long. I remembered briefly waking several times to find the healer hovering over me. She'd been changing my bandages, rubbing a citrusy salve on my burns, or urging me to drink more of the healing tea.

"Four days," he answered. "You're stronger now. Awake. It's good. If you don't come down, I'll bring up the plate. But…" he paused again. "Please, try to put on the clothes. Juniper says I should encourage you to move around today."

He didn't wait for me to reply before closing the door.

I sat in bed while digesting the fact that I'd been in this room for four days. We were in a small brick house located at the far end of the market street. The front of the house was filled with weaving equipment. He'd hurried me through the shop and up a narrow set of stairs that led to this room.

The healer had entered shortly afterward. She'd placed her large basket at the foot of the bed and then pushed Trace out the door. Smiling, she'd introduced herself as Juniper, the village's only healer. She reassured me over and over that she was going to help me feel better before removing the sheer dress that was even more indecent now with a ripped arm strap and the bodice hanging so loose that I was showing off most of my right breast. She'd cooed nonsense words as she'd carefully washed my body with a warm sponge.

Before she did anything, she would explain what she was going to do and had asked my permission before doing it. I'd appreciated that. And I'd appreciated her calm manner.

After she'd coated my burnt skin with a cooling salve and pulled a soft cotton shift over my head, she'd had me drink two mugs of her special healing tea. With my injuries tended and my belly filled, she'd tucked me under a pile of heavy blankets and had left with the promise that Trace would watch over me.

How had that been four days ago? *Soren must be out of his head with worry.* He'd once promised me that even if I ran away from him, he'd come fetch me.

Come find me.

He would come. He always kept his promises.

I eased myself from the bed. Even after four days of healing time, the ripped skin on my neck still stung like fire whenever I moved. My wrist, thankfully, seemed to be mending. While it still pained me, I could open and close my hand, which was a relief. I'd been worried that I'd lose the use of it.

Still, everything hurt, especially my one arm that had been pulled from my shoulder joint when the dragon had yanked me into the sky. I needed to get to Soren. He could heal me.

I groaned as I pulled the thin cotton shift off over my head. It took quite a long time to pull on the clothes Trace had left for me. I fell twice trying to pull up the brown leather trousers that seemed to fit like a second skin.

"Are you okay in there?" Trace had banged on the door each time I'd fallen, but he didn't burst in.

"Just-just getting dressed." Which was hard to do with just one working arm.

It took time, but I finally managed to dress myself in the trousers and warm green sweater Trace had provided. Before heading down to the kitchen, I peered into a small mirror hanging on the wall next to the door. My eyes looked bruised. Heavy bandages encircled my neck. My hair, although it looked clean, was a tangled brown mess. I was sure I had Juniper to thank for keeping me washed. At least, I hoped it was the older, kindly Juniper who'd washed me these past four days and not Trace.

If it had been Trace, dinner was about to be damned awkward.

I made my way slowly down the stairs, taking in everything in the home. There were two other bedrooms on the second floor. And one bathroom, which I made use of. Clearly, one of the bedrooms belonged to Trace. The bed was unmade and there were dirty clothes in an overflowing basket.

But other than that one bit of untidiness, the rest of the house was impeccably neat. Framed paintings of landscapes and dragons in various poses filled the walls in the hallway and stairwell. I studied each one as I made my way to a small living room on the first floor. Once there, I stopped and gaped at the large painting hanging over the fireplace.

It was a portrait of the green dragon...*my* green dragon. The painting depicted the same clearing where the black dragon had landed four days ago. The green dragon stood on his hind legs with his impressive wings spread wide as if about to take flight.

"My mother is a painter," Trace said, startling me. He nodded to the painting I couldn't seem to tear my eyes away from. "She painted that one. And hung it there when I was..." He frowned and paused before mumbling, "When I was away, she hung it over the fireplace. She's put all the paintings up in my house, save for a few. She's run out of room in her own place." He shrugged. "I don't want you to think I'm vain. I'm not. I would never have put a huge self-portrait like that anywhere in my house. Well, maybe in my guestroom when my brother sneaks over to stay while I'm away. He's a thief, and I wouldn't mind him thinking I was watching over him."

"That-that's you?" My breath got stuck in my throat. "You're...?" I shook my head. Trace was the green dragon? *My* green dragon? I shook my head again, having trouble reconciling the two images. My heart started pounding.

My green dragon. I'd pretended and dreamed that he stayed in the valley because he was watching out for me. But that had been a fantasy dreamed up by a lonely girl with a big imagination. It hadn't been real. The dragons had simply lived in that valley near the castle. They hadn't been there for me. Of course not. Because if they had been there to watch over me, why had they left? And why didn't they ever intervene to protect me from Queen Beatrice? No, I couldn't have heard him correctly. I was having a mental breakdown, that was what was happening. I was weak from my injuries, weak from spending four days in a drugged stupor. My mind had snapped.

"I think you need to sit down."

He caught me under my arms just as my legs started to give out. He led me to a cushioned bench that wasn't far from the fireplace. His hand pressed on my back as he directed me to put my head between my legs.

"Breathe, Celestina. Nice and slow."

I tried. It was excellent advice. But I couldn't stop thinking about what he'd said. That painting hanging over the fireplace of my magnificent green dragon with gold-tinged scales was…was this man? And the more I thought about it, the more my breathing felt out of control.

I batted away the hand rubbing up and down my back and sat up. The world wobbled. "You…you're…the…green…dragon?"

Trace nodded.

"Gods." I put my head between my legs again.

"Thank the goddess for your perfect timing. She saw the portrait my mother painted and started hyperventilating," Trace said to someone who'd walked up to the other side of me. From my perspective, all I could see were black boots.

This new person scoffed. "This is our savior?" I recognized the voice from the dungeon.

"Be kind, Amaya." That was Juniper, the healer. I also recognized her voice from when she'd cared for me. "Celestina has been raised to believe she was human. We must give her time to accept her new reality."

Juniper's worn tan boots came into view. Her warm hand gently touched the center of my back as she crouched down next to me. "It's okay, Celestina. You're safe here."

"Do you think she needs more healing tea?" Trace sounded nervous. "I could go prepare it."

"So she can sleep for four more days?" Amaya scoffed again.

"Only if she's in pain," Juniper said at the same time. "Are you in pain, dear? Do you need more tea?"

The thought of drifting back into that black void of oblivion tempted me. But doing that would only delay the inevitable. I needed to face these people—these *dragons*. I needed to hear what they had to say.

And I needed to figure out how to leave here and find my way back to Soren.

By focusing on my desire to see Soren again, I managed to steady my breathing. I needed to get back to him. He'd heal my injuries. He'd know how to make things right.

I lifted my head. "I'll be okay. I don't need the tea."

Juniper gave an approving nod. "You'll feel stronger after you get some food in your belly. Let's go to the kitchen. I'm sure you have questions. And there's much we need to tell you."

Soon, the four of us were seated around an old, well-loved kitchen table. Trace carried four bowls of stew over to us. Juniper handed out spoons and cloth napkins that she'd found in a cabinet drawer. The kitchen had two large windows that looked out onto an overgrown garden. On the opposite wall was a small stove, a double oven, and an oversized sink. Lining the third wall were floor-to-ceiling cabinets that had been decorated with painted climbing flowers, clouds, stars, planets, and silhouettes of dragons. More of Trace's mother's handiwork, I guessed.

"Ohhh, this smells delicious," Amaya said with her nose practically inside the bowl Trace had set in front of her. She looked so much healthier than she had in the dungeon. She wore her long, black hair in a single braid that she'd flung over her shoulder. Her cheeks had a rosy glow that seemed to soften her severe features. She was dressed all in black. Black leggings, black sweater, black boots. After sniffing loudly, she jerked her head up and stared at Trace. "You made this? I didn't know you could cook."

Trace's cheeks flushed as he glanced in my direction before answering Amaya. "I haven't lived in the village for a long time, as you know. I had to learn to care for myself and the others who'd come stay with me."

Amaya turned and frowned at me with a look that felt accusatory.

Instead of thinking too hard about any of that, I tasted the meaty stew. It had a spice in it that I didn't recognize but made my tastebuds dance with pleasure. Soon, my spoon was scraping the bottom of the bowl.

"Do you need more?" Trace had already pushed back his chair and was reaching over Juniper to grab my wooden bowl.

Juniper put her hand on his arm. "She's had enough for now. It's time we talk."

I'd been expecting this. I needed to hear about them...and about myself. Was I a dragon? Was I *the* moonlight dragon?

I wanted answers. And yet, I didn't feel prepared. I drew a long, slow breath and held it as I nodded.

"Let's start with the basics. Do you understand what you are?" Juniper asked.

I slowly let out the breath I was holding. "I was told that I was a moonlight dragon." My body tensed, waiting for the collar to punish me for saying that aloud. One time, when I had tried to tell Soren how I felt connected to the dragons, the collar had hurt me so badly that I'd bled from my ears and eyes. No punishments came now, of course, because the collar was gone. Still, it was hard to convince my body that talking about dragons wasn't going to harm me.

"You are the last moonlight dragon," Juniper confirmed. "That's true."

"And I was stolen? From a cave?"

"You were taken," Trace said. "You hatched twenty-three years ago. You and Amaya both hatched on the same day. A moonlight dragon and a midnight dragon." He smiled at the other young woman. "A few days after the two of you hatched, a woman with strong magic blew through the village and took you. She left ten of our brethren dead. Our leader, my father, was one of the dead."

"So were two of Trace's older brothers and a sister." Juniper squeezed Trace's hand. "Your family lost more than any of the others that sad day."

Trace grunted and looked away.

"My parents recently told me that Queen Frieda had brought me to them when I was a baby. They knew what I was, but they never told me that I wasn't human. Queen Frieda had ordered my parents to keep me safe."

"Those humans aren't your parents," Amaya snapped. "And Queen Frieda only kept you safe because she wanted to use you."

"Who are my parents? Were my true parents one of the ten who were killed when the queen had stolen me?" I asked.

"We don't know who your parents were," Juniper said. "During the Vampiric Wars the vampires had decimated our numbers. Those who remained hid themselves away. Save for a few solitary dragons on the continent, we are the last surviving clan. There are legends of dragons that left the Jayden Continent to find safer lands elsewhere. If the legends are true, hopefully, those dragons were successful in finding a safe place to live. Sadly, no dragon has ever returned from another land. There's just us. And the Vampiric Wars killed off two of our most powerful kind—the moonlight dragons and the midnight dragons."

"I've heard the stories of the moonlight dragons," I said. "But I've never heard about a midnight dragon."

"There's a reason for that," Juniper was quick to answer. "Midnight dragons were our most deadly warriors. They lived in the shadows. Our enemies never saw them strike, never knew their full power, until it was too late."

"If no one knew about the midnight dragon's magic, how could the vampires defeat them in the War of the Magics?" That didn't make sense. Just like it didn't make sense that Juniper didn't know who my true parents were.

"They're the Vampiric Wars to us," Amaya corrected.

"We're not sure how the vampires managed it," Juniper said at the same time. "They used a magic never witnessed before or since. But the legends talk about a magical blanket attack that took out our strongest, our most fierce without touching them, without knowing where they were, or even that they existed."

I tried to imagine such a weapon. None of the stories about the vampires had ever mentioned that level of destruction. But then again, many of the stories I'd been told about vampires had turned out to be wrong.

I supposed the stories about the dragons could be faulty as well.

"After the blanket attack ended, the vampires came in and destroyed all our nests, killed our babies, smashed the eggs. Only two eggs survived the attack. The egg that held you. And the egg that held Amaya. Our ancestors hid those two precious eggs. They watched over them, praying for the return of their most fierce fighters. But the eggs never hatched. Still, generation after generation, the clan guarded the eggs. The elders began to speculate that the eggs were waiting for a time when the world was ready for the return of the fifth kingdom. I'm sure you can imagine the excitement we all felt when the first egg—your egg—formed a crack and we could hear movement inside. What a time to be alive, we all anxiously thought. This was surely the return of the dragon age."

Chapter 16

Celestina

"The return of dragons?" I whispered. Could I truly be living evidence of the start of a new dragon age? And did that also mean the success of this new age depended on my ability to wield magic? The only magic available to me was the ability to compel other magical creatures. It was a powerful magic, but not exclusive to me. Vampires possessed a similar power.

Juniper shrugged. "There's no way of knowing. There are other tales that say the moonlight dragon will return to protect the dragons from a new age of wars, that the moonlight dragon's magic will be the only force that will allow what remains of the dragon clans to survive another wholesale vampire attack."

I couldn't believe that Soren would allow his warriors to attack the dragons. He might be the Beast of Fein who fiercely defended his people, but he was also fair and just. "The vampires wouldn't attack the dragons without provocation."

"Stop living in the clouds. They already do," Amaya snapped. "They killed our main food source and shot me out of the air. Did we provoke them to do that? Did we do something that made them feel justified to hurt us?"

"It was the humans in Tiburnia who attacked you, not—" I tried to argue.

"I was told you bonded with a vampire. Are you seriously going to sit there and deny that Prince Cullen's brother isn't a vampire? Are you going to sit there and tell me that Prince Cullen and your vampire weren't involved with imprisoning me? Because if you are, I can tell you now that you're deluding yourself. The vampires were just as involved with keeping me in those enchanted shackles as *the man* who had shot me out of the sky with a vampire's blood magic."

"I think Cullen was trying to rescue—" I started to say.

"You can't tell me what happened." Amaya shot up from her chair so quickly that it toppled over with a loud crash. "I was there!"

I raised my hands, fully expecting her to hit me.

"Daughter, cease," Juniper said sharply.

Amaya pressed her fists on the table and glared at me.

"Amaya," Trace said soothingly. "Please. Celestina is not the enemy."

"She has bonded with the enemy. She sides with them." Her voice had softened, thanks to Trace's urging. But she still made it clear with her facial expression that she didn't like me.

I didn't know what had happened to her, what the Tiburnians had done to her. Maybe Cullen had taken an active role in torturing her. I hoped he hadn't. But I couldn't forget how he'd drugged me, hit his own brother, and had me locked away with Amaya in the same horrid dungeon.

I'd convinced myself that Cullen had done those terrible things to bring the two of us together and to give Amaya a chance to escape. The explosion of power that happened when I touched her did free me from the collar and her from her chains. But had that been his goal?

Cullen couldn't have betrayed us. The two brothers were close. They clearly loved each other.

Soren. How I ached to go to him. *He must feel like he's in hell right now.*

"Celestina is no one's enemy," Trace said in his even-tempered voice.

Amaya snarled at him.

"Amaya," Juniper said more forcefully. "Behave."

"Yes, Mother." Amaya finally picked up the overturned chair and dropped into it. She angled her body away from me and crossed her arms over her chest to let me know that even though she was giving into her mother's demands, she wasn't changing her mind about me.

"Amaya is your daughter?" I asked Juniper. "I thought you'd said we both came from dragon eggs that had been protected for eons. How is it that you're her mother?" Were dragons immortal? I'd occasionally heard legends that would claim that dragons lived eternal lives, but then again, most people on the continent believed that dragons and dragon lore were entertaining myths and tended to embellish the stories.

Juniper smiled warmly. "She's not my biological daughter. But she is the daughter of my heart." She leaned over and kissed the side of Amaya's head.

I had trouble accepting that Amaya was the same as me, that she was the midnight to my moonlight. If we'd hatched on the same day and were both dragons who were eons old, I supposed we should try to get to know one another. We should try to be friends.

"Amaya is a blessing and a miracle, just like you are, Celestina. If you hadn't been stolen away from us, a dragon family within the clan would have raised you. You would have been loved." Juniper swallowed thickly as tears clogged her eyes. "You are loved, Celestina. We never stopped loving you, never stopped watching over you."

"That's what you did," I said, turning to Trace. "You were in the valley. You and the other dragons. You were there because of me?" Just like I'd dreamed—it had been the truth.

"I was. I'd bring younglings with me. They'd help keep guard and watch over you, make sure no one harmed you, and made sure Queen Frieda held up her end of the bargain."

"Bargain? You made a bargain with the queen? You let her keep me even after she'd kidnapped me and killed so many of your clan in the process? How-how could you do that?" Was this how they showed their love? "Why didn't you come for me?"

"I wanted to," Trace growled deeply.

"We couldn't," Juniper quickly added. "Queen Frieda threatened to kill you if we ever made a move to retrieve you, or if we threatened Earst in any way. She kept you close at hand for that reason. She never let you leave the confines of the castle walls because she feared that we might try to steal you. And she wanted to keep you safe only so she could use you as a weapon against the other kingdoms, perhaps even against us. It took several years of negotiations for Trace to get permission to keep watch, even from a distance."

"And then Queen Beatrice rose to power," Trace added with a snap of his teeth.

Juniper nodded. "The agreement we had with her mother held for several years after her death. But then the new queen threatened to kill you if we didn't leave the valley for good."

"I didn't leave," Trace spoke up. "No matter what Queen Beatrice demanded, I wouldn't leave you alone with that marsh-worm of a queen. I kept to my human form and went to work in the castle stables. Amaya's brother joined me from time to time. And when Queen Beatrice trapped you even deeper with the slave collar and handed you over to that"—his lip curled with distaste—"vampire, I followed. I would have taken you then, but the collar wouldn't allow you to stray far from the vampire without killing you."

"You knew how the collar worked?"

Trace nodded. "Although you may have felt it was true at times, you were never alone, Celestina. You were never without friends who cared for you."

I pinched my lips together to keep myself from sobbing in front of these strangers who seemed to know more about my life than I did.

Juniper smiled broadly. "And now we're all together as it should be. The moonlight dragon is back home with our midnight dragon."

"Has she returned?" Amaya asked. "She's still trapped under Queen Frieda's original spell. She can't access her magic. She can't shift. And she's in league with the vampires. None of that feels like she's with us. None of that feels like a reason to celebrate." Amaya stood from the table, but this time when she pushed her chair back, it didn't topple over. "You're all acting like my bringing the moonlight dragon to Beithiria is a good thing. The way I see it, this is a disaster. She's not one of us. She'll never be one of us. I'm glad she can't access her powers. Just think about how much destruction she and her vampires would cause us if she could!"

"Amaya! That's uncalled for." Juniper rose as well.

The midnight dragon gave a frustrated scream before charging out of the house, slamming the door on her way out.

"I'd better go talk with her," Juniper said, her cheeks turning pink. "Growing up without you has been difficult for my girl. You'll have to give her time to adjust to the idea that she now has someone else she can rely on, that she's one part of a powerful team."

Trace and I sat in silence after Amaya and Juniper left. Finally, Trace sighed.

"I'm sorry about that," he said, quietly. "Amaya has always been...spirited." He stood as if he couldn't contain his restless energy. "Let me brew you some of the healing tea."

"No." I rose from my chair as well, glad my legs felt sturdy. "Thank you," I hastily added. Trace had been nothing but kind, which only made me feel bad about what I had to say.

He stopped halfway to the sink and turned toward me with his head tilted to one side. His bright blue eyes were alive with life and hope.

"Amaya is not wrong." I placed my hand on the back of my chair to steady myself. "I've not returned. I'm sure it's lovely here. But this is not my home. My home is with Soren. My life is with Soren."

Trace drew a deep breath. As he released it, a gentle smile softened his features. "Celestina, I understand your reluctance to accept what we're telling you. I don't want you to think we're trying to rip you away from the only life you've known. We're not. What we're doing is giving you another life, a life where you can grow into the dragon you are meant to be. Whether you can access your magic or not, don't you think you deserve to learn about who you are? To spend time with your own kind?"

"I—" He wasn't wrong. I had longed to find a place where I felt like I fit.

I want to keep you close because I think you and I might fit, Soren had once told me. And those words had served as a balm that soothed deep wounds I hadn't realized had hurt so sharply before he'd spoken them. He was my home.

"Amaya is also correct when she told you that I've bonded with Soren," I explained. "It's an unbreakable vow that tied our lives together. Even if I wanted to, which I don't, I can't abandon him."

Trace gave a shallow nod. "It's understandable that you'd have strong feelings for the first male to offer you kindness. I'd be more concerned if you didn't feel...*something*...toward him." He gestured toward the front of the house. "Take a walk through the village with me? Everyone here is like you. We're all dragons living hidden away from the world. But I think you'll find that the small world we've created on the top of this plateau isn't a hardship. It's quite comfortable. It's a place worth fighting for. I hope once you get to know it like I do, you'll agree."

Since I doubted Trace would lend me a horse or offer to fly me back to Tiburnia or north to Fein, I followed behind him as he led the way through his home, through the weaving shop at the front, and out onto the cobbled market street.

The smell of freshly baked bread filled my senses as we walked down the street. He made no effort to touch me. He kept his hands buried in his trousers' pockets. But every few feet he'd look over at me and the pleasure I saw in his expression sat like a heavy stone in my belly.

The others we encountered on the street nodded and smiled but kept their distance. I felt as if they were all treating me like one of the wild fillies Queen Beatrice would occasionally bring into the royal stables. The kind that might harm itself if you moved too quickly or stepped too close. That, too, sat like a stone in my belly.

This wasn't my home. The plateau didn't call to me like the Yurdu Mountains had when I'd ridden with Soren, Raya, and Gray toward Fein's capital city of Sukoon.

Trace talked in that soothing voice of his as he described what was sold in each of the shops we passed—the bakery that offered the most delicious sugarberry tarts no matter the time of year, the tannery that could make leather clothing that felt like butter in your hands, the seamstress who produced outfits with magical spells stitched into the seams, or the toy shop that made the most imaginative items from wood, metal, and cloth for the children who called the village home.

By the time we'd reached the end of the street, the sun had dipped below the distant tree line, and it had gotten quite dark in the village. The windows of homes we passed as we turned down a street lined with charming cottages glowed with various soft flickering lights, suggesting lamplight and fireplaces. This was so different from the electric lights that lit up the castle in Earst and the palace in Fein.

"If you're up to it, I'd like you to meet a few of my friends." He'd stopped in the middle of the road and had turned toward me. "We don't have to stay long," he added as he raised his eyebrows.

Did I feel up to it? My neck, wrist, and dislocated shoulder still hurt with every movement. And I felt like I could easily crawl back into that soft bed of Trace's and sleep there for another four days.

Honestly, I still found it difficult to believe I was a dragon. I didn't feel like a dragon. I couldn't fly. I didn't have scales. The only fire I'd ever felt burning in my core was from indigestion.

And yet, everyone kept telling me I was a dragon.

"Sure," I said before I found a reason to run screaming toward where the sun had fallen.

Trace nodded to himself as he led the way to a small cottage at the end of a dirt path. The pretty lavender walls vibrated with music and laughter. He paused at the door and pressed a finger to his lips. "My friends can be a little much at times, but they always mean well. It should be fine."

And with that unsettling warning, he pushed open the dark purple door, and entered the cottage's main living area. A large chandelier hung from an arched wooden beam in the center of the room, showering the people crowded together with a warm, yellow light. Two men stood next to a huge fireplace and strummed stringed instruments while singing a lively tune. A half dozen couples had hooked their arms and giggled wildly as they danced in looping circles.

Three people turned our way as we entered.

"It's Trace!" a woman in a long, colorful flowered skirt and white sweater squealed.

A heartbeat later, the music and laughter and conversation all came to an abrupt stop.

Everyone turned to stare at Trace and me. Suddenly uncomfortable, I touched the bandages around my neck and took a hasty step toward the door.

A large hand landed on my shoulder as I bumped into a solid wall of a man with long, red hair and a bushy beard.

"I told them you'd bring her by to meet your best mates," the wall said and then barked a laugh. "But they all said you were too kind to do that to the little one."

"I thought she should meet some of the village and thought of you degenerates. Naturally, I'd forgotten about just how degenerate you lot are." Trace lifted the man's hand off my shoulder and stepped in closer to me. He opened his eyes wider like he was giving the man an unspoken warning. "We don't want to be scaring Celestina off before she's gotten a chance to learn about how special the village can be."

"Don't you worry," said a woman with long blonde hair. She hooked her arm with my undamaged one. "We'll show you how happy we are that you've found your way home. And not just because that means we finally have Trace back with us after keeping watch over you for more than twenty years. We're also excited to get to know you." She patted my hand. "Don't look so worried. We'll be gentle. Gregory, what are you standing around for? Bring Trace and Celestina flagons of ale."

"Of course, my love." The large wall dipped his head to the woman and lumbered off.

"I'm Ivy. And that big oaf is my mate, Gregory. We've been together for nearly as long as Trace has been away looking after you. Oy! Why'd you stop the music, boys? Let's keep the party going." The musicians shook their heads as they picked up their instruments and started up another lively tune. Someone began clapping.

Ivy, stepping to the beat of this new song, spun me away from Trace. "I bet you're tired of looking at his face for the past four days. Let's have some girl talk."

"Um...Ivy, no," Trace said as he hurried after me. "She's still—"

"Pish." Ivy nudged Trace out of her way. "She'll be fine, won't you, dear?"

"I don't—" I started to admit I didn't know if I'd be fine with her or not. But she didn't give me the chance to protest.

"Sure, you do. You'll be fine. We're all friends here. Soon, you'll be as comfortable here as a fuzzy caterpillar is in its cocoon." She pulled me over to a table that was as far away from the two musicians near the fireplace as she could get in the room. She pushed me into a chair and then sat in the one across from me.

Trace grabbed a chair from a nearby table and dragged it over to our table and plopped down next to me. "You okay?" he asked.

Was I? I wasn't in danger. Ivy was...enthusiastic. But her over-the-top excitement had to be far better than Amaya's hostile vibe. And I didn't want to get on anyone's bad side here. Not when every single person in the room had the ability to change into a dragon and roast me.

I still had trouble believing it. *Every. Single. Person. In. This. Room. Is. A. Dragon.*

A month ago, the thought of meeting so many dragons would have thrilled me. Now, it made my stomach twist.

That red dragon had caught our ship on fire. If not for Trace dousing us with that wave of icy water, we'd all have ended up on the bottom of the ocean. Dragons were beautiful and magical and the stuff fantasies were made of.But they were also dangerous.

My favorite stories had never explained just how dangerous a dragon could be.

Before I could answer Trace, Gregory showed up with four clay goblets filled to the rim with a bubbly, yeasty ale. He set them in the middle of the table. Ivy immediately pushed one toward me. "Drink up. It'll make whatever hurts feel better."

She demonstrated this by picking up a goblet and guzzling the entire drink in one gulp. She smacked her lips when she'd finished.

"You have always been the definition of grace, Ivy," Trace said with a laugh. But when he looked at me, his cheeks turned pink. "This isn't like Earst's royal court. We're much more casual here in the village."

"It's—it's fine." I tried to sit back and enjoy myself, but every move felt awkward. And worse. Every move I made felt watched.

"Of course, it's fine," Ivy said, shouting over the music and loud chatter. "Nothing can bother you. You're the moonlight dragon." She shook her head. "After all this time, I still can't believe we finally have you back. Things are going to change now. Things will be better. Just thinking about it gives me goosebumps." She rubbed her arms.

"I'm not sure—" I started to explain that I wasn't whatever they expected me to be.

"It'll take a while for you to get accustomed to us and your homecoming," Ivy said. "But wow, can't you just imagine our bright future? Do you think this could be the start of a new age of dragons? A time when we can come out of hiding and stop living like primitives?"

"I don't know." They did have a simple life here, much simpler than any of the three kingdoms I'd experienced. But what did she expect me to do about it? I leaned toward her and said, "I'm not who you think I can be. I can't take a dragon form, you know. I'm as human as the life I've been living."

"Nonsense." Ivy gave a laugh. "Now that you're back where you belong, the elders will be able to get that sorted. You'll be soaring above the clouds with the rest of us before the next full moon. And what you don't know, we can teach you. Tell her, Gregory." She nudged the giant slouched beside her. "Gregory is our historian and one of the village schoolteachers. Tell her, Gregory. My man could teach a rock to sing if he wanted to."

"That's right, my love," he said after taking a swig of the ale. "The plateau is filled with singing rocks thanks to me." He laughed so loudly that people turned their heads to stare at us. "We'll set you up with a full regiment of study and a tutor. It might take a couple of years, but we'll get you caught up."

"Years?" I felt myself pale at the thought. How did I tell them that I couldn't stay? How did I dash their hopes?

Apparently, I didn't need to say anything. Ivy seemed determined to tell me all about life in the village. She talked nonstop, gossiping about this dragon or that dragon. All the while, dragons constantly interrupted her as they came up and patted Trace on the back or hugged him. Two dragons even pulled Trace out of the chair and kissed him full on the mouth in quite an eyebrow-raising way. The female dragon who'd kissed him was beautiful with blue-green eyes so bright they seemed to glow. The male dragon who'd kissed him had also grabbed Trace's ass and thrust his hips a couple of times. When they parted, Trace's eyes were large and black. And when Trace looked over at me, he shrugged and gave me a goofy grin.

Those same dragons who'd greeted Trace so warmly also introduced themselves to me, shouting their names and offering a hand for me to shake. Their greetings were brief. Unlike with Soren's troops, no one was openly hostile, but at the same time, I felt like an intruder. I felt like they wished I wasn't there. I cradled the goblet of ale with both hands and slumped down a little in the chair, unconsciously making myself smaller. I supposed if I could have gotten away with it, I would have crawled under the table.

Trace leaned toward me and frowned. "You're not having fun."

"I-I—" I gulped the ale. It was nutty and strong.

Trace swore softly. "This isn't the best environment for you to get to know us. It's too loud. Too chaotic."

"Too Trace-centric," Ivy shouted over the music with a laugh.

"That, too," Trace admitted with a lopsided grin.

"You've been gone a long time," I guessed. "You were missed."

"You've been gone longer," he said. "And they've missed you even more."

That might be true, but I wasn't real to any of them. I was an ancient dragon, sprung to life like from a fairytale. These villagers expected me to protect them and to bring about a new dragon age. I'd become a symbol, a vague hope. And—I slumped even lower in my chair—I was doomed to become a disappointment. I had no plans to stay in the village. Could they sense that? Did they know I was planning to run back to their enemy at the first opportunity I got?

Trace took my goblet and placed it back on the table. "Let me take you home."

Home. My thoughts immediately went to Soren and Gray and Raya and Patty and Mary. Those were the family I'd lost when Cullen had drugged me and locked me in a cell with that cranky midnight dragon. Sure, his action had freed me from the slave collar, but at what price?

"We're going," Trace announced to Ivy and Gregory as he stood.

Ivy jumped up from her chair. "But I've barely had a chance to talk to Celestina. I know nothing about her."

"Another time." Trace wrapped his arm around my shoulder and pulled me tight against his side. The movement hurt my dislocated shoulder. I bit the inside of my cheek to hold back a yelp.

"Tomorrow," Ivy insisted. "I'll come by with fresh meat cakes for lunch. We can talk then."

"Meat cakes?" Gregory's head popped up. "I'll be there."

"Very well." Trace gave Ivy a side-hug and Gregory a fist-bump before leading me through the crowded room and out the door.

His hand lifted off my sore shoulder as soon as we were back in the quiet of the evening. He pulled his fingers through his blond hair. "I'm sorry about that."

"Your friends clearly love you. That's never anything you should feel sorry about."

"But they made you uncomfortable."

A dragon shot across the dark sky. It looked like the red dragon that had set fire to Cullen's schooner. I flinched.

"That's Anther, Amaya's brother. It must be his night for patrol duty."

I shivered as I searched the sky for other dragons. "There are patrols?"

Trace nodded. "Ever since Amaya's abduction, we've increased the number of dragons patrolling our borders. Nothing can get close to the village without our knowing about it. Not even a field mouse." He stepped closer to me. "You're safe here, Celestina. We won't let any outsiders get near you again."

I knew he'd meant for his words to comfort me, but they only made me feel as trapped as I'd been in that Tiburnian dungeon. And I worried all the more for Soren and my friends' safety. If they were coming for me—and I knew with all my heart that Soren was out there searching for me—they were walking into a death trap.

Chapter 17

Amaya

"Ivy and Gregory are having a get-together tonight." Anther had nudged my shoulder and had waggled his head back and forth at me several hours ago as he tried to push me to get out of the manor house. "I'm on patrol duty, but you should go."

I'd snarled at him.

He'd raised his hands and backed away. "You're feeling bitey this afternoon. Got it."

Looking to avoid more run-ins with anyone in my family, I'd hidden myself away behind a bookshelf on the second-floor balcony in the manor's library. I wasn't reading. I merely sat in the hard, wooden chair as my emotions boiled.

Stupid Cullen.

I couldn't stop thinking about him. Why put the moonlight dragon in the dungeon cell with me? He'd said if we were still there at dinner time, he'd return. Why had he said it that way? Did he know bringing us together would cause a magical explosion? *How* would he know something like that about dragons? I hadn't even known that, and I thought I knew everything there was to know about moonlight and midnight dragon lore. Maybe I should go to Ivy and Gregory's party. I could ask Gregory about it. He was, after all, the village historian who'd taught me the stories.

Stupid Cullen.

Dammit, he was a villain of the worst sort—the kind who tried to trick others into believing that he was the hero of their stories.

"You might as well stop lurking and come on out," I said to the old lady who still hadn't left the manor house. "Dragons can smell better than we can see. And I can spot a mouse five hundred yards away in the dark."

The old woman emerged from behind the bookshelf. She clutched an old history book to her chest. She tilted her head to one side. "I'm glad you escaped from the Tiburnians. They picture themselves better than everyone else on the continent, but the lot of them are nothing more than a nasty bunch of pretentious bullies."

"I should have heeded your warning more carefully. It was—" A tremor moved through my body as I remembered how helpless I'd felt in those shackles. I violently pushed the memory down. "I will take better care in the future."

The old woman tut-tutted. "While I am sorry you suffered at the hands of the Tiburnians, that wasn't the trouble I saw coming. It may have been the start of the bad times in my vision. But an evil omen still muddies the path before you, child. I fear you will still find yourself standing alone and broken before the dark times have passed, unless—"

"You've got to be freaking kidding me." I couldn't imagine surviving another bout of captivity. Or worse.

"I wish I were. Seers' predictions have been dismissed and disparaged throughout most of the continent as the ravings of mad women, but what I see is real and true and…" She swallowed several times. "What I have seen in my visions lately frightens even me. I'm an old woman who has seen horrors that would make a fierce dragon like yourself lose sleep at night. So, when I say I'm scared, it means something." She set down the book she was holding on a nearby table. "I wish I could provide more help. I wish the visions gave me enough foresight to help me stop it. I've tried to stop disasters in the past. It never works. Knowing that, I still felt pulled to come to this village, to talk to you, to help in whatever way I could, even if it's to offer words of warning so you can prepare your soul."

"I'm going to die?" *Great.* Now I had that to deal with.

"We all die…eventually." She coughed into a handkerchief that she'd dug out of a deep pocket in her raggy dress. "Some sooner than others. It's good to be prepared."

I turned to stare at the half-bare bookshelf. Why did the manor have such a large library when many of the shelves were empty? Were the shelves once full, like the sky was once filled with dragons? The manor house was old, much older than anyone could remember. But not older than the Vampiric Wars. We fled here after our defeat and built this village. An ancestor—well, not my ancestor—must have built the manor house and built this library with the idea of filling it with books. Had that been a fanciful dream? Or had the dragons once owned enough books to fill this huge two-story room?

If the books had once existed, what parts of our past were we missing? What knowledge about our magic were we lacking? We hadn't known what would happen when I touched the moonlight dragon. We didn't know that she could pull my magic to the surface in such a forceful way. What else didn't we know?

And how did I go about learning it?

Prince Cullen seemed to know a surprising amount about the midnight and moonlight dragons. Where did he learn about us? The next time I saw him I would claw that knowledge out of that pretty head of his. *Maybe if I eat his brains, his thoughts will become mine. Goddess, why can't I stop thinking about him? Why can't I stop remembering being weak in front of him?*

"Amaya? Are you crying?"

I hastily wiped my face with the sleeve of my sweater as I jerked my head toward the sound of my mother's voice. She was standing exactly where the old woman had been standing.

"The old woman?" I asked, looking around. "Where did she go?"

My mother frowned. "There was no one here, dear." She placed her hand on my shoulder. "We're worried about you. You haven't been yourself since your escape. Anther told me what happened earlier. How you growled at him. Are you sure you don't need to talk about your time in captivity? Did the Tiburnians hurt you in ways we can't see?"

"Just because I don't want to be around a bunch of drunken jerks doesn't mean I'm injured," I growled at my mother and instantly regretted it.

"If you say so, dear." Juniper stepped away from me the same way Anther had. "I'm here when you're ready to talk about it. Not all wounds are visible on the outside."

"I grew up with a healer for a mother, of course, I know that," I grumbled more to myself than to her. I hated when I got like this, when I pushed everyone away with my angry words. But I didn't know how to stop them from coming. I didn't know how to be someone different, someone better.

Celestina, with her soft voice and cautious manner, would have made a better daughter.

Just thinking of Celestina made me want to tear out someone's eyes. I should fly back to Tiburnia and tear out *the man's* eyes and shove the pair of them down Cullen's throat. I'd like to see the look of shock on his arrogant face when I did that.

I growled again and then prowled up to my bedroom. Without even bothering to remove any of my clothes, not even my boots, I crawled into bed and pulled a heavy blanket over my head. Completely encased in the woolen cocoon, I finally felt safe. My body, exhausted beyond comprehension, shut down.

For the first time since returning home, I slept.

"She's still alive," Cullen's voice cut through the sea of nothingness my slumber had slipped me into. I blinked several times, bringing the forest scene in front of me into focus. Was this a dream? No, it felt too real to be a dream. Cullen, atop a roan horse, was speaking to his brother. And somehow while I was sleeping, I'd slipped into his thoughts. "You know Celestina is alive because you're still alive."

His brother grunted. The two brothers were riding through a dark forest with three others—two males and one female. From the smell of them, all but one carried the cursed blood of a vampire. The other stank like a human.

I thrashed, trying to snap myself out of this connection with Cullen. It had unnerved me that he'd been able to sense me the last time I'd wandered into his thoughts. That wasn't supposed to happen. Others weren't supposed to know that I'd made the connection unless I made myself known. But Cullen had managed to sense me there even though I hadn't wanted to announce my presence. And, I suspected, he knew I was in his head again. I needed to break the connection. But the more I struggled to free myself, the tighter I seemed to connect with him. It felt like Cullen had clamped a hand around my wrist and was holding on to me.

"*Stop*," I forced through the connection.

"*No*," came his quick reply.

We shouldn't be able to communicate like this. He wasn't a dragon. And talking to animals wasn't how my magic worked.

"*This isn't real. I'm dreaming.*"

"*You're not dreaming.*" His voice started to take on that quality that made me think of a burbling brook. "*Tell me where you are.*"

"*I-I'm— No!*"

"I have a connection with Amaya. I'm going to try to use it to help guide us."

"*The hell you will.*"

Cullen chuckled. "She's a feisty one. And as strong-willed as a burl ox."

"*And you're as ugly as a warty monkey.*"

"*So, we're calling each other names now? I hadn't meant what I'd said as an insult. Burl oxen are celebrated for their stubborn natures in our society.*"

"*Liar.*"

"*I have lied to you, but not about this, my pretty dragon.*" His voice in my head seemed to float on calm waters again. "*Tell me about Celestina. Is she safe?*"

Celestina. Celestina. Why was everyone obsessed with her? She was weak. She couldn't even heal her own injuries. And she didn't care for her own kind. If it didn't mean putting the entire village in danger, I would tell Cullen how to find us so they could take the traitor away.

I'd rescued the moonlight dragon. *I'd* returned her to where she belonged. And Celestina had this woe-is-me attitude, acting as if we were holding her here against her will like a freaking prisoner.

If she couldn't see how lucky she was, then good riddance. We'd managed well enough without her. I was more than capable of protecting the village without whatever she could do. What could a moonlight dragon do? I bet Cullen knew, curse him.

"*Tell me about the moonlight dragon powers,*" I demanded. "*How did you know what would happen when you brought us together?*"

"It was more of a hunch about what might happen than hard data," he answered. *"I do have a book or two that helped guide me to that hunch. I could share them with you if you let me know where you are right now."*

I needed those books. My thoughts floated happily within my dream as the pieces seemed to fall easily into place. Cullen's books could be the key to figuring out how to change the old woman's dire predictions. Those books could help save my life. And Cullen wasn't evil. He wanted to help me. All I had to do was meet up with him, and he'd give me everything I needed from him.

Wait. No.

He was trying to compel me to help him again.

Bastard.

"I'm going to twist your head off and give it to the village children to use when they play kick-the-ball."

"I really do have books I could share with you," he said.

"And I really want to twist your head off your neck."

"So vicious. And here I am, trying to help you...again. I did manage to get you out of that dungeon before those shackles killed you."

What did he want from me? A thank-you cake? He could have helped me escape many times over, and he hadn't. No, he wasn't trying to help me. He didn't know anything about the moonlight dragon and her powers. I bet he didn't even know how to read, the barbarian.

"Amaya?" Cullen's voice cut into my seething. *"Are you still there?"*

"No."

Cullen chuckled.

"You were telling me about Celestina." My anger floated away on that lovely calm lake he'd created. *"Is she safe? Is she well?"*

I sighed, too tired to fight the compulsion he had pushed on me. *"She's safe,"* I admitted. *"She's staying with her protector. Because she can't shift into her dragon form, her injuries are lingering. But I don't think she'll die from them. Pity."*

Cullen repeated what I'd said to the others riding with him.

"She's injured?" Soren cried. The man looked ready to fight a wraith. "How injured? I need to get to her, heal her."

"Amaya didn't describe the extent of Celestina's injuries," Cullen answered. *"Amaya?"*

"The slave collar had been embedded in her skin. It took that skin with her when it

exploded," I told him, not because he'd forced me to, but because I could feel Cullen's distress through the connection. And I wanted to reassure him. I knew I shouldn't have felt that way. They were the enemy. I shouldn't even be connecting with him. Still, it seemed cruel not to tell him. *"Our healer is taking care of her."*

Cullen repeated what I'd said, but it didn't seem to ease his worry or his brother's.

The muscles in Soren's jaw tightened. "They had better not harm her."

"She's with her own kind. They won't—"

"You don't know that," Soren snapped. "She's never been with the dragons. All she knows about them is what she's heard from stories or read in those books she checked out of the library. You know how animals react when one of their own acts in a way that isn't expected. They turn violent."

"Dragons aren't animals," Cullen was quick to say.

"Thank you." If he'd agreed with his brother, I would have flown to wherever he was and boiled his bowels from the outside.

"Like us, dragons are one of the original life forces."

"Dragons are the origins from which all life emerged," I corrected. *"Vampires are not an origin lifeform. You're a corruption of nature, not a part of it."*

"Rude."

"Just stating the truth."

"What is Amaya saying?" the female with them asked.

"She's insulting vampires."

"Ah. That explains the look on your face," she said. "I can't wait to meet her. I suspect I'd like her."

"She does have an unconventional charm."

I didn't like the way Cullen had said that. As if he liked me.

"I'm not meeting any of your skanky vampire girlfriends. And when I see you again, I'm going to rip off your head and stick it up your—"

"You're so creative with your threats."

"Promises," I clarified. *"They're promises."*

"I know dragons aren't animals. But I also know the nature of any living creature. They'll attack their own when they don't conform," Soren said. "It happens with the humans. It happens with the vampires. And I'm sure it happens with the dragons. Celestina might be back with her own kind, but she's never been around a dragon. She knows nothing about dragon culture. And her knowledge about dragons comes from stories that have been exaggerated or fabricated from whole cloth. She could easily make a fatal mistake."

"No one will harm her," I assured. I wished they could see me rolling my eyes. *"She's the darling of our village. The golden dragon. The treasure. Everyone is fawning over her and thanking the goddesses for bringing her back alive. Mind, they should be thanking me since I'm the one who did the work to bring her home, but why would they do that when some faceless goddess can take the glory?"*

"Amaya is saying how Celestina is being celebrated in the village. She's fine," Cullen told his brother. "I'm sure she'll remain safe. She's smart. She's not going to—"

Three dragons swooped down out of the pitch-black sky.

The startled horses scattered as the vampires jumped down from their backs and drew their weapons.

The dragons were younger members of our clan. There was a brown sharptail, a yellow, and a sky blue. None of them had trained in direct assaults like this. But when they opened their mouths and sent fire shooting out, the vampires sent their steeds running in one direction while they charged on foot in the other direction toward the cover of the forest's thick stand of trees.

"Did you send these?" Cullen demanded. He sounded angry now.

"I wish!"

"As fun as being insulted by you has been, I'm going to have to release our lovely connection." Almost immediately, that invisible grip on my mind loosened. But I wasn't ready to part ways with Cullen, damn is pretty eyes.

"Wait," I cried out.

A vast void answered.

"Wait!" I shouted as I jolted up in bed.

I screwed my eyes closed and pictured those young dragons who were foolishly attacking the vampires without proper preparation or training. One of those hotheaded lads had to be thinking about me. *Please, be thinking of me and not just of Celestina.*

They must have flown out into the surrounding forest when on patrol and stumbled upon the vampires. And foolishly thinking they were defending their precious moonlight dragon, they attacked instead of flying back to the village to alert the others as they'd been instructed to do. Goddess, the vampires undoubtedly carried the same blood-magic poisoned arrows that had brought me down.

I desperately tried to make a connection with one of the dragons attacking the vampires. I felt my mind slipping past theirs, but I couldn't latch on to anything solid. Those dragons weren't thinking about me. They weren't thinking about Celestina. They'd lost themselves to bloodlust. The bitter metallic flavor of it assaulted the back of my throat.

"Stop!" I sent the order to them as forcefully as I knew how. *"Stop!"*

Those younglings were going to get themselves killed.

I started to shift, my black scales rising to the surface, talons growing in my desperation to get to those fools, to save them. I felt as hotheaded as the younglings, anxious to join them in fighting the vampires. I could drag Prince Cullen into the air by his toes and toss him off the plateau's cliffside to see if vampires could survive having all their bones shattered on the rocks below. He wouldn't be smirking at me then.

But, as anxious as I was to *do* something, I didn't know where the vampires and younglings were fighting other than the vague knowledge that they were in a wooded area of our territory, which described eighty percent of our lands.

I had to go about this another way. I had to be calm…and smart.

I found it ridiculously easy to reopen the connection between Prince Cullen and me.

"I'm busy here, Amaya." He had the brown sharptail in his crossbow's sight and was on the verge of pulling the trigger.

"Don't hurt them!" I screamed at him.

"Don't hurt the dragons who are trying to roast us?" His finger remained on the trigger, but he lowered the crossbow. Not that stopping one vampire from firing their crossbows was good enough. I heard bolts flying from the others traveling with him.

"They're idiots. But they're young *idiots who shouldn't be engaging the enemy. Tell the others to stop firing at them."*

"And do what, Amaya? Let your young friends burn us to ashes? I'm not sure I'd be able to regenerate from that." Even as he protested, he bumped his brother's arm, sending the bolt that had been aimed at the sky blue's neck flying off target.

"Hey!" Soren protested.

"Amaya says these are young dragons who are getting themselves in over their heads."

"Tell her that we're not the aggressors here. I don't care if they're young dragons or not. Their fire is as hot as a full-grown dragon."

The two brothers dove to the ground as the trees above them caught fire. Off to the right of them, the female vampire let loose the string of her archery bow. The sky blue cried out in pain as it swirled large looping circles in the air, desperately fighting to stay aloft.

I screamed my frustration.

There had to be a way to get those idiot dragons to back off before the vampires killed them all.

"Shout my name," I told Prince Cullen.

"What? Why?"

"I need the young dragons to be thinking about me so I can connect with their thoughts. Shout my name."

"I guess it's worth a try." He cupped his hands around his mouth and shouted, "Amaya!"

The two healthy dragons immediately stopped their fiery attack. Their heads jerked in Cullen's direction.

"Shit, now they're coming this way," Cullen cried as he stumbled to his feet and started to run like a rabbit flushed from its burrow.

"That's because you gave away our location with your bellowing," Soren darted after his brother. "Raya! Gray! Cover our flanks. We're heading for the bushes down the hill."

The dragons swooped lower in fast pursuit.

"What the hell, Cullen?" Soren looked like he wanted to punch his brother.

"Amaya told me to do it."

"This advice came from the same dragon who wants to eat your roasted balls?"

"Maybe."

"Here's an important piece of battlefield advice—don't take orders from those who want to kill you."

"Amaya? A little help?" Cullen sounded nearly as panicked as I felt.

The female vampire with the wicked good aim had her bow raised and was in range to take a shot at the brown sharptail.

Thanks to Cullen shouting my name, I managed to slip into the sharptail's mind.

"Victor! Veer off! You're about to get hit!"

He shook his head as if not sure what was going on inside his mind, but he banked sharply to the right. A heartbeat later, an archery bolt sailed past him.

I huffed out a sharp breath.

"Now get out of there! All of you! You're not qualified to take on a troop of vampires."

"Amaya? Where are you?" Victor asked, his head jerking around as he searched the skies.

"At home where you should be heading. And find a safe place for Yarrow to land. He needs to shift and heal before going much further. Can you do that?"

"But we need to stop the—"

"You need to get home and report to the elders what you saw and where you saw them. That's the orders you're given every time you set off on patrol. If you don't want me to go tattling to Trace and Anther that you're breaking those orders, you will do as I say, and you'll do it now."

"Yes, Amaya." Victor gave a low roar that caught the yellow's attention. The two of them turned toward the injured sky blue. Though the sky blue was bleeding and clearly in pain, he'd managed to stay in the air. The poisoned arrow had taken me down immediately. Were these bolts not poisoned?

"Don't shoot them," I cautioned Cullen, still surprised at how easy it was to slide into his thoughts. *"They're leaving."*

"Hold your attack! It's over!" Cullen called to the others. "That includes you, Driscoll."

One of the vampires snarled and showed his fangs, but he lowered the crossbow that he'd been about to fire.

"Is this Amaya's doing?" Soren asked. Even though the dragons were gone, he continued to scan the sky for threats.

Cullen grinned. "Maybe despite her threats, she's not so keen on seeing my balls get roasted."

"Maybe I want the pleasure of doing it myself," I said.

"I'm sure your dragon wants the pleasure of doing that herself," the female vampire said as she jogged up to the two brothers.

"That's what Amaya just said, Raya," Cullen admitted.

"I knew I liked her." Raya laughed. "I hope we get to meet her soon."

Cullen's easy smile seemed to suggest that he thought we would be getting together, partying together like the older dragons all would do at Ivy and Gregory's cottage.

"Cullen, I can never meet up with you or your friends. You must turn back. The clan won't let you get anywhere near the moonlight dragon."

"My brother will never agree to let Celestina go," Cullen cut in.

"You'll have to convince him to change his mind. Pushing forward will only get the four of you killed. Now that the clan knows you're out in the surrounding woods, they'll double the patrols. Triple them. And this time they'll send mature dragons who have years of battle training. They've waited too long to get her back. The entire clan will go to war before losing the moonlight dragon again."

I waited for Cullen to say something. To argue. To agree to leave. To answer. Why didn't he answer?

All I got from him was silence.

"Cullen?"

It grew harder to hold on to the vision of the forest where they were still huddled.

"Cullen! Don't do this! Don't shut me out!"

It was too late. Cullen slammed the door on our connection.

I sat on my bed, staring into the room's darkness. I could no longer feel the icy breeze blowing down from the plateau. I could no longer hear the sizzle from the trees that were still burning from the dragon fire.

After experiencing the battle, the stillness inside my room felt unnatural.

"Cullen?" I tried again to slip into his thoughts. It had been so easy to do, easier than slipping into a dragon's mind even. Of course, dragons are superior creatures, more complex, and smarter. It would make sense that it would be harder to slip into a dragon's mind.

I'd fallen into Cullen's thoughts even when I didn't want to. But now that I needed to get into his head, I kept hitting a steel wall. My inability to reach him wasn't because he was no longer thinking of me. I could feel his thoughts like a soft caress down my spine. He seemed to be thinking about me now even more than ever. And yet, at the same time, he was actively blocking me from getting to him, blocking me from seeing what was happening around them.

Foolish vampire. His stubbornness was going to get them killed. Not that I cared if he lived or died. I didn't. I was simply angry that I wouldn't be the one to have the pleasure of killing him. The clan elders, worried about my safety after nearly losing me to the Tiburnians, would find an excuse to ground me.

"Cullen, don't do this. Please."

Nothing.

I growled.

I had no other choice but to go tell the others. I needed to warn them that it was time to start preparing for war.

Chapter 18

Celestina

"Trace! The clan can't attack anyone who comes looking for me. I'm bonded with General Kitmun," I shouted as I chased after Trace through the tiny downtown as he made his way home from the party. "Soren and I can't be apart. You can't keep him away from here. And you can't kill him. We're bonded. Forever. There's no breaking the connection we have." Not that I would want to. "If he dies, I die."

"Celestina, the collar bonded you to the vampire general," Trace said gently. "And the collar is gone. You're free. You're free of him now. The dragons will protect you from him."

I started shaking my head. "No. No. We're bonded. We had a ceremony where we joined together. He sprang it on me without explaining what it all meant. But he had to link his life to mine to protect me, to keep certain members of the court from trying to kill me. He made a great sacrifice for me…to keep me alive."

Trace stopped walking. We stood facing each other in the middle of the village's downtown. Trace leaned toward me as he frowned. "That's not true. I don't understand why you're lying to me about this. You're no longer his prisoner. You're free. You don't have to feel like you need to protect General Kitmun, not anymore."

"I'm not lying. We're—"

"No, Celestina." For the first time, Trace sounded angry. "General Kitmun is bonded to you. I get that. But it was the collar that bonded you to him. You didn't complete the bonding ceremony. You didn't tie yourself to him. And when your magic broke apart the collar, you freed yourself not only from Queen Beatrice's hold over you, you also freed yourself from General Kitmun's."

"How—?"

"I was watching over you. Even when they took you behind Fein's closed borders, I followed. I have *always* watched over you. I know what happened in Fein's royal court. I know what he did and why he did it. But it doesn't matter anymore. You're here. You're home. You're safe. No one will be taking you away from us. I won't allow it. The clan won't allow it."

As much as I wanted to let his words comfort me, they felt like heavy stones pulling me under the water. I was drowning from them.

"I-I-I can't just walk away from him." A sudden pain flared in my chest like the collar was punishing me. But the collar no longer encircled my neck. It no longer held power over me. And instead of a burning down my back, it was my heart that ached. I rubbed my chest. "I-I-I—they're my friends, my family. They care about me." A sob escaped, and the tears I'd fought to keep at bay started to fall. "I care about them. You can't hurt them for coming to find me. You can't stop them from being just as worried about my safety as you have been."

Trace slashed a hand through the air. "They may have pretended to care. And I understand why you fell so hard for them, especially for General Kitmun. He is handsome and charming. But, Celestina, he's a vampire. Vampires use their charms to trick others, to pull them under their control."

"No, he didn't—"

"They can't help themselves. It's their nature to deceive."

"No," I cried. "No. The stories, they're wrong."

"Are they?" Trace sighed deeply. "Celestina, I hate what has happened to you. Not a day passed that I didn't fight the need to save you from your upbringing. I grieved knowing you were taught to believe you weren't worthy of love. Not a day passed when I didn't want to rip you away from those cold people who pretended to be your parents and, later, to rescue you from the vampires. But Queen Frieda had promised to kill you if we tried to rescue you. She'd tied your life to that spell she'd cast on you, the same spell that keeps you trapped in your human body. And Queen Beatrice only made matters worse with that damned slave collar. You can't imagine the frustration I've felt, the sleepless nights knowing you were at the mercy of those vampires."

"But I lov—"

"Celestina," he groaned. "Celestina." He lightly cupped my tear-dampened cheeks with his large, calloused hands. "Those vampires are not your friends. They were using you."

"No, they were helping me. They were trying to get the slave collar off me."

"Because they needed to free you from Queen Beatrice's control. They needed it off so they could use you against her. She's planning to attack the Fein with a magically enhanced army. The vampires were planning to use you as a weapon against her. They didn't need the slave collar, not when they could use their charms and powers of compulsion against you."

"No, Soren would never—"

"Search your heart, search your memories, I think you'll find you already know the truth. Painful as it is, you know the vampires didn't really love you or care for you. You're nothing but a weapon to them. They are just like the Tiburnians who captured Amaya to use as a weapon for their country. The Kingdom of Earst under Queen Beatrice's rule is attempting to make a big move against the other kingdoms. And as things stand now, she'll win."

"No. That's not true. Her army is weak. They had to call in help from the Fein and from the Asterian armies to push back the Tiburnians for her."

"Her call for help was a ruse. She begged those armies to help her so she could assess their strengths and weaknesses. I know. I was there watching. If you give yourself a moment to think about it, you'll know it, too. General Kitmun puts duty above all else. He'll do anything to protect the Kingdom of Fein and the people living there. That's his way."

"No." Sure, I'd had the same doubts. But my heart knew better. Soren's love for me was true and honest. "He wouldn't…"

The Tiburnian captain had spoken about Soren's plans for using me.

And Soren hadn't contradicted him. But that was simply Soren playing a political game. The Tiburnians were Fein's enemies. He had no reason to be honest with the captain, no reason to tell him anything.

"In time, Celestina, you'll understand." Trace let his warm hands drop away from my wet cheeks. "In time, you'll come back to us."

His vow felt like a manacle closing around my throat.

The red dragon that had flown overhead earlier, shot like an arrow high in the air from somewhere over my shoulder, making me jump. It hovered above our heads for a few seconds before dropping to the ground in front of us.

The movement of the dragon's wings stirred up a wind that had me staggering backward. Dragons were huge, so much bigger than I'd realized from always watching them from my bedroom window in Earst's castle tower. The red dragon towered over Trace and me in a way that made the dark sky disappear. I swallowed hard and fought the urge to run.

A power rippled through Trace as he stood taller, though still dwarfed by the red dragon. He stared directly at the red dragon as if challenging him. The red dragon bowed his head and then, in a shimmering blink, disappeared.

I sucked in a shocked breath.

It took a moment for my eyes to notice the man standing in the dragon's place. While tall and well built, he was a fraction of the dragon's height.

Now that I saw him, I realized I was seeing *all of him*. The blond-haired man wore nothing.

As in nude. Completely. Utterly. Nude.

His blue eyes narrowed. His fists opened and closed as his nostrils flared as if scenting the air. He took a predatory step toward me.

"Are you serious?" Trace said. He stepped in front of me. I peered around Trace's back. I had a feeling it would be a mistake to take my eyes off the nude man.

"What?" The man took another step toward us. "I need to have a word with you, Trace, and I also wanted to meet our mythical moonlight dragon." He gave me a smile that showed off a mouth filled with sharp dragon teeth. "It's a good thing Trace already has you locked down, Moonlight. You'd start a war if anyone thought they could win you as a mate." For a heartbeat, his eyes flashed a glowing red in the darkness.

"I'm sorry?" I didn't need to ask for clarification. What he'd said was pretty damn obvious.

"Gods, Anther, could you just shut up and fly away?" Trace bared his teeth. They were equally as sharp, equally as menacing as the other man's…er…dragon's. I didn't remember his teeth looking like that when he'd smiled before. No, I distinctly remembered them looking like normal human teeth.

These men weren't human. No one in this village was human. That naked one had been a terrifyingly large dragon just a moment ago.

Anther chuckled as he looked me over once again. "One of the patrols just returned from the southern forest. They spotted vampires heading this way. A council is being convened to discuss our response. My father requested that you be there."

"Me?" This could be my chance to convince the village leaders that they allow Soren and whoever he's traveling with—Raya and Gray, I hoped—to enter the village.

"No, darling Moonlight. My father wants to see your mate."

"Mate?" Soren? No. They didn't think of him that way. And Anther was looking at Trace when he said it. I shuddered. Was that what they thought of me? That I was a prize to be awarded to Trace in exchange for him giving up more than twenty years of his life to watch over me?

"Dude, shut the fuck up already." Trace said sounding much less patient and calm as he had with me.

Anther chuckled. "Do you need me to stay and watch over your—?"

Trace growled. It was powerful enough that Anther raised his hands in surrender and danced back several steps. But not so powerful to wipe the smug grin from the naked man's face.

"See you at the manor, then."

In another shimmering blink, the red dragon returned. He stirred up another great wind that threatened my balance as he moved his wings in a graceful arc that lifted him into the air.

"Anther, he is the one who set fire to the ship I was on." The same ship Trace had doused with the wave he'd sent crashing over us. "Was he trying to kill me?"

"He was upset over Amaya's abduction. She's his sister, and he took her capture personally."

"Soren didn't abduct her."

"In Anther's eyes, it didn't matter. We flew to find you, to see if Amaya was somehow with you. When he didn't find her there, he lost it. We'd been searching for her with no luck for days at that point. His sanity had been hanging from a thread." He gestured for me to walk alongside him. "Come. Let's head to the manor house."

The three-story brick manor was located on the edge of the village. It backed up to the edge of the plateau's cliffside, making it look as if it might tumble into a dark abyss at any moment. Lights flickered in the many windows as we approached the home that was far larger than any others in the village.

"Mate?" I asked. "Do I even have a say in whether I want this or not?"

"Celestina, it's not…" He dredged a hand through his hair. "You're a gift to our generation. The last of your kind. But that doesn't mean you have to be *the* last."

"My value to the village is as some kind of broodmare?" That was worse than being thought of as a savior.

"No! No, Celestina. The stories say that you'll bring great changes to our lands and our people. Think of the future—one with the night skies glowing with moonlight dragons again."

"How does this work? If I mate with you, a green dragon, wouldn't we end up with light green dragons? Or—?"

"We don't know for sure, since there hasn't been a moonlight dragon on the continent for eons, but we know from other pairings that when two powerful dragons mate, some of the offspring will be like the father and others will reflect the mother. We expect—*hope*—the same would happen with you."

I started to respond, but what could I say? That I wasn't some object to be handed out to the strongest in the clan? That I didn't want to be used as a baby dragon factory? That I wanted to *leave*? Goddess, I wanted to leave this place.

Trace seemed to take my silence as acceptance. "It'll be nice to finally get back to my weaving. I can have a second loom made. We can do the work together. And my mother, she'll love you to pieces. I can't wait to see what she's been inspired to paint in your honor. Ever since your return, she's kept herself locked away in her cottage and won't let anyone see what she's been working on."

I clasped my hands in front of me. My fingernails dug into the backs of my hands. And I kept walking toward the massive manor house.

Trace talked some more about the weaving shop he owned. He'd opened it on his twentieth birthday. It had been the same year I hatched from that ancient egg they'd been hoarding. He'd barely had the opportunity to run the shop or to discover whether he enjoyed weaving as a career when he left to watch over me twenty-three years ago.

Before then, his family had lived in the manor house we were walking toward, Trace explained. It had been his family's home for three generations. The alpha of the village made the manor house their home. After his father's death at Queen Frieda's hands, a new alpha was named, and his family had to move out.

"I'd already left home, though. I was living above my shop with my brother." His lips twisted. "The one who is now an outlaw." He fell quiet. The only sound was the crunch of stones under our boots. "It was harder on my little sister and mother. While in the depths of their grief, they had to vacate their home, leave the memories of my father behind in the manor house, and watch Drix and Juniper move in with their children. Anther, who's my age, moved back in with his parents to help guard Amaya." He shook his head. "The past two decades have been challenging for everyone in the village."

"I can't imagine how difficult that must have been," I said, meaning it. Just because I didn't want to make my life with Trace, didn't exclude me from feeling compassion for what he'd suffered.

"But you're wrong, Celestina. You can imagine it. You lived it. What we suffered is part of you. It's part of your story, too."

No. I'd been a newborn at the time of his family's tragedy. I had no memories from my life before the abduction. Trace was twenty years older than me. He'd already lived half of his life with a loving family. He was a dragon. And the more time I spent with the dragons, the more I felt tied to my humanness. If he was air, I was soil. What could the two of us possibly have in common? Sure, Trace was handsome with his mane of brown hair, square jaw and shoulders, and kind smile. And in a way he'd been right about me falling for the first male to show me kindness. If

Trace had whisked me away with him before Queen Beatrice had locked the slave collar around my neck, I would have fallen gratefully into his arms. I would have agreed to learn how to weave, to take care of his household, to bear as many babies as he wanted. He would have become the embodiment of my lonely girl's childhood dream.

But, although I'd wished and waited and watched for him, the green dragon hadn't rescued me. Soren had.

And I had no doubt that Soren would come fetch me again and again until the end of time. I *wanted* that. I *wanted* Soren.

I needed to make the dragons understand.

Trace had said that in time I'd come to accept my life with the clan, that my feelings for Soren would fade. When I'd been wearing the collar, I'd worried that the collar's magic had compelled me to feel close to Soren. Now that I was free from its influence, I was finally able to listen to my thoughts and know they were my own. Even without the collar's urgings, my thoughts kept going back to Soren. I needed to know where he was. Was he safe? He had to be just as worried about me as I was for him. Would he forgive his brother? I hoped he hadn't done something rash and killed Cullen. He'd never forgive himself if he had.

I tightened the hands I had fisted together. I was obsessed with Soren, which had to mean my feelings for him had been, and still were, real. My body ached for him.

I needed to make the other dragons understand that my heart—and quite possibly my soul—belonged to Soren. It always would.

Goddess, it wasn't in my nature to allow myself to feel anger. Growing up in Earst, outbursts of anger easily got a person killed. Only the queen could pull off shouting and screaming and killing with no repercussions. And Queen Beatrice did love to vent her frustrations with a great deal of slashing and maiming and bloody killings.

I considered myself a peacemaker. I was as different from the warriors in Soren's army as water was from oil. But as we walked through a long hallway that took us to the center of the manor house, my nerves started bristling. In the flickering light of the wall sconces, Trace continued talking as if our pairing was a done deal.

"I'll make sure the council understands the importance of keeping you safe," he told me as we reached a pair of doors. Amaya, the midnight dragon, was leaning against the wall next to them. Trace gave her a nod. "Stay with Amaya. I'll come looking for you when the meeting is over."

"But—" I tried to protest.

"Don't worry, Celestina. You're safe within these walls." He swept into the room where the council was going to discuss what to do about the vampires. The door closed behind him with a click that echoed in the hall. And a fire I'd never felt before stirred in my chest.

No. I wasn't going to let them keep me out. The council needed to listen to me.

Chapter 19

Amaya

Trace entered the grand dining room where the council elders were hearing the report from those three foolish younglings who'd nearly gotten themselves slaughtered by the vampires. Naturally, the younglings kept quiet about their failed engagement with the vampires. And since they'd listened to me after I'd managed to jump into Victor's vapid thoughts, and they'd succeeded in flying back to the village without any of them dying, I decided to keep their foolish behavior secret.

Celestina tried to follow Trace into the dining room. "The vampires don't mean us harm," she had the audacity to proclaim. "I need to speak up for them."

I caught her arm. "Maybe when we can trust you, you'll be allowed in there."

The door clicked closed behind Trace.

Her amber-brown and jade-green eyes glared at the hand I'd put on her. "Are you going to use your talons to hurt me again?"

"Only if you decide to do something foolish," I answered, not loosening my hold. I leaned toward her and breathed out a wreath of smoke through my nostrils. "I don't trust you."

She didn't quail like I'd expected. With her eyes still as hard as the mismatched gemstones they resembled, she placed her hand over mine. I suspected she was going to try to pry my hand from her arm. Well, that wouldn't work. I had access to dragon strength, and she was stuck in that weak human body of hers.

I started to tell her that she didn't intimidate me when a shock of power jolted through me.

Dammit! She was pulling my magic to the surface. Like what had happened back in the dungeon, black scales started forming on my arms and moving to cover my chest. And we were in the manor house's hallway. There wasn't room for a dragon in here. Not even close. I'd destroy the manor if she succeeded in creating another burst of power like before.

"Stop!" I gritted out. The power surge made all my muscles tense. I could barely remain standing. "You're going to hurt everyone around us!"

Her hand had started to glow yellow like the sun. And her eyes glowed white like the moon.

"Celestina!" I shouted loud enough that the elders and the council gathered in the dining room came pouring out into the hallway.

"What's going on?" my father, the clan leader, demanded.

My teeth and mouth had expanded. My fingers had transformed into talons. Though I hadn't meant to, those talons dug into the skin where I was gripping her arm. I tried to pull away, but her hand on top of mine held firm like a vice grip.

"Can't. Stop. Her," I barely managed to get out. "Turning."

"There's no room here for that," Victor, the young dragon, unhelpfully pointed out.

Trace wedged himself as close between us as possible and put his hands on Celestina's cheeks. He turned her head, so she was looking at him and not at me. "Celestina," he said in that soft-spoken manner of his. "I need you to let go of Amaya."

She didn't flinch. She didn't blink her unnaturally bright eyes.

"I don't think she can hear me," Trace said. Like me, he was trying to lift her hand from where it was still resting on mine.

Her body vibrated from the amount of power coursing through us.

"We need to break them apart," my father said coming to the other side of me.

"I don't think I can." Trace strained as he used both hands and his arms enhanced with dragon power, as he tried to move Celestina. My father joined in. But we remained locked together as the magic in my body built and built. Celestina had turned into an immovable boulder.

It took all that was in me to keep from turning into my dragon form.

"Get everyone out of here," I panted the warning. The manor house would be destroyed when my magic exploded. And I didn't want anyone injured.

"Go! Clear the rooms!" my father ordered. He kept his hands on Celestina's arm and kept pulling. "I'll not leave you, Daughter."

"No…" If he stayed, he'd die. His human form wouldn't survive the explosion of magic. "Go…"

"I won't," my stubborn father said.

"I won't leave, either," Trace said.

"Nor I," Anther added. He placed his hand on my shoulder.

"I. Won't. Die… You. Will… Get. The. Hell. Out." I growled and snapped my sharp teeth at them.

Naturally, none of them obeyed me. That was male dragons for you—too arrogant for their own good.

It was up to me to save them. Just as I felt my human body slipping away, I raised my partially turned hand, the one Celestina wasn't clutching, and swiped my sword-sharp talons at her already injured neck. The talons cut through the bandages there as if they were paper and sliced deeper, through skin and neck muscles.

Blood spurted out of the vein I nicked, spraying me and Trace in the face.

"What have you done?" Trace shouted.

Celestina cried out, her hands instinctively reaching for her neck.

Suddenly free, I stumbled backward. I would have fallen on my ass if not for Anther. He wrapped his hands around my middle and spun me away from Celestina.

"Get control," he commanded. "Get control of it now."

I gave a shaky nod and screwed my eyes shut as I tried to pull all that magic back inside me. Goddess, there was too much. My body couldn't contain it all.

"She's glowing," Anther cried. "The magic, it's still building."

"Get her on the ground outside!" my father shouted. "Move! Now!"

Anther swung me over his shoulder and ran with dragon speed through the center of the manor house. He burst out the front doors with a splintering crash and tossed me like a javelin. I landed hard on the packed earth that served as a walkway in front of the manor. My forehead hit the ground first. My neck snapped painfully back before I jolted violently against the ground.

Goddess, the magic pulsed and screamed and tore at my body. It was too much. I wouldn't survive it. My talons clawed the dirt as I tried to keep from exploding into a million fleshy pieces.

At this point, I wasn't sure if I was in my human or dragon form. Everything hurt.

I opened my mouth and screamed.

Magic poured from my body into the ground, draining me until there was nothing left.

Nothing.

I was air. I was sky. I was darkness. I was night.

And I'd tumbled back into that stupid vampire prince's head.

"Celestina," Cullen's brother was barely able to scrape her name from his mouth. The big warrior tumbled off his horse and crumpled to the ground. His body jerking as if entering death throes.

I was everywhere.

And nowhere.

I was night.

Cullen leaped off his own steed and was at his brother's side in a moment. The three others with him dismounted. The two males pulled their swords as they searched the darkness for the threat that had taken their general. The female knelt next to Cullen. Moving with great care, Cullen gently lifted his brother's head and cradled it in his lap.

"What's happening?" he asked me, because he knew—like he always knew—when I'd slid into his thoughts. *"Talk to me, Amaya. What's wrong with Celestina?"*

The once calm waters of his mind had turned as choppy as a storm-tossed ocean. I didn't like it in there. I wanted his calm waters. I needed his calm.

"If she dies, my brother dies!" he shouted in my mind. *"You promised she was safe with your kind!"*

"She did this to herself. She nearly killed me and half the clan in the process." I looked down at the nothingness that had once been my body. *"Dammit, I*

think she killed me."

"You're not dead."

"Who are you to tell me if I'm dead or not? Jerk. I exploded. I'm a billion little particles now. All of them dead."

"I don't connect with ghosts."

"Oh, so this is a common thing for you? You have hordes of other females sliding into your thoughts?" I should have known.

"You're the first...and only."

"Then how do you know you don't connect with ghosts?"

"I just know. Besides, if you were dead, you wouldn't be able to exact your revenge against me."

"I could haunt you."

"But, Amaya, you promised to eat me alive. You promised twice that you'd do it."

"Aren't you lucky that I'm dead, then? You won't have to suffer the slow, painful death I had planned for you."

"But I've been looking forward to it. Should I tell you what I do at night when my thoughts are consumed with thoughts of you putting your pretty mouth on my body? Should I tell you how I stroke myself until I'm moaning your name?"

I growled.

"That's how I feel at night. Frustrated as hell."

"Sounds like that's about to become a chronic condition for you. I don't have a body—dragon or human. Celestina blasted them both apart. And now I'm dead."

"I've read that when dragons turn from one form to another, there's a moment when you are neither shape. For a stunning, magical moment, you become nothing...and everything."

"Duh. I know how turning works."

"So, it's true? Good. Then you should also know that you're not dead, but only stuck in that in-between phase of turning."

Was I stuck? I'd never spent more than a fraction of a heartbeat in the nothingness that preceded a shift of forms. I never paid attention to how it felt to be nothing and everything, as Cullen had described it. Goddess, if I was stuck, Anther would never let me live this one down. And, if Cullen was right, well, I didn't want to imagine the smug expression that would overtake the prince's already tempting mouth.

Grrr...

"Soren has stopped breathing," the female warned. "What's going on,

Cullen? Why did he fall off his horse? There's no injury. Why the hell are we about to lose him?"

"Something happened with the dragons. Celestina is badly hurt," Cullen answered.

His worry made the violently churning waters in his mind turn acidic. His thoughts burned.

"You need to save Celestina. Please, Amaya. Go back to her. Save her."

Chapter 20

Celestina

Stop! You're going to hurt everyone around us.

No, I wasn't going to stop. It was past time someone else suffered the hurts I'd been forced to swallow in silence. It was time someone else burned in my place.

"*Celestina.*" A welcome voice cut through the darkness calling to me.

"*Soren?*" I floated up on the flames, feeding the fire consuming me until it sent me up higher and higher. I stretched, reaching across the wide distance separating me from him. Soren owned my heart. His love was what kept it beating. *I'm here. I'm here.*

"*Celestina, my princess. Hold on. I'm trying to get to you. I'm—*"

Pain ripped through my neck. I pressed my palms against the ripping agony there.

"*Soren!*"

Nothing.

"*Soren?*"

"No," I sobbed. Hands were on me. Reaching for me. Wrapping around me. Pressing me down. *No. No. No.*

"What have you done?" someone demanded. I didn't think they were talking to me.

It hurt too much to lose Soren again. It felt like the stars had all been ripped out of the sky and brought to earth to burn my heart to ashes.

"Celestina," a mocking voice called out to me in the burning void I must have fallen into. *"Celestina, did you really believe you could find happiness? Did you really believe I would let that happen to you?"*

I recognized that voice. But it was impossible. It had to be a product of my tormented imagination born from the searing pain tearing at my neck and destroying my heart. Queen Beatrice couldn't be here. I refused to accept that she still had any connection to me.

The voice cackled. *"Believe what you will, my ugly dragon. You may have lost the collar, but you'll never lose meeeee."*

Pain rippled through my body as I hit the hardwood floor in the manor's hallway. The heavy scent of the lemon wax that had been used to polish the floor seemed to close in around me like a shroud.

"Put more pressure on the wound!" Juniper's shout cut through the loud buzzing in my ears. She belted out orders like a general. "Get blankets. Fetch my medical kit. More pressure. We can't lose her. I won't lose her."

My eyes involuntarily drifted open. I watched from where I lay on the floor while feeling more than a little detached from the scene as the dragons rushed around me. The ceiling was made from wooden slats that had been stained to look almost black. The clan leader, Drix, was the one who had his hands pressed against my neck. It hurt.

"Dammit. You're a mess."

"Amaya?" I didn't see her, but I could hear her voice more clearly than I could hear Juniper's barking orders.

"Good, you can connect with me. I wasn't sure if this connection would work seeing how I'm not solidly anywhere and you're half-dead."

"Amaya?" We had a connection? I supposed we would. We did hatch on the same day.

"I don't know what Cullen thinks I can do to help you get this sorted. Could you just stop bleeding already? Your human body can't survive losing that much blood. Plus, it's gross. Guess who'll have to clean the floor? Not you, I'm sure. They still treat you like a fucking honored guest. While I'm the problem that needs discipline. So guess

what? I'm going to be the one who'll be handed the mop. That is, if I figure out how to take some kind of corporal form. You did this, you know. You blasted me out of both my human and dragon forms."

"Sorry? Gah! I try to stand up for myself once. Once! And the world explodes!"

"Yeah, you should be sorry."

"Amaya's gone!" Anther shouted as he came to a skidding halt in the hallway. "I got her outside. Got her touching the ground. There was a flash of light. And—" He tugged at his hair. "She disappeared." He sounded out of his head with worry.

I tried to tell him that she was here. That she was talking to me. But all that came out were wet gurgles.

"Hush, Celestina," Juniper cooed. "Anther, I'm sure Amaya took her dragon form and flew off. If there was a bright light, I bet you didn't see her shift forms. That girl of mine has been upset and unstable ever since Celestina was returned to us."

"Amaya did slash Celestina's throat," Drix said, frowning down at me as he continued to put pressure on my neck wound.

"She had better stay away," Trace said, his voice hard. "She tried to kill our moonlight dragon."

"I did what I did because she was trying to kill me and all of you!" Amaya shouted.

I may have been angry but... *"I wasn't trying to kill anyone."*

"Then what the hell were you doing making my magic surge until it made me explode? We're lucky Anther got me away from everyone before I went boom, or else I'd be cleaning dragon bits off the floors and walls in addition to your blood. Besides which, tapping into someone's magic source isn't right. You shouldn't be able to do it. And even though you can do it, you shouldn't do it. You just shouldn't."

Juniper, who'd been kneeling on the other side of me, started pulling supplies from a small leather bag. "Anther, go look for your sister. I don't have time to worry about her right now."

"Yes, Mother," Anther said. But he stayed put, watching with the others who'd gathered around.

Juniper drew a long breath. "Drix, lift your hands. Let's see if there's anything I can do."

Drix gave a nod, and the pressure and the pain slicing through my neck immediately lessened. But a breath later, a hot gush of liquid coated my neck and shoulders. The flickering lamplights in the hallway started to dim.

"Goddess, no." Juniper sat back on her heels and pressed her hands to her face. "I-I can't fix this. There's too much damage."

"You need to turn," Amaya said to me. *"This kind of injury is nothing for our kind. Changing forms will heal you."*

"I can't." I felt woozy. Kind of floaty.

"They're going to blame me. And then they're all going to hate me for killing their shining star of hope. Maybe they'll pretend not to hate me. But they'll hate me. Why did you have to do that thing you do when you touch me? Why did you pull my magic like that?"

"I...don't..."

"Fuck, Celestina, you're not going to die and leave me to take the blame."

Everything was going dark. The voices in the hallway had already faded away to dead silence. And it was even becoming difficult to hear Amaya's voice, a voice that was coming from inside my head. But even with all that happening, I knew I wasn't going to die. Not with this fire still burning in my chest.

The fire felt like life.

"Amaya."

Nothing.

"Amaya."

Still nothing.

I was riding in the wagon with Mary and Patty. I laughed at something Patty had said. I could see their faces, could watch their mouths moving, but I couldn't hear them.

A bright light flashed.

I was back at the court in Earst. I tugged at the sleeves of the heavy court dress, hating how they felt too tight. The fabric pinched. The courtiers behind me pushed and nudged their way forward, not because they wanted to see what was happening in the front of the room. The courtiers kept pushing and shoving each other because they wanted to be seen. The entire room stank of desperation. Some, anxious to be seen by the queen in hopes of winning her favor. Others, slinking away to the back, frightened of what horrors might befall them if the queen did take notice of them. I stood like a wraith in the middle of the crowd wearing that uncomfortable dress as I realized that even though I knew everyone around me, I was alone. I'd always been alone here. The courtiers were always so busy watching their own backs that no one had ever watched out for mine. No one saw me. Not the real me.

But when I looked up, I noticed with a start that Queen Beatrice, still sitting on her throne atop the tall dais, was staring directly at me.

A bright light flickered.

I stumbled as a wave smashed against the side of Cullen's schooner. In the distance, I spotted the small boat Cullen had boarded with a few of his men…all of them spies. As the sun crested over the horizon, Cullen had set out toward Earst. I clutched a small book to my chest. Cullen had handed the book to me right before leaving the schooner.

Once Cullen's small boat was no longer visible, I snuck away. In the silence of my cabin, I leafed through the pages of what looked like an ancient diary. A few of the pages crumbled to dust as I turned them. From what I could tell, a foot soldier had penned his thoughts here. I read a few pages. The soldier talked about the terror he felt when battling the dragons during the War of the Magics. He'd been forced to feed from a fellow soldier after being badly burned in a skirmish. He didn't like feeding on that particular soldier, because every time he took the soldier's blood, he *felt* things for the other male, things he didn't think were right for him to be feeling. He worried that the other man had noticed how his breath had hitched, or how his lips had quivered before sinking his fangs into the tender skin on the man's neck.

I flipped through the pages, skimming over the parts where the foot soldier complained about the rain, about the food, about the lack of action. I then reached a page where the ink was smeared in several places, making it challenging to read.

"My heart weighs heavy tonight. Hortence is dead." The foot soldier's handwriting wavered with every word written. I imagined the smeared ink was from tears that had dropped on to the paper. "A midnight dragon, a beast that can take form from the mist hanging near the ground during the dark of the night, appeared in front of us as we made our way to our tents. It appeared from nothing and lunged. With a snap of its jaws, it tore my friend's head off his shoulders before I could unsheathe my sword. The vile creature swallowed Hortence's head and then vanished back into mist.

If this is the enemy we are fighting, I don't know how we can win. Tonight though, thoughts of death no longer trouble me for I don't wish to live in a world without Hortence."

I stared at the loopy writing on the page while a thought from the present overlapped with my memories of the past. *This didn't happen. It isn't real.*

While Cullen had traveled with a full library, he didn't hand me a diary to read when he'd left the schooner.

The scene flashed and shook, as if angered by my realization.

Suddenly, I was back in the dragon's manor house. I stood in the hallway with my hands clenched. Amaya was again blocking the entrance to the room where the others were meeting. She held up her hands as if preparing to fight to keep me from going through that door.

The anger I'd felt in that moment came flooding back. I'd wanted to strike out at her. I'd wanted to hurt her. She'd been raised with a family who cared for her and in a village that had kept her safe. She'd had everything. And now that I'd found a small piece of happiness with Soren, she was determined to rip that away from me. Amaya was just like the heartless midnight dragon who had killed Hortence and had broken the foot soldier's heart.

She couldn't stand to see me enjoy even an ounce of happiness.

The fire of anger in my chest blazed hotter than ever. "You're the darkness. I'm the light. You're death. I'm life. You're the village's assassin. I'm the bringer of hope."

None of that felt right, but I couldn't seem to stop the words from tumbling from my mouth. I wanted to hit her. I wanted to make her bleed. For me. For the foot soldier.

She didn't respond. She silently stood there with her clenched fists and glared.

"There's already enough pain and hatred on the continent. It doesn't need you!" With a snarl, I slashed at her chest with a hand that had formed sharp talons.

The talons slashed through empty air. I spun around to find her standing behind me. I slashed again. Again, my talons found only empty air. What trickery was this? I felt as helpless as the foot soldier. How does one fight a ghost?

Everywhere I looked, there she was. Glaring. Every time I launched an attack, she disappeared.

"Fight me!" I screamed.

"I can't. I'm not solid anymore. Nor do I understand where we are." Amaya, her eyes wide, looked up.

I followed her gaze. Instead of a ceiling, there was a swirling galaxy filled with stars and colorful planets above our heads.

"What is this?" I asked feeling more than a little alarmed.

Amaya shook her head. "We're somewhere you created...maybe?" She stepped toward me. "I know you want to slash me to bits. But don't."

I growled and slashed at her again. Before my talons could make contact, she disappeared. "I'm here because Prince Cullen sent me to help you." She spoke quickly from directly behind me. "His brother is dying because of you and your bad decisions."

"Soren?" I whirled around to face her. "Soren is hurt?"

Amaya shrugged. "You know, if Cullen is a prince, wouldn't that make your warrior general also a prince? I wonder why no one mentions that when we talk about the Beast of Fein."

"That's none of your business. What's wrong with Soren?"

"You," Amaya answered. "That's what's wrong with him. You need to pull yourself together. I see you managed to shift enough to form talons. That's a good start. You need to keep shifting into your true form—your dragon form—to heal your injuries."

"I don't know how." I shook my talons at her. "I don't even know how to get rid of these."

She reached out and placed her hands over my talons. I didn't feel anything from her touch because, like she'd said, she was no longer solid. "Use your magic."

"I don't have magic. Not anything of any use, anyway. I can compel other magical creatures, but really that's kind of iffy."

"You blasted the shackles off my wrists. You sent that embedded collar of yours flying. And, I don't know"—she tapped her chin—"you freaking made me explode!"

"That was *your* magic."

"That you drew out of me. Rude, but whatever. You could try to do that again to get us back to the real world and give me back a body."

"How?" I demanded. "No one has ever taught me about how to do anything with magic. In Earst, only the women of the royal family have magic."

"The royals have a diluted form of dragon magic because one of their ancestors slept with a dragon. Not that impressive. Human hybrids are so tiresome, thinking they're special when they only have a few drops of what it means to be us."

"Still, that doesn't help us now. I was never taught how to control this power everyone seems to think I possess."

"Right." Amaya frowned. "Let's see. When I was a youngling, Ivy would have me picture a flame in my chest."

"Here?" I touched the spot where I felt the fire burning.

"Yeah. She'd have me picture the flame and try to control it. At first, I'd use it to make a flame on a candle waver."

I looked around. "I don't see any candles in here to practice on."

The hallway wasn't a perfect replica of the one at the center of the manor house. Instead of the wall sconces that had lined the real hallway, this one was illuminated with an eerie light emanating from the center of the swirling galaxy above our heads that made us look as if we both had a blue-green glow.

"I feel you're beyond the flame play anyhow. You did send us to a world you'd conjured."

"Did I?" I glanced at the galaxy above us and cringed. "I didn't mean to."

"When I was learning to use my magic, it felt more like an awakening rather than being taught how to control it. I don't think it was the same for the other younglings. They had to practice the craft of pulling magic through them. For me, that part came naturally. I think that's one of the ways that we're different from the others. Our magic is different. In time, I could use the inner fire to push the magic through me and out into the world around me to wilt a plant or break a vase. I wasn't very popular in the village when I was first exploring my powers. I made cakes fall and kitchens explode and—" She snapped her fingers, which strangely made a snapping sound even though she was made of nothing but air. "Oh my goddess, why didn't I think of it sooner? I'm death. You're life."

"I didn't mean—"

"Yeah, yeah." She waved her hand in a rolling gesture.

"I don't want to be your enemy." I felt the need to tell her.

"You only want to run back to help our enemy."

"I…um…Soren's not our enemy."

"He's a vampire." She lifted her eyebrows as if to suggest that she'd said all that needed to be said about that. "Let's get back to saving you and worry about how the vampires have completely twisted up your thoughts later. As I was saying, when you channeled my magic, you destroyed things. That's how my magic works. It breaks things apart. Sometimes violently."

I was starting to catch on. "We were protected together, hatched together, because our magics complement each other. We're a set. Light and darkness. Life and death."

"Everyone prefers the light," Amaya softly grumbled.

"What?" It seemed as if a lifetime of pain was connected to what she'd just said.

"Nothing. You need to use your powers, not mine."

"But I don't—"

"Beg to differ." Amaya pointed at the swirling galaxy.

"Right. I don't know how I did that. But I guess since we're stuck here, it wouldn't hurt to try to do something to get us out." I closed my eyes and pictured returning to the hallway, the *real* hallway. I kept my eyes tightly closed for a long, long time. "Nothing's happening," I whispered.

"Try focusing on that flame you feel in your chest. And on your emotions. I always get myself into the worst binds whenever I let my emotions take over. Since you're the light to my darkness, your strong emotions might undo bad things."

"Or I might create more galaxies that we don't need." Goddess, I hoped I hadn't conjured an actual galaxy from nothing. "Do you think there might be civilizations up there?" I pointed to where the ceiling should have been.

Amaya made a face. "Let's just focus on saving ourselves. If there are civilizations in that swirling mass of stars, they're going to have to watch out for themselves. Now, work on pulling the magic that's all around us through your flame. That's what shapes the magic. That's what makes it go where we want and do what we want…mostly."

"Mostly?"

"It's never perfect. It is, after all, a force of nature that we're trying to control."

"And there's no sure way to control nature. I think I'm beginning to understand." I drew a long breath and pictured the hallway as it should be—with a ceiling. The flame in my chest wavered.

"Don't forget to make me solid again," Amaya interrupted.

I nodded and started over. My body went still. The flame in my chest grew a little larger.

"Don't forget you also have to heal yourself," Amaya interrupted again. "The swiftest way to do that is to take your dragon form. Turning from one form to another heals our ailments. It's great for when we feel a cold coming on."

"Okay. I'll…try." I started over yet again. Drawing in a deep breath, picturing the flame, feeling the magic travel up from the ground, through my toes, up my legs, and—

"Oh! Is that a lizard?" Amaya squealed.

"Amaya!" I huffed. "Please, I'm trying to concentrate."

"Right. Right." She reached down and picked up the little green lizard and let it run up her arm. It looked exactly like the pesky lizards that followed us from Earst and had traveled everywhere with us. The lizard crawled on to Amaya's shoulder just as the midnight dragon pressed a finger to her lips. "I'll not say another word. Promise."

Yet again, I tried to concentrate on the hallway, on the movement of the magic through my body, on Amaya's human form becoming solid, and my neck being healed. The flame wiggled but seemed content to remain steady.

Gah! Why did I think this could work? I had absolutely no experience with magic. Plus, hadn't Queen Frieda used her magic to bind up my powers? Maybe my approaching demise had released a magical explosion that had created this place. Whatever had happened earlier, I had no clue how to repeat it…or even undo it.

Which meant I would remain forever stuck in this strange hallway with a formless dragon who didn't like me. Soren had promised that no matter where I ran, he'd find me. But he couldn't come here. I'd put myself in a place that was beyond his ability to reach me. I'd never see Gray scowl at me again. Never get to enjoy girl talk with Raya. Never laugh with Patty or run away from Mary's oversized spoon. And this was my own doing. Queen Beatrice had been right about me all along. I was useless. Beyond useless, since my ending up here endangered Soren's life. Could our bond stretch out across dimensions? Or had it snapped? Had I already killed him?

Have I already killed him?

I couldn't—I couldn't catch my breath.

"Soren." If my runaway emotions and uncontrollable magic killed the only man—er, vampire—I'd ever loved, I'd never forgive myself. He deserved better than me. He deserved to have a life.

Don't be dead.

Don't be dead.

Don't be dead.

The ground shook. Or was that just me trembling? I reached out to catch myself as I stumbled. My hand hit not the smooth surface of the hallway's wood-paneled wall, but the rough surface of…what was that?

I opened my eyes and stared at the small tree that had helped steady my balance. It wasn't just one tree. There were hundreds of them…and no hallway. I looked up and spotted the night sky. A few stars winked at me.

Just past my hero tree, four horses were milling around a narrow forest trail. My gaze, as if pulled from a power outside of me, jerked sharply to the right. I sucked in a breath when I saw Soren sprawled on the ground. His head rested in Cullen's lap. His black hair was loose and formed what looked like an ominous shadow against Cullen's leg. Raya knelt next to Soren. She had his hand pressed to her chest. And even from this distance and despite the darkness, I could see her cheeks were shiny from tears.

"Is he…?" Raya asked, her voice sounded husky and rough.

"He doesn't smell dead yet," Amaya answered. I wasn't surprised to find her standing next to me, and back in solid form. I'd been thinking about my need to rescue her as strongly as I had been thinking about saving Soren.

Cullen turned his head sharply toward us. Amaya had spoken loudly. His eyes widened with surprise when he spotted us standing under the trees. "Amaya? Celestina?" He shifted Soren's head in his lap as if considering a need to get to his feet. He then adjusted his glasses. "How are you here?" he asked with deliberate care.

Raya scrambled to her feet, gaping at us. "Celestina? We—"

"Soren isn't breathing," Cullen said, his brows furrowing. "If you're here, Celestina, and uninjured, my brother shouldn't be like this. Amaya?" He settled Soren's head on the ground and stood. "Amaya? What's happening?"

"It's complicated," Amaya said. "Celestina is somewhere where she's not breathing."

"I'm right here," I said. And I was breathing. Wasn't I? I pulled in a deep breath of air to prove it.

"She's right there," Raya agreed as she pointed to me.

"She's here and…somewhere else," Amaya corrected.

"What?" I demanded. "I'm right here."

"We're working on getting it all sorted," she said, not glancing in my direction.

"Do it faster," Cullen demanded, his hands clenching into fists.

Amaya lurched forward and hissed. "You don't get to order me around, *vampire*."

Gray scowled quite brilliantly as he put himself between Cullen and Amaya. When Amaya took another step toward them, Gray rushed toward us, his twin swords coming out of their sheaths, prepared to fight Amaya. I was trying to decide if jumping between the two of them would save Gray or save Amaya when he suddenly stumbled to a stop. "Celestina? What's going on? Why are you glowing?"

I glanced down at my hands. Gah! They were glowing like the moon. So were my arms. And my legs. And-and the rest of me.

I didn't have much time to ponder that I'd never again need a candle or electric light when I walked to the bathroom in the middle of the night. Driscoll, dressed all in black, had crept up as silently as a cloud. He emerged from the shadows next to me. His beady black eyes flashed in the darkness a moment before he grabbed my wrist and jerked me away from Amaya.

"Got her!" he called in his deep, gruff voice. Just as his words emerged, he released me. He howled as he clutched his hand to his body. The acrid scent of burnt flesh curdled the air.

I rushed toward Soren. "He's not breathing? Is he…dead?"

"Not yet," Cullen said, still not taking his eyes from Amaya. "Vampires can exist like this for several hours. But"—he shook his head—"if you can't find a way to recover, he won't either."

"I'm fine. I'm right here."

"*I'm* here." Amaya grabbed my arm. I winced, expecting her to sink her talons into me again. But her hands were human hands. And though she tightened her fingers firmly around my wrist, it didn't hurt. "You, unfortunately, Moonglow, still need to find your body. This isn't where you belong. These vampires aren't your family."

With every word she spoke, I could feel the magic swirling faster and faster. The flame inside my chest burned so hot I was convinced my organs were melting. How did anyone survive channeling magic? This felt like torture of the worst kind. Amaya must be pulling my magic like I'd done with hers. And, yeah, I now understood why she'd been so angry about it. This did feel like a violation.

"All vampires are our enemies." Amaya glared at Cullen. *"Stay away from us!"* Her scream tore through the night as the magic she was pulling through me burst out of my eyes. With a deafening explosion, we shattered into light and air.

Silence.

Blessed.

Silence.

I groaned when I managed to pry open eyelids that felt like they'd been glued closed. Pain smacked me hard in the…everywhere. My neck especially burned. And my arm felt like someone had ripped off my skin.

I blinked as I stared blankly at the wood slats that made up the ceiling in the manor house's long hallway. Whatever Amaya had done with my magic, it'd brought me back to the plateau, back to the manor, back to my broken and bleeding body.

I took a shallow breath, wincing as the slight movement made everything hurt even more.

"Celestina took a breath!" Juniper shouted. The older healer was kneeling beside me. Much like Raya's face had been in the forest, hers was shiny from tears. "She's breathing!" I wished Juniper's voice wasn't so loud.

Trace dropped to his knees next to her. His hand went to her shoulder as he peered at me. "She—she's alive?"

Juniper nodded happily. "She's still bleeding, but it's slowed. And her injuries look—" Juniper shook her head. "It looks as if she partially shifted. Look at that. She's healed enough that I can stitch up the wound."

While everything still hurt, I could feel the difference. My neck was bleeding, but it was a slow ooze instead of the gushing of blood leaving my body like it had been before.

"Let me get started on stabilizing her," Juniper said.

Amaya fell to her knees next to me. She was laughing.

"You did it!" Her jubilant voice sounded distant even though she was leaning directly over me. She grabbed one of my hands and held it in front of my face. "Look! You're no longer glowing. You no longer have talons. And I'm able to pick up your hand." She laughed again. "I'm solid."

You are. We did it. You and me. Those are the words I tried to speak. But I only gurgled troubling noises. And I felt woozy.

"Get her away from Celestina!" Trace shouted.

Arms reached down and pulled Amaya away.

"Don't you dare touch her." Trace rose to tower over me. "I'll not let you harm my girl again." He growled. It was a low, inhuman sound that made my skin prickle.

"I didn't—"

"You slashed open her throat. We all saw you!" Trace shouted. "If you weren't *important*, I would insist your father call for a tribunal to hold you accountable for your actions. You've been allowed to get away with too much. You're dangerous, Amaya. You shouldn't be allowed to be around the other dragons. If it were up to me, I would seriously consider whether you should be allowed to exist."

Amaya folded in on herself.

"Come along," Anther said as he wrapped his arms around Amaya's chest from behind. "There's nothing for you here to do anyway."

"I didn't—"

"I know," Anther said, cutting her off. "You never mean to do harm. It's simply who you are."

Amaya shrank into herself even more as she allowed her older brother to pull her away.

"Put a guard on her door," Amaya's father said quietly to another dragon I didn't recognize once Amaya was gone. "Make sure my daughter stays in her rooms until we can figure out what to do with her."

"Drix," Juniper cried. "I'm sure she didn't mean to harm the girl."

"She never means to do harm," he said, his expression grim. "But things always seem to fall apart, and dragons get hurt whenever she's around. Now that we have the moonlight dragon back, we might need to rethink how we handle Amaya. Trace isn't wrong. The few stories we have of the midnight dragons have always emphasized how dangerous they can be."

I wanted to defend Amaya. I wanted to tell them how Amaya had saved me from myself. But I could only manage to make more gurgling sounds. I thrashed a bit and tried again, only to slur a few unintelligible words.

"Are you sure she's going to survive this?" Trace asked as he placed a steadying hand on my shoulder. He pushed me back down to the hardwood floor.

"She's a dragon," Juniper said with considerable pride in her voice. She poked my neck with a sewing needle and started to stitch up the gaping wound. I jerked from the sting of pain. But her movements were swift and sure. "She's one of us, Trace, which means our Celestina is going to be just fine."

Trusting in her confidence that I'd survive the pain and blood loss, I closed my eyes and allowed my tired body to rest. I could figure out the rest another day.

Like how to tell them that I'd never be Trace's mate.

And how to convince them that Amaya wasn't a danger to them.

And how to get back to Soren. I needed to get to him, to see that he'd recovered from the damage my bond had caused. If I had the strength, I would have run through the village, searching for a way off the plateau that didn't involve tumbling off a cliffside. My need to get to him was that great. Goddess, I hoped my returning to my body meant Soren had started breathing again.

But, right now, my body simply needed to…heal…

Chapter 21

Amaya

A week and a half had passed since *the incident*—that's what Mother called it. As soon as Celestina grew stronger, she explained to Trace and my father how I'd helped her find her way back from that strange dual existence she'd created for herself. Even so, Trace still watched me as if he expected me to lose my temper and rip out Celestina's throat again. Not that he let me get in scratching range of the village's precious moonlight dragon.

My father, on the other hand, didn't believe what Celestina had told them. He insisted she'd suffered from some kind of fevered dream brought on by a near-death experience. It didn't matter that I had the same story to tell. Dragons couldn't exist as air. And dragons couldn't split themselves in half and exist in two places at once—not even accidentally.

They kept me locked in my room with a guard outside the door and two more outside my window. During that time, I overheard too many whispered conversations thanks to my ability to drop into the mind of anyone who was thinking about me. And most of the clan were thinking about me lately.

"She's a danger to us all."

"It's her nature to destroy."

"She needs a firmer hand controlling her."

"She's being who she was born to be."

"She's death."

They weren't wrong. My solution to every problem was to crush it, which was why when they'd locked me away, I'd wanted to smash down my bedroom door, shatter all my windows, and tear out the throats of the dragons prowling outside my room as guards. I would have done it if Anther hadn't been out there serving as one of the guards.

I didn't want him to see me losing control like that.

But while I stopped myself from tearing apart the world, that didn't settle the raging firestorm that burned inside me.

The same destructive magic that had once given the others in the village a sense of safety and protection now frightened them. Since their beacon of hope had been returned in the form of the moonlight dragon, they no longer needed a trained assassin.

I returned her to you! I wanted to scream in their already wary faces.

Discussions in the village turned to how they could best use the moonlight dragon's powers to protect the village. While I'd been kept locked up in my room for so long, I'd started to worry that they might forget about me. Not that servants didn't bring me food and hot water for the bath. And my parents would visit every day. But the door remained locked.

Until one morning when I woke up to find my bedroom door open. The guard was gone. The guards outside the window were also nowhere in sight.

I cautiously crept down the stairs, keeping alert to any strange sounds. All the worst scenarios ran through my mind as I made my way through the house. Had the manor been attacked while I slept? Had my family been murdered in their beds? Would I be blamed for it? Was this the moonlight dragon's doing? She might seem all sweet and ignorant on the outside, but I knew—I knew what terrible power lay just beneath her pretty surface. And I knew her heart lay with the vampires. Celestina was the dragon they should be worrying about.

As I padded down the hallway, I heard voices coming from my father's study. I tiptoed closer.

"My daughter has been asking to talk with Gregory again," Drix said. "She's questioning whether he's told her everything we know about midnight dragons and their powers."

"What did you tell her?" Sires, one of the elders and a rare purple dragon, asked.

"I've not told her anything. But we can't keep her locked up forever.

And she'll talk to him as soon as she's out of her rooms." Drix grumbled something I couldn't hear. "Juniper has insisted I unlock her door."

"Is that safe to do?" Trace demanded.

"I imagine letting her out is safer than trying to keep her caged," Sires said with a nervous chuckle. "I'll talk with Gregory and warn him that he should use a goodly amount of…discretion…when Amaya comes to him."

"Thank you," Drix said. "Gregory does get carried away when talking about history. Trace, you might want to warn our moonlight dragon that we're no longer holding Amaya. I wouldn't want her to be frightened if she sees her around the village."

"I'll make sure she's made aware. And you'll caution Amaya to keep her distance?"

"I'll talk with her." Drix sighed, not sounding at all happy about the thought of speaking with me. *What a way to make a girl feel loved, Dad.*

"Now about the other issue, have you given it more thought?" Sires asked.

"I have. I don't like it. Nor do I think Juniper will agree to let us do it."

"It's for everyone's safety," Trace was quick to say. "Even Amaya's."

Anxiety clawed at my throat as I crept closer. Whatever they were discussing couldn't be good.

"I agree with Trace," Sires said. "Amaya said it herself. The moonlight dragon can grab control of the midnight dragon's powers. Maybe, for the safety of us all, we should encourage Celestina to grab ahold of it and keep it."

Had they already forgotten the absolute explosion of power Celestina had caused the last time she'd channeled my magic and how I'd had to scramble just to keep her alive?

"Celestina's magic is more stable than Amaya's," Trace agreed. "And she's mentioned that she's able to use compulsion to control other magical creatures."

"I don't like what that would do to Amaya." At least my father wasn't jumping on board with their plan. "I don't think she would agree to being controlled."

"Now that we have the moonlight dragon, do we really still need Amaya's erratic magic?" Sires asked. "The prophecy never mentions the midnight dragon."

"But Amaya's egg was protected alongside Celestina's. There must have been a reason our ancestors did that."

"Clearly, she was saved so the moonlight dragon would have access to the destructive power of midnight," Sires said, sounding alarmingly ready to dismiss my existence. "It's the moonlight dragon who the storytellers glorify and the other kingdoms fear. It's the moonlight dragon who will usher in a new age for the continent. She's our future. She's the one we need to protect."

"I'll think about it," Drix agreed.

The crinkling of fabric signaled movement in the study. I whisked down the hallway and around a corner before any of them came out and spotted me. I spent the rest of the morning sulking in the library. Sadly, this time the old woman never came to comfort me.

That night, now that I'd been released from the confines of the manor, I took my dragon form and soared through the star-speckled sky until exhaustion had me landing in a thick forest. This part of the forest was a fair distance from the plateau, but it looked familiar.

I sniffed. Vampires had stopped here. More specifically, Prince Cullen had camped here. His was a scent I'd never forget. *Stupid vampire.* This part of the forest was where Celestina and I had landed when she was trying to heal herself, which was telling. She felt closer to her vampire lover than she did to her own body. *Foolish, brainwashed dragon.*

I recognized that spindly tree over there. It was where Cullen had been standing.

But his scent was faint.

Did I come here by chance or did a part of me want to find this spot? I snarled. I did want another chance to rip out Cullen's throat. The next time I saw him, I wouldn't be so cautious. I planned to strike first and let him talk *never.*

The thought of killing the smug Prince Cullen made me remember how Celestina believed I could hold on to the nothingness that happened while shifting between my human and dragon forms. Was that a third form? One of nothingness? That would come in handy.

I shifted and attempted to grab on to the in-between shape. I tried to hold it. But it slipped through my grasp like water. I landed on the forest floor as a human. Naked and helpless. I quickly shifted back to my superior dragon form. I never wanted to turn back to my human form. I felt much more like myself as a dragon than I ever did living as a human.

Because the clan was in hiding, the council and elders always preferred that we lived as humans. That way, if a human did come across us, they wouldn't ask too many questions, and we wouldn't risk having a human reveal that dragons were still living on the continent.

I rolled on my back, letting the leaf litter scratch my wings.

While living as a human chafed, I did understand the importance. Our numbers were small. We might be able to take out an army or two. But we wouldn't be able to defend ourselves against an entire continent, and certainly not against a continent filled with magical defenses.

I wondered what the elders thought one moonlight dragon could do for them against such magical foes. The prophecy was vague. There had to be more information about it that I didn't know about. I launched into the sky and headed back to the plateau.

I needed to talk to Gregory, and despite the council's warnings, I needed to convince him to tell me everything.

Chapter 22

Amaya

I landed near a small gardening shed on the manor's property where I kept a stash of clothing. Once back in human form and dressed in a black sweater and leather pants, I took a cliffside trail that wound around the periphery of the village.

No one walked this trail at night. Barely anyone used it during the day, either, which was one reason I preferred it. But tonight, I came across my mother on the trail. I swiftly turned away from her, but she'd seen me and called out.

"What are you doing?" I asked once we'd closed the distance between us. "Are you searching for me?"

"No, dear, I knew you were out flying. I was…" Her eyes glided over to where a shadowy figure was walking much closer to the edge of the cliff than the trail ever went.

"Is that Celestina?" The shadow moved along the edges of the plateau. The silhouette reminded me of a tragic heroine that would wander through muddy moors in those overly dramatic human gothic romance novels Trace would bring back to the village from Earst.

"It is. The poor dear has been sneaking out every night." My mother clicked her tongue behind her teeth.

Quite a distance away from Celestina I spotted a tall figure. He moved only when Celestina moved. "And that's Trace following her?"

"He is her protector."

I had a feeling Celestina didn't see it that way. "She doesn't know he's there, does she?"

"He's in a tough spot with her. She wants her freedom, but she needs to be protected. He's trying to give her that."

"She feels trapped here." I could feel her panic like tiny pinpricks against my skin.

"There's an emptiness in her that she's looking to fill. Trace thinks she comes out to the edge of the plateau because she's trying to connect with her dragon form and doesn't know how. It makes her restless. It must be hard for her to be around so many dragons who can shift forms like water pouring from a pitcher while her dragon side is bound up like a block of ice by that evil queen that stole her from us."

I watched Celestina move slowly and carefully along the edge of the plateau's cliff. "That's not why she comes out here," I said.

My mother put her hand on my shoulder. "I think you're right. I believe our dear Celestina takes these nightly jaunts because she's aching. Part of her soul is empty, restless. She's searching for a way to connect with this place. What she needs to do is resurrect long-buried memories of the village from before her abduction. Then she'll be a peace."

No, that wasn't it, either. But I didn't tell my mother that Celestina was scouting the edge of the cliff, searching for a way to escape.

The plateau had steep cliffs on all sides, making it a perfect place for dragons to hide. But that didn't mean humans never stumbled across our village. There was a hidden and mostly overgrown path that rose sharply up the southern side of the plateau. It was the same path the old lady had taken to reach the manor house during the storm.

Since we were all dragons in the village, we rarely needed that trail. If we wanted to leave the plateau, we flew. I had asked the old lady more than once how she happened to find our hidden trail, but she'd never given a clear answer. She would mention the storm and wave her hand as if that were all the answer I needed. The old nameless human had been good at gathering information from us but never giving anything specific about herself.

I wasn't surprised Celestina had failed to find the trail. She would have to push through heavy bushes and blackberry brambles to find the opening.

"Why don't you go to her?" my mother suggested. "She could use a friend."

Was my mother serious? Trace would rip my head off if I dared approach his precious dragon. "I was heading to Ivy and Gregory's."

"Wonderful. Take her with you. She needs to hear Gregory's tales."

I reeled back. "Trace would never allow that."

"I'll handle Trace. Go on." My mother gave me a gentle shove toward Celestina. "She needs you."

I doubted that. But I crossed my arms and headed toward the cliffside where she was leaning precariously over the edge, peering down.

"You'd die if you tried to escape that way," I said as I approached her.

She spun around. "I wasn't—"

"You totally were. But I get it. You've been brainwashed by the vampires to see us as the villains and them as the heroes." I kept more than a few arm lengths away from Celestina so Trace wouldn't worry that I might push her over the edge. Even so, I heard scuffling and angry whispers behind me. "I'm heading over to Gregory's cottage. He's the clan's historian. You're welcome to come along."

I walked away, not waiting to see if she'd follow. I expected she wouldn't. She was too charmed by her vampire to want to listen to the truth. But after I'd gone a few yards, I heard her barely-there footfalls and the swish of her long woolen skirt behind me. "Gregory and Ivy, they're not…" She walked a little faster. "They're not having a party at their cottage, are they?"

I tilted my head toward her. "You've been to one of their parties?"

She shuddered. "Trace thought it'd be a good way for me to meet his friends."

"He did? I got the impression that he'd be more protective of you than that. Taking you to one of their parties is the same as throwing one of our lambs to the wolves that hunt the forest below the plateau. The younger dragons don't always school what they do with their hands."

"It wasn't like that. Everyone was nice." She fell in step with me and rubbed her arms. "I'm sorry about what happened. I've been meaning to talk to you about…everything. But you haven't been around."

"I've been locked away."

"You've been busy?"

"Yeah, something like that." I guess no one had thought to tell her that I'd been locked away for her safety.

"I wish I had more to do to occupy my time and thoughts. Trace has given me a few lessons on his loom, but he's been busy with clan matters. He hasn't had much time to show me much more than how to set up the threads. And he keeps telling me that I need to rest, to heal."

She still had a heavy bandage around her neck and a sling on her arm.

"You aren't healed yet?" Come to think of it, she did look unnaturally pale. Dragons could heal themselves so readily, I found it impossible to believe she wasn't better. The younger dragons suffered much worse injuries during combat training, but then again Celestina wasn't like the others. And she was more important.

"It's—" She shrugged. "It's fine."

"Sorry about digging my talon into your neck." She had almost died. I hadn't really thought of the damage I'd cause. Getting her to stop channeling my magic had been my only priority.

"I'm sorry, too. I promise to be more careful around you. I wouldn't want to accidentally channel your magic and endanger any more lives."

"I suppose you wouldn't want that. Your vampire nearly died. What a shame that would have been." What was wrong with me? Why couldn't I keep the bite from my voice?

"He isn't your enemy, Amaya."

Gods, she actually believed that. We were getting close to the cottage. "How about this? I don't touch you, and you don't touch me."

"Seems like the safe way to go." She clutched her hands behind her back.

"I don't want to be your enemy," I admitted.

"You're not."

We'd reached the cottage's front stoop, but neither of us knocked.

Celestina shifted nervously from one foot to the other. "Trace says that I'm meant to channel your magic. He thinks I should practice controlling your powers"—she drew a long breath—"and you. He says that's the way we were made."

"And what do you think?" I was interested to know.

She snorted. "What he says doesn't make sense. Maybe Gregory can help. I do want to learn more about this clan and about dragons and how dragons interact with others on the continent. Maybe then I would understand."

Celestina

Gregory was thrilled to find us both at his door. The large, friendly redhead ushered us inside while calling for Ivy to put the kettle on.

Once we were in the living room, Gregory crushed Amaya against his chest in a massive bear hug. "I'm so glad to see you, Amaya. We've been worried, haven't we Ivy?"

Gregory's equally friendly mate came into the living room from the direction of the kitchen. "I never thought you meant to cause Celestina harm. And look at the two of you together. It's as it should be." She poked Gregory's shoulder. "Let the girl loose already so I can have a go at her."

She gave Amaya an equally enthusiastic hug. She then framed her hands on Amaya's chiseled cheeks. "You know we love you to pieces. I told your father he was overreacting when he locked you away." She glanced over at me. "And look at you, coming around to our humble cottage with Celestina as if the two of you are sisters. I suspect Trace is outside. Should I invite him in?"

"No!" Amaya answered before Ivy even finished that question.

"I don't think Trace wants me to know that he's been following me everywhere I go," I said. "He wants me to think I have the freedom to move about the village."

"You knew he was there?" Amaya pried herself out of Ivy's hug.

"Someone as tall as Trace is kind of hard to miss." And I supposed I shouldn't mind his presence. While I might have felt anxious to get back to Soren and my friends, I was enjoying getting to know those living atop this desolate plateau. Many of the dragons were like Gregory and Ivy, genuinely friendly and kind. Amaya must have had an incredible childhood being surrounded by a community that loved her. I'd started to envy her until something Ivy had said to Amaya sank in.

"Drix—your father—locked you up for what happened two weeks ago? That's why I haven't seen you?" I demanded.

"Trace wanted to execute me, so I think my father was taking the less bloody option when he put me under lock and key."

How could Amaya sound so nonchalant about members of the village discussing killing her?

"No one would have allowed Trace to harm you." Gregory tossed his arm over Amaya's shoulder to give her a quick side hug. I noticed how she flinched from his touch. "You're our secret weapon. The continent doesn't know about the terrible power of destruction the midnight dragon wields."

"That's why I came to you," Amaya said. "I have questions."

"So I heard." He rubbed his hands together. "Sit. Sit. The tea should be ready soon."

"I don't want you holding back information, especially if it concerns me or Celestina. Don't you agree that we deserve to know? Aren't you always saying that knowledge lets us become better decision-makers?"

"I am always saying that. And I'm glad to know you've been listening," he said as we all settled into a set of comfortable overstuffed chairs arranged around the blazing fireplace. Ivy left only briefly to fetch the tea kettle. She returned with a tray filled with primitive teacups, a delicate teakettle that bore Earst's royal seal, and plates of a seeded cake that smelled as if they'd been taken fresh from the oven.

"What kind of information are you searching for?" Ivy asked as she poured the tea.

I lifted the cup and took a tentative sip. The hot drink had a smooth, slightly fruity flavor with a touch of mint. I took another sip and let the drink's heat fill me.

"Soothing, isn't it?" Ivy asked.

I nodded.

"It's my own blend. Good for promoting restful sleep. I'll send a jar over to Trace's tomorrow. I have a feeling you could use it."

I didn't want to tell her that I wandered at night only because I was searching for a way to get off the plateau, so I nodded and thanked her instead.

"So," Gregory's voice boomed. He clapped his large hands together. "What do you want to know?"

"The prophecy," Amaya answered immediately. "I know it's vague, but stories never are meant to be taken alone. There are histories and related stories that help give us a clearer picture of the past. The same must be true for the prophecies. So, tell me some of that. What stories were told at the time of the prophecy's origins? What was happening on the continent when the prophecy was first spoken?"

"I wish the others listened to my lessons as keenly as you do," Gregory said. "Most of my students dismiss my teachings as useless prattling. Perhaps because you are from the past—as well as you, my dear Celestina—you have a unique interest in the tales from that time."

I sat forward. "I have always been drawn to the stories about magic and magical creatures, including dragons."

"I'd be interested in comparing the human's stories to ours. The victor of any conflict always paints history differently from those who suffer." Gregory tapped his lips. "But we'll have plenty of time to chat now that you're back where you belong."

I forced a smile to my lips. "There's a prophecy?"

"A most wondrous one. Would you like to tell it, Amaya?" Gregory leaned over his mate and took a plate of seeded cake from the small table where she'd set the tray. "These smell delicious, dear." He kissed Ivy on the cheek. The woman flushed pink.

Amaya rolled her eyes. "The two of them are disgusting like this all the time. Like a pair of younglings experiencing their first spring heat."

Gregory boomed a laugh and then nuzzled Ivy's cheek. His sinewy movements looked otherworldly, reminding me that while these creatures in this room with me looked human, they were something different, something ancient and primal.

I guzzled what was left of the calming tea. "The prophecy?"

"Right." Amaya's eyes glittered. "The moon will burn—twin magics will rise causing borders to shift like sand in a desert when the moonlight dragon returns."

"With your knowledge of human stories and human histories, what does that prophecy mean to you, Celestina?" Gregory asked. He'd settled back into his chair and was regarding me with a serious expression.

"I'm not sure." I hurriedly ran through the tales of the War of the Magics and how the vampires defeated the moonlight dragons with a mysterious weapon. The dragons were wiped out. The vampires went on to terrorize the continent until magical humans rebelled and defeated the vampires, beginning an age of humans. Magic was held only by the ruling classes, and the other magical creatures on the continent had retreated into the shadows or disappeared altogether.

Even knowing that the stories weren't completely correct—Vampires weren't creatures that only could walk in the night and didn't live in nests scattered throughout the continent, that they held a kingdom that rivaled the others in wealth and size—I couldn't picture a future where humans weren't the dominant power.

The others in the room remained silent, waiting for me to say more. When Amaya started to speak, Gregory raised a staying hand. The silence stretched so long that it began to feel itchy and awkward.

"I'm not sure what it could mean. However, while the dragons hide themselves away because they're afraid the outside world will destroy the few that remain, the humans and vampires live in terror of what the dragons can do to them." The vision the seer had forced on me where the capital city of Sukoon was burning, and all my friends were dead, flashed in my mind. I hugged myself. "It wouldn't take many dragons to decimate a city."

"Interesting." Gregory finished off his piece of seeded cake and licked the crumbs from his fingers. "I think fate had a hand in causing us to lose you to the humans for such a long time. You needed to live with the humans for the prophecy to bloom. No one in the village would ever suggest waging war on an entire continent like you just did. But perhaps that's exactly what is needed to shift the borders."

"I-I wasn't suggesting…" Watching any city burn—witnessing the deaths of countless innocent lives—was the last thing I wanted to happen.

Amaya smiled. Her teeth had elongated into sharp weapons. "So begins the new age of the dragons."

Chapter 23

Amaya

The next morning, I rose before anyone in my family and shuffled to the kitchen expecting it to be empty. It was market day. The household cook would be in the village buying supplies for the week. I wanted the alone time so I could sort through my thoughts.

All my life I'd been taught that I was special, a gift to the village. I'd been trained in the most efficient ways to kill. It was my duty to put the village's welfare before anything else, including my own safety.

Villagers had loved me for the sense of safety I provided. At least I'd believed they'd loved me. They'd allowed me to be the chaos-bringer that was innate in my nature. But now, with the moonlight dragon's return, the once indulgent villagers wanted me leashed, contained.

Goddess, that stung.

How did I process this without wanting to burn down the manor?

I felt a flash of annoyance when I found the old lady sitting at the scarred wooden kitchen table that was used as both a work surface and an informal dining table.

The old woman had her tatty shawl wrapped around her bony

shoulders and was sipping a cup of hot tea. Her tired eyes softened when she saw me.

To be honest, I was glad to see she was still in residence. Like a favorite chair or a cozy knit blanket, I'd grown used to having her around. Her dire predictions gave me an unsettling sense of reassurance. Like I'd been holding my breath my entire life waiting for the bad things to come, and because of her, I'd been finally given permission to exhale since she let me know that the bad things were finally here.

A woven basket perched at the end of the table next to the old woman. I peered inside it. My eyes nearly dropped out of my head at what I saw.

"Are these cloudberries? Where did these come from?"

"Oh. Here and there." The old woman waved her hand.

"But they don't grow on the plateau." The sweet berries only grew on the north side of the cliffs where there were no paths.

"Is that so? Well, I found a small bush during my ramblings yesterday. I decided to pick what berries I could find this morning as a surprise for you. You've been such a generous hostess, my dear. Would you enjoy having them in muffins with breakfast?"

I frowned, still staring at the basket filled with the delicate ripe fruit. "Cloudberries don't produce fruit until the end of summer. And because they grow on the windy side of the plateau, they rarely produce any fruit at all."

"If you don't want them in your muffins, I could make—"

"No, no, no, no, no. I would never pass up a chance to enjoy a cloudberry muffin. They're my favorite." And incredibly rare. I could count on one hand the number of times I'd eaten them.

"Splendid!" The old woman's face suddenly looked decades younger as she smiled at me. "Sit, child. Let me work, then. Would you also like eggs? I could poach them."

"Would you? I love poached eggs. The cook rarely makes them, since everyone else in the family prefers their eggs fried."

"Glad to do it. Glad to do it." She moved around the kitchen with her familiar stiff gait. "You provided for me. I'm pleased to return the favor." She lifted a bowl from a kitchen shelf, set it on the table, and then looked at me. Her brows furrowed, deepening her already impressive wrinkles. "Is something bothering you?"

Where did I start? Did I tell her how I resented Celestina because everyone fawned over her, even Gregory had gushed about how she brought a fresh perspective because she'd been raised by stupid humans? I hated that I resented the moonlight dragon because she seemed so...*nice*. Did I tell her how I was worried that Trace and the elders might succeed in convincing Celestina to take control of my magic? If I didn't have my powers, what did I have?

I slid into the chair the woman had left. It was still warm from her body heat. And I blurted out something I hadn't even realized I'd been obsessing over. "None of the patrols have spotted the vampires or even seen evidence that they have been in the forests surrounding the plateau. I think they left the area."

"And that's good?" The old woman didn't pause in her task of gathering ingredients.

"I suppose it's good. I know I shouldn't feel disappointed that Prince Cullen has heeded my advice and has turned back. But I do. And I feel sad that Celestina's Soren has so easily given her up. Not that it wasn't the right thing to do. I just..."

"You just what?" the old woman asked.

"I wanted to believe in true love, all right? If not for me, at least for someone in this world." I banged my forehead against the table. "I know it's stupid."

"It's not stupid," the old woman said. "Love is never stupid."

"It's always stupid. And it doesn't matter, does it? Vampires can't love dragons. Moonglow's Soren won over her affections only because he was using her. I heard him say so when I was in Prince Cullen's mind."

"Did you ever think you might have misunderstood what he meant?"

"Even if I did, it doesn't matter. There's a war coming. The village is expecting Moonglow to bring forth a new age of dragons and to repopulate that world with moonlight dragons. And I suppose I'll be expected to provide some little midnight dragon warriors for the clan as well."

"That's a heavy load for you and for Celestina." The old woman cracked several eggs into the bowl. "Your family shouldn't have locked you in your room."

I made a rude sound.

"Your mother and Anther both fought on your behalf the entire time. Their faith in you never wavered. You're lucky to have allies like them." She pushed the bowl in my direction and slapped a wooden spoon into the palm of my hand. "Stir."

"I-I can't." I was more likely to blow up the kitchen than to do anything useful in it.

"Oh, for goddess's sake." She roughly grabbed my hand and had me swirl the spoon around the sides of the bowl, mixing the flour and eggs and whatever else she'd put into the mix. "It doesn't take magic to bake a few muffins. Just your hands."

She released her hold, and I tentatively started stirring. I held my breath, fully expecting the bowl to go crashing to the floor. She picked up the basket and poured the cloudberries into the bowl.

"Don't do that!" If I smashed the bowl now, the cloudberries would be lost. "I'm going to mess it up." I always did. While I was an expert at destroying things, putting anything together never worked out right.

The old woman put her hand on mine, steadying my stirring, which in my panic, had turned erratic. "You have more facets to you than a shimmering diamond. There's nothing wrong with you. Yes, you're a powerful dragon. But there's beauty in that power...and life."

I pulled the spoon from the bowl before I destroyed a breakfast treat that already had my mouth watering. "That's the moonlight dragon you're describing. She's beauty and life. I'm destruction and death."

"No, child. The same magic that flows through the moonlight dragon flows through you. And trust me, baking doesn't involve magic. You've been allowed to believe for so long that you are something dark and dangerous, that you've forgotten that you're also a dragon with a heart, a dragon who opened your home to a lost and weary old woman, who rescued your moonlight dragon and took the blame for the destruction *she* caused in this very manor. Now stop fussing and get mixing."

The old woman muttered to herself as she moved around the kitchen, checking on the batter, poaching eggs over the wood stove, and directing me to pour the batter into metal tins. By the time she'd finished with the cooking and the baking, the entire kitchen was warm and smelled of sweet spices, fruit, and love.

"The muffins need to cool." She slapped my hand when I reached for a muffin before waiting for her to remove them from the tins. "Now go fetch a pile of plates while I put the muffins in the basket. Your family will be joining you soon enough." She drew a long, shuddering breath. "Amaya, I don't blame them for what they did. So don't you blame them, either."

"I don't," I answered as I went to the cupboard. I didn't blame them for locking me away. They'd done what they'd thought necessary to protect the others from my destructive nature.

"And one more thing, child." She took the plates from me, set them on the table, and cradled both my hands in hers. Her touch felt cool. Her rheumy eyes held steady on mine. "The prophecy and the fates may have set the future into motion, but that doesn't mean you're a mindless puppet in this tale. You can decide to take a different path." Her grip tightened. "The decisions you make—you, specifically, not the moonlight dragon—have the power to rewrite the lines that the fates put down eons ago. You, my beautiful dragon, can save countless lives, but only if you decide to follow that amazing heart of yours." She dropped my hands and, before I could ask any of the questions that flooded my mind, she put me to work gathering napkins, silverware, and crystal glasses for my family to use. "Hurry. Hurry. You'll want everything to be ready."

I obeyed her. I could always ask my questions later.

I had just finished setting the table when my mother came into the kitchen. She'd braided her blonde hair in a spiral on the top of her head and was dressed in a rainbow sweater and long skirt with a rainbow of tiny dragons stitched into the hem. She didn't get far into the kitchen before she stopped and sniffed deeply. "I thought it was cook's day to go to the market." She headed straight for the muffins that were still cooling in the basket.

"It is."

My mother stumbled to a stop and whirled toward me. "*You* made breakfast?"

"No, of course not. The kitchen's still standing, isn't it? The old woman made it for us as a thank you."

"Who?" Mother looked around.

I turned a full circle to discover I was standing alone in the kitchen. "The old human woman. She came to our door seeking shelter when you and Father were gone. She's not left."

Mother shook her head. "I haven't seen an old woman in the house."

"That's ridiculous. She's been sitting in on all our meetings."

"Who's been sitting in on our meetings?" Anther asked as he entered the kitchen. His hair was still mussed from sleep. His loose pajama pants hung low on his hips.

I slapped his bare chest. "Can't you put a shirt on? No one wants to look at all that skin when they're eating."

He playfully pushed me out of the way and then took a deep sniff the same way our mother had. "Do I smell cloudberry muffins? I haven't had cloudberries in years."

"Amaya says a human came to stay at the manor during a storm," Mother said as she stepped between Anther and the muffins. "What is she talking about?"

"The old woman?" Anther paled.

"Yes." I gestured to the muffins in the basket, the poached eggs under the covered platter, and the fresh bread on the cutting board. "She's the one who cooked breakfast."

His hand had a tremor as he took a muffin from the basket. He sniffed it. "You think the old human who came to stay with us baked this?"

"I helped her stir the batter," I sheepishly admitted.

"You—?" My brother grimaced as he bit into the muffin. As he chewed, his look of disgust gradually lifted. "You didn't bake this. It's good. Who made it?"

"The old woman." I couldn't figure out why this was so difficult for them to understand.

"Amaya," Anther said and then stuffed the rest of the muffin into his mouth. "That's impossible. That old stray died the day after you were abducted. Gregory took care of her body since I was busy searching for you. I think he incinerated her and spread the ashes in the flower garden you keep forgetting to tend." He gestured with his neck toward the side of the manor house where the gardens were kept.

"No. You're mistaken. She's been here at the manor. And she baked muffins this morning."

Mother placed her hand on my forehead. "You don't have a fever."

"She was here. Right there. She picked the cloudberries."

"Who was?" my father asked as he came in. "Oooo, cloudberry muffins. What a treat! Are the berries even in season?" He grabbed one and carried it over to the kitchen table.

"Amaya is seeing dead people," Anther teased. "And they're cooking meals for her."

Father looked at me as if he were concerned about my mental stability. But I was used to that. He'd looked at me that way ever since I'd returned with Celestina.

"Ha-ha, Anther, I'm not seeing dead people."

That's when I noticed that Anther wasn't smiling. He hadn't been teasing. His entire body had gone stiff as he stared at the breakfast spread out for them.

"The old woman prepared the meal," I said with great care. "I don't know why you are all acting so surprised. She sat in on the family meeting we had shortly after I escaped. She was in the chair by the fireplace. And she's been around ever since. I've spoken to her. Anther, why are you looking at me like that?"

"Amaya." He dragged his fingers through his already messy hair. "After you were abducted, I killed the old woman."

"You did what?" I screeched.

"I killed her." He clearly had no remorse for attacking a defenseless old lady. "Humans took you mere days after you opened our home to her. I had told you to send her away, told you that I didn't trust her. And I was right. She led the other humans here, didn't she? She was the reason you were taken. I did what needed to be done."

"No! That's not what happened! She didn't—"

"Doesn't matter," my father said. "Humans aren't trustworthy. You know that, Daughter. Taking you was an act of war against us. Anther did the right thing by executing one of theirs."

I couldn't believe what I was hearing.

I don't blame them for what they did, the old woman had told me. I'd misunderstood what she'd meant. But of course, I'd misunderstood. I had no way of knowing that my brother had killed her. I had no way of knowing that she was dead. She'd cracked eggs, measured flour. She'd held my hands.

"She came back from the dead to bake cloudberry muffins for me."

Tears burned like acid in my throat. "I can't imagine anyone in the village doing that. Not now that you have the moonlight dragon to fawn over." My magic pressed against my edges, searching for a way to explode out. I snatched the basket of muffins off the table and clutched it to my chest.

With an ear-piercing crack, the large table that had held the basket fractured down the middle. The crystal glasses and plates shattered as the two halves of the heavy wooden table toppled. Perfectly poached eggs slid off the clattering platter and slithered over the stone floor. That, I regretted.

"Amaya!" my father barked. "You have to calm down."

"No!" Still clutching the basket of precious cloudberry muffins to my chest, I ran from the room, leaving a trail of broken stone floor tiles in my wake.

Chapter 24

Amaya

"Go away." I stuffed an entire muffin into my mouth. It would have tasted delicious if I hadn't been sobbing too hard to taste anything. I really shouldn't have been wasting the muffins like this. I should have been eating them slowly, savoring every last crumb as a way of honoring the old woman's memory. I didn't even know her name. How did I not know her name? What the fuck was wrong with me?

"Are you okay?" Celestina asked as she crouched down next to me.

I was huddled inside a cavity of an ancient tree. For as long as I could remember, this had been where I'd go when I didn't want anyone to find me. I should have figured Celestina would be the first one to find my hiding place.

"I'm eating breakfast." I stuffed another muffin into my mouth. It was either do that or blast fire at the too-perfect-for-words moonlight dragon. I hated her.

But trying to roast the village heroine would only get me locked up in my room again.

"I see." She sat on the ground, which she would regret because she was getting mud all over her pretty pink skirt. She crossed her dainty ankles and stared at me with those brightly colored mismatched eyes of hers that only made her look that much more unusual and perfect. "Do you usually leave a trail of uprooted ground wherever you go?"

She glanced over her shoulder at the small mountain range of overturned dirt. Plants, trees, fences had all toppled over thanks to my rage. "I was upset," it didn't hurt to admit.

"What happened?" Celestina asked, but quickly added, "You don't have to tell me. I know we're not friends."

"We're more like quarrelsome sisters." I handed her a muffin. "A ghost baked this."

"There are ghosts in the village?" Her eyes grew impossibly wide. "I shouldn't be surprised," she muttered under her breath.

"Apparently there are now." I sniffled. "She bakes the best muffins despite being human. Someone should enjoy them."

"You don't like how they taste?" She studied the muffin.

"I'm grieving." As if she couldn't already tell that by the tears falling from my stupid leaky eyes.

Celestina nibbled the muffin, sighed loudly, and then took a big bite. "These are the best muffins I've ever tasted." But then she frowned. "You're grieving the ghost? Who was a human? But I thought the clan didn't allow outsiders to enter the village."

"She was an old woman who'd lost her way during a storm. I gave her shelter. It's our way to be hospitable to those in need." I told her all about the old woman, how she wouldn't tell us her name, how she'd given me advice and warnings. "She was a seer."

Celestina's shoulders hunched at that news. "Seers are charlatans. I had one call me a monster. And she tried to have me killed more than once."

"To humans, you are a monster."

She thought about that for a moment and nodded. "I'm sorry your friend died," she said after a long span of silence that, oddly, didn't feel awkward at all.

"Anther killed her. He did it soon after that awful man, the one who was Cullen's friend, abducted me." I hugged myself and rocked a little. *"We are monsters,"* I whispered.

Celestina pressed a hand to her mouth. Clearly, I'd shocked her. She'd lived in a human world with human royalty. She must have felt like she'd been dropped into a pit of vipers when I brought her here. No wonder she'd been plotting her escape back to the vampires. Even those bloodsuckers had to feel safer than living with a bunch of monsters who saw nothing wrong with killing a helpless old woman. And I was the worst of the worst? The most violent of our clan? *Goddess, help me.*

"She must have liked you very much to come back from the dead to bake muffins."

"Cloudberry muffins are my favorites," I admitted.

"I've never had a cloudberry before. I like the tart flavor."

"They're rare. And they're not even in season. She shouldn't have been able to get them, but I guess if you're dead you have some leeway on how things get done."

"More proof of how much she must have liked you." A smile sneaked its way onto Celestina's pretty face.

"At least someone does...*did*." As soon as I'd said it, I recognized that it was a lie. Despite my prickly and (let's face it) deadly nature, everyone in the village treated me with respect. I tilted my head back and stared up into the hollow center of the tree. The view always reminded me of a dark, swirling vortex. "Father says the nature of a dragon's unique powers affects our individual personalities, and that's why I'm, well, the way I am. Unfortunately."

My heart was like the inside of this tree. An endless swirl of darkness.

Celestina punched me in the arm. Hard!

"What the hell?" I growled. "You want to start something with me? After everything that has already happened between us, you think coming at me is a good idea?"

The demented moonlight dragon was still smiling, like she thought this was funny. "I think you need someone to punch you every time you get down on yourself, Amaya. And since we're sisters in a way, I'm appointing myself the one to do the job."

"Until you leave," I snarled, unable to simply accept that she was trying to be friendly.

She punched me again.

"Ow!" I rubbed my arm. "That one actually hurt."

"Really? Sorry. Soren was training me to defend myself before..." She shrugged. "Anyway. Even if I do find a way off this plateau, you'll still be my quarrelsome sister. There's no changing that," she said, throwing my own words back at me.

We sat in silence for a while longer. I liked being around someone who didn't feel like she needed to natter on and on. But then she ruined things by starting to talk again.

"What Gregory told us last night about that prophecy, it's—" she said and lifted her hands to her head and made an exploding sound while spreading her fingers as if her head were splattering.

"Now you understand why you're so popular with everyone. 'The lost heroine returned home.' Dragons will sing ballads glorifying your accomplishments for a millennium or more."

Celestina pulled her knees up and hugged them to her chest. "Yeah." She rocked a bit. "I don't see how anything in the prophecy is going to happen. Queen Frieda has done a good job making sure I would never be a threat to anyone or anything. I'm not even a threat to these lizards that follow me around." She brushed aside a green lizard that had crawled across her boot. I scrunched my nose as I watched the lizard scurry away. "I'm more human than anything else. And not a very accomplished human at that."

I hadn't really taken the time to consider how heavy a burden the prophecy must feel to her. The old woman had said she felt sorry for the moonlight dragon. "Look at us having our first pity party as if we were truly sisters."

Celestina gave a little laugh. "I've always wanted a sister."

I handed her another muffin and took one for myself. This time when I bit into it, I was able to enjoy the sweet and tart flavors.

"Things aren't perfect in the village," I said after I'd finished the muffin and licked any stray sugar off my fingers. "But you need to give us a chance, Moonglow. You did hatch here with me. We'd been held in stasis, waiting for the time when we'd both be needed. Apparently, you more than me. But that's not the point. The prophecy says the clan needs you."

"Prophecies aren't always right." Celestina backed up. This wasn't what she wanted to hear, and she was getting ready to bolt.

"It's not all about the prophecy. Even your precious vampires know that war is coming. Honestly, I'd be fine letting the vampires and humans battle it out. But we can't. Because we hatched after an eon of waiting, it means this war that's coming is one that will threaten the dragons. Look around you. This village is a fair-sized one, true. But this plateau is all we have. The days when flights of dragons would blot out the sun no longer exist. We're the original species, and we're on the verge of extinction. It's disgraceful. Are you willing to let the dragons die out without giving us a chance to show you who we are? To show you who *you* are?"

Celestina started shaking her head. She'd back away from me even more. "Maybe I don't have to be here on the plateau to help. Maybe I'm meant to be with the vampires, to convince them to leave the dragons alone."

"The vampires have twisted up your thoughts, Moonglow. That's what they do."

"No. No. I love Soren, and he loves—"

"A vampire can't love a dragon!" I don't know why I shouted that, or why I felt like I'd been punched in the gut after I'd shouted it. "They just can't," I said, my voice softer. "I'm sorry. Soren was using you. One of my magical talents is the ability to connect with anyone who is thinking about me. I've connected with Prince Cullen several times and overheard conversations he was having with your general. I heard Soren say it himself. He needs to get you back so he can use your magical abilities against Queen Beatrice."

"No." She touched the heavy bandage on her neck. "He wanted to get the slave collar off me. He even went against his…"

"What?" I asked when she didn't finish.

"He didn't go against his father," she muttered more to herself than to me. "That had been a lie. But he still traveled all the way from the Kingdom of Fein to the southern tip of the continent so I could question my adoptive parents. He'd been trying to help me get rid of that slave collar."

"He doesn't need you in the collar. He's got you in a much more powerful way. He tricked you into falling in love with him."

"It wasn't a trick. And he didn't know what I was until after we fell for each other. He loves me. I know he does."

"Then where is your perfect vampire? They were in the forest two and a half weeks ago. Do you think a little dragon fire scared them away? Or was he scared away because your magical explosion nearly killed him? Maybe he went running home to break the bond he made with you."

"It's an unbreakable bond." Her voice sounded hoarse.

"They told you it was unbreakable. And you believe them. But how do you know that's true?" I felt angry about this on her behalf. "The clan has been sending out extra patrols day and night, and no one has spotted humans or vampires or anything that shouldn't be in the forests surrounding the plateau. Face it. Your vampires decided it was too dangerous to try and get to you. It's not as if you can access your powers anyhow. I think they decided you aren't as valuable to them as they once thought you'd be. And that's why your precious Soren has given you up."

Tears brightened Celestina's eyes. She quickly blinked them away.

"Dammit. I'm sorry. I didn't—I didn't mean to—" I growled. "I stink when it comes to talking to others. It's part of that destructive personality that comes with my destructive powers. I'm just trying to tell you that you have us. We *want* you here. We *need* you here. There's a war that will threaten us. We need you to help us defend ourselves against both the human and vampire armies."

"Yeah, well…" She cleared her throat. "I'm not going to fight anyone, especially not the Fein. I-I-I won't fight—" She jumped to her feet and ran off as if a nest of vampires were chasing her. The haunted look in her eyes worried me more than her words.

"I thought I told you to stay away from her." Trace crouched down and peered into my tree-cavity hideaway.

"She came to me. What did you want me to do? Send her running away crying. Well, I did that. I doubt she'll willingly talk to me again." The thought of losing her made the muffins in my belly sit like a lump of paste.

Trace stood and walked away from the tree. But then he abruptly turned back around. "Did she say why she was upset?"

"Something I said upset her, as usual. You already know I destroy everything I get near."

He tugged at his neatly combed brown hair, tangling it. "No, it's not you that has her like this. Not this time." He started to pace. "Celestina has been living like a shadow. She barely involves herself with village life. She spends most of her day reading history books and spends her nights wandering along the cliffside. I follow her wherever she goes to make sure she stays safe. Most nights, she stays out all night, Amaya. I won't lie to you, I'm tired. I have a full schedule of work to do in addition to keeping an eye on her. Plus, I'm trying to set up the weaving shop. And then when I desperately need to rest, she heads outside. She won't talk to me. Whenever I ask her what's wrong, she tells me she's fine. But she's anything but fine. And I don't know how to fix it."

"You can't fix this. She's lovesick and desperate to get back to her vampire general."

Trace closed his hands into fists at his side. His eyes turned feral, and his teeth went all pointy as he growled. "I'll never let that bastard touch her again. Never."

Chapter 25

Celestina

"I would prefer it if you didn't go out tonight," Trace said when we met in the hallway of his home. "I'm too damned tired for it."

I tilted my head and studied him. "You don't have to follow me."

He barked a tight and angry laugh. "Celestina, my one task for the past twenty-three years has been to keep you safe. I'm not going to let you tiptoe along an unstable cliffside in the dark without keeping watch and making fucking sure you don't die within the first few weeks of your return to our village."

I swallowed hard. "I-I'll stay inside." Clasping my hands in front of me and with my head down, I started to make my way toward the bedroom I'd been using. "I-I'm sorry, Trace. I didn't mean to appear ungrateful."

Even if I did find a way to climb off the plateau—there had to be one since Amaya's human friend had somehow found her way up here during a storm—I wouldn't be able to escape, not with Trace watching my every move, counting my breaths.

I *hated* him.

No, hate was the wrong word.

Other than following me around everywhere, Trace had been nothing but patient with me. He never touched me, not even in a casual way.

Every couple of days, he'd bring me a small stack of history books from Gregory's personal library to read. And when we had meals together, he'd talk in a soft voice, recounting daily happenings in the village as if trying to lure me into his life with his homey stories of families and friendships.

But despite his kindness, my heart remained cold. Toward him. Toward the village. Toward everyone except Amaya, the one dragon Trace had expressly told me to avoid.

"Well, good night then," I said as I stepped into the bedroom.

"Yes, good—" He gave a little cough. "He's not coming for you."

"What?" I spun around. Had Trace done something? If he'd harmed Soren, I didn't know what I would do, but it wouldn't be pretty.

"There's been no sign of him or his warriors in the forest for weeks. Back when you were in Fein, I watched him as carefully as I watched you. He's a brilliant strategist. Which means he realizes that you're back with your own kind, you're back where you belong. He must also realize that if he tries to get close to the village or you, I will end him."

"You think telling me that makes me feel safe? Makes me feel protected?"

"No, Celestina. I know it does not, dammit. As I already told you, I'm tired. And I know I'll never have the perfect words for you. I'm not a vampire. I don't have the magic of charm on my side. I'm simply a dragon trying my best to show you that you can be happy here, if only you would give us a chance."

I couldn't think of anything to say to that other than, "I'm sorry."

"I'm sorry, too." His shoulders dropped. He turned away from me and walked down to his bedroom. He stepped inside and closed the door behind him.

After a few tense moments, I closed my bedroom door. And locked it. Not that I needed to. I knew I was safer here than anywhere I'd ever been in my life. Still…

I padded across the room to the small window that looked out over a patch of wild grasses. The room was on the second floor, too high to contemplate safely climbing through. I pressed my forehead to the cool glass and allowed the tears that had been burning in my eyes for days to finally fall. Whether I liked it or not, this was my life now.

The moon had set by the time I'd finally drifted off to a fitful sleep. I hadn't even bothered to remove my clothes. I'd pulled off my boots and collapsed on to the bed. My temples throbbed from crying too much.

As I'd slept, images of war and death and friends being burned by dragon fire troubled my dreams. And because I was this mythical, long-awaited moonlight dragon, I was the one leading the charge to destroy all I'd come to love.

"No!" I cried out in the dream. I didn't want this. I never wanted this.

Queen Beatrice, in her rage, bound my hands and tied a long rope to the bindings. "No one wants you," her sharp words stung. She gave a guard a nod. The hulking beast picked me up and tossed me over the side of the castle wall. I fell until the rope came to a jolting end, nearly pulling my shoulders out of their sockets and breaking my wrists.

"Stone her!" she shouted down to the courtiers who had gathered below to watch the queen's latest spectacle.

Soren stepped forward. He held a pebble in his hand. He looked up at me, grimaced, and then tossed the small stone.

Ping.

It missed.

He picked up another pebble from the ground.

Ping.

Another miss.

Was he even trying?

Ping.

"I'm going to have to go up there," he said, and after picking up yet another pebble, he started to scale the castle wall, scraping his boot against the stone with each step.

I woke up with a startled gasp. That scraping noise wasn't part of my dream. I jolted up and grabbed the heaviest history book from the stack on the bedside table to use as a weapon. My gaze traveled the room and stuttered to a stop when it reached the window. It'd been closed when I went to bed. But now, the windowpane was swung open, leaving a gaping hole to the outside. A cold breeze swirled into the room as a dark, booted leg stepped through.

A scream rose in my throat, I opened my mouth to let it out when a burst of movement blew through the room. A black gloved hand smashed against my face.

"Stay quiet," came a harsh whisper against my throat made me whimper until the owner of that hand added, *"Sky Girl."*

Soren?

He was dressed all in black. Black boot, black tunic, black leather pants, black hooded cloak. His face was shielded with shadows. But I didn't need to see his face to know him. Not when I'd memorized the shape of his body, the timbre of his voice, and the scent of his embrace. With a gust of excitement, I tackled him in a hug that carried such force, he lost his balance and tumbled on to the bed with me. I pushed his hand away from my mouth as I sprawled on top of him and rained kisses all over his face.

"As much as I like this position and, goddess, I'm starving for those kisses, we don't have time for me to properly make love to you. Not here." He wrapped his arms around my waist and stood, bringing me to my feet with him. "We have to move quickly."

"What? How? How?" In this room. With me. *How in the blazes did he get past the dragon patrols and the villagers to be here?*

"I'll explain later." He disentangled my arms from around his neck. "We need to go. Now."

I nodded so hard I felt the stitches in my injured neck pop. "Yes. Yes. Let's go."

When I started for the door, Soren caught my hand and led me back toward the window. "Um…we're on the second floor," I reminded him.

"I know," he rumbled, his voice a balm to my nerves. He scooped me into his arms. "Hold on tight, Sky Girl," he said as he ducked through the window to balance on the sill.

"You-you're not going to—?" He stepped off the skinny ledge before I could finish the question. His gloved hand covered my mouth the entire way down, muffling my screams. He landed with such a jarring lurch, I knew that if I'd been the one making such a leap, I would have ended up with multiple broken bones in my feet, ankles, and legs.

He lifted his hand and replaced it with his mouth. "Goddess, how I missed your taste," he murmured between drugging kisses.

"Kiss her later," Cullen cautioned. Sweat beaded his forehead. "It's nearly impossible to hold on to my cloaking charm with so many dragons around. It feels as if their magic is pushing against mine, which according to the books shouldn't be happening. But that's what feels like is happening."

"You can write a scientific dissertation about it when we get back to the capital," Soren said as he started to run with me still cradled in his arms. He moved with blurring speed toward one of the most dangerous parts of the plateau.

"You're not expecting me to fly us out of here, are you?" I squeaked. I'd fallen off the side of a cliff once before. An angry warrior had tossed me over the edge of a ravine. And I had no desire to repeat that experience.

Soren looked down at me and lifted one eyebrow. "You can fly?"

"No!" I swatted his chest. "I'm still the same as I was before Cullen stuffed me into that dungeon."

"Except you no longer have that wretched slave collar," Soren said. "I saw the pieces of it on the floor of what was left of the dungeon after that black dragon flew away with you."

"Amaya," I said. "She's a midnight dragon."

"That's what Cullen told me." He didn't sound pleased.

We were at the cliff's edge. "How-how are we getting down?" I asked, not sure I wanted to know the answer.

"Are you sure you can't fly us?" he asked. But when I started to fight him, he winked. "Don't worry. There's a trail."

"Not here there isn't. I looked. Soren! It's a sheer cliff face!" That he was about to tumble over and at a hard run. At the last moment, he shimmied around a thicket of thorny bushes. On the other side, hidden by those prickly bushes, was the trail I'd spent weeks searching for. About as wide as my bedroom windowsill, the trail hugged the cliffside, zigzagging on switchbacks down the side of the plateau. "Oh my goddess, you found the trail!"

"Didn't I say that already?" He was smiling down at me. I placed my hand against his chiseled jaw, loving the roughness of his stubble and the warmth of him below it.

He ran as surefooted as a goat down the harrowing trail. There were parts where I buried my face against his shoulder so I wouldn't have to see how we were often just a step away from plunging to our deaths. As we continued down, he gave me encouraging words for me to cling to like, "We're nearly to the base," and "I've got you," and "We'll be away from here soon."

After a thousand stuttering heartbeats, we reached the bottom of the trail. Soren kept running. From there, he darted through the forest like an acrobatic deer leaping over felled trees and giant roots. The tree canopy above us made the world seem that much darker, more ominous. I flinched at every sound, certain that Trace would be racing his way across the sky, coming after me.

"We're far enough away now," Cullen said as he caught up to us. Soren kept a dizzying pace. "The cloak is holding."

"Finally." Soren slowed to a trot and then stopped altogether. He set me on my feet but kept his strong fingers curled around my shoulders as if afraid that if he took his hands off me, I would disappear. He flicked a glance in the direction of his brother. "Find somewhere else to be."

"I'm not sure that's—" Cullen started to say.

"Go." Soren sounded on the verge of committing violence.

Cullen lifted his hands. "Leaving. Not far. But far enough that I won't be able to see or hear anything you two might—"

Soren dropped his forehead to mine and groaned. "That brother of mine is never going to stop talking."

"I think he's moving away, though."

"Thank the goddesses."

"I heard that," Cullen's voice carried through the trees. But that was the last thing we heard from him.

Soren lifted his head and backed up, putting a little distance between us. His green eyes, eyes that seemed to glow in the dark, crinkled at the corners. "Hello," he said, a smile coming to his mouth. "I missed you."

I tossed my arms around his neck, certain I was choking him. But, goddess, I needed to hold on to him as tightly as possible. "If this is a dream, don't you dare wake me up. Not ever."

"I'm real." He wrapped his arms around me and held me so close against his chest that I could feel the way his heart raced. "It took us so damned long to figure out how to get to you."

"How did you manage to get past the patrols?" I still couldn't believe Soren had his arms around me and my arms were around him.

"I'll explain it later."

Were we already back to his old habit of refusing to tell me anything important? I growled.

But then he added, "Right now I need to look at you, feel you, make sure you're okay. You are okay, aren't you? They…they didn't hurt you?" His body trembled as he pulled out of my embrace. His eyes trained on the bandages around my neck and wrists. "They hurt you?"

"No! I'm fine," I protested. "The dragons all treated me with extra care."

"Then why the hell are you bleeding?" He reached up and started to unravel the heavy bandage protecting the many wounds around my neck. I was amazed at how gentle his warrior-hardened fingers could be with me. He muttered what sounded like a violent curse in ancient Eirid under his breath once he had the bandages off. "Did they make you sew your own stitches?"

"No. Why would you think that?"

"Because the last time I saw such sloppy work was when Gray took a spear through his arm and had to sew himself up to keep from bleeding to death. And he did a piss-poor job of it. But he had an excuse." Soren's voice was growing tighter and tighter. "He was bleeding to death and didn't have a village who were supposedly looking after him. Why wasn't anyone looking after you? The stitches are all torn out from that wound. You're bleeding. And that deep wound near your collarbone has become infected. It's all red and puffy. Doesn't it hurt? How can you turn your head? Gods, what even happened? Some of these are clearly wounds from the embedded collar coming off. But the really deep gashes look like an animal attack or like—" His expression hardened. "Did one of the dragons attack you?"

"It was a mistake. It wasn't—"

"A mistake?" Violence glittered in his eyes. "Who? That green dragon? Did he hurt you?"

"No! Soren, please."

"This is why we almost died, isn't it? Because the dragons attacked you? Which ones?" He looked ready to return to the village and wreak vengeance on the clan.

"I'll explain it later," I threw his own words back at him.

He jerked as if I'd struck him. "Celestina—"

"No, Soren." I put my hand on his arm. "Don't fret for me. I'm here. I'm alive. And the clan honestly did their best to take care of me. The act of shifting from one form to another heals a dragon's injuries. And because they heal so easily, their medical knowledge is limited. The female who took care of me, Juniper, cleaned the wounds and applied a salve. But she wasn't sure if the injuries were healing or if something was wrong with them."

"Something is most definitely wrong." He pressed his palm to my forehead. "And you're running a fever. I should have gotten you out sooner. I'm sorry it took us so long to rescue you. But I'm going to make it better." He bared his fangs and tore into his own wrist. "Drink my blood. Let me heal you."

I stared at him for a moment watching the blood dripping down his wrist and heard Amaya's snarky voice, *Soren uses his charm and his blood to control you.* And I couldn't move.

He seemed to misunderstand my hesitation. "We're going to be traveling quickly through this forest. We need you to be healthy, Celestina."

Although the sight of his blood did make me crave him, could I risk it? Sure, I had felt my body weakening ever since Amaya had struck me. And my neck often throbbed. It hurt when I made quick moves. His blood would fix all of that. So, unless I wanted to be carried back to Fein like some fainting damsel in distress, I'd need to take his blood.

"Thank you for not using compulsion on me." He was giving me a choice.

"If you refuse, I might feel…" He looked at the blood still oozing from his wrist. "I need to know you'll survive this. But I'd rather you willingly let me help you." He held out his wrist for me. "Please."

I don't know why I kept hesitating. It wasn't that I didn't want to be with him or to have my hands all over him. It was just that niggling voice—the voice that sounded annoyingly like Amaya's—that continued to warn that Soren was lying to me, that he was using me.

Let him use me.

With a frustrated growl, I grabbed Soren's arm and pressed my lips to his bleeding wrist. His blood tasted citrusy and spicy and like the best parts of home. I closed my eyes and drank.

The magic in his veins moved through my body, warming me on that chilly night. It pulsed in my neck. The pain I'd been ignoring there started to fade away. For the first time in weeks, I could draw a full breath without wincing. And the feverish buzzing in my head fell silent.

My body was also heating up. Goddess, how I'd missed Soren. I'd missed the way he made my body feel alive. I'd missed how he touched me and how he liked to play rough with me.

I opened my eyes and looked up at him. His pupils had gotten so large, that his eyes had turned black. He was watching me like a predator, and I knew how this would end up. The muscles in his arm tensed as I lifted my mouth from his wrist. He bent down and licked the corner of my mouth where I imagined his blood had smeared.

"*Sky Girl,*" he groaned with pleasure.

He held me with one arm slipped behind my back as he raised his hand—the one with the still bleeding wrist—so he could tilt my head to one side, inspecting my damaged skin there. The light touch of his trailing fingers over my vulnerable neck made me shiver.

"There's still some redness, but the wounds have closed. Do you feel any pain?" he asked.

"No." But even if I were in pain, I would have lied because all I wanted to do in that moment was to climb him like a tree and wrap my legs around him.

He gave a stiff nod and then brought his wrist to his mouth. With his tongue, he sealed up the wound and cleaned off the blood that had spread on his skin. Watching him lick himself with that talented tongue of his made my breath hitch and my heart pound. I knew my mouth-watering reaction to his every movement was partly due to his magic-endowed blood rushing through my body, making me want. But I didn't care.

"I need you," I confessed.

"I'd promised myself that I wasn't going to...that I was going to give you time..."

"No," I growled. I would do him serious harm if he tried to deny me.

"I need you."

"Thank fuck, Sky Girl, because I need you impaled on my cock more than I need anything else in the world right now." With vampire speed, he made his move. My back slammed against the nearest tree with enough force that it knocked the wind from my lungs. His body pressed against mine. His hands lifting my ass, pressing me against the hard ridge in his pants as I got my wish and wrapped my legs around his waist.

A second later, he nudged my head to one side and struck.

"Gods," I hissed at the pain of his fangs digging into my barely healed neck. But then he started pulling my blood into him, and a wild heat replaced the sharp pain. I rubbed against him with a frenzied motion as I chased a release that felt impossible to find.

While still feeding on me, he reached between us and freed his cock from his pants. His hot skin brushed against my naked thigh as he bunched up the pink skirt I was wearing. I helped push my panties to one side as he lined himself up with my opening.

With one thrust, he buried himself deep inside me. I gasped from the sting of being stretched so suddenly, so completely.

He lifted his mouth from my neck and looked at me. The world seemed to hold its breath as neither of us moved.

"Celestina?" His breathing was ragged. His eyes filled with questions. "Are you—are you up to this?" he asked softly.

I nodded. But that wasn't enough for him. He brushed his mouth against mine. I could taste the bitter tang of my blood on his lips. I could feel his desperate need in his shortened breaths. "I need the words. Is this still what you want?"

"Yes, I want—I want *everything* from you, Soren."

Hearing that, he pulled out and pushed in again in two long, torturously slow strokes.

"Hold my shoulders," he warned. "Hold on as tightly as you can."

And that's when it started. He made love to me like a vampire possessed. His thrusts were hard and fast and everything I needed. They reminded me that I was alive, that I was wanted. While he laid waste to my pussy, he bit my neck and shoulder, again and again, blending pleasure with pain. Marking me as vampire-owned.

My release bordering on agony, I convulsed on his cock. He tossed back his head and groaned as he followed me over the abyss.

In the aftermath, a wild piece of me stirred for the first time. I opened my eyes. What did that wild feeling mean? The question faded as fast as it had come. My head dropped on to his neck as I waited for my out-of-control breath to settle. Soren hadn't simply given me an incredible orgasm with his forceful lovemaking. He'd given me back my world.

Chapter 26

Celestina

"I missed you," I confessed once I found the strength to talk. "I missed this."

"I'm sorry I didn't protect you better." He growled deep in his throat. "I never expected I'd have to protect you from my own fucking brother."

"While I don't agree with his methods, he did get rid of Queen Beatrice's collar."

Soren shook his head. "He should have never—"

"He was desperate to save Amaya," I needed him to know.

"Not an excuse." He kissed me hard, thrusting his tongue deep into my mouth as his cock, still buried deep within me, stirred. "I was so frightened that I'd lost you when that dragon flew away with you." He kissed me again. "I can't lose you."

"I'm right here."

"Yes, you are." He grabbed my hips, pulled out, and then thrust inside me again. "You're exactly where I need you to be."

"Before the two of you start up again," Cullen said as he emerged from the shadows of the trees, "let me remind you that we need to get moving. We want to have as much distance between Celestina and the dragons when they discover she's missing."

Soren made a rude sound.

"He's not wrong," I said, wiggling to separate myself from him, but only succeeding in pushing his cock deeper.

Soren cupped both my cheeks and kissed me again with such fierce longing that, in that moment, I forgot where we were and what we were doing.

Cullen cleared his throat.

Right.

Dragons.

Escape.

Need to move.

With a long-suffering sigh, Soren turned away from Cullen to block his brother's view. He lifted me and set me on my wobbly feet as my long, pink skirt fluttered down around my legs.

"Shall we go, my princess?" Soren offered his arm.

I'm a princess. How could I have forgotten? Tiny dragons fluttered in my belly. I smiled as I placed my hand on his arm as if we were about to walk into his father's court or into a ballroom instead of making our way through a hazardous dark forest.

Cullen kept several steps behind us. His lips compressed to an unhappy line. He remained so silent that I looked over my shoulder to reassure myself that he was still there. We walked for what felt like hours—though it wasn't that long—before we came upon a flickering torchlight within a tight thicket of trees on the far side of a hill.

"Sky Girl!" Raya, dressed in black battle leathers, ran toward us. She grabbed my shoulders and pulled me into her strong embrace. "We all missed you something awful. Especially Patty. She strapped on one of Gray's swords and was ready to march across the continent on her own to fetch you."

"I missed her, too. And you." I hugged Raya back with just as much enthusiasm as she'd shown me. "And even you, Gray."

Gray, also wearing black battle leathers, scowled. "Are you sure we should take her?" What did he want Soren to do? Take me back to the village?

"We're not having this conversation." Soren made it sound as if they'd already discussed my rescue several times before.

"I think we need to." Gray blocked my path forward.

Stealing me away from the dragons would cause them to retaliate. Cities could be burned. Lives lost. Was my rescue the trigger for the destruction I saw in that nightmarish vision? I hugged myself.

Was I worth it?

Soren moved to stand in front of me. "Celestina belongs with us."

"Hell, Soren, I know there are *feelings* involved. But someone needs to say this." Gray flung his arm out, pointing in the general direction of the plateau. "Celestina was back with her own kind. She was back with the ones who would have raised her if Queen Frieda hadn't kidnapped her. How can we take Celestina away from what should have been her home?"

That argument went in a different direction than I'd been expecting. Gray was worried for my wellbeing instead of worried about the security risk I might present?

"She is mine." Soren bared his fangs. "She belongs with me."

Gray held his ground. "We don't know that."

There was so much tension that the air crackled with unspent violence. Both Cullen and Raya stepped in between the two warriors.

Gray made an angry sound in the back of his throat. "I know what it's like to live as a minority in Fein. I know what it's like to be an *other* in your society, Your Highness. While the vampires try to treat the humans fairly, and I do like where I live and what I do, there aren't many of us. And we're spread out from each other. Our rituals and holidays aren't recognized. Our traditional foods aren't served anywhere. If we want to make it ourselves, the ingredients for those foods are damn near impossible to come by. Celestina, you have an opportunity to discover what it means to be a dragon. You have this chance to immerse yourself in dragon culture. If you leave, you might never get that again."

"Gray," Raya breathed as she reeled to face him. "I never knew that you…"

He slashed his hand through the air. "This isn't about me. And I'm sorry, Soren, but this isn't about you, either. This is about Celestina cutting herself off from her own kind. Forever. It's not a decision that should be made *for her* nor should it be taken lightly."

"If we don't get moving, the dragons will make that decision for us,"

Cullen warned. "And we won't care, because we'll be dead. Except for you, Celestina." He bowed his head in my direction. "What do you wish to do?"

Soren turned toward me. He didn't say a word, but I could read the determination on his face. He'd fight for me. He'd fight to keep me. If I told him I wanted to go back to the village, I doubted he'd allow it.

And, yes, part of me ached at the thought of leaving. I did want to nurture my budding friendship with Amaya. I wanted to learn dragon lore from Gregory. Drink ale with Ivy. And learn gardening from Juniper. But on the other hand, if I stayed, they would expect to use me to attack the humans and the vampires. If I stayed, the vision of Fein's destruction by dragon fire would become a reality, because I'd be the one leading the charge.

I couldn't allow that to happen.

"My heart wants to be with Soren," I told Gray. I reached my hand out to my battle-hardened warrior, who gladly accepted it. "I'm not being abducted." Soren twined his fingers with mine. The tension tightening his features eased. "I consider all of you my family, my *chosen* family. My support. My future. You are where I want to be."

While Gray wasn't happy about my decision to run away from the continent's last remaining clan of dragons, he gave me a nod as if to say he respected my decision to return to Fein with them.

I looked around, searching the thick copse of trees for where they'd hidden their horses. "We're not walking back, are we?"

"No, Sky Girl." Raya hooked her arm with mine. "We're going to fly."

"Fly? You do know I don't have the ability to change forms. And even if I did, I wouldn't want you riding on me, because that's just weird."

Cullen led the way. I noticed that Soren and Cullen kept their distance from each other.

Gray followed Cullen. Soren stayed at my side. And Raya took up the rear. It felt all so familiar traveling like this. Having them surround me made me feel safe, protected.

Dawn was nearly breaking when we reached a clearing filled with heavy morning mist.

"Here we are." Cullen had to stop to wipe dew off his glasses.

I looked around. "Where?"

Raya chuckled.

Gray scowled.

"You're going to love this," Soren whispered with enough heat that I shivered.

"This is one of Cullen's side projects," Raya offered. "The fog included."

I didn't want to walk into a place I couldn't see. When the others went forward, I tried to hang back. Soren put a comforting hand around my shoulder. "It's safe."

Together we entered the thick curtain of fog, turning the dimly lit morning into an indistinguishable sea of white. Who knew what manner of beast hid within that mist? I'd been taught all my life to avoid misty areas because that was where the vampires hid when the dawn was cresting. I knew it was irrational—I was safe with these vampires—but I couldn't seem to help myself. How did one fight what amounted to a lifetime of bloody warnings? My heart raced because that was what my legs wanted to do. Run. Run as far away as I could.

"Did you secure our dragon?" I recognized Driscoll's arrogant voice even though I couldn't yet see him.

"Celestina is safe," Cullen answered the spy who worked for him.

"It's a magical shield?" I asked as we passed through the heavy fog. From the hill, the fog looked as if it covered the entire clearing. But from the center of the clearing, I could now see that it encircled the field to hide our massive escape vehicle. "An airship?"

I'd only seen them from a distance. Queen Beatrice supposedly owned one, but never used it. A metallic balloon towering several stories above me was tethered to the ground by six long ropes. Below the balloon sat a wooden structure that resembled an oversized egg. There were round windows like one would find on a sailing ship and a door with sturdy hinges.

"Are the currents holding?" Cullen asked Driscoll.

"They've been steady for the past hour. But there are signs that the winds will start to shift to the west. There's no time to tarry."

"Very good." Cullen turned to me. "Everyone in. Driscoll and I will start unlatching our anchors."

"An airship." There was no stopping the smile from coming to my face even if I'd wanted to, which I totally didn't. This was…this was… I was going to fly again. And this time I wouldn't be half-conscious and bleeding.

"Told you that you'd love it," Soren said as he brushed a gentle kiss against my temple. "How are you feeling? Do you need more blood?"

"I'm fine." This time it wasn't a lie. It was amazing what a little blood and sex could do for a girl.

Gray held the airship's door open for us. I couldn't wait to see what it looked like inside, especially since the airship belonged to a royal family. "Is it ridiculously lavish?"

"My sister decorated the interior." Soren rolled his eyes.

"So it's…?" Princess Priscilla wore beautiful gowns and had a comfortable bedchamber, but she also opened medical clinics throughout the kingdom and championed equality, which meant her decorating style could go either way.

"It's ridiculously lavish," Soren finished for me, his voice filled with fondness for his younger sister.

"Splendid!" I hurried to get inside.

"You're not going anywhere, Moonglow." Amaya materialized from the air. Her voice crackled with cold rage. She stood like a warrior goddess with a proud tilt to her head. She wore not a stitch of clothing and didn't seem bothered in the least at her stark nakedness as she blocked me from getting near the airship's entrance. She raised her large taloned claws.

"You held the third form!" I was so pleased to see that she'd materialized from air that I forgot about the danger she posed to us and the damage those claws had done to my body in the past. "Can any of the others do it? Or is it truly a talent only you possess? What did you do to master it?"

Instead of answering my barrage of questions, she glared. "If you value your life, Invader, you'll drop your swords," she warned Gray, who'd already pulled both his short swords from their scabbards. She kept her back to him as if she didn't consider him a threat. Surely, an insult to Gray. "Unlike your neutered moonlight dragon, I can conjure fire while in any shape. I can end you before you touch me. Or perhaps I'll end your precious prince's life instead." Her gaze shifted from me to Soren. "He's the one who's bewitched our savior."

Raya, who was standing beside me, slowly moved her hands away from her body to show that she wasn't a threat. I couldn't see either Cullen or Driscoll. I hoped neither of them planned to do anything that would cause Amaya to overreact and harm Soren.

"Everyone, hold your positions." Soren raised a fist. He tightened his grip on my shoulder, pulling my side flush with his. "We're not stealing Celestina. You're the one who stole her. And you can go back and tell the tribe that she wants to come with us."

"You mean you—" She sniffed the air and then twisted her face to show her disgust. "You fucked her and drained her until you weakened her resolve to stay where she belongs? Excuse me for not believing anything she says is what she really wants. Or needs."

"You know this is what I want, Amaya," I said. "You know I wasn't happy. The village isn't my home."

"The hell it isn't! The clan has dreamed of this moment, the moment when their precious moonlight dragon returned to fight for them. You represent our only hope for a better future. I'm not going to let your lust for rutting on some vampire's cock destroy that."

"It's not lust—" I tried to tell her that what I felt was love, and not just for Soren but for everyone I'd met in Fein. Love drove my need to return to them. But Amaya refused to let me say any of that.

"I might have believed what you feel for your vampire could be something other than lust if your neck wasn't covered with bite marks. Fuck, Moonglow, you haven't been gone for more than a few hours. How the hell did he have time to feed on you that many times? How the hell do you have enough blood in you to even be standing?"

I put my hand on my neck while my face burned like fire from embarrassment.

"I may have gotten carried away," Soren said for my ears only. My skin still tingled where he'd bitten me repeatedly when we were…getting reacquainted. And he hadn't healed the marks. He liked to leave them visible whenever he wanted to make sure others knew that I was his possession. "Sorry."

Unfortunately, the fact that they were there and so visible and that there were so many of them meant I had to work twice as hard to show Amaya that I could make clear-headed decisions. I removed Soren's hand from around my shoulder and took several steps away from him. He didn't try to stop me, but he did rumble his displeasure.

I squared my shoulders. "Amaya, if you harm anyone here, I swear I will grab on to you and siphon your powers until the world unmakes itself."

"You wouldn't."

"Try me."

Amaya gave off the kind of reckless energy that suggested she would strike out at one of my friends just to see if I had it in me to fight back. I fisted my hands at my side and didn't dare breathe. I didn't dare blink. Because I was serious. I would show the world my rage if Amaya took Soren away from me. I needed her to feel that.

It took everything in me not to react when the fog that had ringed the clearing flooded the space behind Amaya.

"I don't want you harmed," I told her as a warning to whoever—either Cullen or Driscoll—was using the fog to sneak up behind her: *Don't harm her.* "But, Amaya, this is my life. I'm not a symbol. I'm not an ancient idea come to life. I'm simply me, an imperfect creature trying to make the most of her life. And right now, I'm choosing to have a life with these vampires. When the clan is open to accepting that decision, I will come back to talk with them, learn from them, help them if I can. But if they continue to dictate the decisions I make, who I mate with, and what my life will look like, I can't be around them. I need space to grow, to discover who I am." I pointed back toward the plateau. "I barely had space to breathe back there."

Amaya snarled leaving no doubt that she wasn't human but a deadly creature of the night and sky. "You would doom us to—?"

Cullen moved with the kind of dizzying vampire speed that still startled me. One moment Amaya was alone with the mist creeping up behind her. The next moment, Cullen was in front of her with his hands on her cheeks. He didn't strike her or try to do anything to restrain her.

He spoke only one word. But it was a word that reverberated with such a strong pulse of compulsion that hearing it had my legs collapsing beneath me and Soren racing to catch me. And I wasn't his intended target.

"*Sleep.*"

Chapter 27

Amaya

I woke with a startled jerk when one of those invasive green lizards—
where are they coming from?—scurried over my boot.

"Dammit."

The airship and Celestina were gone. Someone had draped a black,
hooded cloak over me. The cloak held the remnants of the spicy scent that
I associated with...

"Prince Cullen." I spat his name from my mouth.

When I saw him again, I planned to chop off those warm fingers that
had caressed my cheeks as if he cared for me, and stuff them up his—

"Amaya? What are you doing sitting on the grass way out here?" Anther's red
scales glittered in the morning light as he dropped out of the sky and
landed on the grass a few feet away.

He took a sniff and stiffened. *"Humans."*

"Mostly vampires."

Anther showed his teeth. *"Why didn't the patrols sense them?"*

"Not a clue."

"What were they doing here?"

"Stealing Celestina."

Anther shifted into his human form and grabbed my shoulders. "What do you mean, stealing Celestina?" he shouted in my face.

I gave him a shove. While we were used to seeing everyone else in the clan in their altogether, I didn't enjoy being so close to my brother with all his nasty dangly bits hanging out like that. I pulled Cullen's cloak around my body. "It means she's gone."

"Are you sure?" He kept his distance, thank the gods. "You must be mistaken. She can't be gone. She's sleeping in Trace's home above his shop. He watches her day and night. There is no way someone could have taken her from under his roof."

"I don't know how it happened—blood magic, I imagine—but I saw her with the vampires. They had an airship."

"Impossible," he snapped. "And you just happened to stumble upon them here? In the middle of the forest? Why didn't you stop them?"

"I tried!" I snapped my sharp dragon teeth at him. He was smart enough to back off. "I woke up last night and felt a strange pull to fly into the forest."

Anther nodded. "Because of your connection with the moonlight dragon?"

Yeah, let's grab on to that explanation.

But I knew something else had led me to this clearing, the same something that had been tugging at me ever since that cursed vampire had saved my life. *Stupid Prince Cullen.* I wondered how he'd react if I grabbed him by the ankles and flew him over to the nearby Flaming Basin and dropped him into one of the geysers. Could vampires survive being boiled alive? It'd be interesting to find out.

With an angry curse, Anther shifted back into his dragon form and took to the sky. *"Can you communicate with her?"*

I closed my eyes and tried to follow the pathway to Celestina. *"Moonglow?"*

Nothing.

I tried to follow the well-worn path I'd been using to try and connect with Prince Cullen. Almost immediately, our minds touched, but I couldn't get past the wall he'd built around his thoughts. *"I'm being blocked,"* I told Anther.

"There's no sign of an airship." Anther continued to curse as he soared above the tops of the trees. He swooped and set this part of the forest on fire with his fiery rage. *"Why the hell are you still here, Amaya? Send out an alarm! Tell as many in the clan as you can reach. This is war. Go! Go back to the village to prepare with the others! Move fast. We must get the moonlight dragon back. Go!"*

I shifted to my dragon form, spread my leathery wings, and shot into the air like a meteor hurtling across the sky. But I didn't do as my big brother had demanded. No. While Anther raged and set more of the forest ablaze, I flew in the opposite direction from the village.

I set out toward the Kingdom of Fein…and that bastard Prince Cullen.

Celestina

I enjoyed pretending.

Pretending meant I didn't have to think about the lies that still hovered between Soren and me. It also meant I didn't have to wonder about the troubles the dragons would make when they realized I was gone. There was going to be fire and deaths because of me, and I dreaded that more than anything else. When I pretended, I didn't have to think about any of that.

Pretending also meant I could enjoy this quiet time on the airship as we flew over some of the prettiest landscapes I'd ever seen. Even the Rainbow Desert, which had looked so bleak and foreboding from the ground, glittered from this vantage point. Heavens, I enjoyed flying.

Soren hadn't been joking about the airship's lavish interior. It reminded me of one of Reinheart Palace's plush royal chambers. There were sofas in the main cabin, bed chambers in the back, and food everywhere. The amount of food waiting for us had made me wonder if I hadn't somehow drifted into the Great Beyond. Or perhaps I was dreaming.

Don't you dare pinch me!

Soon after we'd soared into the air, Soren had tugged me onto his lap as he sank on to the nearest sofa. He hand-fed me sweets and little bits of meat that had been waiting for us on the silver trays scattered throughout the ship.

In that moment, we were a bonded pair, happy, and together in a way no one could pull apart. We had our entire lives in front of us. We were heading to Soren's home to start our new life. Together. I trusted him, and he trusted me. Completely.

It was a beautiful lie, one that made me happy.

"I still can't get over seeing you without that awful collar," Raya said as the capital city of Sukoon glinted in the distance. She dropped on to the sofa next to Soren and me, making the overstuffed cushions bounce.

"I'm still getting used to being able to say and do things without the collar punishing me for it," I told Raya and leaned toward her to whisper, "I'm a dragon."

My muscles tensed, expecting the worst to happen.

And…and nothing bad happened.

I leaned back against Soren's chest. "See?" I said with a smile that was a mixture of relief and joy. "I can talk about dragons. I can talk about anything I want. I can do anything I want. I'm free."

"You still have that binding charm holding back your magical powers," Driscoll reminded us with that gruff voice of his as he walked over toward us. He stopped near the sofa, hovering in a way that felt as weird as it looked.

"No." Soren draped his arm over my shoulder and planted a sweet kiss against my cheek. "She's been feeling her magic lately, haven't you?"

He didn't know the half of it, and I didn't want to tell Soren what had happened between me and Amaya when I was living with the clan. Not when I was still pretending that everything was perfect.

Driscoll sat down next to Raya, who glowered at him so hard, her expression mirrored Gray's scowling face. Driscoll didn't seem to notice, or if he did, he didn't care.

"So, Celestina. Tell us everything you learned about the dragons living on the plateau."

Soren shook his head as if to say *not now*. I wondered if Soren was also pretending.

Undaunted, Driscoll pressed on. "We've never been able to get much intel on the dragon clan. They protect their secrets with deadly ferocity. Tell us, do they live as humans, or do they stay in their dragon form? Where do they live? How do they provide food for the clan?"

He'd shot so many questions at me, I didn't know where or how to start. For one thing, I didn't want to think about Amaya or the dragons I'd left behind. I didn't want to think of how I was failing them.

"We need this information to help us form battle plans, attack strategies," Driscoll persisted.

"No." I jumped up from Soren's lap. "No, I'll not help you harm them."

"Driscoll," Soren warned.

"Putting together a battle strategy now is vital. The dragons won't let you go easily, you know that. It's morning already. You tell me, Princess Celestina, do you think they've discovered that you're gone?" Driscoll continued.

"No," I repeated more forcefully than before. Why couldn't he let me enjoy this time on the ship? Tears filled my eyes as I whirled around to plead with Soren, "I'll not help you with this. I can't."

Soren nodded. "Now is not the time." With a gentle tug, he had me back on his lap. The warmth of his body calmed me. "We can protect ourselves against the dragons."

"We can?" Driscoll's eyebrows shot up into his hairline. "May I ask how?"

"No." Soren pressed his lips together and gave Driscoll such a sharp look, I felt like I'd been cut. Driscoll merely shrugged and walked away.

"May I ask how?" I repeated Driscoll's question. Raya leaned forward as if she, too, wanted to hear Soren's answer.

"It's nothing I want you to worry about." His arms tightened around me. "I'm going to keep you safe."

A loud bang had us all jumping to our feet. The airship lurched. A heartbeat later, Gray came running out from the pilot's area where he'd been watching Cullen fly the ship.

"Cullen says there's nothing to worry about. We hit some air turbulence."

"Didn't sound like turbulence," Raya muttered. "It sounded like we hit something."

"Or something hit us," I added.

"I'm sure it's fine," Gray said, although he did look paler than usual. "Prince Cullen started smiling after that thump."

I peered out the nearest window, wondering if we'd banged into the side of a mountain. But there was nothing outside other than blue skies and high wispy clouds. Below us, Fein's capitol city of Sukoon spread out like a necklace in a jewelry box.

Not long after, the airship set down on one of the military training fields outside the city. A small army of King's Guards and two horse-drawn carriages were waiting for us.

"If you don't go and find Patty right away, I'll never hear the end of it," Gray warned as we approached the carriages.

"Is she back in the city?" I asked.

"She is. We all returned to Sukoon on Cullen's schooner after dragons chased us out of the forest when we were searching for you. And, let me tell you, Patty fought like a wild weasel, trying to come with us on this rescue mission."

"Well, then tell her to come see me," I told him, knowing Patty would love it if Gray showed up at her house. "I want to see her, too."

"Is that a royal order?" Raya asked as she came up behind me. She nudged my arm with her elbow and smirked at Gray who'd started to scowl again.

"A royal what?" I asked the same time Soren said, "Yes, anything Sky Girl says is a royal order."

I opened and closed my mouth like a stranded fish.

Soren looked at me and shrugged. "That's how being a royal works, Princess Celestina."

"Don't look so horrified," Raya said. "Enjoy having some power for a change."

I didn't feel worthy of the power. Was it even mine to take? I was a princess only because Soren felt the need to bond with me to prevent the other members of the royal court from killing me.

He also loves you, a voice in my head reminded me.

He's using you, another intrusive voice put in.

And wasn't it funny (not in a ha-ha sort of way) that the first time I had access to a little power, I questioned whether I deserved it? What was wrong with me that I needed to put myself down like that? I was just as deserving as anyone else…wasn't I?

Yes, I was.

I was a moonlight dragon, for goddess's sake, one of the most revered dragons to ever exist. I didn't need the title that came with Soren's bond to prove I was deserving. I held power all on my own. And I needed to start acting like I believed it.

"Your father wants to see you right away," one of the guards informed Soren. "He wants to brief you about what has been happening at the border while you were gone."

"I was gone from the palace for less than twelve hours." Soren sighed. "Very well. I'll attend him as soon as I wash off the grime and change my clothes."

"What's happening at the border?" I remembered that Queen Beatrice was bringing her army to the border. "Is it still Queen Beatrice?"

"It's nothing. Let's talk about it later," Soren said as he guided me toward one of the waiting carriages. The toe of his boot dislodged a rock that glinted in the sun as he crossed the field. I scooped down and picked it up without breaking my stride. The yellow-blue stone had sharp edges but a glassy surface that glinted as I turned it. The stone smelled sweet. *And so shiny.*

"Later had better come soon," I warned Soren. I tucked the pretty stone into my skirt's pocket. "Otherwise, we're going to have a serious problem."

Soren raised his hands. But a corner of his mouth lifted as if he were looking forward to a fight. "I'm not trying to keep secrets."

I harrumphed. "Prove it by talking to me." I paused. "And that's a royal order. I can make those, right?"

"You can. We'll talk in private," he promised.

When I was wearing the slave collar, I'd been forced to accept that "later" might never come. "When?"

He paused by the open carriage door and studied me, maybe to gauge how serious I felt about this. "Tonight," he finally answered. "We'll talk immediately after dinner."

I gave a tight nod and started to step into the carriage. I barely had a foot inside the contraption when a loud, animalistic scream sounded from inside it.

Soren grabbed me around the waist and pulled me away from the carriage before I had a chance to react. A scaley arm with blood-red claws swiped at where I'd been standing not even a heartbeat earlier.

"What is that?" I screamed the question at Soren's face.

Soren shook his head as if I'd rendered him temporarily deaf. "A rat-viper. What I want to know is how the hell something like that has gotten into a royal carriage."

"Maybe it crawled in looking for warmth while the carriages sat empty?" I guessed as I pushed Soren further away from the carriage.

He shook his head. "Those nasty bastards aren't native to our area." Gray and Raya now flanked us with their swords drawn. The rest of the King's Guards had fanned out around the carriage. "They live only in the Kingdom of Tiburnia."

Chapter 28

Celestina

"Tiburnia? How did it get all the way to the most northern kingdom?" I demanded, still not sounding the least bit calm.

"Someone must have put it there," Soren said. "Someone who wants us dead."

"But we're well armed and protected." Certainly, an overgrown rat couldn't harm a large group of highly trained vampire warriors.

Gray circled around to the rear of the carriage.

"Rat-vipers are nearly impossible to kill," Raya said as she lowered her sword in front of me. Soren did the same. "Those scales are as hard as steel. We're in serious trouble."

"And the claws and fangs are coated in deadly venom. If it breaks through our defenses, you need to run," Soren said. "Don't look back. Just run."

I shook my head. "Not going to happen."

"Please, don't argue with me." The rat-viper sprang out of the carriage. Its long tail undulated from side to side like a snake. It held its front claws up near its body, ready to strike. Its wide mouth gaped open, exposing long viper fangs. Soren and Raya both backed up as the rat-viper slithered toward us. "You don't even have a sword."

"I don't need a sword." I snarled at the revolting rat.

The small, beady-eyed variety of rats made my skin crawl, and this one was a hundred times worse. It was as tall as I was. And the stench. It smelled like a pile of rotting meat.

"Stop!" I told the beast in my most growly and magical voice. I felt the magic flow up through my feet and out of my mouth. The sensation made my entire body tingle.

That was new. Did that extra awareness of my magic mean I was starting to break free from Queen Frieda's magical curse?

"It worked." A little too well. Everyone in the field stopped moving, even Driscoll and Cullen who were still near the airship, which was a fair distance from the carriages. They'd been busy securing the anchors. Cullen was partially bent over with a rope in his hand. Driscoll had another rope and had been moving toward the far side of the airship.

"The rat-viper," Soren muttered through lips that didn't move, "isn't magical."

The gray scaly beast crouched as it tilted its head and stared directly at me. Crap. Crap. Crap. It was going to leap at us.

"Move! Move! Move!" I growled. My powers of compulsion only worked on magical beings. In my panic, I barely managed to get a ripple of magic moving through my body. But it was enough to counteract my earlier compulsion. Both Soren and Raya sprang into action. They struck with their swords. But their weapons scraped uselessly against the rat-viper's impossibly hard belly as it launched itself into the air and toward me!

Soren tossed me to one side, putting himself in the path of the rat-viper's deadly claws.

"No!" Raya shouted and jumped in front of Soren.

I hit the ground and rolled.

No. No. No. The rat-viper's venom-soaked claw was going to dig into Raya's chest. Its deadly claws would kill her. And I couldn't do anything to save my friend.

No. No. No.

The rat-viper had raised its claw. Raya didn't have time to do anything. She was dead. Or would be as soon as that claw struck her.

But before the claw moved, the rat-viper exploded.

Bloody bits of rodent (or was it a reptile?) rained down on the carriage, the practice field, the airship, and on us.

I would have screamed and danced around, trying to rid myself of the hot, bloody carnage that had landed on me if this had been the first time I'd been splattered with fleshy gore. Thanks to Queen Beatrice's violent spectacles, I merely brushed what appeared to be part of the rat-viper's ear from my cheek and stared at the spot where the nasty creature had once occupied. In its place—for the briefest of instants—I'd seen a dragon. It hadn't been fully visible. Just the outline of a long, graceful neck, outstretched wings, and a tail that could easily break a leg. A shimmering, see-through dragon. And then a blink later, it was gone.

"Did you—Did you see—?" My heart thundered in my chest. "Was that—Was that my dragon? My moonlight dragon?" The legends spoke of the moonlight dragon being luminous and see-through. Had I conjured my moonlight dragon as a separate piece of me? Was that even possible?

Soren wrapped his arm protectively around my shoulder while holding his sword in his other hand. "That was an assassination attempt. We need to get you out of here."

The King's Guards who'd come to meet us had spread out to search the area for additional threats.

"How would someone get a beast like that into the carriage without being killed themselves?" It seemed impossible.

"They're trainable," Raya said as she jogged toward the carriage that had once held that stinky rat thing.

"Gross."

"I agree." Gray ran up to us. "Nasty beasts. I searched the carriage over there." He pointed to the one he meant with the tip of one of his swords. "It's clear."

"Let's go then."

"What about Cullen?"

"He'll be fine. We need to get you to safety, Sky Girl."

"You don't think that rat-viper-thingy was sent to attack me, do you?"

"It was either me or you, and I'm not willing to risk you. There might be more of those things out here," Soren answered.

"More?" I squeaked.

"We should be safe once we get to the palace."

I was now the one tugging him to go faster to the other carriage. I didn't even use the stairs that had been put down. I jumped inside, landing sideways on one of the cushioned benches. Soren came in right behind me. And then Gray entered, closing and latching the door behind him. Almost immediately, the carriage jerked into motion.

"What happened to the rat-viper?" Gray asked swaying with the carriage as it picked up speed. "I was on the far side of the carriage and couldn't see how you killed it."

"It exploded," Soren said.

"Yes. I'm wearing parts of it," Gray flicked at what looked like a piece of the hairless tail stuck to his arm. "*How* did you make it explode?"

Soren looked over at me. "Did you do that?"

"Honestly? I have no idea." I hadn't felt the tingling of power push through me like I had when I'd used my compulsion. I hadn't felt anything. And the explosion had come as a complete surprise. "In the aftermath, did you see a dragon?"

"No," both Soren and Gray said.

Had I imagined it? The dragon had been visible for less than a blink.

"We're almost to the palace," Soren said. "Hopefully, we'll be able to get some answers there."

Amaya

"That was a clever trick." Cullen lifted his head after finishing off the knot he'd been tying as he secured the airship. He looked directly at me. I knew he couldn't see me. I was nothing more than invisible particles and pieces of air. I had no form, no weight, no outline.

I'd started to follow the moonlight dragon as she rode away with her vampire toward the capital city. But a niggling feeling made me turn back to the field. And stupidly, I'd floated over to Cullen. I couldn't seem to keep away from him. Pathetic.

"I know you're there." Cullen dusted off his hands and placed them on his hips.

"If I was here, your penis would have exploded along with that naked rat monster," I told him. I was surprised I could drop into his mind like this. After all the times he'd blocked me, I'd expected to keep hitting that wall he'd built around his thoughts.

"You're always so bloodthirsty and vicious, Darkness." A smile creased the corners of his mouth.

"I'm not going to apologize."

"I don't want you to apologize. I like how you talk to me. It's sexy." He moved forward. I floated backward to keep my distance, not that I needed to. It wasn't as if he could grab on to me. Not when I *was* the air. "Plus, that trick you did with the rat-viper saved the lives of probably everyone who was in this field. I'm grateful to you for that."

"Who sent the beast? And what do you plan to do to keep the moonlight dragon safe from future attacks?" I demanded.

"Clearly, our friend Captain Proctor is angry at us for your escape. His interest in training wild beasts for warfare is well-known."

I should have figured I wouldn't be done with that bastard. "What do you plan to do about it?"

Cullen's eyes flashed black. "I will end him."

The vampire who was working on the airship with him snapped his head in our direction. "Cullen? Is everything all right over there?"

"I'm good," Cullen called back. He kept his gaze locked on the empty air I was occupying. "I'll make him suffer as I pull his life from his body while letting him know I'm doing it for you."

Gods, that sounded sexy. I wanted a body so I could rub against him, scrape my claws down his back, and dig my teeth into his neck.

Dammit. I should have kept my distance from Prince Cullen. He was water to my fire. We couldn't be near each other.

I needed to watch over Celestina and figure out how to get her to return to the village before the dragons started a war. I didn't have time to play games with Cullen.

With a snarl, I sailed away from him.

I hadn't moved far when the air around me froze. I couldn't move forward, or sideways, or any way.

"Not so fast," Cullen put the words directly inside my mind.

"How did you—?" I struggled against his hold. How the hell was he

holding air?

"You've been banging around trying to get inside my head so often lately, trying to spy on what we've been doing, that you've blazed quite a strong connection between us. And the wonderful thing about connections is that they always go both ways. I'm curious, my sweet Darkness, how did you blow up the rat-viper?"

I'd acted mostly on instinct, but I was so proud of the way I'd dispatched that ugly creature that I didn't see anything wrong with bragging a little. *"I floated over to the—what did you call it?"*

"It's a rat-viper, the deadliest rodent to roam the continent. And the largest."

"Lovely. I hope to never see something like that again. When it went after Celestina, I floated over to the creature and let it breathe me into its lungs. Once I was inside it, I shifted to my dragon form." I became a dragon just for a heartbeat. But that had been long enough for my powers to do what they did best— destroy the rat-viper, utterly and completely.

"Gods." Cullen breathed. His expression turned hard. "I won't let you hurt my family."

"I'm here to keep death from happening, not to cause it."

"I'd find it easier to believe that if you weren't a midnight dragon."

In a fit of anger, I wrenched myself free from his magical binding.

"Don't. Hold. Me. Like. That. Again." I should roast that smug grin off his handsome face. I wondered if I could produce fire in this form. I'd have to test that sometime. But not right now. Not when I needed to protect Celestina. I hated to imagine what trouble she might stumble into next. No wonder Trace felt the need to watch over her all the damn time. The moonlight dragon attracted danger as if she were a magnet.

"There's a palace ball tomorrow night. I expect you to attend as my guest."

Was he unhinged? I wouldn't go to a vampire ball. I'd get massacred.

"If you don't show up, I'll know how to find you." He pushed power into that threat, power that made my many particles shiver with fear…and, disturbingly, with an unhealthy amount of delight.

Goddess, why did I lose my mind whenever Prince Cullen was near?

It was because I liked him.

Dammit.

Chapter 29

Celestina

The haughty, overdressed, backstabbing lifestyle of court life in Fein felt more like home than the quaint village life the dragon clan lived. And yes, I did recognize how troubling that was. It wasn't as if I enjoyed court life. I didn't. But growing up in a court that operated in one similar to the Fein court meant I understood what was expected of me.

When Soren and I reached his bedroom chambers, Goldie, the royal maid who'd helped me prepare for events in the past, was already waiting in the chamber. Impeccably dressed in a golden gown, the gray-haired woman looked more glamorous than most of the ladies who'd ever stepped foot in a royal court. She'd brought with her a collection of dresses and shoes for me to choose from. She took one look at Soren and pushed him back out of the room.

"She doesn't need you distracting her," she scolded when he protested. "This is important business we're undertaking. Not that you need many enhancements for your already lovely face, my dear princess. But we do want to put our best foot forward to silence any gossips who want to find a reason to think less of you simply because you're not of the same species as the royal family."

"No, Goldie, I'm not leaving this chamber. I need to clean up and change as well." Soren charged back into the room while giving her a fierce look that would have frightened the rat-viper back into the carriage.

"Not here, you don't." With an impressive shove, she pushed Soren out of the bedchamber and slammed the door in his face.

"Was that wise?" Although I'd rarely seen Soren lose his patience with insolent staff or his seconds in the army, he was the crown prince and a powerful vampire. If this had been Earst, Goldie and I would have been waiting outside the room until Soren finished preparing for his audience with his father.

"I'm not worried about that boy. He'll go to his brother's chambers and get ready there." She puffed out a loud breath, reminding me once again how the royals in this country weren't nearly as fierce as they liked the world to believe. "And, princess, I know what happens when the two of you are around each other. If he'd stayed in here, no one would have seen either of you for days."

Heat raced to my cheeks. She wasn't wrong. I didn't want to face his father in front of the court or confront the reality of our relationship. All I wanted was to be with Soren. In every position possible.

"Things seem to go best between us when we're ignoring the real world," I muttered.

Goldie patted my cheek. "Challenges can be the spark that keeps a relationship interesting. Sometimes you'll want to chop his head off and other times you'll ache to be under him, like you're aching now. Neither one of those things fully defines either you or your relationship. Since the beginning of time, relationships have always been an ever-changing river, rife with rocky hazards. But there are also calm shores." She straightened her shoulders. "Listen to me prattling on when I should be dressing you. Turn around, let's get you into the bath."

An exhausting hour later, I looked like I belonged in a royal court. I wore rich blue silks that shimmered with silver embroidery. The formal gown had a scalloped neck, cinched tight at the waist, and flared into a long, full skirt with tiny dragons stitched into the hem and down the sleeves. It was quite a daring statement. I wouldn't have chosen it.

But all the gowns Goldie had presented had been embroidered with similar dragon designs. According to Goldie, Soren had requested these gowns be made for me with that specific dragon motif before we'd set sail for Tiburnia.

I was on the verge of telling Goldie to find Soren's sister and ask her if I could borrow one of her court dresses when Soren returned.

"Gods," he breathed. His face lit up when he saw me. "How did I get so lucky? You, my princess, are fucking radiant."

He'd washed and changed into a black court suit trimmed in silver, which matched my gown's stitching. His dark hair was still damp and pulled back into a neat queue. He wore a silver open crown with a simple geometric design etched into the metal.

By all accounts, he was the radiant one.

"Are you sure about this dress?" I gestured toward the dragon stitching on its sleeves. "Aren't you worried this will send the wrong message? We might be fighting the dragons within the next day or so." I prayed we wouldn't be, but I wasn't naïve.

"You look gorgeous." He stepped closer to me. "Especially with my bite marks decorating your neck." He crushed his lips to mine and started ushering me back toward his private bedchamber.

"Oh, no you don't, boy." Goldie swatted Soren's backside with a wooden hairbrush. "It took me too long to achieve this level of perfection. I'll not have you ruin it for a quick poke and grab."

Soren peeled his lips from mine. His pupils were blown wide from lust. He turned his head toward Goldie, bared his fangs, and hissed.

Goldie wasn't the least bit intimidated. She didn't say a word. All she did was lift her wooden hairbrush like she was brandishing a sword.

"Very well," he said softly as he straightened. "My father is waiting. Impatiently, if I know him."

"Gray?" He held out his hand toward the open door.

Gray, who'd also cleaned up and changed his clothes, hurried into the chamber. He wore a neatly pressed King's Guard uniform with a single sword hanging from his belt.

"I thought you were no longer a King's Guard." Gray and Raya had stood with Soren against the king. To protect them from retaliation, Soren had moved them out of the King's Guard service.

"The king wanted Raya and me to wear the uniform while we stood beside you and Soren as a show of unity." Gray scowled and tugged on the uniform's ornate collar as he said it, which made me smile. He then handed Soren a plain black box.

Soren peeled back the lid. Inside, nestled in a blanket of black velvet, sat a second silver crown. A shiny, sparkly crown that had my fingers trembling to touch it.

"For you, my beautiful dragon princess." Soren lifted the crown out of its box.

"Me?" I squeaked, deliriously happy to have the shiny object touch my body. Instead of geometric patterns, the crown he placed on my head had been etched as if a flight of dragons soared around the shiny, metal circlet.

So many dragons. How would the court react to my blatant reminder that I wasn't one of them? I was a dragon. I was the vampire's mortal enemy. My stomach lurched at the thought of representing the one thing the vampires seemed to fear the most.

"I don't see how this is going to go over well," I muttered. Not that I'd willingly take the *shiny* off my head. I liked how the pretty metal vibrated and sang up there.

But what kind of statement would I be making to the court by keeping it on? Would the court view my choice of clothing as a threat?

"The statement you're making is that you stand with me, and that we hold the power. It's a reassuring message of unity. At least, that's what Priscilla tells me. She's the one who told me to order the gowns and this crown. And you and I both know she's much better at navigating court life than I could ever aspire to be." Soren loathed political games and wasn't afraid to admit it. "I'd much rather show those popinjays how proficient I am with a sword and leave it at that. But swinging my sword around in the middle of court would make my family howl at me—as we already know—so I won't be doing that. At least not this evening."

"There's no need to fret," Goldie said as she adjusted my hair around the crown. "You, my dear Princess Celestina, look as regal as a natural-born queen. And, besides which, you should be proud of who you are. There's no reason to hide your true, powerful nature."

I wasn't sure if that was right. In Earst, anyone in the court who was the slightest bit different would be picked apart for it. My mismatched eyes caused no end of torment because I was the only one who had them.

Soren took both of my hands in his. "Come on, Sky Girl, be my princess. Be my helpmate. Stand by my side and show everyone how lucky we are to have you in our midst."

The Fein court fell silent as we entered, which was quite a feat considering the size of the crowd.

"Why is everyone acting so weird?" I murmured.

"There's never been a dragon in the court before," Soren answered.

"I've been here before," I reminded him.

"But they didn't know you were a dragon then. It's all new and different now. You're all new and different to them."

"You say it like it's a good thing." I fought an urge to turn around and walk back out the doors. I shouldn't have worn clothes with dragons plastered all over them.

"It's a very good thing, Princess." He kissed the back of my hand.

The courtiers, dressed in what looked like their silkiest and most ornate court outfits, parted as we made our way through the crowd and toward the dais where Soren's parents sat, waiting for us.

Gray and Raya, wearing the formal black and gold King's Guard garb, flanked us as we went. My heart started to pound, which was ridiculous. I had nothing to be worried about. Soren had bonded with me. Our lives were linked in a way that couldn't be undone. His parents couldn't steal that from us. No one could.

Sensing my growing alarm, Soren threaded his fingers with mine and gave my hand a gentle squeeze. "Tonight," he promised, his soft voice rumbled deep through my body. "Tonight, you will be mine and mine alone, and I'm going to"—he licked his lips—"bury my face so deep between your legs you'll be screaming my name."

My body responded to his words even though my brain was still panicking. "Do you promise?"

"Try and stop me."

A half smile tugged at my lips. "Now why would I do that?"

We reached the double golden thrones at the front of the room.

Soren's parents, dressed in shades of gold and wearing golden crowns, looked down at us with severe expressions.

"You're late," his father admonished.

"I beg your pardon," Soren said as he bowed deeply. I quickly remembered my court protocols and curtsied. "We were delayed by a rat-viper in our carriage."

The court gave a collective gasp.

"You're joking." The queen had a soft-spoken voice that made her sound so serene and innocent. She wasn't. Not that long ago, she'd tried to have me killed because I was some nobody from a foreign kingdom, and not the high-born vampire she would have chosen for her eldest son.

"I wish I were." Soren straightened. "You didn't send the rat-viper as a test for *Princess* Celestina, did you, Father?"

"Goddess no. She's too important to risk like that. Besides, the Tiburnians aren't our trading partners anymore. Not after we supported Earst against them."

Important? The king thought I was important?

Soren's grip on my hand tightened. "No tests, Father. She's more than proven herself. We're lucky to have her back with us. Agreed?"

The two men held each other's glare for several moments before the king relented. "Agreed." He cleared his throat. "We're lucky to have a dragon, especially with the troubles on our border."

"We'll leave for the front immediately after tomorrow's ball," Soren confirmed. "I hear there's news to be shared."

I frowned.

They were lucky to have a dragon?

We were heading to the front?

What did they think I could do?

"Good." The king finally smiled. "I've already had our spies leak the news we'll be adding a dragon to our defense. Hopefully, that'll make Queen Beatrice rethink her aggressive attacks."

"What exactly is happening at the front?" I asked, hoping I'd finally get some of the answers Soren kept promising would come later.

"You don't know?" The king leaned forward to peer down at me.

Since the answer was obvious, I stared back.

One of his advisors whispered in his ear. The king nodded before taking a deep breath. "Your queen—"

"Your wife?" I interrupted.

"No, not my wife!" The king violently shook his head. "*Your* queen."

I'd known who he'd meant, but I didn't want the court to think I held allegiance to Queen Beatrice. The collar was gone. I had the freedom to speak however I wanted. "Queen Beatrice, then?"

"Yes, Queen Beatrice," the king snapped.

"I see." I refused to back down. I understood court life well enough to know when a little insolence was needed to prove you deserved to hold a position of power. I gave him a rolling gesture. "Go on. What is Queen Beatrice doing?"

Soren watched with widening eyes.

The king's cheeks reddened. "The queen is attempting to invade our southern border. Her human troops should be no match for our vampire warriors. But Queen Beatrice is using a magic we've never encountered before. It enhances her army's ability to… Survive isn't the correct word." His advisor whispered something else in his ear. "The men fighting for the kingdom die when we kill them. But I'm told that they keep moving even after they're dead. Worse than that. They become more dangerous after being killed. They're being sent out on missions where they're certain to be slaughtered just to turn them into these unkillable abominations."

"That's gruesome." The nonmagical Tiburnians used blood to conjure powerful magical spells. I wondered if Queen Beatrice had used blood to augment her already strong magic. Was that the reason for her bloody spectacles? Was she testing out ways to strengthen her powers?

No, she might have stumbled upon the side effects of gaining stronger power from bloodletting, but that wasn't the reason she tormented her subjects. Ever since she was a child, she'd enjoyed making others suffer.

"That's not all," the king continued. "The queen now knows what we are. She knows what we can do, what our blood can do. Her army—the ones who aren't mindless killers—have been capturing our warriors and draining them."

Gray swore softly but viciously. Raya, I noticed, had tensed up. Nervous murmurs rose in the room. This must have been the new information the king needed to share. It made me wonder why the king had decided to talk with Soren about these matters in such a public forum.

Soren—I looked up at him—hadn't reacted. He kept his expression carefully neutral. He hadn't tightened his hold on my hand. Was he acting this way because he already knew that Queen Beatrice was harvesting vampire blood? Was this yet another piece of information he was keeping from me?

Goddess, I wished my mind could trust Soren the same way my body trusted him.

"How did she find out?" I asked.

As if feeling the press of my stare, Soren slowly turned his head toward me. The look I saw in his eyes made my heart sink.

"It doesn't matter how she found out," Soren said. "All that matters is that she knows, and that she has plans to enslave us."

"We have to stop her." I don't know why I said "we." There wasn't anything I could do.

"I'm glad you're on board with the plan. Soren wasn't sure if you'd willingly agree to assist us." The king settled back, making himself more comfortable on his large golden throne. "As soon as you get to the front, you'll use your powers to—"

"I don't have access to my powers." He had to know that. It wasn't something we'd kept secret.

"But you do, Dragon Princess." The king looked beyond me. "Isn't that right?"

I turned and watched as Prince Cullen, still dressed in his dusty battle leathers walked up through the center of the court. "She does," he said as he adjusted his glasses. "Moonlight dragons have the power to control other dragons. And I've seen Celestina use this power."

"I don't—"

"I'm sorry, Celestina. You do," Soren said quietly. "And if we're going to stop Queen Beatrice, we need that power. The only way to stop her dead warriors is to burn them."

"Then use fire. You don't need dragons."

"Queen Beatrice isn't our only threat. The Kingdom of Tiburnia is angry about everything we've done to them. Where do you think that rat-viper came from? Tiburnia would be my first guess. And according to our spies, the Tiburnians have started to rebuild the army we defeated so they can move in after Queen Beatrice's *dead-but-not-done* warriors have weakened us—that is, if we manage to defeat Queen Beatrice's forces. And not only that, the dragons will try to get you back by any means necessary." Soren opened and closed his fist. "You can use your compulsion to stop the dragons from attacking us. You can also compel those same dragons to fight Queen Beatrice's army for us."

"Why do you think I risked both of my sons to fetch you, Celestina?" the king asked. "We need a powerful dragon if we're to survive this conflict."

Oh.

My.

Gods.

My mind froze. My body turned to ice. I untangled my fingers from Soren's and took several steps away from him.

"This makes sense now," I said, my voice flat.

"What makes sense?" Soren asked, wary.

"This." I gestured to the court dress covered in tiny, embroidered dragons. I reached up and pulled the dragon-etched crown from my head, tugging loose the elaborate hairstyle Goldie had spent so much effort on. "This!" I tossed the crown at him. It bounced off his chest and clattered as it hit the black onyx floor.

Soren had dressed me in clothes that shouted "dragon" not because he loved me and wanted to shower me with beautiful gifts. No, Soren and the rest of his royal family wanted to show the court how they controlled a dragon.

And Soren claimed he didn't know how to play the court's games. I bet he was playing me every time he said something like that.

While I was wearing a slave collar, he'd never made me feel like I was an object to be owned and used. But I sure felt that way now. Wouldn't Queen Beatrice be pleased?

"Celestina." Soren sounded calm, too calm. I wanted to rage at him. Hurt him.

In a flash, my heart went from frozen and barely beating to thundering. The sudden change made my chest burn. Or perhaps that pain was from my heart tearing apart.

I was a fool. The biggest fool to ever walk this world.

But that didn't mean I needed to stay that way.

Chapter 30

Celestina

You've been brainwashed by the vampires to see us as the villains and those bloodsuckers as the heroes, Amaya had warned me.

And I'd refused to listen to her. Her rightness sat like a pile of smoldering ash in my throat, burning away the unshed tears I wouldn't let fall.

It's understandable that you'd have strong feelings for the first male to offer you kindness, Trace, who'd been nothing but patient, had tried to explain.

Soren had charmed me into falling for his too-handsome warrior self.

He didn't want me, the "nobody" of a court lady. No one had ever wanted me. Why should I believe that a good-looking, powerful general of a foreign army would see me differently than anyone else had ever seen me? Why believe I was no longer being overlooked? I'd been foolish to…

I shook my head.

"Celestina," Soren said quietly. "It's not—"

"Isn't it?" I snapped.

He closed his eyes and sighed. "Celestina. You've been through a lot."

"Oh, so this is my fault? I'm the one who doesn't understand? Or maybe you forgot to tell me? But that promised conversation is no longer necessary, is it? I understand too well, now. I'm *important* because I'm the dragon you own. And Prince Cullen wasn't doing a good deed when he used me to free the dragon the Tiburnians were keeping in captivity. He was making sure they didn't have a weapon equal to yours."

The court gasped at that news.

"That's not why I helped Amaya," Cullen said, but I didn't want to hear it. I didn't want to hear anything anybody had to say.

"I'm done letting you tell me what I think I know is wrong!" I'd been starved for such a long time that a little praise and attention had made me punch-drunk, had made me stop questioning intentions. I'd wanted their friendship and love so badly I would have done—and apparently *had* done—anything to make myself believe I had won it.

"Celestina." Soren moved toward me. I skittered backward, nearly tripping over a man dressed in a bright pink silk suit. "I had planned to—"

"You'd planned to do what?" I shouted.

"Celestina—" He held out his hands as if trying to warn me to calm myself. But it was too late, wasn't it? I could never be calm again. And I wasn't done with my shouting because the anger burning inside me sure as hell demanded release.

"Don't you say my name! Don't you say anything other than the truth! That you…" Anger made my voice breathy. The words felt torn from my throat. "That you've been tricking me! That you've been using me! That you're only with me because you want me to control the other dragons for you! How—how dare you lie to me and manipulate me like that!"

"It's not—"

"Did you ever have any feelings for me?" *Ugh!* I couldn't keep the sob out of my voice. And I hated that. I blamed him for that, too. It was his fault I was falling apart in front of everyone. That I sounded weak and hysterical. That I sounded like he'd hurt me as sharply as he had.

I hated that I couldn't even have the dignity of hiding my feelings from his court.

"I love you." His voice, barely a whisper, was filled with all the vulnerability I felt.

"*How dare you,*" I growled.

General Kitmun puts duty over everything else. He will do anything to protect the

Kingdom of Fein and the people living there. That's his way, Trace had warned. And even when Trace had said it, I'd known it to be true. Soren hadn't hidden that piece of himself from me. Over and over, he'd told me how he put duty to his country above everything, even his own feelings. And I'd thought that was a strength to be admired. But now I knew the truth of those words. Even if he loved me, that wouldn't stop him from betraying me, from using me.

Soren reached out to take my hand.

In a burst of rage, I spun away from him. I don't know where the sword came from. Did I yank it from Raya or Gray's scabbards? Or did my dragon magic let me conjure the weapon from thin air?

The sword weighed heavy in my hand. My gaze narrowed—all I saw was Soren—*damn him*—as I charged across the distance between us with the sword raised.

I would make him hurt as keenly as I was hurting.

I wanted him to hurt.

He whirled in a circle to avoid my berserker attack. In the process, he grabbed Raya's lightweight sword.

The blade in his right hand rang like a chime as it blocked my wild slashing blade that would have sliced into his chest.

"Keep your head," he whispered.

Like hell I would. I needed him to feel my rage. I went after him, my sword slashing wildly as I desperately tried to slice off the pieces of him that had made me love him and that now made me hurt.

They didn't need the slave collar, not when they could use their charms and powers of compulsion against you, Trace had tried to warn.

Soren's efforts to sneak me away from the clan hadn't been a rescue. It had been a recapture. Only, I was too stupid, too charmed by Soren's sexy body to realize I'd never broken free from his captivity.

"Keep your tip up," Soren whispered when I went after him again.

I screamed and swung like a wild woman. Soren had only taught me defensive moves. I wasn't sure how to initiate a proper attack. But somehow, my sword found its mark. It slammed into his upper arm. The razor-sharp edge sliced through the silk of his court jacket and didn't stop moving until the blade struck bone.

Blood oozed from the deep wound. I froze. Our eyes met.

"That's my Sky Girl. Fight me," he gently urged, while waving off a couple of approaching King's Guards.

I pulled my blade from his arm. His ripped flesh made a sickening squelching noise. The blade was now smeared with deep, red blood. My stomach churned at the sight of it.

This was what his manipulations and lies had created. The Fein wanted a killer dragon? Well, I'd show them. I'd make them regret turning me into something vicious and dangerous.

With a shout, I swung, aiming for his side.

Soren easily blocked the blow.

I swung again and again. Soren kept blocking the strikes even though he was losing too much blood from his wounded arm.

"You lied to me!" I jabbed straight for his chest.

He easily blocked the attack.

"You made me believe you cared for me, but you only wanted me for the destruction I could bring you. I was nothing but a damned weapon to you." I slashed wildly down from above my head.

Soren quickly sidestepped. My sword clanked against the sleek black floor.

"You stole me from the dragons!" I spun a circle and used my momentum to hit his sword's blade hard enough that he backed up a step. "You stole me! And you made me feel like I should be grateful!"

"You think I'm the villain?" His voice turned as hard as the blade in his hands.

I screamed and rushed at him again, our blades crashing. I suspected he could have easily ended this at any time. He had the skills that would allow him to strike me in a way that would wound…but not kill. And yet, he used the defensive moves he'd taught me. I'd practiced them enough that I recognized each one.

And not once did he strike back.

Was it self-preservation? He had, after all, tied his life to mine. If he struck me down, he'd be killing himself. Or was it something else? If he wounded me, if he acted like the villain, he'd never have my cooperation. He might be able to compel me with his vampire magic, but all he'd win would be an empty-headed puppet dragon. One that he'd have to compel over and over and over.

Because there was no way in hell that I would help him enslave and destroy my brethren.

I'd run from the dragons because they saw me as their best weapon in the fight against the humans and vampires. They wanted me to lead the way in remaking the realms and in bringing back the fifth kingdom. They wanted death and fire.

That wasn't something I was willing to do for the dragons…and I certainly wasn't going to go to war *against* the dragons.

"When Queen Beatrice put that slave collar around your neck, she weaponized you. She then sent you with me to my home so you could kill my friends, my family, my people. And you're angry with me for trying to protect those I care about?" Soren asked. "You're angry that I put my country's needs in front of my own? In front of my own feelings? You're angry that I tricked you into leaving Fein before you and the other dragons succeeded in burning all that I love?"

"You used me!" I swung the sword three times in quick succession. Left. Left. Right. He moved in harmony with my moves, blocking every attack.

"I'm trying to do the honorable thing here, Celestina."

"Honorable? You fuck me until I can't think straight while plotting with your father all the ways your pet dragon can be useful. Is that what you call honorable?" I punctuated each sentence with a strike that made my sword clash against his.

"I. Am. Not. The. Villain." He didn't strike out at me, but when I sent the blade slashing against his, he held still, causing my blade to hit his so hard the muscles in my arm screamed with pain. I stumbled but caught myself.

"You think *I'm* the villain?" I quickly recovered from my surprise that not only was he holding back with his attacks, but he was also moving with mine to make things easier for me. How. Dare. He. My anger flared back to life. "You're the one who's been lying to me, who's been playing with my emotions, and who made me fall—" No, I wouldn't say that last part. I loved him. *Still* loved him. I wouldn't let him trick those words from my mouth. It would hurt too much.

"I'm trying to do the impossible," he roared. "I'm trying to save everyone…including you, dammit!" He protected himself from another flurry of my wild perries.

"Why should I believe you? Every time I've asked you to tell me the truth, you have either refused to talk to me or answered with lies." I thought I'd made a clever move, twirling and swiping low to slice through his ankles.

He jumped over my blade.

"That attack would have worked, Sky Girl, if you hadn't telegraphed your intention by staring at your target area." His voice had softened. He danced back a few steps, taking himself out of striking range. "I wanted to tell you everything. It killed me to lie to you." He lowered his sword as if he no longer saw me as a threat. "How do you think Queen Beatrice learned that the Fein are vampires? How do you think she now knows what our blood can do? Why do you think she moved her forces to the border after we staged what looked like a major rift in the royal family? What? No answer? I'll tell you why.

"Not only could Queen Beatrice control you through that slave collar, but she could also see, hear, and know everything you could see, hear, and know. We didn't understand that this was how the collar worked until it was too late. And when we did figure out what was happening, I couldn't tell you about it without letting Queen Beatrice know that we'd figured it out, could I? And I had to lie to you when we wanted to feed false information to Queen Beatrice. We had to keep information from you when we didn't want Queen Beatrice to know that information. I had to stage that fake escape when I wanted Queen Beatrice to believe there was a weakness in our command structure that she could exploit. And yes, I lied to you more than once about that, because Queen Beatrice was listening to every damned word I said to you."

He finally swung his sword. It hit the blade in my hand with such force that both his and my sword shattered. The bones in my hand felt like they had shattered as well. The hilt of my now-broken sword clattered to the ground as I stumbled from the blow. I ended up falling on my ass.

Soren, breathing hard, towered over me. His broken sword rested at his side. Blood sluggishly oozed down his arm from the one injury I'd inflicted. He held a dagger in his opposite hand, raised as if primed to continue this insane, unwinnable fight. If he killed me, he would die. If I killed him...let's be honest, I couldn't kill him. I lacked both the skill and the desire to best him. *Damn him. Damn everything about him.* Despite everything he'd done to betray me and the other dragons, the stupid Beast of Fein still owned my heart.

I threw my head back and, as I screamed my frustration, fire exploded from my mouth.

Chapter 31

Amaya

"Are you searching for secret documents?" Prince Cullen asked in an "I'm merely curious" tone of voice.

My heart stuttered. I jumped up and spun to find him still dressed in the same black tunic and leggings he'd worn when orchestrating Celestina's escape from the plateau. I couldn't stop wondering how Cullen and his brother had managed to get Celestina away from the plateau without any of the dragons seeing them coming or leaving.

His clothes were now singed in several places from Celestina's fiery explosion back at the court. Her use of her fire had been a surprise. She hadn't pulled that power from me. I would have felt it if she had.

"If I were interested in finding secrets, I could dive into your thoughts," I said softly, tauntingly. "You're the kingdom's top spy, I hear." I'd thought I'd found a good hiding place in the shadowy alcove tacked away in some royal snob's private library.

"You must be a talented spy yourself, what with being able to become air *and* the ability to tap into anyone's mind."

"The individual has to be thinking about me for me to visit their thoughts, which must mean you're pretty obsessed with me." I wouldn't have had such easy access into his head otherwise.

"Right." A faint blush colored his dark cheeks. He adjusted his glasses before tilting his head to one side. "What are you doing here, Amaya?" The crease between his eyebrows deepened. "And where did those awful clothes come from?"

I glanced down at what I was wearing—a gold brocade jacket with the most ridiculous epaulets and a King's Guard's pants, no shoes, no underwear—and winced.

"I hope the owners of those clothes are still alive and breathing," he added, sounding more serious now.

"That's offensive. I'm a dragon, a superior being in every way. I move like the air. You should be able to deduce from that fact alone that I can filch a few clothes without having to resort to murder."

"You've also promised destruction with nearly every breath."

"They're still living, I suppose." I shrugged. "I didn't take the clothing off anyone's dead body if that's what you're wondering. Though, if I had, I might have incinerated the one wearing this jacket on the spot for crimes against fashion. It's quite…" I made a rocking movement with my head that would have made more sense if I were in my dragon form. I then turned my back on Cullen and wandered over to one of the room's many bookshelves. I ran the tips of my fingers over the leather spines, inhaling the sweet scent the books released in response to my caress. "To answer your question, I don't know why I escape to a library when I need space to think. It's not like I'm a big reader."

"You like the silence."

"It's quiet in other spaces," I pointed out.

"True. But the quiet you find in a library is different. It's the kind of silence someone experiences when a mentor or a scholar pauses to take a deep breath before imparting an important piece of knowledge. It's a silence rich with the best kinds of anticipation."

I chewed on that thought for a moment. "I suppose that makes sense." This room, with its dark paneled bookshelves covering every available wall and crammed into the spaces in the middle, felt safe to me. Even safer than the library back at my family's manor house. There was something soothing about it. Perhaps how it smelled—slightly spicy. Perhaps the cluttered organization made it feel as if this were a library that was well-used and well-loved.

"I'm glad you like it here." Leather creaked as he settled down in a deep burgundy chair next to a large window. The sky outside was turning several shades of orange as the sun began to set over the ocean. I hadn't turned back around, but I watched his movements from the corner of my eye. "It's interesting how you chose *this* library from the nearly five dozen libraries scattered throughout the palace to hide in."

"Hmm?" I pretended to be extremely interested in the titles of the books on the shelves in front of me. *The History of Aquamining. The Migration of Chorts. The Personal Diary of Private Draver.* I pretended I was too interested in these mind-numbing titles to pay any attention to the pretty vampire behind me.

"This is my personal library." He swung his legs up and onto the arm of the chair as he lounged sideways on the seat like an idle lord.

His library. Of course. I closed my eyes and berated myself for not realizing I'd slipped into Cullen's private domain. Now that I knew better, I recognized the comforting scent as his.

"These aren't yours, are they?" I asked gesturing to the jacket with enough glitter to lure ravens into a trap.

He chuckled. "Good gods, you must have a low opinion of me if you think I'd wear that."

I turned to openly glare at him. "You helped a human scramble my thoughts and kept me captive even after I'd begged you to help me escape. You also helped kidnap the moonlight dragon. Do you really think there's any *good* involved when it comes to my opinion of you?"

He waved his hand as if he really didn't care what I thought of him. "You'll have to excuse me for not being a better host. I haven't slept for two days, and I'm tired. I hope you don't mind, but I came in here to take a nap." His eyes drifted closed. "I assume you're here to try and kidnap Celestina, so you can return her to the dragons."

"You kidnapped her! I freed her from the dungeon you dumped us in." And I followed Celestina here. Not to force her to return, but to make sure the vampires didn't harm her.

I'd nearly revealed myself after Celestina had made that spectacular outburst of flames. I'd expected the vampires to descend on her like a pack of wild animals with their fangs bared. But even though she'd singed half the court with a huge fireball, no one had attacked her. Soren had given a cry of pleasure when her rage had exploded, like a male cheering on his female's accomplishments. I'd seen the same look on Gregory's besotted face whenever Ivy brewed a new flavor of ale.

Soren's look of pride then crumpled when, her fire spent, she'd collapsed. He'd rushed forward with dizzying speed and wrapped his arms around her, catching her before her head hit the floor.

Celestina's rage had punched a hole through Queen Frieda's muting spell, but the muting spell had recoiled, hitting Celestina with twice as much magic, and slamming the hole closed. Even in my air form, it felt as if someone had punched me in the gut from the magical reverberations that had rocked the royal court.

And, although I'd expected Celestina to be punished for destroying the gilded throne room, Soren had petted her head and whispered how much he loved her as he'd carried her back to his chambers.

The clan had locked me away for two and a half weeks when I did what had to be done to save my fellow dragons from Celestina's out-of-control magic. And the vampires hadn't punished Celestina for her wholly unnecessary—but fun to witness—outburst. Why weren't they punishing her? They should be locking her in irons. Not kissing and petting her.

After leaving Soren's bedchamber, I'd whirled like a confused tornado through the palace, only stopping when I'd reached the calming silence in this library.

And since I couldn't sit in a library in the nude, I had to go search for clothes. But I returned after I'd taken my human form. I needed the quiet of this place. I needed time to think.

Celestina's vampire warrior had treated her with kindness. Trace had been kind, too. But…

Fine. Perhaps Soren wasn't completely evil. Yes, he was trying to use Celestina. And his *niceness* could be a trap to brainwash her into believing he loved her and wanted to protect her. But what I'd witnessed, the tender way Soren had carried her and whispered to her, he didn't have to do any of that. She'd been unconscious. So, why would he fawn over her like that? I'd stared into the silence of the library trying to figure out why seeing Celestina so well cared for hurt like a thousand pins in my heart. If only I could talk to the old human woman. I wished her ghost would find me here, bake me more cloudberry muffins, and offer me more words of wisdom.

The decisions you make—you, specifically, not the moonlight dragon—have the power to rewrite the lines the fates put down eons ago. You, my beautiful dragon, can save countless lives, but only if you decide to follow that amazing heart of yours. She'd already returned from beyond the grave to tell me what I needed to do.

But hell, couldn't she have been more specific? I had no idea what my rusty heart wanted me to do.

My gaze drifted over to where Prince Cullen was resting as if nothing in the world could harm him. He'd been working against the dragons, helping *the man*, putting Celestina into the dungeon, and helping Soren steal Celestina away from the clan. I'd promised him that I'd kill him the next time we were in the same place. I'd let him get the best of me back in the field with the airship. I wouldn't make that mistake again.

Like a silent predator, I circled his chair. "Something is troubling me." My fingers elongated, noiselessly transforming to sharp talons. "How did you and your brother evade our patrols?"

"Ah-ah, my lovely menace, that would be giving away secrets," he murmured without bothering to open his eyes.

I kept circling him. "You used blood magic." My teeth sharpened into deadly points.

"I've told you more than once that vampires don't use blood magic. Don't need to. The Tiburnians, however"—he did that hand-roll thing again—"did you know their magic doesn't come from dragons?"

"I didn't know that." *Should I slit his throat or bite off his head?* What did it take to kill a vampire? "I should have smelled the lack of dragon ancestry on *the man*. But he stank so much of pig, I didn't really wish to take a more thorough whiff."

"Tiburnian society is much different from any of the other kingdoms. It's really rather interesting. The Tiburnians overthrew their magical royal family with dragon ancestry during the War of the Magics. Their kingdom is now ruled by elected tribunals. And magic is available to anyone…well, anyone"—he gave a jaw-cracking yawn—"with the money to pay for a mentor or who can afford one of their exclusive magic academies. Very few in their society possess natural-born magic. That's why they use blood magic."

"Vampire magic," I corrected.

He still had his eyes closed as he turned his head drowsily from side to side. "It's not at all the same."

"Isn't it? You consume blood to allow you to have the power to draw magic into your body so you can direct it. Those who practice blood magic use blood to capture magic and trap it in objects. Like those manacles that nearly killed me." Blood magic was a corrosive deviation of a powerful and beautiful force in nature.

His eyelids opened just a smidge but dropped closed again. "I am sorry about that. I allowed myself to get put into...into a bad position, one that made it impossible to help you."

I sniffed, not willing to let him off the hook for what he'd done. I continued to circle him. I could go feral and eat him raw. I'd like to see how he would react to that. Would he quiver and cry? Somehow, I doubted he'd give me that satisfaction. He'd likely enjoy it.

"The Fein have never used blood magic. I agree with you that it's corrosive, especially to the wielder. Shortens their life."

"I didn't say it was corrosive."

"But you thought it."

He had to be guessing. It wasn't as if he could hear my thoughts. And why was he still breathing? Why was I hesitating to use the skills I'd been born with? I could shift into air and let him breathe me into his lungs like I'd done with the rat-viper. A vampire wouldn't survive being blown apart. But blowing him to pieces felt too quick, too impersonal.

I moved so there wasn't the slightest jingle from the heavily spangled jacket and continued to circle my prey.

What I really wanted to do was to tear open his chest with my talons. Feel his warm flesh as I dug into him. Watch as his eyes grew wide with shock. While he suffered, I'd lick his blood from the tips of my talons. I could almost taste the spicy tang of his blood now.

I looked down at him. He had to be sleeping now. His hands rested on top of each other on his chest. They were too far away from any concealed dagger he might be wearing to be of any use. The tension in his face had smoothed out. A slight smile tugged at the corner of his mouth, making me wonder what he was dreaming about. Foolish vampire prince, he shouldn't leave himself vulnerable to me, a superior predator. The clan would be pleased that I'd struck back at the vampires after they'd taken Celestina from us. Just like Anther had killed the old woman because the humans had taken me. This was our way. This was our justice.

A red haze coated my vision as I raised my arm.

His arm shot out and, before I could react, he grabbed my taloned wrist. "You don't want to do that, my beautiful, bloodthirsty Amaya. If you kill me, all the fun we've been having together would come abruptly to an end." He opened his eyes. "You'd miss this." That damn smirk returned. "You'd miss me."

"How did you—?"

"Amaya."

"No." I tried to back away from him. He tightened his hold on my wrist.

"Amaya." He sounded so damn calm. He caressed the back of my hand with his thumb. The tender motion settled my boiling blood and caused my talons to return to my fingers.

"How dare you be kind to me." He'd caught me in the act of plotting to rip out his chest. He should be furious. He should be shouting for the King's Guards to come and drag me away. Not that they'd be able to. I'd turn to air before anyone could touch me.

"Why aren't you turning to air to escape me?" he asked.

I looked at my wrist still trapped in his warm hand. His thumb continued to trace those silly little circles. Why wasn't I running away? "Turn to air and lose this stylish jacket? Never!"

Prince Cullen snorted.

It was such a surprising and welcoming sound, that I couldn't help but smile...and laugh, just a bit.

"Was that—?" Cullen jerked upright in the chair. With one hand, he adjusted his glasses. He kept hold of my wrist with his other, tugging me a little closer as he peered at me. "Was that delightful sound a midnight dragon's laugh?"

My smile faded at his teasing. "No."

He pulled me even closer. I nearly tripped and landed in his lap. "No, no, no, Amaya, don't stop smiling. Please. You haven't smiled or laughed in my presence. I'm thrilled to see you can."

I bent down and pressed my nose to his. "I would have laughed my head off if you hadn't stopped me from tearing out your entrails."

His lips curled up into a look of delight. Not the reaction I'd been going for. His warm brown eyes sparkled. "I would have liked to hear that."

"Hear what? Your entrails being torn out?" He was demented.

"No, I would have liked to hear you laughing so hard your head fell off. And to know I caused you such joy doesn't make me demented. It means I like you, my sharp-fingered Darkness."

I spun away from him so quickly, I snapped free from his grip. "You can hear my thoughts!"

He shrugged as if it wasn't important. "You grabbed for my mind so many times over the past two weeks, you blazed a permanent connection between us. Can't you hear my thoughts?"

"Not unless I'm trying!" This was so, so unfair.

"Not unfair, Amaya. We have a connection. Which means you can hear my thoughts as clearly as if I were speaking to you…"

"Like this."

I moved closer to him. "That-that shouldn't happen. That's not how my powers work."

He looked absolutely pleased by that. "The two of us must have rewritten the rules."

"Or you broke the rules."

He reached around me, pulled open a desk drawer, and stuck his hand inside. After a moment of rummaging around, he withdrew his hand. He had a triumphant look on his face as he opened his palm to reveal a small golden box. It shimmered in a way that made my dragon heart beat faster.

"What is that?" I demanded at the same time the door to the library swung open.

A woman wearing a sunny yellow dress breezed into the room. She had finely chiseled cheekbones, a pretty pink mouth, and the most glorious head of black hair. It made my hair look like a tangled mess. At the first sight of her, I panicked and dissolved into air.

"Dammit," Prince Cullen growled as the clothes I'd been wearing clattered to the ground at his feet. "Haven't you ever heard of knocking, sister of mine?"

The beautiful princess glanced around the room. "Why? No one's ever in here with you except for me or Soren."

"Did you ever stop to think there might be a reason for that?"

"I already know the reason for that." She crossed the room to him and kissed the top of his head. "It's because you don't have any friends."

He pushed her away. "No, it's because I don't want anyone coming into my library." He didn't sound angry with her, just annoyed. "What do you want, Priscilla?"

She looked down and kicked the pile of clothes I'd left behind. "What in the four kingdoms are you doing with Sir Godfry's ugly blazer and a pair of one of the King's Guard's pants? You aren't planning on wearing that mismatched outfit for a spy mission, because if you are, you'll immediately be found out. Oh! Is that Fireborn Chocolate?" She made an obscene sound in the back of her throat. "You said you didn't have any left."

She tried to snatch the box from him. But he snapped his hand closed around it. "The chocolate isn't for you." He glanced around the room as if searching for me. "I was saving it to give to a friend."

"A friend?" She stamped her pretty foot.

"Yes, Priscilla. I do have one or two of them."

"Who are you looking for?" She turned a full circle. "You don't have a female hiding away in here somewhere? Lady Smythe? Are you in here? I've seen the way she looks at you, like she wants to—"

Cullen jumped out of his leather chair and slapped his hand over his sister's mouth. "That's inappropriate. And wrong. So wrong. You're my sister. I'll not talk about *that* with you."

"That's not fair," she said after she'd shoved his hand from her face. "Just because I'm a female, I don't get to have the same conversations you and Soren have?"

"I don't talk to Soren about my personal life, either. Are you happy?" He pushed her toward the door. "Now, if you don't mind, I was trying to get a few minutes of peace so I could rest."

"But, Cullen, you need to talk to someone about your personal life…or apparent lack of one."

"No, I don't." He swung the door open. "I'll see you in the morning, Priscilla."

She opened her mouth as if to argue, but then smiled. "You do realize you've never thrown me out of here before? And that, my dear brother, is telling."

"I realize that. Good night." He closed the door on her smiling face and turned a key in the lock. After a few moments of silence, he walked back to his leather chair.

"Amaya?" He tossed the box of chocolate in the air and caught it again. "She won't be coming back."

That didn't matter. I refused to reappear in front of Cullen without clothes. Usually, nudity didn't bother me. And just that morning, he'd seen me...*all* of me. So, I didn't understand why I felt all hot and nervous about standing in front of him naked now. *I must be too close to a heat source.*

"I know you're still in here," he said, slowly spinning in a full circle as if he might be able to catch sight of me. "I'll turn my back and promise not to peek, even though you have nothing to be embarrassed about. You have a lovely body."

I stilled my thoughts. I didn't want him to hear them, especially when I suddenly started to picture what his fit body might look like if he stripped off all his clothes.

"Amaya?" He sighed. "About tomorrow's ball. I'll leave a gown and dance slippers in this room for you, so you don't have to come dressed as raven bait."

He walked over to one of the many bookcases and pulled a book bound in blue leather from one of the higher shelves. "I don't ever give out books, and I'm breaking at least three laws by sharing this one with you, an outsider and enemy of the Fein. But you deserve to have this one, even if you say you aren't much of a reader."

He set the book on his desk. He placed the golden box next to it and gave it a light pat. "Until tomorrow, my lovely Darkness," he said softly. He walked toward the door but paused for a moment. "And Amaya? Please, don't roast or maim anyone in the palace before then."

After he was gone, I turned back into my human form and rushed over to the desk. I ripped the box open and popped the chocolate into my mouth. The treat exploded with a rich symphony of cacao flavors. Gracious, that was good.

After I'd licked the box clean of chocolate crumbs, I opened the book he'd left on his desk and read the title page aloud, "A Compendium of Dragon Lore and Facts, translated by Cullen Kitmun. The original text penned prior to the War of the Magics by Draco Falco, a self-proclaimed midnight dragon."

While I didn't like books all that much, I sat down in his leather chair, turned the page, and started reading.

Chapter 32

Celestina

Some days you're tired and want someone to come and rescue you. Today was one of those days. Did I really want my green dragon to come blasting into this room to take me back to the plateau and the unfamiliar life with the clan? Maybe?

I didn't have the energy to figure out what I wanted. I'd been taught my entire life just how tricky vampires could be. And yet, I'd let myself be fooled by Soren's charm. I'd let myself believe that they loved me. That *he* loved me.

The slave collar and its connection to Queen Beatrice put Soren in an impossible position, the part of me that still loved my prince pointed out.

A soft knock on the door pulled me out of my thoughts. I'd sent back my breakfast untouched. I wondered if someone had noticed and was worried about me. Someone like Soren.

Stop it! He was angry with me. I'd tried to kill him. And I was still angry with him. I didn't want him in my room. *His room. Dammit.*

This morning, I'd woken up in his bed alone. Not under the covers, but tucked under a soft, wool blanket. And there'd been a breakfast tray waiting for me, steam curling up from a dainty teapot. There was no evidence that Soren had spent the night in the room with me. But someone had removed the court dress and had taken my hair down. They'd put me in a simple cotton dress.

I shook my head trying yet again to remember what had happened after I'd blasted the court with fire. I had no recollection of anything beyond seeing Soren jump out of the path of the worst of the flames. His clothes had caught fire. The walls, too! The entire room had turned into a blazing inferno.

My head suddenly turned cold at the thought that jumped into my mind—*What if I'd killed Soren?*

If he were dead, I'd be dead, too.

No, that wasn't right. That wasn't how the bond worked. I hadn't bonded with him. He'd only bonded himself to me. The slave collar had bonded my life to his. But the collar was gone.

Was Soren now gone too?

The soft knock came again, and then the door opened.

I clutched the wool blanket to my chest and scooted up as high up the bed as possible, trying to put as much distance between myself and whoever was coming into the bedchamber. My heart beat a wild tattoo. I wasn't safe here. I wasn't safe.

Princess Priscilla stepped lightly into the room. A trio of armed King's Guards followed closely behind. The guards eyed me with great caution. Did they think I would open my mouth and burn them (or their princess) to ashes? They probably did.

They probably *should.*

The princess looked behind her and sighed. "Where is the tea I ordered?"

"It's coming, Your Highness," the guard nearest to her answered. The way he said "Your Highness" sounded suspiciously disrespectful. I fully expected her to reprimand him for his insolence. But she merely laughed softly before turning back to me.

"Please"—she gestured to the bed—"may I sit? I wish to speak with you…if you'd let me."

"Of course." What else could I say? I'd attacked her brother. I was a prisoner if the guards in the room with me were any indication.

The princess wore a lovely blue gown that complimented her dark features. Like her brothers, she had silky black hair that flowed down her back unbraided. Her deep brown eyes were lined with kohl, making them look even larger. She was a tad shorter than me, but she was by no means insignificant.

Before she crossed the room to the bed, a small, wizened human woman charged into the room, pushing the soldiers out of her way with her slightly hunched shoulders as she carried a tray holding a teapot and two delicate cups.

"Mary?" I'd thought I'd never see the old army cook again. Wearing the blanket like I would a cape, I crawled out of the bed to get to her.

Mary set down the tray on a small bedside table before she launched herself at me. She hugged me so hard, that I worried she'd crack all my ribs. I hugged her back just as tightly as tears filled my eyes. I hadn't realized how much I'd missed the old, cranky cook. She scowled when we finally released each other.

"Don't you go getting yourself kidnapped again. I'd never hear the end of it from Patty. My ears are still aching from how she complained and complained. She still wants to come see you. But I told her that you needed time."

"I would like to see her, too." I swallowed over a lump in my throat. "If I'm allowed."

"If you're allowed?" Mary clucked her tongue. "Child, you're a princess and the bonded partner to the kingdom's crown prince. You can order those oversized knuckleheads to do anything you want."

"Soren?" At the mention of him, my worries for him exploded again. Why wasn't he here? "Is he well? I didn't—?"

"You didn't do anything that boy couldn't handle."

"But I—"

"From what I've heard, you showed everyone that you're different from the rest of them. That's not a bad thing. You also showed them that you're someone worthy of their respect." Mary glanced over her shoulder at the guards. "Your fire was much more effective than my spoon, I suspect."

I didn't know what to say to that. Princess Priscilla, who'd started to pour the tea, smiled in my direction. "Much more effective," she murmured.

"Listen to me blathering on when I have work to do. You should see the incompetent lads assigned to assist me. They're worse than worthless." She patted my cheek. "Don't be a stranger, girl. You're welcome to come and peel carrots and chop onions anytime."

My heart squeezed. I gave Mary another tight hug before she bustled out of the room.

"Please leave us," Princess Priscilla said to the guards.

The one who'd spoken to her earlier tried to object. But when she looked his way and lifted her eyebrows, he closed his mouth and gave her a bow. "We'll remain outside this door, Your Highness." Again, his use of her title dripped with contempt.

The princess' cheeks darkened. "He can be trouble, but he's..." she said once we were alone. She shook her head and blushed a bit harder. "Tea?" She held up a steaming cup. "I heard you'd sent your breakfast tray back to the kitchen untouched. You should drink something."

My throat still ached from breathing fire, but I wasn't sure if my nervous stomach could handle the tea.

She didn't wait for me to answer. She merely set a cup in front of me and took her time pouring tea into a second cup. Her head was tilted to one side as she went about her silent task.

"Have you ever wondered why Soren's eyes are green when Cullen's and mine and our parents are brown?" she asked. Her voice was soft and measured.

I shook my head.

"Please, drink the tea." She gestured to the delicate cup she'd filled for me. "It's a honey-lemon blend, soothing for sore throats."

"Why would you think my throat would be sore?" My voice did sound scratchy.

"You did breathe fire out of it. For the first time, perhaps? I would think it would ache. Doesn't it?"

"It does," I admitted.

"Then drink the tea." She smiled at me.

"Aren't you angry with me?"

"For what?"

I sat on the edge of the bed and picked up the cup. "For trying to roast your brother."

"Angry about that? No, Celestina. I'm sure it was justified. And you didn't actually roast him. So…" She lifted her shoulders in a small shrug. "I still would like to be your sister. I hope you still would like to be mine as well." She settled next to me on the bed. Her arm pressed against mine.

Her kindness made me uncomfortable. Not because I didn't trust it. Oddly, I did. Although I suppose I shouldn't have. I felt uncomfortable *because* I trusted her. Trust was such a foreign concept in the Earst court where courtiers and royals were always plotting ways to backstab one another. Tearing someone down was one of the few ways a courtier could move up in the ranks.

I took a sip of the tea she'd poured. The hot lemon and honey soothed.

"Is that valerian root I'm tasting?" I asked when a slightly bitter flavor bloomed on the back of my throat.

Princess Priscilla seemed pleased I recognized it. "To help settle your nerves. Now, keep drinking. And I'll drink mine while I tell you about Soren's green eyes." She took a sip of the tea, holding it in her mouth for a few moments before swallowing. "This is one of my favorite blends." She took another sip and then set the cup back on the table. "Now, this is a tale that has been banned from our land." She pressed a finger to her lips. "Being a younger sister, it's a story that would shock my parents if they ever learned I knew of it. They can be terribly protective. And before I tell you, I'll ask that you promise to keep the tale to yourself, unless you see an important need to share it. Can you do that?"

"Of course." With that kind of opening—a secret tale—it was enough to whet my appetite. "Especially if it concerns Soren. I think I deserve to know it." I added that part in case she decided to change her mind about telling me.

She smiled with the satisfaction of a sailor who'd felt a tug on a fishing line. "Do you remember the old, blind woman who came into the royal dining room when we were all attacked?"

"The seer." I shuddered at the memory. I hadn't told any of them what had happened when the old woman had touched me. I hadn't told them about the vision of the buildings in smoldering ruins. And all my friends, all my found family, including Princess Priscilla, dead. It was a vision of a future I never wanted to see realized.

"Yes, she's from a long group of seers who used to be trusted advisors to kings and noblemen for as long as the continent has existed. What they saw could change the course of a war, could change the minds of men. Could save lives." She paused and gave me a long look. "Or cause parents to kill their children."

What?

She nodded knowingly. "That's what happened. For generations, the seers of our kingdom held positions of power. They'd give vague predictions and repeat the same grim prophecy. *'When the green-eyed child born to the king reaches adulthood, that ill-fated royal progeny—the Beast of Fein— will cause the Kingdom walls to come tumbling down.'* It's the stuff of nightmares, right? When I first heard it, I lost sleep for more than a week."

"Soren has green eyes," I whispered. And his own people called him the Beast of Fein.

Princess Priscilla nodded. "Every couple of generations such a child has been born to a king."

"If it's happened before, the prophecy must be wrong." Soren couldn't be the bringer of destruction to the kingdom he loved.

"We don't know if it's wrong or not." The princess angled her body, so we faced each other even though we were still sitting side-by-side on the bed.

"But if there have been other green-eyed children born to your ancestors, wouldn't it have to mean the prophecy is wrong? You still have a kingdom. What am I missing?"

"No other royal child born with green eyes has been allowed to grow up. In ages past, as soon as a new royal was born, the seer would be the first to hold the baby. She'd peer at the baby's face and then announce the eye color. The king's advisor would slit the throat of any royal baby born with green eyes."

"Gah!" I couldn't imagine killing a baby because of the color of its eyes.

"My parents were just as horrified as you are now. Their marriage was a love match. And their first child—Soren—was such a blessing to them. But then the seer announced that Soren had been born with green eyes. My father's advisor already had a dagger pressed to my brother's throat when my father ripped Soren from the old crone's arms. *'You must kill him,'* the seer warned my father. *'The kingdom cannot survive him.'* My father took one look at the tiny, helpless baby and another at my mother, who'd started to sob, and he tossed the seer out of their chambers." Priscilla looked at me. "My father then banished all the seers from the palace. He had his spies and agents spread rumors about them. People throughout the continent started to believe that seers were agents of the devil, that they ate children, and that none of them could be trusted.

"Soon, no one listened to a word the seers said. They laughed at the prophecies and portends of doom the seers would shout at anyone who'd listen. And for the first time in nearly twenty generations, a king's green-eyed child was allowed to grow up."

"Does Soren know about this?" I asked.

"He's the one who told me. My father taught Soren about the prophecy on his ninth birthday. He wanted to make sure Soren wouldn't be troubled by what some random seer might shout at him. My father also wanted to make sure that Soren would never act in any way that might inadvertently harm the kingdom. You see, while my father didn't completely believe in the prophecy, he decided that schooling Soren to put country above all else would be an important safeguard for the kingdom."

"Poor Soren. He must have felt so alone. How could your father do that to his son?" I pictured Queen Beatrice's spirited boys and tried to imagine how one of them might react if he learned he should have been killed at birth.

"My father did what he thought was best for Soren and our kingdom. The prophecy is a heavy burden. My brother constantly worries about what his existence means."

"He puts country first." I'd heard him say that more than once, especially whenever someone had accused him of falling under my thrall.

"Exactly. He's had that duty to protect the Fein people drilled into him for two decades. He never does anything for himself. It's country, his family, and, if there's ever anything left, himself. Believe me when I tell you that there's never anything—time, energy, resources—left for him to enjoy. I believe this is why he's refused to bond with any of the women Mother paraded, barely dressed, in front of him. He worried that taking a bonded partner might be the thing that triggers the wheels of the prophecy to start rolling. Because by taking a bonded partner he might learn to love would mean taking something for himself."

"He bonded with me because he saw what I could do for his kingdom. He has always acted with honor." I set the teacup aside. "Thank you for telling me this."

"I don't believe it's something Soren would talk about. Especially, not with you." Her words dug like a dagger into my flesh. "Let me tell you what he said to me after he told me about the prophecy." She squeezed her hands together. "He told me that if I ever saw him doing something I thought would endanger the kingdom, he wanted me to kill him. He knew my father and mother wouldn't do it. He thought Cullen was too young, too bookish, and too soft to do it."

"But Soren says you're the compassionate one of the family. You open health clinics. You look after the poor."

She nodded. "Yes, I do those things. Like Soren, I've been raised to put the needs of the kingdom, the needs of its people, before my own. He knows I would do anything to protect the people of Fein, even if it means killing someone I love the most."

I glanced over at the teacup, remembering how Cullen had drugged the wine. Had his sister done something similar, but with poison and tea? "Was that bitter flavor really valerian root?" I asked softly, not sure I wanted to know the answer.

"What?" She jerked back as if I'd slapped her.

Priscilla had also been drinking the tea from Mary's pot. But perhaps she'd slipped something deadly into my cup when she was pouring.

"You kill me, and you manage to get rid of both me and your brother," I said. "You save the kingdom from its enemy. And I get it. I destroyed the royal court yesterday. Perhaps, I even killed a few people."

"No one died!"

"I'm what the Fein fear most," I continued. "It would be wise to get rid of me."

She grabbed my hand. "Celestina, is that why you think I told you about the prophecy? So you'd understood why you were about to die?"

I nodded.

My stomach twisted. Was that the poison starting to do its work?

"Oh my goddess, that wasn't my intention at all!" She tightened her hold on my hand. "Celestina, I want to love you like a sister. I came here this morning only after bullying my hardheaded brother into staying away from you for a few more hours. I wanted to try to get you to understand why he sometimes acts the way he does. He's terrified of letting himself have this one thing for himself, terrified that it'll cause him to make a decision that will destroy the kingdom." She drew in a long breath. "He loves you. He loves you more than I've ever seen him love anyone…even his family. You should have seen him when he'd returned to the palace without you. He was broken. And scared. And he fears the love he feels for you, fears what it will do to the world. But at the same time, he's unwilling to give you up. My parents tried to convince him to leave you with your own kind. But—" She closed her eyes. "He loves you, Celestina. And that's all I wanted you to know."

"You told me this, so I won't roast him when I see him again?"

She chuckled. "Something like that." She picked up both teacups as she rose. "I've never seen him so stupidly in love."

"I've tried not to love him." I wasn't sure why I needed to tell her that. "But I can't seem to help myself."

"I'm glad." She placed her cup and mine on the tea tray before walking to the door that led to the outer chamber. "You're good for him, Celestina, and I'm thrilled to be able to call you sister."

Chapter 33

Celestina

Patty, dressed in a pretty knee-length flowered dress and pigtail braids, came bounding into Soren's chambers with the energy of an excited puppy. She squealed so loudly when she saw me, I wondered if I'd ever get full hearing back. In the time since Priscilla had left, I'd taken a bath, styled my damp hair into a single braid that hung down my back, and changed into the comfortable black leggings and black tunic I'd worn when I'd traveled with Soren's army.

Patty hugged me and made me promise to never leave her like that again, complete with pinky swears and bumping elbows to seal the deal.

"Don't be too mad at Soren," she begged as she clung to me. "You don't know what he had to do to get you back."

"What did he do?" I asked as I flicked away a lizard that had dropped from the ceiling to land on my shoulder.

"What didn't he do," Gray grumbled as he entered the chambers. He was back to wearing the all-black uniform preferred by the members of Soren's army. Gray's twin swords hung from his back. Raya entered closely behind him, dressed the same way, but with a sword sheathed at her hip. Neither looked worried that they'd need to use them against me, I was glad to see.

Raya kissed my cheek as she greeted me. "That was some display you put on last night."

"Certainly reminds us hapless males not to underestimate the power of a female's wrath," Gray said with a mock scowl.

"I'd never burn you!" Patty untangled herself from me and leaped on to Gray's back, making him scowl for real this time.

"Yes, you would." He wiggled as he peeled her off. "The first time I angered you, you'd fry me up in one of your grandmother's big pots."

"And you'd hit him over the head with Mary's spoon," Raya added.

Patty thought about that for a moment, and then nodded. "True. But only if you made me really angry." She pantomimed swinging Mary's spoon around in the air.

A loud laugh burst from my mouth. But then Patty started to laugh with me. Gray joined in. And finally, Raya chuckled a bit, too. This felt so much like before I'd been taken—like I was surrounded by family and not by *others* who wanted to use me—tears burned in the backs of my eyes.

Embarrassed by my emotional outburst, I spun away from them. My watery gaze collided with Soren's as he entered.

My handsome warrior was carrying a large platter piled with pastries, sandwiches, sliced meats, fruits, chocolates, and cakes.

"I heard you sent back your breakfast, so I had the kitchen fix a little of everything." He set the tray down on the round table in the corner. He'd changed out of his shimmering court suit. (I'd likely burned most of it off him.) He was wearing the same type of black tunic and leggings as the rest of us. He had his hair tied back with a simple leather strap and wore no weapons.

He stepped toward me, and then stopped himself. His hands closed into fists at his sides like he was keeping himself from reaching for me.

His green eyes shimmered as we watched each other. I wanted to hate him. Every piece of me shouted that I should hate him for bringing me back to Fein like a prize to be displayed and used in his battles.

But Soren's very existence predicted his kingdom's doom. And he'd been told over and over since he was a small child that unless he schooled his actions, he'd be the one who'd bring destruction to his people. Every decision he made had to be made with the prophecy in mind.

Perhaps he had made mistakes when it came to us. But he was trying to make our doomed relationship work.

And, honestly, I didn't hate him. I doubted I could *ever* hate him.

I closed the distance between us, lifted one of his tightly held fists into my hand, and gently unfolded his fingers. He held his breath as I lightly traced the scarred skin I found. I did the same to his other fist, opening it, and massaging the taut muscles. I then pressed a kiss to each knuckle, while silently telling him that it was okay. That I understood. That I still cared for him.

His shoulders dropped as he brushed his rough thumb along my jaw, tilting my head up. "Celestina," he whispered my name. "I am sorry."

"I may have overreacted yesterday…a touch." I quirked a smile. Those dang tears still glittered in my eyes. I tried to blink them away, but they were as tenacious as those lizards that followed me everywhere. "Is there anything left of the throne room?"

"Two half-melted thrones," Soren said. "Did you learn how to do that from spending time with the dragon clan?"

I shook my head. "I didn't know I could do anything like that. I felt so angry with you that it all exploded."

"Hmm." The furrows in his brows deepened. "You'd better take some of the food before Gray eats it all."

Gray had two honey tarts in one hand and a small strawberry cake in the other. Patty was next to him, picking through the pile of goodies to find another honey tart for herself. Raya stood back with her arms crossed, watching us all with a strangely pleased expression.

While I did love honey tarts, I feared the sweet treat wouldn't sit well in my nervous stomach. Everyone was acting so nice. They should be angry with me. Were they pretending? Was this a manipulation? Did the king tell them to charm the scary dragon that they were hoping would slay their enemies?

The twist in my stomach tightened.

Yep, I wouldn't be able to enjoy any of the food Soren brought. A shame. The tarts and fruit did smell delicious.

"You need to eat," Soren said softly. He plucked a honey tart from Gray's hand and held it out for me.

"I—" I was about to explain about my sour stomach when Prince

Cullen, dressed in blue leathers, entered the chambers without knocking.

"Sky Girl!" He'd balanced a tower of books in his arms. "There's the heroine of the hour! Nice show, yesterday. You proved to the court that the Beast of Fein bonded with a lady who is truly his equal. Everyone in the palace, in the city even, is talking about you this morning. Next time, though, save the fireworks until you're outside. Father is trying to salvage the thrones, but they're hopelessly melted. *'Five generations of royals have used them,'* he keeps muttering."

I gulped. "Your parents are never going to like me, Soren!"

"Those ugly relics were oversized and pretentious." Soren placed himself between Cullen and me. "It was past time someone melted them down." He crossed his arms over his chest. "What are you doing here, Cull?"

Gray and Raya swiftly flanked me. Gray had even abandoned his remaining honey tart. Patty snatched it up and made a show of finishing it off.

"I wouldn't drink anything the younger prince offers you, Patty. You know what? Keep away from him altogether." Gray threw out his arm to prevent her from getting close to him. "The bastard's not to be trusted."

Cullen tsked. "Is that how you speak to royalty?" He glanced around the room before settling on a spot in a far corner near the sofa. A smile creased his lips for just a moment. It vanished when he focused on Soren again.

"I've been researching the dead soldiers that refuse to stop fighting, and I have some thoughts." He gestured with his chin toward the sofa. "May I?"

"No." Soren stood his ground.

"We don't want you around our Sky Girl," Gray growled.

"I helped you get her back."

"Only after you orchestrated her abduction in the first place." Raya stepped forward to stand directly in front of me.

"Celestina"—Cullen peered around Raya—"I truly didn't mean you harm."

"You didn't?" Gray snorted. "You tossed her into a dungeon with a dangerous dragon. What outcome did you expect?"

"What happened was what I'd hoped would happen."

Soren's eyes narrowed.

"She's free of Queen Beatrice's slave collar," Cullen reminded them.

"You let the dragons know we have their moonlight dragon!" Patty shouted.

"And by stealing Celestina away from the clan, we have likely started a war, a war we don't have the resources to fight. Not with Earst throwing an endless supply of undefeatable dead soldiers at us," Soren added somberly.

Everyone fell quiet after that.

I was sure they were all thinking what I was thinking—that this could be the prophecy of the green-eyed royal coming to fruition. Soren didn't have to come after me. That had been his choice. He'd allowed his emotions to take over when he should have gone to fight with his army at the border. Even if he'd convinced himself that fetching me was necessary for the war against Earst, it had been a misstep.

"The dragons already knew I was with Soren," I said breaking the tense silence. "They've had dragons watching over me ever since Queen Frieda took me. That was why the dragons lived in the valley next to the castle while the rest of the continent believed dragons were nothing more than myths.

"Queen Frieda had placed safeguards on me to both prevent me from accessing my powers and to keep the dragons from rescuing me. The slave collar must have destroyed some of the safeguards. I wouldn't have been able to leave the castle with Soren otherwise. But while I could leave the castle, the slave collar assured that I wouldn't be able to escape Soren's side without the collar killing me. The dragons knew that. And they were actively trying to figure out how to break the collar's hold on me.

"As soon as we figured out how to release me from the slave collar, they would have come for me. The dragons are also working to figure out how to break Queen Frieda's muting enchantment so I can access my powers...*for them*. They want to use me to protect the clan and to usher in a new age of the dragon. They want me to lead the fight against the humans and the vampires."

Cullen nodded. "You seem to be chipping away at the spell keeping you from your magic all on your own."

"I'm not sure the fire breathing was my magic." It was most definitely my rage. But was that destructive burst of power mine? My magic was supposed to be light and goodness, at least that was what Gregory and Trace had told me. It was Amaya's powers that carried a destructive punch.

I'd been able to siphon power from her when I was touching her. Was it possible that I could draw on her powers even when we weren't touching? "It's frustrating not knowing how my magic works."

Gray shot a disgruntled look at Soren that seemed to say *I told you so.*

"I might be able to help with that," Cullen said. "May I sit down?" When no one budged and no one said anything, Cullen shifted unhappily from foot to foot.

"You need to forgive him," I said.

Soren whipped his head in my direction.

"Cullen hurt you, but his heart was in the right place when he rescued Amaya. I don't think Amaya would ever admit it, but she needed his help." A frigid wind blasted through me. I rubbed the chill from my arms. "He's your brother. You need to forgive him."

"No. I don't." Soren bit off the words. But his fighting stance relaxed. "But I will. In time."

"That's the best I would dare ask for." Cullen gestured with his chin to the sofa again. "May we talk about what I found in these books?"

At Soren's curt nod, Cullen crossed the room and dumped his books onto the sofa.

"Should Patty leave?" Gray asked. "She's—"

"She's one of us." Raya put her arm around the teen's skinny shoulders. "If she wants to stay, I think she should."

Patty squealed and stuck her tongue out at Gray, who took his trademark scowling to an entirely new level of grumpiness.

Cullen sat on the floor in front of the sofa and patted the carpeted floor beside him as an invitation for me to join him. Before I could, Soren sat between us. "Just in case," Soren muttered. Raya and Patty sat near me. And Gray stood at the door with his arms crossed over his chest.

"Talk," Soren said.

Cullen gestured to the books. "I've been looking into the source of power behind Queen Beatrice's army of the dead. Necromancy hasn't been a talent she's exhibited in the past." Culled raised his eyes and looked over at me for confirmation.

"Not that I've ever seen," I said.

"Not that any of my spies have seen either. And lately, Queen Beatrice has tightened her security. I've lost three men while trying to get more information about how she's creating her unbeatable army from the grave. She sent my spies back to us in very small, bloody pieces."

"Queen Beatrice likes to make a statement," I muttered.

"But you have an idea how she's making the dead walk?" Soren asked his brother.

"I do." Cullen picked up a book from the top of his stack titled, *The History of Tiburnia*. When he noticed my frowning at it, he explained, "Sometimes the most important clues come from the most unexpected places. As is the case here, I remembered reading something a few years ago and went back to look it up today." He flipped through the pages until he came to the one he wanted. "Here." He adjusted his glasses. "As you know, other than the royal Tiburnians who were overthrown and killed, most of the Tiburnians can find a vampire somewhere in their ancestry."

"I didn't know that." No one bothered to tell me anything.

"Sorry about that," Soren said. "I would have talked to you about the people of Tuburnia before our ship docked at its capital, but I couldn't since Queen Beatrice was listening in. And we didn't want her to know what we knew about the other kingdoms."

"I get it." I didn't like it, but grudgingly understood.

"Anyhow," Cullen continued, "the Tiburnians have a history of vampire lineage. It's similar to how the royal families in Earst and Asteria can trace their magical lines back to dragon hybrids. Only, the Tiburnian hybrids aren't royal, and they aren't magical." He paused to make sure we were all paying close attention. "This next piece of information doesn't leave this room." He glanced at the ceiling above us as he said, "It's important to our survival that we keep this part of our past secret."

I nodded. "Does this have to do with the fact that the other kingdoms don't know that most of Fein is populated with vampires?"

"It does," he agreed. Finally, I knew something. "It's a piece of our past that allowed us to create the Kingdom of Fein while erasing large chunks of the continent's history. And keeping this secret is vital to our future."

Chapter 34

Amaya

I hovered in the corner of the chamber, floating on a small current of warm air that had formed from the body heat of the room's inhabitants. Holding my air form for an indefinite amount of time came to me easier now that I'd read the book Cullen had given me. It contained various tips and techniques that the ancient midnight dragon, Draco Falco had written about as if it were common knowledge.

I'd learned more in one night about midnight dragons and dragon history than I'd learned from years of Gregory's tutoring sessions. At the end of the Vampiric Wars, the dragons must have lost much of their knowledge and traditions when the clan escaped to the plateau. This book, this gift Cullen had handed me, would change our clan for generations to come.

Why did Cullen give this to me? What did he expect in return?

If anything, his kindness had made me trust him less. And it troubled me that he could find me even when I was nothing but air. His warm, bespectacled gaze had traveled unerringly to my corner of the chamber. A corner of his lips tilted up before he continued to talk about those evil Tiburnians.

Of course, the Tiburnian who'd captured me had vampire ancestors.

"The Tiburnians' have to trace their line back many, many generations before they can find any vampire ancestors. They're essentially descendants of humans," Cullen said as if he could hear what I was thinking.

Dammit, he can. I made an extra effort to tamp down any thoughts that came into my mind.

"The Tiburnians cannot access magic the way dragons and vampires do." Was Cullen explaining this exclusively for my benefit?

His deliciously calm voice lulled the angry beast inside me, the beast that seemed to always be thrashing and searching for ways to burst free. Ways to be destructive. He glanced in my direction again before continuing. "Now here's the interesting secret—the Tiburnians don't know that the Fein are vampires. Before the War of the Magics, vampires were hunted, enslaved, and drained by humans. They used the healing powers in our blood. This continued until one day our ancestors rose up and rebelled. The uprising triggered the War of the Magics that blazed like a wildfire across the entire continent.

"After the war, the best of our kind, those who had the strongest powers of compulsion, came together and collectively wiped the memory of vampires from human minds. Our ancestors then went from kingdom to kingdom, gathering all the books, stealing away centuries of knowledge, to keep the survivors of the war from remembering why they had once hunted vampires. We went from being slaves to becoming the stuff of legends. We became the monsters that lie in wait in the dark shadows."

He took off his glasses and used his sleeve to clean the lens. "That is how the Palladian Library was created. It's stuffed full of stolen books and scrolls. And yes, Princess Celestina, Soren told me how you think hiding away all that knowledge is a crime. And you're not wrong. But our ancestors went to such extremes because they knew what it was like to live as you once lived—collared, controlled, a life to be taken at a whim. They created our closed society here in Fein because they wanted to protect their descendants from suffering as they had suffered. And that is why slavery in any form in our culture is considered a great evil and a crime punishable by death."

I floated on the ebbs and flows of his voice. Gentle waves tugging on me, making me feel his voice like a caress. It was like when he tried to use compulsion on me. But this time his voice felt softer, safer. And not like he was trying to lay down traps to ensnare me.

This, I thought, *is his passion. Research and sharing knowledge. It must kill him to live in a society that hides all its knowledge from the rest of the continent.*

"It does," he answered.

I slammed down a wall around my thoughts, using a method Draco Falco had described in his book. But I kept listening to his voice, enjoying the stillness in the sound of it.

"How does this history lesson help us fight Queen Beatrice's already dead warriors?" Gray asked from where he stood at the door, stiff-legged and looking as unhappy as I usually felt.

He's getting to that, you impatient oaf. I let that thought sneak over the wall I'd built.

"Thank you." Cullen smiled down at the book in his lap and then cleared his throat. "I needed to make sure we were all on the same page and understood the background before diving into new information. Context matters." He adjusted his glasses, which he seemed to use as an excuse to glance in my direction. I wondered what he saw. I was formless, clear air.

"I see you, my beautiful Darkness," his voice came as another sweet caress. *"Always you."*

"Whatever." If I'd had eyes I would have rolled them.

Cullen chuckled.

"What's funny? Don't tell me. I think I already know. You're losing your mind," Cullen's brother grumbled.

"I think I am," Cullen agreed, but then he gave his head a hard shake. "But back to the research. Shortly after the War of the Magics, the Tiburnians discovered the power of blood magic. Perhaps some of the Tiburnians had clung to the memory of harvesting vampire blood for its healing magic and decided to see what they could do with blood from other living sources. That's conjecture on my part. The origin of their knowledge has been lost to time. But we do know that the Tiburnians have been perfecting and expanding their blood magic for generations. This hasn't come without a cost. Blood magic is corrosive magic. It takes from the user and the recipient, shortening both lives. That's one reason why there are very few elders who use blood magic in Tiburnia. They don't live to see old age.

"I suspect that modern legends of vampires have their roots in Tiburnians who wield blood magic. Their skin color turns a dusty pallor that burns easily in the sun. Their magic demands high quantities of blood, which can mean draining multiple victims dry. And they operate in secret, hiding that their magic is stolen from spilled blood."

"My parents are with the Tiburnians." Celestina pressed a hand to her mouth. "They could be in danger. Should I warn them?"

Those aren't her parents. They're her villainous abductors, I wanted to scream.

"They're the only parents she remembers," Cullen replied. *"It's only natural that she'd feel an attachment for them. And wow, that was loud."*

Whoops. I guess I did scream it.

"We'll warn them." Soren took Celestina's hand in his own. "I'll send men to get them out, if that's what you wish."

Celestina nodded. Seeing her with her stupid warrior should have made me rage. Cullen's calming presence must have stopped all that. Also, Soren hadn't punished Celestina for exploding with a *literal* fiery rage. Instead, he'd brought her extra food.

I—I didn't understand why he'd do that. I understood very little of what the vampires were doing. Was this their way of charming us to do their bidding? Was this how they dragged us under their thrall?

Possibly.

Possibly? No! Probably. Undoubtably. Absolutely.

Goddess, it was already happening. I was already softening toward our mortal enemies. Fuck Cullen and his soothing voice. I would not let them wreck my defenses like they did with Celestina's.

I started to move toward my fellow dragon. I needed to get her out of here. Even if I had to fight my way out, I needed to get us out before I turned as moon-eyed as she had.

But then Cullen said, "The Tiburnians aren't our biggest concern, at least not right now. While I believe they're helping Queen Beatrice create her undead army. It's Queen Beatrice who's the real threat. Not just to us, but to the entire continent, including the dragons."

"No, you lie." I materialized with my face directly in front of his, which meant I was kneeling since he was still sitting on the floor. Not the best defensive position, I knew. But I wanted him to feel the words in my breath against his face. "That human queen isn't a threat to the dragons, not if our fire can kill them."

His cheeks darkened. *"Amaya,"* he said my name so gently it made my chest ache.

"I'm not going to let you use your vampiric compulsion to lull

Celestina and me into believing we have no choice but to help you. Not when it's a lie."

"Amaya!" Celestina launched to her feet. "You're wearing clothes! How did you manage that?"

I *was* wearing my own clothes. And I was clutching Cullen's dragon book to my chest. I wasn't about to leave that treasure in the library for him to steal it away from me. I planned to return the book to the clan where it belonged. The book had taught me how to conjure clothes when I shifted to human form. It'd been a simple conjuring that pulled matter through magical currents. I'd pulled a black sweater and black wool leggings from my bedroom.

"Is this the other dragon you were talking about, Raya?" the younger woman with braids shouted. "She's beautiful! You're beautiful!"

I turned my head and snapped my razor-sharp dragon teeth at the girl to get her to back away from me.

Gray jumped between me and the girl, the metal of his twin swords singing as he drew them from the leather sheaths he wore on his back.

"Easy, now," Cullen warned. He rose to his feet just as I did. But instead of taking a fighting stance—which he should have done, seeing how I could detach his head from his neck with one swipe of the talons I snapped together in warning—he held up both his hands as if wanting to surrender. I supposed that would be smarter than fighting me.

"We're not your enemy, Amaya." His voice eased into my head like a gentle summer rain and the soft rumble of distant thunder.

I swayed with the rhythm of the soothing sound. We weren't enemies. I don't know why I ever thought—

"Cullen." Soren was now on his feet. Celestina wrapped her arms around the warrior prince's chest. "Don't."

"You don't want to harm anyone, Amaya." The voice in my head tugged at me, daring me to run with him through open fields filled with spring flowers. Daring me to smile at him. How could I think this kind, bookish man was my enemy?

"Noooo!" I screamed, the compulsion snapping. I swiped at him with my talons.

He moved lightning fast, dancing out of the way. My talons hit empty air.

"I'm going to take Celestina home and let you vampires and humans and hybrids with blood magic have fun without us." I held out my hand to Celestina, my fingers were still deadly sharp talons. "Come on. Let's get out of here."

"No." Celestina tightened her arms around Soren. "I'm where I want to be. Where I need to be."

"They're using compulsion to make you think that!" I growl-shouted my frustration.

"Soren wouldn't do that."

My poor delusional moonlight dragon seriously believed that. She blinked at me with those giant mismatched doe-eyes as if trying to will me into believing it, too.

"Why wouldn't he use compulsion to secure your cooperation? His brother has been trying to compel me to follow his directions from the moment we met!"

"And he's going to stop doing that now." Soren punched his brother's arm. Hard. Cullen winced. "That's not how we treat our friends, Cull."

"I'd like to remind you that *our friend* has been plotting violent ways to end me ever since we met." Cullen rubbed the spot where his brother had punched him.

"Maybe if you'd treated her better from the start," Raya said, "she wouldn't be angry all the time."

Unfortunately, anger was pretty much a steady state for me, except for when Cullen was trying to enthrall me. "What that girl said." I flicked my talons in Raya's direction.

She backed up a few steps.

"Let's put away our swords." Soren gave an open hand "cool it" motion to Gray. "No one wants to force you to do anything, Amaya," he said. His voice sounded flat and devoid of any kind of power except for the kind that came with being a natural-born leader. "We were discussing Queen Beatrice. I'd like to finish that discussion before we prematurely start another War of the Magics with the dragons." He turned to his brother and raised his brows. "Cullen?"

Cullen clicked his tongue. "I'm sorry, Amaya. I shouldn't have tried to use compulsion. That was a mistake on my part. Unless we're in a life-or-death situation, I won't do it again."

I didn't like that he'd added a caveat, but I was glad that he'd apologized. "Thank you. I still plan to take Celestina home with me."

"But you can't leave us again, Sky Girl!" the girl-child shouted. "We need dragon fire to fight the undead army. And I need you to—" She abruptly cut herself off as she flicked a glance toward Gray.

Ah.

"At least stay for tonight's ball," Cullen said. That calming quality stayed in his voice, but I felt no push of compulsion hidden underneath the calm.

Even so, I found myself nodding. I did want to go to this vampire ball of his and see what their rich, royal celebrations were like.

"Thank you," Cullen said softly as the child shouted for joy and hugged me.

I'm so not a hugger. Having this strange girl's arms wrapped around me felt like I was being attacked by a giant tangle tree. But, for Celestina's sake, I didn't swipe my talons through the child's middle in a desperate attempt to escape. *You're welcome.*

Chapter 35

Celestina

Knowing how volatile Amaya could be whenever we were in a room together, I tried to push everyone out of Soren's chambers before she killed Cullen or anyone else. Also, I wanted to talk with her alone, woman to woman. I wanted to convince her that I was happy and that she should go back to the clan and explain to the other dragons that I belonged here.

But before I could do any of that, I needed to pry Patty's clinging arms from around Amaya's middle. It took a little doing, but I managed to free Amaya from Patty's sweet show of affection. I shoved Patty over to Gray's care. Patty squealed with delight.

"Gray, escort Patty back to her home," I said with what I hoped sounded like a regal command. Not that I had practice with issuing regal commands. I figured it involved holding my chin up and speaking in rich, round tones. "Everyone else, leave us. We need to speak with Amaya in private." I tossed in the royal "we" for emphasis.

No one moved.

Amaya snorted.

Raya stepped toward me and asked quietly, "What are you doing?"

"Issuing a royal decree," I snapped, frustrated that my first real attempt at wielding my princess powers wasn't working. "You have to do what I say because I'm a princess." And yes, I did realize how pretentious that sounded as soon as the words left my mouth.

Raya glanced over my shoulder to look to Soren for guidance. Neither Gray nor Raya took orders from me when it came to watching out for his safety.

I spun to face Soren. "I want you to leave, too. I want *everyone* to leave so I can have a private word with Amaya."

Soren tilted his head to one side. "That's not going to happen."

"You told me I could issue royal decrees, and that they had to be followed. Was that a lie?"

He crossed his arms over his chest. "As crown prince, I can outrank you, Princess."

"As prince and the younger son of the king, I outrank you as well," Cullen added.

Ooohhh! They were making up these rules of royalty to fit their needs!

Fire stirred in my chest as my rage lit up. I hadn't realized the power was still there. But it must have been. A wisp of smoke curled from my nose. I swiftly waved it away, hoping no one had noticed.

Soren shot me a look of surprise. When it came to me, that man of mine noticed everything.

"I could use my growly voice and force you to leave," I threatened.

"Your dragon powers of persuasion don't work on non-magical creatures like me," Gray reminded me.

"That's not helping," Raya sang.

"Now, Sky Girl." Soren sounded amused even though I suspected he knew I wasn't kidding. I would use compulsion if they forced my hand. "We just made a point of how we don't use compulsion to force others to do our bidding. Is that a rule that should apply to everyone but you?"

Dammit. I closed my eyes and drew in a steadying breath. Ever since last night's explosion, my emotions had tilted from one extreme to the other. I needed to pull myself together. "Then, I'm asking as a friend since I hold no power in this room. Or am I not allowed to do that because I'm nothing more than a tool for your kingdom?"

Soren sighed. "Leave us," he said.

Both Gray and Raya protested. Soren cut them off with a shake of his head.

"Come on, Patty," Gray said as he plucked handfuls of the sweetest treats from the tray. "Let's share this feast with your family."

Raya squeezed my shoulder before she left.

"Would you like me to take Amaya with me?" Cullen asked. He moved toward the midnight dragon who was giving Cullen a look that suggested that if he got any closer, she would slay him.

"No," Soren said softly. "Sky Girl wants to talk with her."

"Then I wish to stay." Cullen glanced over to where Amaya was still glaring at him. "If Amaya and Princess Celestina are agreeable, of course." Amaya bared a mouth filled with sharp dragon teeth at Cullen. He smiled as if pleased by her reaction. "I know what Amaya wants, and I believe I can help her find a solution."

"You're offering your own head on a platter?" Amaya purred in a low, seductive voice. "Splendid."

"Depends on which head—"

"Cull!" Soren snapped. "You're not helping."

"Please." I put myself between Cullen and Amaya. "Give me a moment."

"Very well." Cullen winked at Amaya. She snarled. And he laughed as he left Soren's chambers.

Once the door was closed, Soren suggested we sit down to talk. Amaya sat at the edge of the sofa. I pulled a chair over from the small dining table and placed it across from her.

Soren stepped back and, after picking up a book from the small bookshelf in the chamber, chose a chair at the dining table. "Pretend I'm not here." He opened the book and started to read.

"He can be overly protective," I said.

"I suppose that's a good thing." Amaya watched him lick his finger before turning a page. "The clan needs you safe."

I leaned forward. "I am safe. I might not be sure of everything that's happening. And I still need to clear up some matters with Soren. You may have heard about that."

"About how you conjured your fire? I witnessed it. Impressive. If any of them had raised a weapon against you, I would have killed them." She glanced over at Soren again. "Their reaction confuses me. *The man* in Tiburnia—my abductor—was never so…" She shook her head. "But that doesn't mean the vampires aren't using you."

"I know," I hated to admit. "I—" I'd wanted to tell her that I felt more at home, safer, more loved here in a kingdom that might love me only for what I could do for their people than I ever would feel living with the clan. But I didn't think she'd accept that. "This is where I'm meant to be. I feel it"—I touched a finger to my heart—"here."

Amaya rolled her large silver eyes. "Look, Celestina. I get it. You're a princess here. Back at the clan, you're simply the chosen one, the promised savior of our kind. If I had to choose between the two, I'd pick princess, too. Well, only if wearing fancy dresses all the time wasn't a requirement." Amaya shuddered. "I didn't follow you here because I wanted to ruin your fantasy life. I'm here because I'm trying to save lives. Dragon lives. Vampire lives. Even some human lives, apparently."

"What do you mean?"

"Do you really think the clan will peacefully let their damned savior go live with the enemy? And more to the point, do you think the clan imagines you went with the vampires willingly? They think he stole you!"

I glanced over at Soren. He set down his book. "I could talk with the council, make them understand that no one is forcing me to be here."

"Celestina, they all believe you've been mesmerized, brainwashed. And even if you do convince them that you've not been tricked into falling for a vampire, you've been living as a captive your entire life. No one is going to believe you're capable of making *any* decisions on your own. That's why they've already decided where you'll live and have already picked your mate, heck, they've even picked out your clothes."

"Hold up." Soren leaned forward. "Picked her mate?"

"Yes, she's been promised to the green dragon who has been watching over Celestina her entire life. When I returned her to the clan, they set her up in his home."

The chair scraped on the stone floor as Soren abruptly stood up. His gaze flashed to me. "You said they didn't hurt you."

"They didn't. He's been…patient with me."

A muscle in his jaw worked furiously. His fists at his sides opened and closed several times. I could tell he wanted to know more and break open a few dozen heads. But he didn't force me to talk about what happened between Trace and me. "I'm not going to let you steal her from me."

"And I'm not here to kidnap her." She stood. "Celestina, I've watched you search the plateau for an escape route enough times to know that tactic won't work."

"If you're not here to force her to go back with you to the clan, why are you here?" Soren demanded.

"I already told you! I'm here to stop a war. The clan is coming. And they plan to ride in on the currents provided by the ever-hungry Goddess Perth. They mean to bring death to your land. And Celestina, you're the only one with the power to stop it." Amaya dissolved into nothingness after delivering what felt like a death blow.

In the silence that followed, I folded over my legs and buried my face in my hands. I should have known this fairytale I was trying to create with Soren couldn't last.

Soren crossed the room and placed his hand on my back. "We'll figure this out, Sky Girl. Together. We'll find a way I can keep you."

"Keep me?" Lowered my hands from my face, I sat up. "How do I know you aren't manipulating me?" He'd explained last night how he'd both loved me *and* wanted to use me. And while I believed him, that still didn't sit right.

He crouched in front of the chair and took both of my hands in his. "Celestina, my feelings for you are bigger than this kingdom. I wish they weren't." He shook his head. "I—There's a reason why I must put the kingdom first, and I am sorry for it. It's..."

Was he trying to tell me about the prophecy? "Princess Priscilla told me about your eye color and what it means."

His grip on my hands tightened. "There is that. Plus, I have a duty as general, as crown prince, as a son to follow my king. And still, part of me wants to throw all of that away and run away with you to a place where we can start fresh, where we can be a team and not enemies—not a warrior with his weapon—just two lovers forging their own path, creating their own kingdom." He lightly brushed his lips over mine. "I loved you even before I bonded with you. But I bonded with you, because of my love for you, but also because I knew you were a dragon. I knew what that could mean for Fein's defenses."

I tried to pull away from him. But he wouldn't let me go.

"Celestina, after the bond took hold, my love for you changed. I changed. My priorities shifted away from putting the Fein first and toward putting your wellbeing first. Would I welcome your help in protecting my kingdom? Yes, of course, I would. But only because you're in this kingdom with me. If you asked me to leave, I would leave. I'd follow you anywhere you wanted to go. My life is yours. And maybe that's what the prophecy has been warning us about all along. Maybe your egg hatched because my father didn't kill me. I don't know. And at this point, I don't care. I once promised you that I'd free Earst's slaves, and I still intend to do that. But other than that, I don't know what will happen or how our relationship plays into some ancient prophecy. All I know is that I will fight to keep you because that's what my heart is telling me to do."

Someone knocked on the chamber door. Banged on it so hard, it rattled in the frame.

"But what about your family and the dragons?" My heart ached for him….and for me. The only way out of this mess we'd created involved blood. So. Much. Blood.

Whoever was on the other side of the door started to hit it with their fist.

"Is there a way to avoid a war?" I whispered the question, not sure I wanted to know the answer.

He didn't answer right away. "I'll need to pull back some of my warriors from the border. With two fronts to contend with and one coming from the air, things will get tricky. We'll need a strategy that keeps the conflict as brief as possible."

But would the dragon clan give me up? Ever? That wasn't a question I dared ask because I already knew the answer. "I think you should see who's at the door before they knock it down."

Soren huffed, but he rose to his feet.

"Stop blocking the doorway. I'm here to prepare Princess Celestina for tonight's ball." Goldie pushed her way into the chamber.

"We haven't finished breakfast," Soren complained. "You can come back later."

"Beauty takes time, Your Highness. Something you don't have to worry about since you could show up in your battle leathers and have all the ladies salivating. But the ladies must select the perfect dress, have it altered so it fits just so, wash in just the right oils, paint our nails, paint our faces, and style our hair."

"We're not doing any of that today," Soren growled.

"You're not doing what?" Goldie went back outside and returned with her rolling wardrobe. "The ball is being held in Princess Celestina's honor. You must let me make her look perfect."

"No, I don't." He blocked Goldie's path to me.

"Boy, I've been keeping royalty in this palace looking their best since before you were born. I know what must be done and how long it takes to do it."

"Not today, you don't."

They stared at each other for so long that I was certain Soren would be the first to break. He had a soft spot when it came to the older ladies in his life.

"Hand me the gown," he finally said. "*I'll* get her ready." When Goldie started to protest, Soren held up a hand. "That's the best you're going to get from me today. Hand me the gown."

"I brought several for Princess Celestina to pick from."

Soren opened the rolling wardrobe and sorted through the gowns hanging inside. "None of these will do."

"But-but they were all specially created for—" Goldie sputtered.

"The princess does not want to wear anything with images of dragons stitched on the gown. Bring me something simple, but elegant." He looked over his shoulder at me. "Silver?"

I nodded. My heart clenched, but in the best way. Soren understood why I didn't want to be trotted out as the kingdom's token dragon. And he was standing up for me.

"Silver," he said. "Like moonlight. And simple. If you bring anything different, Sky Girl will go to the ball dressed in what she's wearing now. And she'll start a new fashion trend in the kingdom. The ladies will all start coming to the balls dressed in tunics and black leggings."

"Your parents will hate this," Goldie grumbled. "But I'll bring a simple gown."

"Good. I'll call for you when we're ready for you to return." He pushed the wardrobe back into the hallway and, despite Goldie's objections, slammed the door shut. He turned the key in the lock and gave it a toss, sending it flying across the room.

"What if we need to get out?" I asked, looking around for where the key might have landed.

He took my hands in his and lifted me from the chair. "We won't need to open that door for several hours." He started to kiss me. And Goddess, I wanted to kiss him back. My body arched into him. We were like two magnets pulling toward each other.

But I forced my lips to peel away from his. "Should—shouldn't we be spending this time preparing for an aerial attack?"

"We will. And I promise you'll be involved with every part of the planning. But first, I need to do this." He lifted me into his arms and carried me into his bedchamber.

As he'd predicted, we didn't emerge until several hours later.

And when we did, my body ached in the best way.

Chapter 36

Amaya

The ballroom outfit waiting for me in Cullen's personal library wasn't the elegant gown I'd expected. No, what he'd left for me was infinitely better—a silky white pantsuit. The top consisted of several strips of shimmery material that wound around my torso, covering my breasts and shoulder and not much else. The loose-fitting pants were made from the same soft material and came with pockets. For my feet, he'd given me the most delicate pair of white slippers that would surely fall apart before the end of the night.

In a small box, I found a delicate filigree necklace studded with a rainbow of gems that made my dragon heart patter. It didn't matter if this piece of jewelry was a loan, he was not getting it back. While my hoard back at the plateau contained several large stones, nothing in it rivaled this necklace's artistry. I couldn't stop looking at it in the mirror as I wove my black hair into a neat topknot.

A gong that rang through the palace halls announced the start of the ball. I emerged from the library to find Cullen leaning against the hallway wall, waiting for me. He looked dashing in a dark blue suit. It was the same intricate fashion I'd seen in drawings in magazines Trace would bring to us from Earst. Cullen had tamed his dark, wavy hair and had changed out his glasses for a pair with dark blue rims that perfectly matched his suit. He was handsome in a way that made my chest ache.

I didn't like it.

"You look ravishing, my lady Darkness," he murmured before kissing the back of my hand.

"I know," I wasn't too proud to admit. "Thank you for the...pockets in the pants." I didn't want to give him too much credit even though I was immensely pleased with the pantsuit he'd selected.

"The pockets do look fantastic." He held out his arm. "Shall we go and dazzle everyone?"

He led me to a set of double doors that two human men dressed in ridiculous red and white suits opened for us as we approached. "This is the royal entrance to the ballroom," Cullen explained as he swept us through the doors. "Which means we can avoid the crush of courtiers waiting to enter on the opposite side."

Gentle strains of music carried through the air from a small stringed quartet set up on a raised platform in the far corner of the massive room. The king and queen's raised dais and twin brocade chairs (Celestina had destroyed their thrones) were set up near the doors we'd just passed through. The floor, made from polished black onyx, glittered in the soft lights coming from the line of chandeliers that ran down the center of the long space. One side of the room was defined by an impressive glass wall that looked out over the ocean. The glass wall arched up overhead to create a ceiling that provided a view of the night sky. The other side of the ballroom was lined with a series of archways and doorways that led to what I could only assume were secret places where vampire revelers could find a little privacy to feed on their victims.

"Only on *consenting* victims," Cullen corrected.

I swatted his arm. "Stay out of my thoughts."

"Stop projecting them into my head," he said with a light chuckle.

A hush passed through the crowd as we walked further into the opulent room. Heads turned and murmurs rose.

"Everyone is wondering about the beautiful mystery lady on my arm," Cullen said.

I scoffed. "They're looking because they're curious about having yet another dragon in their presence. We inspire awe wherever we go."

"Ah, that may be true, but no one in this ballroom knows, save for a select few, who or what you are. Here, you are truly anonymous. Does that bother you?"

Does it? I turned my head away from him to watch a group of dancers—ladies dressed in elaborate gowns and gentlemen dressed in ridiculously elaborate suits—twirl around one of the three dance floors that had been set up in the room. A few of the dancers took notice of us and stopped to stare. "Why aren't you dressed like those men?" I asked instead of answering his previous question.

"Because I'd rather be comfortable."

I couldn't argue with that. "Thank you for not bringing me a dress like one of those monstrosities. Gracious, that gown must weigh a ton."

"You once told me you never wore dresses."

I was surprised he'd remembered. "Do you think I'm causing a terrible scandal by showing up in pants? Is that why everyone is staring."

"I'm sure you're causing the worst scandal ever to rock the walls of our hallowed palace. I've witnessed at least four ladies swoon at the sight of you, and three of the men have collapsed as well."

I liked his dry humor. It made me smile despite my determination to only show him my snarls.

"Truthfully, though, Lady Darkness, I've seen several ladies eyeing you with interest. And the gentlemen…well, I don't wish to have to punch anyone—my mother would scold me in the worst way if I did—so I'm trying to ignore how they're looking at you."

"Men are looking at me?" I knew I wasn't an ogre. Back at the clan, I had no shortage of bedmates. But to find myself an object to be watched in a sexual way by the enemy was unnerving.

Cullen tightened his grip on my arm. "There are a few of my friends over by the punchbowl. Should we go meet them?"

"You have friends?"

"I am a prince." He said it in the most arrogant manner that I nearly hated him for it. But then he added, "My parents pay scores of gentlemen to pretend to like me. And over there are some of their highest-paid employees."

I recognized one man from Celestina's escape. His hair was slicked back, and he wore a black suit that was as plain as Cullen's blue one. He raised a single eyebrow as he watched Cullen approach with dangerous-little-me on his arm.

"Crispen, Driscoll, and Bower," Cullen said once we'd joined the small circle of men. "Let me introduce my date, Miss Amaya…" He looked at me and frowned. "You know, I have never learned your last name."

"Nor have you ever had reason to know it."

He continued to stare at me as if I had more to say. The moment should have turned awkward with his friends gawping at us, but I was rather enjoying myself.

Cullen ruined my fun by grinning as if he approved of my stubbornness and had even encouraged it. "Let's call her Lady Mystery tonight."

"I wouldn't expect any other kind of lady to grace your arm," Crispen said. He was a good-looking vampire with dark blond hair and sparkling blue eyes. "It is a pleasure to meet you, Miss Amaya."

Bower, who had close-cropped black hair, a round face, and thick neck, was quick to agree. Driscoll, however, crossed his arms and looked about as pleased as my brother would look whenever I went on a rampage, which wasn't happy at all.

"How are matters faring tonight?" Cullen asked his friends once there was a lull in the conversation.

"Nothing new to report, Your Highness," Crispen said. "After last night's fireworks, this ball promises to be a damned dull evening. Well, perhaps not that dull now that Lady Mystery has joined our ranks." He winked at me.

"Is everything well with you, Prince Cullen?" Driscoll asked as he moved closer to me.

"It's fine." Cullen shrugged.

"Is it?" Driscoll pressed. "Do we need to worry that Lady Mystery has the same abilities as another in her ranks?"

"Excuse me? What are you implying?" I demanded.

"There's more like her?" Crispen cried as his gaze roved over the ballroom.

"Driscoll is worried you've used your beauty to ensnare me." Cullen kissed the back of my hand. "And I don't mind admitting that you have."

Crispen and Bower both chuckled.

Driscoll looked like he would run me through with a sword if he could. He started to say more, but Cullen—still clasping my hand—whirled me toward the dance floor.

"This is one of my favorite songs. Do you dance?" he asked.

"Not in such a stiff manner." The dancing that took place at Ivy and Gregory's parties came from our emotions. The movements were fun and sometimes erotic.

"Stiff? I suppose the waltz could be described that way." We arrived at the dance floor. He placed one hand on my lower back and held up his other hand. "Touch your palm to mine. And put your left hand on my back as I've done with you."

"But I don't know the steps." The other dancers on the floor had already begun to rotate around us. "Are you trying to make me look like a fool?" If he was, I planned to bite his head off and feed it to the palace rats.

"You might have trouble finding enough rats to devour my head. Vampires are bad for the vermin population," Cullen answered. "But I appreciate the thought." He leaned in closer and whispered, "I'm not trying to embarrass you. If you trust me to take the lead, I promise you'll enjoy dancing with me." When I didn't lift my hand to meet his, a thread of tension pulled through his handsome smile. "Please, Amaya. If you trip, I'll make it look like it was my fault. And if you hate it, we can stop at any time."

"Very well." The longer he stood there with his hand in the air staring at me like I was the only person in the room, the more awkward I felt. I placed my hand in his. "Maybe I can find some other disgusting beast within the palace walls that will eat your severed head. Are there ants? I hear a hungry colony of ants can clean bones in a matter of hours."

He swirled me around so swiftly, the room seemed to tilt to one side. "Careful." He pulled me in a little closer. "Think less with your head, especially when it comes to my body parts. Instead, feel the movements of my body and try to match them."

I moved when he did, mimicking his steps. Gradually, the dance, though regimented, started to feel indecent. He stepped toward me. I stepped toward him. Our hips would brush, and then we'd whirl around the room. The rest of the dancers seemed to fade away. My body and Cullen's melded together as we danced as one as the rush of music grew louder and louder. His lips skated over mine several times before he twirled me to another part of the dance floor.

Suddenly, I stopped.

"I-I can't."

Cullen and his relentless charm were making me forget myself.

"Are you dizzy?" Cullen pulled me so my body was flush with his.

I pressed my palm against his chest. "You said we could stop if I didn't like it." I pressed even harder against his chest. This time he let me go.

"It seemed like you were enjoying yourself."

"I don't like it." I moved away from him. "I didn't enjoy dancing with you. Not like this. Not here." *Lies. Lies. And more lies.*

Not long after, the music came crashing to a halt. Had it stopped because of me? Had I made a social blunder?

A trumpet near the royal entrance blew a sharp note and the ballroom fell silent.

"King Devon and Queen Leona," a herald announced. As if in unison, all eyes turned to the royal entrance as the doors slowly opened. An older version of Cullen and a lovely older woman held hands as they entered the ballroom. A man dressed in a puffy purple suit shouted for the loyal subjects to make way for their king and queen.

The men bowed and the women curtsied as if part of the choreographed dance. I didn't bow or curtsy. Those vampires weren't my monarchs, and dragons didn't bow to anyone.

No one seemed to notice. The king and queen, as if moving in tandem, walked gracefully to their waiting chairs and sat down. The queen's gaze searched the ballroom. Whatever she saw made her expression turn sour.

Worry prickled the back of my neck.

"What's wrong?" I whispered as the king's booming voice rang out over the ballroom. "Let the festivities continue."

The music resumed. I made a quick retreat off the dance floor. Cullen chased after me.

"Are you thirsty? Can I fetch a lemonade?" he asked. "Or something stronger?"

I ignored him. My gaze scanned the room, much like the queen's had, as I tried to puzzle out what was bothering her. Then it hit me. "Where's Celestina and your brother?"

Cullen rolled his eyes. "Whenever Soren gets in a room with a bed and his Celestina, it's difficult to lure him back out again. Hell, he doesn't even need a bed. He's been known to disappear with her in his chambers for days at a time."

"But this ball is for them."

"I know." He glanced over his shoulder toward his parents. "Look at how tightly my mother's lips are pressed together. She's furious."

"I noticed. Will she take that anger out on Celestina?"

"She would if she could. But Soren would never allow it. He's super protective. No one can speak ill of his princess without facing his wrath. Not even Mother."

"Good. Celestina needs to be protected."

"How about you?" Cullen dipped his head and brushed the question against my neck in a way that made my entire body tingle. "Do you need to be protected?"

I jerked away from him. "Certainly not! I'm the embodiment of destruction. Others need to be protected from me."

"Do I need to be protected?" His voice dipped lower. And he stepped toward me in a move that resembled the dance steps that had made my heart pound and my body feel needy. "Do I need to be protected from you?"

"You already know what I want to do to you." *Another lie.*

Under the sparkly lights of the chandelier, with the music playing in the background, and feeling like I looked as beautiful as the decorations in the ballroom, I wanted to lean into him and press my lips to his. I ached to discover what a vampire tasted like, to lose myself in the web of desire he was weaving all around me.

Was he doing this to me on purpose? Was this a trick? Seduce the dragon and win her favor?

"Don't!" I snapped at him when he tried to touch my hand. Several heads turned in our direction. "You think you're so clever."

"I am clever, but I'm sure that's not what you're talking about."

"Cullen?" The prince's black-haired sister hurried over to us. She was dressed in an elaborate gown with a huge yellow skirt and tight golden bodice that would have looked ridiculous on me but looked elegant on her. "Crispen told me you'd brought a mystery date?"

She looked at me and smiled. It was the same dazzling smile Cullen had used.

"Now is not the best time, Pris," Cullen warned.

"Nonsense." She hugged my arm to her side to avoid the wave of vampires (and a few humans) suddenly crowding all around the refreshments table after the music ended. "I'm Princess Priscilla, Cull's older sister. And you are?"

I twisted free from her grasp and stepped further away from the refreshments and the crowd. "I'm the shadow in the night that is about to murder your brother."

Princess Priscilla's smile gentled. She turned to Cullen. "What have you done this time?" she asked, but before he could answer, his overly friendly sister slipped her arm through mine again and went with me a few more steps away from the crowd. "You'll have to forgive my younger brother. He's hopeless when it comes to courting eligible ladies. He keeps telling them that he has no desire to take a partner. That's why it's so surprising to find him here with you. I haven't seen you around the palace before. Are you from the city? Or is your family part of the visiting gentry hailing from the Southern Hibrides?" She patted my arm. "You'll have to forgive my brother for not introducing you. He can forget his manners sometimes. Not that manners weren't drilled into that thick head of his from the moment he was born. But his research and dusty books can make him forget himself. I hope you're from the city. I would love to find out who made your ballroom suit, is that what it's called? A suit? It looks amazing on you. I bet my brother didn't even tell you that you look amazing, did he?"

"He did," I admitted. These vampires were good. I bet he'd telepathically sent for his sister to come over and told her to be nice to me. Compulsion didn't work on me. But their *niceness* was chipping away at my defenses. "You're charming and beautiful, I'll give you that," I told his sister. "But it's not going to work."

The princess' smile faltered. "What's not going to work?"

"Your brother has been trying to seduce me so I'll turn against my own. Chains didn't work. Compulsion doesn't work on me. So, he clearly decided to try flirting. Like I'd believe someone like him would fall hard for me." I snorted.

"Cull, no." Her pretty brown eyes widened. She grabbed her throat. "Chains? You put this delicate creature in chains?"

"I'm not delicate," I said at the same time Princess Priscilla said, "Is that what you do when you go away on your missions? *You torture women?*"

"What? No! I would nev—" Cullen, who'd followed behind us, protested.

"And now you're practicing your spy craft in the palace? During Princess Celestina's ball? Does Dad know about this?"

"No! No. I'm not…" He turned to me. His voice softened. "Amaya, I'm not attempting to do anything other than hope you enjoy this evening."

"Don't lie to me," I growled while keeping my attention on his sister. "Your brother is a monster!" I shouted that last bit. Even though we'd walked away from the crowded refreshments table, we hadn't gone far enough. At least two dozen fussily dressed vampires (and humans) turned to watch the unfolding drama.

Cullen grabbed my arm. "Excuse us," he said tightly as he marched me away from his sister. He headed directly toward one of the many shadowy archways.

"What are you doing?" I had to run in the thin-soled slippers to keep up with him.

"I'm taking you somewhere private so we can shout at each other without causing a scandal." He slowed down when we entered a darkened corridor that appeared empty. He opened a door and peeked inside before deciding to go somewhere else. We walked in silence and passed several closed doors until he stopped in front of a door left partially ajar. He pushed it open and ushered me inside a spacious parlor with soft lights and a small fire blazing in the fireplace. There were several seating areas, each with sets of cushioned chairs, loveseats, and chaise lounges.

Cullen closed the door behind us and turned the key in the lock. His breathing was faster than normal. His eyes glittered in the candlelight with fury.

He had every right to be angry. I'd embarrassed and insulted him in front of his sister and half the court.

I should have felt nervous locked in a room with him. But, honestly, he didn't pose a threat. Not to a dragon. I could roast him with my fire, lop his head off with my talons, or simply turn to air and float away.

"Don't turn to air." The words came slowly like a threat, or a seduction. "Stay with me, Amaya. Shout at me. Fight me." He peeled off his suit's coat and tossed it over the back of one of the chairs. He then spread his arms wide. "Do what you want to me."

I hated how quickly my body responded to that taunt.

I shouldn't want to kiss him. I shouldn't want to rub against him like an overheated cat. But I do.

Instead of following any of my body's instincts—*stupid instincts*—I fisted my hands to keep from reaching out to him. I should have killed the stupidly handsome prince when we were alone together in his library. He deserved to be cut from this land like a cancer. There had never been anyone with a blacker heart than his. No one was more deserving of the title of the villain of this story.

"I'm a villain?" he spat.

"You're a vampire, aren't you?" I wasn't shielding my thoughts from him. At. All. While I didn't want him to know how I wanted to rip off that shirt and lick his bare chest, I did want him to know that I thought he was the most repulsive, vile, villainous—

"Do you want to see how villainous I can be?" Cullen shouted a moment before he launched himself at me. His hard body knocked me back onto the nearest chaise. His weight pinned me in place. Before I had a chance to react, he grabbed my wrists and trapped them between our bodies.

"Mia kaida, I am not a nice man," he growled a moment before his fangs sank into my neck.

I hissed at the piercing pain and thrashed my head from side to side, desperate to escape from what could easily turn into a fatal bite.

I could have escaped. I *should have* escaped. I could have turned to air before his teeth had touched me. But my traitorous body had kept me there and allowed this *vile* vampire to bite me. Because I was feeling curious. And needy.

Dragons and vampires were mortal enemies for a reason—when the two creatures came together, one of them killed the other. I didn't want to die here. On this *human* sofa. In the middle of a *vampire* ball. Goddess, no. I wanted to be the one killing him.

But with his teeth buried in my neck, he had complete control here. His fingers pressed against my temples, trapping my head in place, stretching my neck so he could deepen the bite. A sound rumbled deep in his throat.

I suddenly realized his bite no longer hurt. He licked the twin wounds with his hot tongue. That felt...that felt...good. His warm lips closed over my skin, and he started to suck. Surely, he was pulling, pulling the blood from my body. And...it felt... *"uhhnnn"*.... Heat puddled in my core. I stopped struggling and settled into that heat like one of those strange green lizards bathing in the sunlight.

Ohh...I should fight him. Instead, I was acting like a deer that had given up as it faced a predator. I hated that. But at the same time, I wanted to let him take as much of me as he wanted. My legs were wrapped around his middle. *When did that happen?* I bucked my hips against the hardness pressing against my core.

"That's right, *kaida*," he murmured. "Ride me."

I rubbed shamelessly against him. But it didn't bring me any satisfaction. The friction between our bodies only made me feel more desperate.

He was going to drink me dry, and I was loving every minute of it.

I pumped wildly against him, crying out in frustration, as he continued to hold my head in place. Not that he needed to. I didn't want him to stop.

"I've got you, my pretty menace," his deep voice rumbled, sending shudders all the way through my body and to my core. "I'm going to take care of you."

He put his lips back on my neck and resumed feeding. But he released my temples. That wicked hand of his trailed down my torso and then wedged its way between our bodies. He eased his hand past my silky pants' waistband and worked his fingers into the heat of my panties.

"So wet for me," he purred softly. I stilled my frantic bucking and let my legs drop open wider. "That's my good girl. Let me do this for you. Let me give you everything you deserve."

With his mouth back in motion, feeding on my neck, he pressed past my folds, easing a finger into my slick opening. He hummed with satisfaction as he pressed another finger inside me. He pumped slowly, in and out.

"Let's see if you can take three," he whispered before going back to what felt like his feasting on my blood.

Yes, let's do that.

"How does that feel?" he asked after he'd buried three thick fingers into me. He paused his feeding to search my eyes.

What was he looking for in my expression? Consent? A feeling of superiority? Reasons to torment me?

His eyes widened, and he smiled before his hand started to move. He hooked his three fingers, pumping them roughly. His lips sank back onto what must now have been a gushing wound on the side of my neck. I bucked and twisted and rode his hand.

"Ahhh, Amaya," he whispered against my skin.

My body was tightening, and I was getting close to exploding. Instinct took over as I continued to buck, his hand rubbing against my tight bundle of nerves.

Goddess.

If this was what it was like to have a vampire drink me dry, I was all there for it. More than willing to give everything up for him. The mating instinct clawed at me. My teeth transformed. I lurched up and dug my mouthful of sharp, pointy dragon teeth into his neck.

He hissed a breath, and his muscles grew taut. But he didn't let up. He kept working my body until my muscles tightened. My eyes rolled back. A voice in my head screamed. Out of fear or pleasure or both. All I knew was that I was on the cusp of what was going to be the best orgasm of my entire life.

Chapter 37

Celestina

Soren's parents glared when we finally arrived at the ball. Hours late. Oh, his father tried to hide his displeasure as we climbed the dais to bow and curtsy to them.

When Soren briefly explained the reason for our tardiness, the older vampire nodded. "Give me a full briefing of your plans immediately after the ball. I'll make sure the festivities end early."

"Thank you, sir." Soren loathed official parties. He smiled when his father suggested he end this one early.

The entire time Soren was speaking with his father, Soren's mother had been shooting daggers at me with her sharp brown eyes. I wasn't the princess she'd wanted for her son. Not even close. But I was the princess her son had chosen. So, I smiled demurely, curtsied prettily, and let Soren handle his mother. Her disapproval wasn't my problem. I couldn't change who or what I was. She was the one who was going to have to change her opinion of me. Luckily, I had Soren's support in this.

After Soren had kissed his mother's cheek, he whispered something in her ear. I don't know what he said, but the queen plastered a fake smile on her face before rising from her throne. She embraced me and kissed both my cheeks.

Perhaps he'd reminded the queen how I'd saved her life even after she'd tried to kill me.

Families. They're fun.

"Everyone is expecting us to dance," Soren said, looking adorably uncomfortable as we descended the dais' steps. He could cut through a throng of heavily armed men without breaking into a nervous sweat. But put him in a formal suit—tonight's was a creamy white with silver trim—and he quailed. "If we give them one right away, the palace advisors might leave us alone for the rest of the evening."

I doubted that. And besides which, I was looking forward to dancing with him.

He frowned as he held out his hand for me.

"I'm an excellent dancer," I promised as I pressed my hand against his palm. A rush of heat flowed through me that I'm sure showed on my cheeks. "And a good actress. No one will ever suspect if you happen to stomp on my toes."

That made him smile. "My feet are like clouds when I dance, thank you very much. I just don't enjoy it."

I chuckled softly. "You'll enjoy dancing with me."

"Only if we do it alone and naked."

"That's not dancing."

His eyes darkened with lust. "Apparently, you're the one who needs dance lessons. I could show you how to—"

"General Kitmun," Driscoll rushed over to intercept us just as we descended the royal dais. "Thank goodness you're here."

"What's going on?" Soren reached for the sword he hadn't worn.

"It's your brother. He's in trouble." Driscoll glanced warily at me before continuing. "You must stop him before he does something incredibly foolish, something that'll get him killed."

"Where is he?" Soren sounded more resigned than surprised.

"In the retiring parlor. He's locked the door," Driscoll explained.

The retiring parlor was a room off the ballroom where ladies could go when they needed to fix a hem or get away from the crowd.

"I'll see what the trouble is." Soren took off toward the parlor at a fast trot.

The spy caught my arm when I tried to follow.

Was Soren anxious to save his brother or running away from having to dance a waltz with me in front of this huge crowd of courtiers?

Likely both.

"If Cullen is in danger, why didn't you go save him." While Driscoll wasn't a warrior, I'd seen him fight. He knew how to hold his own. He didn't need to wait for Soren to help Cullen.

Driscoll shook his head. "I don't have the ranking to interfere with a prince. And Prince Cullen made it clear that he didn't want to be interrupted."

"But you are interfering by bringing in Soren, aren't you?"

He thought about it for barely a second before deciding, "Technically, no."

Ranking and overstepping their place was never something either Gray or Raya ever worried about. And, as irritating as their stubborn presence had sometimes been in the past, I was glad they watched out for Soren with or without Soren's permission. The only reason Gray and Raya weren't trailing after us now like a pair of angry guard dogs was because they were busy preparing for later tonight.

It hadn't been merely sexy-fun-in-the-bedroom that had made us late to the ball, although that was why my legs and wrists felt sore...in the best way. After we'd finished our bedroom games, Soren had kept his word and included me when he'd called Gray and Raya back into our chambers to plan what to do about the impending dragon attack. He involved me in the discussions...even letting me hear secrets known to only a handful in the palace.

While waiting for Soren's return now, I went over those plans in my head. Parts of them would work. Other parts were *problematic*. I was so caught up in thinking about what needed to be done tonight that I barely paid attention as Driscoll introduced me to a few of his friends, which I took to mean they were also spies within Cullen's inner circle. Everyone was exceedingly friendly—even the ladies and lords who came up and asked for introductions—which was a relief. I'd been worried that those in attendance would fear and hate me for turning last night's court into a bonfire.

Things were going so well that I started to believe that I could make this place my home. I belonged here.

Amaya

Cullen knew what to do with my body.

It had been right there...

Ready to explode...

Into something mind-numbingly beautiful...

Until something ripped Cullen's hand away.

Cullen's entire body flew off me. That same something tossed him clear across the room. He crashed against the wall and slid to the floor.

No! my entire body screamed. *No...*

I was still struggling to catch my breath, and my body still buzzed with unsated heat.

"What the hell, Cull?" a deep male voice growled.

What was Cullen's brother doing here? It looked as if battle-boy Soren was seconds away from slamming his fist through my prince's pretty face.

"This isn't who we are. This isn't how we act."

"She—" Cullen looked at me and then dragged a hand through his black hair.

"You might want to watch what comes out of your mouth carefully," the crown prince's voice was low and deadly. "Because if you're about to blame Amaya for your actions, you're not going to leave this room in one piece."

"I wasn't going to blame her." Cullen climbed to his feet. He shook his head several times before he turned toward me. Blood gushed from his neck where I'd bitten him. He pressed his hand to the wound as if pressure alone would staunch the flow. I touched my neck, expecting to find a similar ragged, bloody gash. But there was no wound. When I pressed against the spot where he'd bitten me, the unblemished skin tingled and heat coiled through my body reigniting all my sensitive spots. I sucked in a trembling breath. Even from across the room, Cullen had noticed. His gaze darkened as he spoke. "Amaya and I were working through this toxic attraction we seem to be feeling toward each other."

He stumbled a step as his skin paled.

I sat up. I supposed I shouldn't have bitten his fragile neck that deeply. What I'd done had come so naturally, I hadn't stopped to consider if I was harming him. When dragons mated, they would walk away from the encounter with fierce battle wounds. It wasn't anything that a quick shift through our forms couldn't fix. Only occasionally, something would happen that would require the services of the healer. But Cullen wasn't a dragon. His skin wasn't fireproof or as tough as thick leather. And he couldn't shift to heal himself.

But when his gaze landed on me again, he gave me the cockiest smile I'd ever seen.

Even bleeding, even on the verge of getting murdered by his own brother, Cullen thought it wise to grin at me like that? To run his tongue suggestively over his fangs? To look at me with eyes so blown with lust they looked pitch black?

Apparently, my beautiful prince had no sense of self-preservation.

I jumped up off the chaise and rushed across the room before Cullen's brother committed murder. *Foolish.* Vampire affairs were none of my business. I needed to convince Celestina to come back to the Andalotian Plateau with me instead of wasting time with either of these two idiots. Even knowing that, I grabbed Soren's arm before he slammed his fist through his bookish brother's head.

"I-I wanted—" I stammered. Damn, this was embarrassing. And unbecoming of a dragon. I shook my head in disgust and raised my chin. "He is mine to punish as I see fit." I bared my pointy dragon teeth. "But if you wish to challenge me for that right, I will gladly fight you."

Soren raised his hands. "I'm trying to avoid fights of any kind, Lady Amaya. The Fein hope to be your ally."

"I'm not a lady or any kind of royalty. Beithir society is above such frivolous hierarchy games."

"I stand corrected." Soren stepped back, bowing as if that kind of formal behavior would impress me. "If you wish to remain in this room and punish my socially deficient brother, I'll let you have at him." He looked over at his bleeding brother and raised an eyebrow in question, telling me all I needed to know. He wasn't really going to hand one of his own over to a dragon to be slaughtered. At least, not without his brother's permission.

Cullen nodded. "Amaya and I could use a few minutes."

"Very well." Soren started for the door but paused. "Your neck. It's bleeding heavily. Do you want to take care of that first?"

"No, I'm fine."

Cullen didn't look fine. He looked the opposite of fine. He needed the services of a healer or a blood donor, or whatever vampires did to keep themselves from bleeding themselves dry. Blood had coated his hand and arm and was now dripping on the floor.

"Very well. I'll bid the two of you a goodnight then. Amaya." He gave another shallow bow in my direction. He then left the room and silently closed the door behind him.

"You don't look good," I said in the awkward silence that followed Soren's exit.

"Ah, Amaya, you are terrible for my self-confidence." He leaned against the wall.

"I mean you look like you're going to collapse from blood loss. Isn't there anything you can do to stop that?" I waved toward his neck. "Not to mention the mess you're making all over the floor. Some poor servant will have a devil of a time cleaning all that up, you know."

"Do you think I should send that servant some of my secret chocolate stash as an apology?" He slid down the wall a good inch. I moved closer in case he collapsed altogether. "My body should have healed the bite by now. But as you might have read in that book I gave you—the book I translated when I was a lad—dragon bites can be deadly to vampires. There's something in your saliva that keeps the wound from healing."

"Oh." I think I'd forgotten that part. "I-I didn't mean to. I mean, it's what dragons do when we mate. We bite." And the fact that he was bleeding and hurting from that bite, a bite I'd made because I'd lost myself to lust, made me want to beg his forgiveness.

Imagine that. A dragon begging a vampire's forgiveness? That wasn't going to happen…even if I'd wanted to do it. I did have my pride.

"There is something you could do for me." He suggestively ran his tongue over his fangs again. How could he be thinking about *that* when blood was gushing like a damned geyser out of his body? "But you won't like it. And I won't ask it of you."

"You want me to get you off one last time before you die? Give you a hand job? Or service you with my mouth? Sheesh. That's such a guy response. I don't think turning your body into a playground is the best use of our time here. Let me fetch you a healer." I started for the door.

He caught my wrist. "I don't need a healer, Amaya. I need you. But only if you're willing."

Chapter 38

Amaya

"What do you need me to do?" I stared at the wrist Cullen held in the shackle of his hand. "I can't talk to you when you're looking all bloody and pale enough to be half in the grave."

"The murmurings of a lady in love." He wavered again. I wrenched my wrist free so I could steady him. "What I need, Amaya, is blood. Your blood."

My hand flew to my neck where he'd already bitten me, not that there was a gaping wound. "You already have my blood." Clearly dragon blood—at least my destructive *midnight* dragon blood—was worthless when it came to healing vampire wounds.

"I didn't take your blood, Amaya. Not without your permission. I just—" He turned away from me. "It was compulsion—a trick I played to make you believe I'd bitten you. I shouldn't have done that. It's just—" He looked up. "When I'm with you, I make poor decisions. You—I'm not blaming you—but whenever you're around, I feel like my mind glitches. I need you. I don't want you. But I can't stop thinking about you. You shouldn't exist. And here you are, a threat to our kingdom. And I don't care. The thought of never seeing you, never trading barbs with you, never kissing you again, breaks me." He put both his hands on my face. "You break me, Amaya. But goddess help me, I never want you to stop."

My heart hammered in my chest.

I didn't—

I didn't—

I didn't know what to do with that.

I pushed his hands away. "You're getting blood all over me. And the floor. And this lovely pantsuit. Stop it. Take my blood and stop bleeding everywhere already."

"Are you sure?" He started to slide down that wall again.

"Goddess, yes. Do it before you fall over dead. And don't blame me if our blood is incompatible. All my magic is good at—all *I'm* good at is tearing things apart, not putting them back together."

"Amaya." He leaned forward and kissed me, while herding me until my back bumped up against the nearest wall and until he had my body tightly wedged between the wall and his hard planes. His lips felt cool against mine when earlier the press of them had seared my skin. "If for some farfetched reason your blood doesn't work," his voice weak, barely a whisper, "please, find my brother. He'll know what to do."

I nodded and steeled my nerves as he tilted my head to one side. His breath tickled my neck before he struck.

I gasped at the pain. The bite felt sharper than before. Pain lanced through my entire body, causing me to jerk. I dug my fingers into his shoulders. But just as quickly as it hit, the pain vanished. There was a gentle tug on my neck as he lapped up my blood. The sensation curled its way down to my core.

I needed him.

We hadn't finished what we'd started, and my body was gearing up as if this second round would give me the release it desperately wanted. As if sensing my growing arousal, Cullen leaned his hips into mine, spreading my legs with his knee.

His lips tugged at my blood, pulling it out of my body, making my head spin. I rocked against the hardness he'd pressed against my core.

I tightened my grip on his shoulders. Suddenly, this didn't feel sexy. I was no longer a few thrusts from coming apart.

I was scared.

"*Sorry. That's because I'm scared,*" Cullen pressed into my mind.

"*You're scared? Aren't you the one who's supposed to know what he's doing?*" I was totally going to die here. I shouldn't have let him talk me into this. If he hadn't looked so pitiful, I would have left him to bleed out on the parlor's floor.

"*I do know what I'm doing. But I'm scared I'll hurt you. My need… I've never felt like…*"

"Like what?" My voice rasped. Terror pulsed through my veins, and my heart started hammering again.

He eased his hand between us to place it flat on my chest. "*Be calm.*"

He pushed his compulsion on me. My heart almost immediately slowed, and I could draw a steady breath.

"Like what?" I repeated without panicking this time. "You've never felt like what?"

"*I've never felt like I could lose control when feeding on someone.*"

"*What?*" I started to panic again.

"*Be calm.*" He pressed the compulsion on me again. "*Calm, my gentle Amaya.*"

And I did feel calmer, but not nearly as relaxed as I had the first time he'd willed calmness on me.

"*I won't lose control. I promise. I care for you too much to let that happen. But still, I—*"

"*You shouldn't care for me,*" I interrupted. We were enemies.

"*But I do.*"

"*You're a fool.*"

"*For you.*"

I snorted.

He slowly dragged his lips—lips that now felt warmer—from my neck. "That's enough," he murmured against my skin. His tongue brushed against where he'd bitten me. And I moaned as warm tingles spread all the way down to my toes.

I rubbed against the hardness still pressed against my core.

I wanted—

I wanted—

I needed—

Dammit. I forced my body to go still as I drew a long, slow breath.

The jagged wound on his neck was still there, but it was no longer bleeding. And his skin had gained color. Still, he wasn't in any kind of condition to do what my body wanted me to demand of him. Disappointment clogged my throat. I quickly cleared it. "How do you feel?"

"Better." He nodded, as if reassuring himself.

I put my hand on his cheek. His skin still felt cooler than expected. "Are you sure?"

"Nothing a good night's rest won't fix." He stepped away from me, leaving me suddenly feeling as cold as his skin had felt. "I do thank you for letting me—" He pointed to my neck. "I'm sorry I ruined your pantsuit. If you'd allow it, I'll escort you back to my library. I assume that's where you left your clothes?" His voice grew colder and harder with each word. His brown eyes no longer held any emotion. He looked at me with the same assessing expression as he had when we'd first met.

"What's happening?" I asked him. Had my blood poisoned him? Was he now, like me, a bundle of angry kindling searching for a spark?

"I'm afraid you can't return to the party. Not looking like that." He gestured to the wettest bloodstain on the pantsuit's white silky material. He wasn't wrong. I looked as if I'd vanquished my enemies with no care for my personal appearance. Blood was smeared and splattered all over me. His hands curled into fists at his sides. "Please, let me escort you back to the library."

"No." I folded my arms in front of my chest.

"No?" He tilted his head to one side. Did he look *pleased* that I'd resisted him? Did he like poking the dragon to play with its fire?

"I'm not going anywhere with you until you tell me what's going on." We'd battled each other so much that this did feel like our unique way of flirting.

"I'm trying to take you back to your clothes."

I reached into his mind to search his thoughts. And my head was flooded with embarrassment. Deep. Coiling. Grinding. Embarrassment.

My cheeks burned as hot as dragon fire as soon as my mind brushed up against the emotion. I immediately pulled back. And even though I was no longer feeling his emotions or listening to his thoughts, the burning lingered.

"That was rude," Cullen grumbled. "Those are my thoughts."

"Oh? You're angry with me about that? Well, Prince Moody, I'm the one who should be testy. I was the one who had been at the brink of orgasm when your brother intervened. Denial of pleasure has never been a game I enjoy."

"Denial of—?" Cullen dredged his hand through his hair. He walked away from me but didn't get far before he turned around and marched right back. "I'm trying to be the gentleman here. And I have every right to feel embarrassed. I assaulted you…twice!"

"Everything we've done in here has been consensual. If you had stepped one toe out of line, I would have set your pretty hair on fire and used the flame to roast your balls that I would have twisted clean off—"

Cullen smashed his lips against mine. His lips were warm again and tasted of promises.

"Goddess, I love it when you threaten me," he murmured against my mouth. "If I weren't still weaving on my feet from blood loss, I would have you wrap your legs around my waist and demonstrate exactly how much I love it."

"I don't need all that." I looped my arms around his neck and nipped his earlobe, careful not to break the skin. "Just kiss me."

While our lips tangled—and my heart spun like a top—I gently pushed him across the room until the backs of his knees knocked against the sofa where I'd nearly found paradise not that long ago. He lost his balance and plopped down onto the cushion, pulling me down with him.

We both laughed, and his eyes sparkled. The corners of his mouth pressed into one of his infuriatingly smug grins that made him look like an indolent god as he gazed up at me. I was half-sprawled across his lap, my core pressed to the bulge in his pants.

"Amaya," he groaned as I rubbed myself against him. "You make me feel like I've made my way to the feasting table in the Great Beyond."

He untied the knot that kept the crisscross straps of my silky top. The loose fabric parted, baring my breasts to him. While he'd already seen me naked, his heated gaze caressed me.

"Beautiful." The word purred in my head. He lifted my hips and eased out from under me, so I was lying on my back on the chaise, and he was

straddling me. He dipped his head down and sucked a nipple into his warm, moist mouth.

"We need to get these off you," he murmured against my breasts as he struggled with the thin, cord holding up my wide-legged pants. Frustrated, he ended up snapping the cord.

"That's one way to do it," I said feeling downright bubbly, which knocked me off balance. I never felt bubbly or giddy or anything resembling a fizzy emotion. "Hey." I sat up a little as I helped him push my pants off. "When you took my blood that didn't change me, did it?"

"You're not going to become a vampire, my deadly menace." He playfully nipped my breast. "Those rumors are ridiculous. Vampires are born, just like dragons."

Pressing both my breasts together, he sucked on one and then the other while he rubbed against my now bare core. My body zinged to life from the sensation of his hot mouth tugging and teasing me.

"That—that's not what I meant," I managed to get out the words between halting breaths. And then he did something with his tongue that made tears well in my eyes from a flood of emotions that I had no hope of processing.

He lifted his demanding mouth from my breasts. "Amaya?" His voice was soft. "What did you mean?"

It took me several tries to get my breathing back under control. "I feel—I feel"—this was damned embarrassing to admit, but at the same time, I wanted to know if he was to blame for this. Because if he was responsible, I was totally going to bite his pretty head off his pretty body—"I feel giddy."

"Giddy?" A single eyebrow quirked up. "Lightheaded, you mean?"

"No. Giddy, as in stupidly happy. Is this your doing?" My arousal throbbed harder, as if demanding to know why I'd stopped him from playing with me.

"You're blaming me for feeling happy?"

"*Stupidly* happy. I'm never—"

"I'm sure that's true." He kissed my belly. "But you've never been with me before. I'm really good." He kissed the tender space below my belly. "An expert." His hot kisses moved lower. "I'm a genius at making your body feel things." He licked my damp seam, and my head fell back. "All the things your body needs to feel." His hot tongue flicked over the tiny bundle of nerves down there. "Especially the feelings you're not used to feeling."

And then he began feasting. His mouth devoured me in the absolute best way. His tongue. Oh my goddess, his talented tongue had my toes curling and my back arching off the sofa. His fingers pressed into my hips as he held me steady.

"Mia kaida," he whispered against my heat just before he thrust his tongue into me. He didn't let up until the world burst into a rainbow of colors that left me panting.

And I still felt embarrassingly *giddy.*

Bastard.

He pulled me into his arms and kissed me. His lips tasted like exotic spices as well as my own musky essence. And gracious, wasn't that now my favorite flavor? I could spend the night here kissing him, on this sofa, as long as he held me in his arms like this.

Amaya. My name echoed like a groan through my head as we kissed. His voice sounded far away, muffled, which meant Cullen wasn't projecting them into my mind. I must have accidentally slipped into his thoughts. *Amaya. You make me need. You make me want more than I should ever dare ask for. Your fire calls to me like nothing ever has. Yet if I dared tell you that, I know you'd vanish on me. But, gods, I want to tell you. I want to tell you how much I've fallen in love with your prickly bits. You're not nice. You're rough and mean. I see through that. Did you know? That's my talent. I see through to the pure essence of an individual. I see you, Amaya. From the first time we met in that cheap inn, I saw you. You are amazing. I should tell you that. But again, I know that if I did, you would vanish on me because you wouldn't believe it. And I need you to believe me. I need you to share with me a little of that bright spirit of yours. You can't begin to imagine how much I need that from you.*

If he'd said that aloud, I would have panicked and vanished on him. But because I was in his mind, listening in on thoughts that weren't meant for me, I held him tighter and kissed him with more urgency. True pain had been woven into his thoughts. He was hurting. Not physically, but in the same way that I often ached. Soul deep. Like we'd never be able to live up to the expectations of the perfect world we'd been born into.

"I need you, Amaya," he admitted aloud as his deft fingers unbuttoned the flap of his trousers. He pulled his shaft from its confines and then maneuvered himself to be positioned between my splayed legs.

It was one thing to play with each other with our hands and mouths. It was quite something different to let him—

Was I ready for this level of intimacy? With my mortal enemy?

Sensing my hesitation, he guided my hand to his shaft. "We don't have to do anything you don't want to do." He felt warm and velvety. And, gracious fuck, I moved my hand along his length. I couldn't decide whether the size of him was impressive or intimidating. And that was coming from a girl used to superior dragon parts.

I'd already told him that I didn't enjoy playing denial games. And that shaft of his did have me intrigued. What would it feel like to have that much of him stuffed inside me?

Yeah, I *needed* to know.

"I want you," I said guiding him to where I needed him to be.

He nodded. The head of his shaft was wide, stretching me in a way that hurt but I also welcomed. He pushed himself deeper. Deeper. Deeper. I sucked in a sharp breath certain I couldn't take any more. But he had more to give. And I was still curious to know what taking all of him would do to me.

His fingers threaded with mine. His warm, brown gaze watched me as he slowed his movements. A ghost of his smug smile tugged on one corner of his lips.

"My beautiful Amaya." The voice he projected into my mind made me think of spring and flowers and hope just as he thrust hard. The hilt of his shaft slammed against my already over-stimulated clit. My entire body shuddered with an orgasm while stars blinked in and out of my blackening vision.

"Stay with me," he urged. And then he started to move.

Chapter 39

Celestina

"Sorry about that," Soren murmured when he returned. He bent and kissed me deeply in front of everyone. "My brother…" He shook his head. "He's fine."

Driscoll's mouth dropped open with disbelief. "But he's with—"

"With exactly who he wants to be with," Soren finished for him. "And I believe discretion on his behalf is what the kingdom needs right now."

"Yes, Your Highness," Driscoll bowed. But he didn't look happy about Soren's decision to leave his younger brother alone.

I had to agree with Soren, though. Cullen was an adult. He should be allowed to make his own decisions. After living as a slave and then living under the overbearing rules of the clan, I fervently believed in individual freedoms. Even if those freedoms meant making poor decisions.

The string quartet began to play a pretty tune I recognized from balls in Earst. "Shall we get our one dance out of the way, my handsome prince?" If I had my way, we were totally going to dance until my feet gave out, but Soren didn't need to know that yet.

Thankfully, for my toes' sake, he hadn't lied about his dancing ability. He moved with grace around the dance floor, sweeping me into intricate twirls. His eyes reflected the delight I felt with him taking the lead. The rest of the revelers seemed to disappear as he held me in his arms. I imagined we were floating on sound waves as the melody swirled through the ballroom.

Goddess, I loved my vampire.

Every moment with him felt like magic.

Amaya

That vampire had wrecked me. I lay boneless on the chaise, staring at the coffered ceiling, wondering if I was dead.

His hands had clenched mine when he'd followed with his own release. His hot throbbing cock had had my body pulsing and clenching on him as he'd peppered my face with sweet kisses and the most scandalous promises for future couplings. At the end of it, we were both breathing hard. And he'd collapsed on top of me. But instead of feeling trapped or crushed underneath him, I felt safe. And happy.

A lizard caught my attention as it scurried across the ceiling. *Where are those little pests coming from?* The entire continent seemed suddenly infected with them.

Cullen traced the contour of my face with a fingertip. "What are you thinking about?"

"Lizards."

He frowned. "Not what I expected."

"Have those green lizards always been in the palace, or are they new?"

"Hold on, you're actually thinking about lizards? And not about us and what just happened?"

"Sorry." I wasn't sorry. "The lizard on the ceiling was staring at me and, well—"

He kissed me. I kissed him back. And since our bodies were already touching in the most interesting places, I forgot about the lizards and focused on the vampire prince who was too handsome for *my* own good.

Afterward, Cullen framed my face with his hands. There was still dried blood staining his fingers. We seriously needed to get cleaned up. I didn't even want to look in a mirror. He'd touched me everywhere with his blood-smeared hands.

"I'm making sure you're keeping your attention on me this time," he said when I squirmed underneath him.

"We're filthy. This sofa, the rug, our clothes, there will be no cleaning them. They'll all have to be thrown away. And then someone is going to ask you why."

"Darling dragon, I'm a prince. They can ask, but I don't have to answer." He sucked my lower lip into his mouth. My lips already felt bruised and swollen. How noticeably bruised and swollen were they? Would I be the talk of the palace in the morning? Would everyone be wondering if Prince Cullen had ensnared a dragon of his own? Was that his plan?

And if I returned to the plateau, what would my parents or Anther or the others say about how I looked? Would they be able to smell the spicy, slightly metallic scent of vampire on my skin?

"Let's get you back to my chambers. I'll call for a late-night snack to be brought up. Fruit? Or do you need red meat to replenish your blood? We can clean up"—he kissed me senseless again—"and then we'll get filthy all over again."

Cullen didn't ever need to use compulsion. All he had to do was ply me with his drugging kisses. I lost myself in his mouth for a while. It didn't matter that my lips were sore. I wanted to keep living this forbidden fantasy…with him. Forever.

"I'm leaving with Soren to head to the front tonight," he said when we finally came up for air. "I'll make sure the staff takes care of you in my absence. I can talk to my sister, too. She'll make sure you have everything you need."

He…he expected me to stay? And wait for his return like one of those silly helpless damsels in the horrid novels Trace would bring back from Earst? The damsels who'd drone on endlessly, whining about how lonely their lives were while waiting for their simpering lovers to return from war?

"Why are you scowling? You don't want to stay in my chambers? They're comfortable and spacious, I'll promise you that. I try to keep the bulk of my books in the library. Or, if you'd prefer, I could arrange for you to travel with us. But I doubt the situation at the front will be pretty, or safe. Not that you couldn't hold your own."

Cullen expected me to stay? With him? We-we couldn't.

No. No. No. What have I done? We. Were. Enemies. His people and mine. Were. Enemies.

I slapped his chest and wiggled out from underneath him. It wasn't a graceful escape. I ended up landing hard on my hip.

"What are you doing?" He sat up.

"I'm leaving."

"Leaving? Why?"

"Why?" I flapped my hands and paced while searching for where he'd tossed my pants. I must have been quite a sight, marching around the fancy (but now blood-splattered) parlor, wearing a blood-stained top that was nothing more than dangling straps and no pants or underwear. "Why?"

"Yes, why, Amaya?" He stood and buttoned up his trousers. "What did I do that's making you want to run?"

My heart started to pound so hard I could hear it.

"Amaya, talk to me. Tell me what I did wrong."

"You called me dragon!" I screamed. I didn't care that there was a crowded party happening just outside that door that might overhear me. I didn't even care that this wasn't the thing that had my heart beating like it wanted to break free from my chest. Those were the words, the emotions that needed to come out. "*The man* called me dragon! He never cared about my name! He only cared about what I could do for him!"

"Goddess, Amaya, I would never..." He closed the distanced between us.

But before he could touch me, I turned to air.

I knew I shouldn't have done it. Not after overhearing how his soul found relief in just having me around...just like I found calm in his voice. But I couldn't. I couldn't stay here. This thing between us—whatever it was—could never find a happy ending.

My life had never been my own. Celestina and I had been protected for hundreds of years until a shift in the fates caused our eggs to hatch. We existed *for* the dragons. We belonged *to* the dragons. And right now, my only focus should have been on ways to remind Celestina of her duty to her own kind instead of chasing an orgasmic high that would never last, not even with a vampire prince who liked to play mind games.

As air, I passed through walls, through crowded halls, out a window, and into the cool night where the ocean winds ruled by the ever-silent and often cruel Aquas, God of the Waters, wanted to take me.

"You promised to stay with me."

I never promised anything.

"You made that promise with your body."

I scoffed at that.

"Amaya?"

The ocean below me glittered in the starlight like someone had sprinkled diamonds on the surface of the undulating waves. It was perfect in its beauty. I would have preferred a storm.

"Please, Amaya. Curse me. Threaten me. Talk to me."

I'd let him take my blood. No wonder I'd started experiencing all these *unnatural* feelings. I'd taken his blood. And now he had mine. We'd formed a bond. One I didn't know how to break.

He was the enemy. He only wanted me for what I could do for his kingdom.

"I need you. I need your—"

I slammed a barrier down between us. I couldn't let him tempt me with his calming voice, not when I was feeling emotional and weak because of him. Because of *him*. First, he made me feel giddy. And now I was feeling guilty for running away like a damned coward. I should have skewered him like a hunk of meat instead of running.

I'm sorry. I'm sorry. I'm sorry. I whispered in my head, even though I knew Cullen wouldn't be able to hear it. My mental walls were too strong. Maybe I was whispering the apologies to myself.

I could never come back.

Not for him.

Not when he was poison.

The worst kind of poison.

The kind that had made me care.

Chapter 40

Celestina

The time I spent at the ball sped by. Soren and I socialized with so many courtiers, their names and faces blurred together. We danced a few additional sets together, turning down invitations to dance with others—shockingly rude, but neither Soren nor I wished to dance with anyone else. And we enjoyed refreshments with Soren's lovely sister Princess Priscilla.

Despite the fun I was having, I was anxiously waiting for the evening's end. The sooner we could get our plans into motion, the safer everyone would be.

Our travels toward the border would begin as soon as we left the ball. Soren didn't want a battle with dragons to take place in the middle of a busy city where hundreds of innocents would be harmed, which made moving me away from Sukoon our priority. While we'd been doing our part on the diplomatic front, Raya and Gray were prepping for travel.

Soren hoped the dragons didn't attack until we reached the border. He wanted to use the conflict with Queen Beatrice as cover and let the dragons roast some of Queen Beatrice's undead warriors for us, maybe even get those undead warriors to go after the dragons. According to him, complicating the conflict by making our enemies split their efforts would benefit Fein's position.

Going against the dragons—*my* dragons—didn't feel right.

I hoped I'd be able to talk to Trace and the others and convince them that I was happy with Soren, that this was my life, my choices. If they'd listen to me, truly listen, I believed they could accept that, while I didn't live with the clan, I'd always be looking out for them. But the vision I'd had of the dragons destroying everything in the city and killing my loved ones kept replaying in my mind.

I still hadn't told anyone about it. Not that I needed to. I was sure Soren and Gray and Raya were already picturing something similar in their own minds.

The "how" we planned to fight a kingdom of dragons—if my attempts at diplomacy didn't work—was a trickier matter.

Soren's ancestor had been the one to decimate the dragon population after the War of the Magics. He'd done it by having his warriors ruthlessly kill any dragon they encountered, young and old included, destroy dragon eggs, and burn dragon villages. His goal had been extinction.

"We can't do that. That's barbaric," I'd warned during our earlier planning session.

"King Frendrik the First did what he needed to do to protect the vampires," Gray quickly pointed out. "He did it to create a safe haven, a kingdom for the vampires."

"He tried to wipe out a magical species!"

"The dragons killed scores of innocents," Gray said as if that excused the massacre that had followed. "And none of the vampires could trust that the dragons wouldn't attack again."

While I understood the need to protect one's own, the wholesale killing of a species—a magical species at that—wasn't right. It would *never* be right.

At the ball, the quartet played a lively waltz. The three dance floors were so crowded, several of the pairs bumped into each other.

"That's the last song of the evening," Soren said with obvious relief as he took my hand and led me toward the double doors that opened into the royal apartments. "We're done. If we slip away now, we can be on our way as soon as I finish briefing the king regarding our plans."

"Thank goodness." The back of my neck had been prickling with worry for the past several minutes. "We need to lead the dragons away from the city."

Soren's hand had just touched the door handle when a loud crash, like the shattering of a thousand mirrors, reverberated in the ballroom behind us.

And then the screaming started.

My movements felt painfully slow as I turned around. Soren's arms went around my shoulders, holding me back. Three dragons had broken through the glass ceiling. They flapped their massive leathery wings while breathing fire, burning everything beneath them.

Chaos erupted in the ballroom as courtiers, nobles, and guests dashed for the doors. The screams increased when people caught fire. The King's Guards flooded into the space from every corner. They herded guests toward the exits while holding their shields above their heads, as if those thin metal pieces could stop dragon fire.

Soren's grip around me tightened.

"This is happening sooner than we anticipated," he said. My heart was beating faster than it should while he sounded so damned calm. "We need to get you out of here." Soren tugged me toward the doors.

"Your parents!" I tried to hold my ground.

"Will get themselves to safety." He threw the doors open and pushed me through.

"Your brother!"

Soren slammed the doors closed, muffling the destruction exploding inside the ballroom.

"Can fend for himself."

"But I need to stop them!" How was I going to stop rampaging dragons without getting roasted myself? They weren't searching for me. They weren't attacking only the armed guards. They were killing indiscriminately. "I could use my growly voice."

"Will they hear you over all that screaming?" Soren shook his head. "I can't take that risk. I *won't* take that risk with you."

Gray and Raya ran up to us in the elegant corridor. They wore battle leathers and traveling cloaks. Raya thrust a traveling cloak at me. "There's no time for either of you to get changed."

"The horses are ready," Gray reported. "There's a change of clothes for each of you in their packs."

"Do you think the dragons can sense you?" Soren asked as he helped drape the cloak over my shoulders. "Do you think they'll know if we leave the city?"

I had no idea. "I'm going to have to show my face."

"No. That's not going to happen."

It would if I used my growly voice to compel him to change his mind. But I didn't want to do that. Not yet. He'd always been so careful not to issue orders that compelled me to do whatever he said. Another idea came to me. "Amaya. We need to find her. She can help."

"She's likely out there helping them destroy us." Gray gestured toward the ceiling.

"She wouldn't—" But I didn't know that. She'd warned us that this would happen, but she'd also made it clear that her loyalties would always remain with the dragons.

"She was with Cullen in the ladies' retiring parlor not that long ago," Soren said. "They were..." He flicked the thought away with a wave of his hand. "We need to find them. Follow me. We can use a servant's passage to get there without entering the ballroom."

Soren slid open a panel in the wall and took off jogging down a long, undecorated corridor. "Gray! Fetch my sword."

"Not happening. I won't be leaving your side with those dragons in the palace," Gray said as he kept pace with Soren.

"The dragons are too big to get into the passageways. Get my sword."

"You're forgetting they can take human forms," I reminded all of them. "The attack on the ballroom could be a diversion." I didn't recognize any of those three dragons that had crashed through the ceiling. Dragons shaped as humans could be entering the palace even now.

"Even more reason that I need a weapon."

Gray grunted and handed Soren one of his twin blades.

"I'd give you one of my daggers," Raya said, "but I'm guessing you're wearing at least one with that fancy suit."

Soren nodded as he skidded around a corner.

I was breathing hard and close to stopping to put my hands on my knees. I wasn't used to running like this. Also, these flimsy slippers weren't meant for mad dashes around the palace.

Raya slowed her pace to meet mine. "Lose the shoes."

"What?"

"You'll do better barefoot."

"And what will I do once we reach the horses?"

"Let's get you out of the palace alive first."

"The dragons won't kill me." I was fairly certain of that. If the dragons had crashed through the ceiling a few minutes earlier, I would have still been in the center of the ballroom. And dead from that blast of fire. Maybe the dragons had written me off as a lost cause. Maybe they'd realized that I wouldn't help them fight against my friends. And they'd decided to take me out along with half the city.

Oh! I wanted to scream. All of this was happening because of me.

I should have never left the plateau!

"Focus on surviving," Raya cautioned. She must have noticed that I'd started to spiral into a panic attack. "We're in crisis mode. Don't think about anything other than living to see the next minute. And the next. And the next. Now is not the time for big picture thinking."

A few yards down the hall, we ran into Cullen. He stumbled and Soren caught his arms.

"What the hell happened to you?" Gray demanded. Cullen looked as pale as milk. His neck was raw with a barely healed wound and bloody. His clothes were disheveled and soaked through with blood. "Did the dragons already get to you?"

Cullen shook his head. "I'm fine."

"You're not fine." He could barely stand, but he didn't need me telling him that. "Where's Amaya? She can stop the attack."

Cullen looked away from us. Soren shook him harder.

"Answer Sky Girl. Where did Amaya go? We need to find her."

"I scared her away." He closed his eyes and trembled in silence. When he opened his eyes, he looked even more frustrated and defeated than before. "She's left the palace. And the city."

"Why would she leave?" I demanded. I found it hard to believe she'd leave just as the clan started to attack.

"I asked her to stay. With me. Here. I scared her."

He wanted her to…? "She's the one who attacked you?"

He touched his neck. "This wasn't an attack. It happened in the heat of—" He straightened. "Never mind. Our parents, Soren. Are they safe?"

"The King's Guards surrounded them when the ceiling came down. I'm sure they got whisked off to the underground passages and are on their way out of the palace."

"And Pris? Did you see her?" Cullen's voice grew more strained.

"Pris is no wilting flower. She can take care of herself." Soren sounded so sure of it. I hoped he was right. "Besides, Tristan that King's Guard she allows to crawl into her bed never strays far from her side. She'll be well protected as she directs efforts to tend to the wounded."

"She allows *who* to do *what?*" Cullen shouted. "Never mind. As long as she's safe."

"She's tougher than you give her credit for," Soren said as we moved quickly down the hallway.

"I hope so." The palace shook with a loud boom. "Sounds like the guards pulled out the cannons."

A cannon could shoot a dragon out of the sky. "I need to get out there. I need to command the dragons to stop before anyone else gets hurt." Especially the dragons. There were so few of them...of *us*...left already.

"Celestina." Soren turned his head to the ceiling as if keeping himself from shouting at me.

"If I can talk to them, I can stop them."

"They might kill you," Soren warned.

"Or take you," Raya added.

"I think we should let her do it," Cullen said. "It might be the only way to stop this before the entire city catches fire."

Soren's outraged gaze shot to his brother's. "I can't put her at risk."

"It's a risk you have to make if it means saving your kingdom." I put my hand on his arm. "You told me that you were loving me *and* using me. Let me do this."

"Dammit, I did say that." When he looked at me, his eyes hardened. "But I was wrong, Celestina. I can't. I can't use you in any way that puts you in danger. Every instinct in me is demanding I take you down to the underground passages to get you out of the palace using the same route my parents are using."

"But your honor won't allow you to run while your kingdom is torn apart. Mine won't, either. Let's do this together, Soren. Let's stop the dragons from destroying your city." I swallowed hard. "Please."

His jaw tightened as he gave a stiff nod. He held my hand so tightly, my bones ached. But I didn't want him to loosen his grip. I never wanted him to let go.

Chapter 41

Celestina

The five of us—Soren, Cullen, Raya, Gray, and I—stood outside the palace and watched the night sky in silent horror. Every dragon living in the Andalotian Plateau must have come. All around the city fires blazed, lighting up the night with their destructive glow. It was worse than I'd feared. This *was* the vision come to life.

Cullen looked at me and shook his head. He walked away from us, his eyes tightly closed, his hands curled into fists. Had he given up?

Was this where we'd all die? Was this both prophecies (mine and Soren's) coming together to create one spectacular disaster?

Soren never let go of my hand. "We'll figure something out," he said as if he could hear my thoughts. He couldn't. But I was sure he was thinking the same things. The dragons would destroy the city. Queen Beatrice would lead her unnatural army of undead warriors into the Fein kingdom, take the land as her own, and exploit those who lived here.

Vampires would be drained for their healing blood.

Humans used as slave labor.

Goddess, how I wished things could be different. But there was no going back in time, no changing reality.

This was our ending.

I supposed I should have always known it would never be a happy one.

Amaya

Come.
Back.

The words whispered in my mind. They shouldn't have. I had all my barriers up. Doors closed. Windows latched. Flues covered. Cullen shouldn't have been able to get in.

"Leave me alone."

He'd said that I'd forged this pathway between us. Well, he'd helped. Our constant thinking of each other, constant dipping into each other's minds, peeking into each other's worlds had worn a path—much like the worn away fibers on a well-traversed rug—the barriers where we'd traveled had been eroded. Not completely gone. But weathered enough that his plea had been able to slip through.

I tried to tighten things up, to block him. I needed time away from him. He confused me. Being near him made me want things I shouldn't want.

The.

Dragons.

His disjointed message continued to leak in.

I turned to my dragon form and instead of simply following the eddies of air above the ocean, I flew faster, further out over the open water. Maybe distance would relieve me of my desire to rush back to him, to spar with him, to tease him.

To kiss him.

Dammit. I was a dragon. I was above all those messy feelings.

Am I? Wasn't this *need* exactly how all the other magical creatures were made? Dragons couldn't help themselves when it came to mixing with the other creatures on the continent. There were the magical humans, the mammoth cats, the venomous bungeroos, the chorts. All dragon-made from a lustful encounter with one that wasn't our kind.

But I was a *midnight* dragon. I was better. Harder. Crueler.

I didn't want to rush back to him. I couldn't want that.

Celes—

Nnn—

Help—

Not a coherent message, but enough had leaked through to get my attention.

"Celestina? What's wrong with Celestina?" I turned around and started the journey over the ocean back to Sukoon, cursing myself for having flown so far.

"Protect her," I pushed the message toward Cullen. *"I'm on my way."*

"Thank the goddess." I could feel the surge of relief in his thoughts in response to my reply. I threw open the pathway between us and looked through his eyes. And saw my fellow dragons scorch the buildings all around Cullen. Celestina was there, huddled next to Soren. If the fire didn't get them, the smoke may choke them to death. Did vampires need air to stay alive? Celestina did.

"What the hell are you doing?" I sent the message to Anther. *"You're going to*

kill the moonlight dragon!"

No reply came. He wasn't thinking of me.

"Stop the attack! You're going to harm the moonlight dragon!" I sent that message to as many dragons as I could picture in my mind at the same time.

Silence answered me.

"Do you need me to shout your name?" Cullen asked after I'd cursed in frustration.

"Will they be able to hear you?" If the dragons could hear Cullen, they could hear Celestina. And she could use her powers to compel my idiot clan to stop their attack.

"No. The dragons are flying too high. And the noise on the ground is too loud."

The sound of a cannon blast reverberated through the pathway I shared with Cullen. I watched through his eyes as the dragons scattered out of the way of the slow-moving cannonball.

The lights of the capital grew brighter as I shot like an arrow through the sky back toward Sukoon. I hoped I could get there in time.

Celestina

Short of climbing up to the highest tower and tossing myself off the side, I didn't know how to catch the dragons' attention. They weren't here to save me or to return me to the clan. They were here to destroy the place that had dared to help me. I could feel their fury pounding against my skin. My own magic fought against the bonds that kept it caged. It wanted out. It wanted to take to the skies and rip those other dragons' throats out for daring to touch the sparkly treasure that belonged to me.

This place. These vampires. They were my hoard. *My* hoard.

I tossed back my head and screamed.

Soren wrapped his arms around me. A spark shot between us. It blasted him away from me. He landed on the ground several yards away, dazed, shaking his head.

Gray rushed to Soren. Raya ran to me.

"What the hell was that?" Gray shouted as he scanned the area, searching for invisible enemies.

Soren rubbed his arm. Were those burns? Had my touch burned him? "Our Sky Girl is furious, and we already know she's dangerous when that happens." He didn't sound worried or scared of my out-of-control powers. He sounded...*pleased?*

His gaze locked on to mine as a smile creased the corners of a mouth I suddenly wanted to lick.

"What can we do to amplify it?" Raya pointed to the smoldering sky. "To get your rage up there?"

Soren rubbed the back of his neck as he pushed to his feet. "I'm not sure we can." He looked over at me. "Can you think of a way?"

At that very moment, a dragon soared overhead sending out a spray of white fire that set the royal stables blazing.

"Shit. The horses!" Gray shouted.

The four of us set off running in that direction. Soren kept pace next to me.

"I can't control it," I told him. "I wish I knew how."

"We'll figure it out."

If we live that long.

With all of us working together—I wasn't sure where Cullen had disappeared to—we managed to clear the stables, saving the horses and the stable hands who refused to leave until every last horse was moved to somewhere safe.

Posey, the horse I'd ridden to reach the capital, nudged my hand as if thanking me as I led her to a stable yard. I pressed my forehead to her long face and soaked in the simple warmth of her spirit. I drew strength from the connection.

I didn't know how to stop the dragons, but I did know how to help minimize the damage. "We need to get out into the city and help fight the fires," I called to the others.

"Agreed!" Soren barked orders at anyone he spotted as we ran toward the palace gates, directing them to join us in helping the citizens of Sukoon.

"What about the library?" I shouted as we climbed a long ladder to help a café shop owner put out a blaze on the roof of a neighboring apartment building. The café had already been lost.

The Palladian Library spanned an entire block and was several stories high. To lose that library would mean losing huge chunks of the continent's knowledge and history.

"The library is fireproof," Soren shouted over the roar of the fires popping up all around us. He tossed a huge bucket of water over the roof, making the fire sizzle and pop. I took the empty bucket and handed it to the person next to me to be handed back down the line to be refilled. "Also, the mages are instructed to go straight there and set up an impenetrable ward if the city is ever in danger. The books are safe."

"All the mages?" I glanced over my shoulder at the palace that already looked half-destroyed. "Hopefully, these aren't the same wards the mages constructed to protect the royal properties."

"Kings and queens can be replaced." He tossed another bucket of water on the roof. This one washed over the rest of the smoldering flames, completely extinguishing this fire. "The knowledge in those books cannot. The mages are sent to protect the irreplaceable."

It hurt to hear Soren calling his parents replaceable. But I supposed on a grander scale he was right. And he'd seemed confident that his parents were on their way a to safe shelter.

"I'm glad." We climbed off the roof. Raya surged ahead of us, scouting out where we were needed most. Cannons continued to boom from the palace. Still, none of the dragons seemed to care. They raged as if their fire had no end.

We went from building to building. Helping. Providing words of comfort, whatever small snippets of support we could offer, and letting people know where safe shelters could be found. The library, with its impenetrable wards, was one of the many shelters the royals where the citizens were being sent. There was also a warren of tunnels underneath the city where the Fein could escape the fires above.

Helping others helped me calm the pulsing magic battering against Queen Frieda's bindings. I could draw a deep breath again without feeling as if I would be torn apart from the inside out.

A dragon screamed overhead as we moved through a narrow alleyway. We were helping a young family search for their youngest child who'd run off in terror when the attacks had first started. It wasn't the first dragon to swoop above us. But as soon as it had moved on, Cullen came running from the opposite direction. We'd not seen him since he'd wandered off outside the palace.

"There you are!" he shouted at us. "You shouldn't have left the palace. Took too damned long to find you."

"In case you haven't noticed, there's an entire city in crisis." Soren gestured to the buildings around us. "You're welcome to join in and help."

"We're searching for a four-year-old girl." I explained how she'd run away when the dragons had started their assault. "She's alone and terrified."

Cullen closed his eyes and rubbed his temples. His arm shot out to the right side of the alley. He pointed at a wooden box meant for the storage of rubbish containers. "There." He opened his eyes and adjusted his glasses. "I need you to come with me, Celestina. Amaya is back, and she might be able to help us. But she won't do anything until she sees that you're safe."

We followed Cullen to a city park where Amaya was waiting. She was in her human form and pacing. When she saw me, she rushed across the distance between us. Thinking she might attack me, I froze. But when her arms tightened around me and the warmth of her hug surrounded me, I relaxed. And thankfully, no magical explosions happened from our touching.

"You're safe," she whispered. "You're safe."

I wiggled out of her embrace and pointed to the sky. "Can you stop them?"

"I've already tried. The clan has been worked into a frenzy, thinking they've lost you. There's no reasoning with any of them, not even my brother will listen to me."

"How about your mother?" I couldn't imagine the soft-spoken healer of the clan agreeing to attack innocents.

Amaya shook her head. "If she's here, I couldn't find her. Something tells me she decided to stay back at the plateau." She gestured to the sky. "The ones who have never left the plateau and have lived their entire lives in fear of a world they'd never seen are the ones doing the most damage now."

"Fly me up to them. I'll compel them to stop."

Amaya shook her head. Soren was shaking his head, too.

"That's a temporary fix," Amaya said. "They'll only come back and start again once the compulsion clears."

"Then what can we do?" Raya shouted.

Amaya looked at me, and I knew the answer. My stomach clenched.

"No," Soren said. He took my hand as if he planned to never let me go. *Don't let me go.* "No. There has to be a different way."

"What?" Gray asked. "What needs to happen?"

Raya smacked his arm and gave him a look.

Cullen bit his lower lip and turned away.

I drew Soren away from the others. Several yards to the left of us sat a bench surrounded by tall hedges on three sides. It would give us an illusion of privacy. The vampires had excellent hearing and could easily listen in on our conversation if they wanted to. But I needed to feel like we didn't have an audience for this conversation.

A part of me didn't believe Soren would give me up, not even if letting me go would save his own kingdom.

"I won't *ever* give you up," he said as if he'd heard me. I knew he hadn't. But he had to know what I was thinking. He had to know what needed to be done. "I can't."

I reached up and cradled the sides of his face in my hands. His scruffy whiskers made me want to rub my cheek against his. He smelled of pine and snow and caramel, my favorite scents in the entire continent. I breathed in deeply, trying to memorize his scent. "Soren, I love you."

He closed his eyes and pressed his cheek into my palm. "No, Celestina, *please.*"

"My life has never been my own. I was born to serve a purpose, to serve the dragons. They have waited generations for the promise of me to come to them. And they will burn the world to the ground until I agree to fulfill that promise."

"There has to be another way." His voice sounded husky. He still had his eyes closed. He held on to my hands so I wouldn't move them away from his face.

Goddess, I wished for *any* solution other than the two of us having to live our lives apart, to live as enemies. "What other way? I'm not willing to fight the dragons. There's a part of me here"—I touched my hand to my chest—"that feels the dragon fire, that feels the magic that I don't know how to unbind, that knows I belong with the dragons." I dragged in a shaky breath. "Before I met you, I knew this with my whole heart. My entire being would ache to go to the dragons who'd kept watch in the valley. They were the missing pieces from my life. What I'd once believed to be the imagination of a lonely child, turned out to be the longings of a creature being kept hostage in a world that wasn't hers."

"And then you met me?" he guessed.

"And then I fell in love with you," I corrected. "I fell so hard that my yearning for my dragons got pushed aside. But not lost. Only muddled within the haze of love. And the dragons, the clan, they never forgot about me. They never questioned where I belonged. Would you ask me to turn my back on my own kind? To wage a war against the blood of my blood?"

He opened his eyes. The gold flecks in his eyes sparkled like we were standing in bright sunlight even though it was a moonless sky. "I will go with you."

How I wished he could come with me and stay with me forever.

"If you came, you couldn't be there as my mate. Or my bonded anything," it hurt to admit. The dragons expected me to produce a new generation of moonlight dragons, which would mean I would have to mate with a dragon. Perhaps even mate with multiple dragons throughout my lifetime. It would be hell for Soren to give up his life, his family, his commitments to this kingdom to come with me to the plateau only to watch me go to another male's bed. "My future has already been cast."

"Recast it."

"Soren."

"I don't want to let you go. I can't let you go. I love you, Celestina. I love you so much that the thought of losing you tears a hole in my chest that I don't think will ever heal. And that's just from the *thought* of losing you. What will losing you do to me?" He stopped himself and pressed his lips together. "You are—and have been ever since I met you in the bailey yard protecting Queen Beatrice's young sons—my guiding star, my hope for tomorrow, the reason to smile in the morning. You, Princess Celestina, are as beautiful as a sunrise with the heart of a warrior. I will never love another as purely or as completely as I love you."

"Oh, Soren." How could I leave him?

I looked over my shoulder at the burning city behind us. I needed to leave for his kingdom, for his people. It would be beyond selfish to do otherwise.

"Goodbye, my love," I barely managed to whisper as tears clogged my throat.

Soren cupped my face and closed his lips over mine. His kiss was brutal and demanding and a silent reminder that he had no desire to live in a world without me.

But he couldn't rewrite the laws of nature like he'd once promised to do for me. He couldn't keep me with him without threatening his kingdom, his family, our lives. I wouldn't want him to.

Slowly, his lips pulled away from mine. I cried out as cold air rushed in, chasing away the heat we'd shared.

"We need to go," Amaya said. Her hand tightened around my wrist. I hadn't even heard her creep up behind us. "We need to stop them before they destroy everything here."

I let her pull me away from Soren.

"I'll never stop loving you." My voice was rocky with emotion. "I'll never stop—"

Soren reached for me. But Amaya wrapped her arms around my middle and shot into the air, changing into her dragon form before she started to fall. Her leather wings filled with air and lifted us higher.

"I've told Trace and the others that I have you. They should back off their attacks now."

I nodded as I watched my infuriating green dragon incinerate a farmhouse on a distant hillside. How could he do that? People lived in that house. Children lived there. From this great height, I could see the silhouette of a family with several small children fleeing the blazing house.

"Please," I thought as strongly as I could. *"Please, get him to stop."*

The green dragon was swooping down as if he planned to kill the helpless farm family. If I were closer, I would have used my powers to compel him to stop.

"Get me closer!" I growled at Amaya, compelling her to move faster to get me to shouting range. *"Go fast!"*

"Stop using compulsion!" Amaya complained, but she pressed her wings back and stretched out her neck. The wind hurt as it rushed past us.

"Stop!" I shouted in my growly voice when we were close enough. *"Stop! Don't hurt them! Don't hurt anyone! It is OVER!"*

The green dragon screeched. The sound sent a chill down my spine. But I noticed that he'd changed his direction. He screeched again, sounding like he was in pain. If pressing that compulsion on him had hurt him, I regretted it. But if my actions saved the lives of the innocents in Fein, I would do it all over again.

"It's over." Amaya sent the message to the dragons who were still attacking the capital city. *"I have Celestina. We're all going back to the plateau."*

I watched with growing relief as the dragons flying over the city rose higher into the air and away from the city.

"We did it," she sent the words into my mind. *"It's over."*

Those words rang true for me in more ways than one. My heart cried as I absorbed them. It *was* over. I'd never see Soren again. Or if I ever did, we'd be facing each other from opposite sides of a battlefield.

I'd fallen hopelessly in love with the wrong male and have destroyed my chance for happiness.

Chapter 42

Celestina

Barefoot and wearing nothing more than my sleeveless silver dress, I was freezing by the time Amaya crashed down on the plateau. I rolled in the grass, scraping my knees and elbows, tearing the skirt of the dress. Trace landed next to us and immediately took his naked human form. Breathing hard, he towered over me. His eyes flared with rage.

I screeched and scooted back as he reached for me.

"Don't—!" I started to command him not to touch me. I used my growly voice. Before I could get all the words out, he slapped his hand over my mouth and dragged me to my feet. He pressed my head to his bare chest to keep me from being able to speak and grabbed a cloth handkerchief from one of the lads running up to greet us. He stuffed the cloth into my mouth so deep I was gagging on it. He then grabbed another handkerchief and tied it around my head to hold the gag in place.

"That'll keep you from trying any of those dirty tricks of yours."

"Where are you taking her?" Amaya demanded. She'd shifted into her human form, pulling on black pants and a black sweater through her magic. This seemed to surprise a few of the dragons who landed around us. She clutched a book to her chest with her left hand and held a dagger ready for battle in her right.

Trace only growled as he dragged me down the street and toward his shop. She ran after him, but he threatened to break my arm if Amaya didn't stay back. He pulled me into his shop and locked the door behind him.

"You can't hurt her!" Amaya pounded on the door. "She willingly returned to us!" There was more pounding. "She's the clan's savior!"

Trace didn't react. He closed his hands over mine like manacles as he pulled me toward the stairs. I fought with all my strength to keep from being taken up to the bedrooms against my will. I'd agreed to come back to him. I'd agreed to let this be my life. Why was he making my return violent?

"Come away from here, Amaya," Drix shouted at his daughter. There was what sounded like a scuffle outside the door. "He won't kill her," his voice sounded strained. There was a thud against the door. "But he will teach her a lesson in obedience." There was another thud against the door. "As is his right."

No one had that right, not over me, not over anybody. I managed to kick Trace in the shin hard enough that he stumbled. In retaliation, he slammed my head against the nearest wall. The room spun in and out of focus.

Taking advantage of my disorientation from the blow, he moved quickly, dragging me up the stairs, down the hallway, and into the bedroom I'd been using.

The lone window in the room, the same window Soren had used as our escape route, had been boarded up. Trace tossed me onto the bed, which had been stripped down to the bare mattress. He grabbed a length of rope that had been left on the bed and wrapped it around my wrists. With quick movements he secured the rope to the heavy wooden bedframe, leaving me very little slack. He'd tied the rope so tightly, my fingers immediately started turning blue and my hands throbbed. I knelt on the bed and pressed my hands to the bedframe to give the rope as much slack as possible.

I'd freed myself from ropes before when I was with Soren. But I had no idea how I'd managed to break through the binding spell to get my magic to work while we were in that ship's cabin together. And because I'd slipped free from the ropes without having to practice untying Soren's impossible knots, I never did master the skill Soren had been trying to teach me. Even so, I twisted and turned my bound wrists, hoping to spark my magic and free me from the tight bindings.

My head was still spinning from being slammed against the wall, and my stomach was now rebelling. If I threw up, it would be all over myself. And I had a feeling Trace would end up blaming me for it and leave me wallowing in my own sick. I took long, slow breaths, hoping to keep from vomiting.

After testing the bindings to ensure I couldn't escape, he ripped the rag from my mouth.

The first thing I did was summon my growly voice.

He slapped his hand over my mouth so fast, I didn't manage to utter a sound. "If you try to use your magic to compel me, I'll cut out your tongue. Nod if you understand."

He sounded so hard, so angry. My entire body started to tremble as I carefully nodded.

"Good girl." He lifted his hand.

I licked my sore lips. "If you cut out my tongue, I'll lose the only power I have. I'll be useless to you."

"Useless, Celestina?" He tilted his head to one side as he peered at me so intently, I shrank back from him as far as the rope would allow. "Even if we never figure out how to free your dragon form from Queen Frieda's bindings, the clan will still be able to use you, or more precisely, use your body to create more moonlight dragons."

"I'll not consent to that."

He curled his lip. "You are the last of a powerful line of dragons. If we have to strip you naked and tie you down, you will fulfill your role as the future of our kind."

"You—you promised to protect me." My voice broke. And I hated that. I didn't want to show him any of my vulnerable pieces.

"I promised to protect the future of our clan from our enemies. I wasted twenty-three fucking years following you around, making sure you were safe. I didn't do that for you. I did that for the clan. I did that to secure our future. You, my pretty dragon, dove out that window, rushed straight to our enemies, and handed your body over to the worst of their kind."

"Soren is the best…of any kind."

Trace dug his nails into his palms as he squeezed his hands into tight fists. "Don't. Ever. Say. That. Bastard's. Name. Again."

"Or you'll cut out my tongue?"

"I will. Silence is what I want—what I need from you right now."

I pressed my lips together. I'd willingly returned to stop them from attacking the Fein. And still, Trace acted like they'd had to drag me back to the plateau.

He moved about the room, righting a bedside table that had toppled. Using his fire, he started a blaze in the fireplace. He then dug a blanket from a trunk and laid it across the foot of the narrow bed.

Once he'd done all of that, he stood in the middle of the room, naked and angry. He glanced over at me and then at the boarded-up window. His hands flew up to his head and tugged at his hair as if he was trying to pull it out. "This wasn't what I wanted," he muttered to himself. A tremor passed through his muscles. "As soon as we figure out how to get you to take your dragon form, you'll change your mind about us. You'll accept that this is where you belong. And you'll regenerate that tongue I'm sure I'm going to be forced to slice from your mouth tonight."

"And until that happens, you're going to keep me tied up like this?"

"It's unfortunate. But yes." Trace crouched next to the bed. He reached out to me like he was going to touch my face. I flinched away. His hand closed into a fist that he rested on the mattress next to my knee. "This isn't your fault, Celestina. I don't want you to think I blame you. Not completely. You were raised with lies and handed over to those who wanted to exploit your powers. I can't blame you for believing those who pretended to love you any more than I would blame a thirsty horse from drinking water from a contaminated pond."

He didn't blame me, and yet he still abused me? The bastard.

"I used to love watching the dragons in the valley. I used to dream that one day I would join with them, live with them. You showed me today that my believing I could be happy with any of you was the lie I'd been telling myself."

"You weren't raised to be who you should be. You don't understand what it means to be a dragon."

"What it means to be a dragon?" I scoffed. "You mean what it means to be like you? I will never want to be like that. You killed so many innocents tonight. Vampires and humans who had never done anything to you. Many who once believed dragons were a storyteller's myth. And now those who survive will fear and hate you. They will come and hunt you."

"None of those deaths would have had to happen if you hadn't run from us."

"No." The word felt ripped from my tear-drenched throat. "No. I won't take the blame for your actions when all I did was stand up for myself. I have a right to live my life on my terms."

"A right? You are a gift to our clan from our ancestors. You have no rights. And if you refuse to accept the blame for your misguided actions, that's fine. But I guarantee that the vampires knew that taking you from our land, from this fucking room was an act of war. If they didn't want fire to rain down on their cities, they should have kept their asses out of clan business."

"No. Those who came to rescue me are my family. And families stand up for each other. The clan should have done better, made a different choice." I swallowed down the sob that was threatening to choke me. "By choosing wholesale violence, you've become the monster you set out to slay."

Amaya

I managed to kick the door one last time before my father pulled me away from Trace's weaving shop. All that accomplished, though, was a bruised big toe. I still had Cullen's book clutched to my chest. My father was scolding me for rushing into enemy territory instead of waiting for the clan to move in as a unified front.

I wanted to tell him about my interaction with Prince Cullen and how we'd helped each other. But I could feel the aggression beating off him like heat from a fire and shut my mouth. He'd been part of the force that had attacked the capital city. And even though he was older, he'd trained me. I knew how skilled a fighter his dragon could be. If I told him that I'd gone to the palace, that I'd befriended the vampires, even danced with one of them at a ball, he'd likely handle me just as roughly as Trace was handling Celestina.

"I brought Celestina home without anyone having to force her," I pointed out, not letting the man who'd raised me intimidate me. "You're welcome."

I spun out of his hold and ducked down a side road.

"Where are you heading now?" Drix sounded exasperated.

"To Ivy and Gregory's," I called over my shoulder. "I found a history book that Gregory will want."

That was likely the only answer I could give him that wouldn't get me dragged back to the manor house by my ear. "Come straight home after you're done there!" he called. I raised my hand to let him know I'd heard him.

I made it halfway to Ivy and Gregory's cottage when I stopped in the middle of the path. I stared at the book in my hand.

I was *so* not a reader. I'd told Cullen that, and yet he'd still gifted me this book. Gregory would know what to do with it.

Although it had been written by a midnight dragon and it had instructed me on how to shift clothes onto my body and pull objects to me when moving from one form to another, it wasn't something I should keep.

Gregory would love the history that I'd scanned in the book's pages. He'd know what to do with the knowledge packed in every sentence. This was a great treasure for the clan. I really should take it straight to him.

I opened the book to a random page and tenderly ran my hand over the slightly raised letters. Prince Cullen had translated the book from Draco Falco. He'd written these words with his own hand. I felt a push of warmth through the pathway that still existed between us.

"Missing me already?" The teasing words flowed like a gentle summer rain into my mind.

"Missing you? That's insulting." I couldn't stop myself from answering when I knew I should try harder to block him.

I could feel his pleasure fill my thoughts like the tickle of bubbles against my skin.

"How is Celestina faring?" He had to go and ask.

I slammed the connection between us closed before he could feel my distress about what Trace was possibly doing to Celestina right now. I hadn't given up on helping her. But I needed to figure out how to get her into a better situation without getting myself locked away in my room for another several weeks.

What I really needed to do was figure out how to free Celestina's bound up dragon. If she had the ability to fight back, she wouldn't be so helpless around the rest of us. We were all a rather feral bunch of creatures. But despite our wild natures, Trace had stepped well over the line with that possessive shit he was pulling with Celestina.

I looked at Cullen's book again. I hadn't had a chance to read the entire thing. And I wanted to. *Not because reading the book would make me feel closer to Cullen and his stupid handsome face.*

Instead of making my way to Gregory's cottage, I changed course and stomped toward the manor house. It didn't take long to get to my favorite spot in the library.

Before opening the book, I sat in silence for a few minutes, hoping I could feel the old lady's presence. Hoping she'd have a few words of wisdom for me.

The silence stretched on unbroken. The library felt cold and empty.

She must have stuck to her word and moved on.

With a sigh, I finally opened the book and proceeded to read every translated word Cullen had written down. The first chapter discussed the differences between male and female dragons and their relationships with their mothers. The passage reminded me how strong the maternal figures were in our society. I sat back and smiled. I suddenly knew exactly what I needed to do to rescue Celestina from Trace without starting another war.

Celestina

I needed to pee.

I didn't know how long I'd been left alone and tethered to this bed.

With the window boarded closed, I couldn't see the sun to mark the passage of time. The fire behind the grate had long burned through its fuel.

I'd slept uncomfortably and fitfully on the bed. Alone. *Thankfully, alone.* My hands throbbed like a heartbeat from the tight rope. My arms ached from not being able to move them into a comfortable position. And I shivered from the cold since I couldn't use my hands to put the blanket over me.

Had he laid the warm blanket on the foot of the bed to torment me?

Somehow, I doubted it. It felt as if he hadn't thought through any of his angry actions.

I'd tried calling for him to come help me, to untie me, to let me go pee. Trace either couldn't hear me, or he refused to come.

No matter how many times I tried to conjure my magic throughout the night and that morning, it refused to answer me, refused to slip through Queen Frieda's binding spell to free my hands from the ropes.

"Please!" I begged, becoming desperate. I hoped Trace wouldn't lose his patience and cut out my tongue. "Please!" I really didn't want to empty my bladder on the bed.

The door swung open, allowing in a stinging shaft of bright light. I turned my head away from the door.

"I have to pee," I rasped. "Please, don't punish me for—"

"We're not here to punish you." That wasn't Trace's furious voice.

"Amaya?"

"I brought some friends to help clean you up and get you fed."

"I have to pee."

"We'll get you taken care of." I recognized that voice, too.

"Juniper?"

"That's me, dear." Warm hands deftly untied the knots holding my wrists hostage. "I have a salve that will help with those rope burns and slow the bleeding." I hadn't even noticed that my wrists were oozing blood.

"Let's get her to the bathroom first," a third woman said. By that time my eyes had adjusted to the light streaming into the room from the open door. This woman had the same brown hair and crystal blue eyes as the male who'd tethered me to this bed.

"You're Trace's mother." I couldn't remember her name, or even recall if I'd ever been told it. "The artist."

"Yes, dear. I'm Gwen." She hooked her hands under my arms and gently helped me to my feet. "The washroom is this way."

After I'd taken care of business and washed my face and raw wrists, I stepped out of the washroom to find Gwen standing outside the door waiting for me.

"Look at you!" Gwen had a warm smile that held no expectations. "You look so different from when you were a hatchling. Especially, your eyes. I don't believe I've ever seen a pair of mismatched eyes. They're so pretty. You'll have to let me paint you."

I briefly considered using my powers of compulsion to force her to help me escape. But where was the need? The three had already promised to help. And if I were to escape, Trace would only convince the clan to attack the Fein again.

I couldn't allow that to happen, which meant I had to stay and make the best of this horrible situation.

"You don't have to tie me to the bed or anywhere else again," I said when Gwen returned me to the bedroom. I couldn't manage to look any of them in the eye. I'd messed up. If I hadn't run away, none of those lives in Fein would have been lost. Running hadn't solved anything. Here I was, back in the same room where I'd started. Only now, everyone hated me. "I don't plan to leave here. Ever."

"Oh, Little Moonglow, we're not here to abuse you," Juniper said, using the nickname Amaya had been using for me. "Amaya explained how you willingly came back to us. We're here to make sure no one harms you."

Her gentle voice nearly broke me. The memory of the fires and deaths in Sukoon—that had looked so similar to the vision the old seer had forced on me—flashed in my mind. I wanted to curl into a ball and hide. At least my friends hadn't died. "I am sorry for the trouble I caused."

Gwen sighed. "Celestina, dear. I'm not excusing my son's abhorrent behavior toward you." She gestured to my mangled wrists that Juniper had started dabbing a cooling salve onto. "But I would like to explain it. When you were taken as a baby, Trace lost his entire family. His father, two older brothers and, his eldest sister died. I retreated into my painting. His younger sister mated with a family friend, choosing to start a new life with him. And his younger brother turned to a life of living outside of clan laws.

"Trace hadn't even begun to process his grief for his lost family when he volunteered to go after you. At first, he'd thought he'd be able to steal you back from Queen Frieda. Later, he volunteered to watch over you, to do everything in his power to keep you safe. You were the hope for our future, so he didn't see this as a great sacrifice. But it was a sacrifice. More than twenty years living away from the clan. Twenty years denying himself the chance of finding a mate who would love him. Over time, the clan leaders began to recognize Trace's sacrifice. No mate. His shop shuttered. His life on hold indefinitely. And while he trained young dragons about life outside the plateau, he'd had very little interaction with his own kind. It was rare that he'd return to the plateau. And when he did come, he never could stay long.

"It was the clan council, worried he'd give up watching over you, that started to make promises. They're the ones who put in his head that you would be his once we rescued you. At first, he'd balked at this idea. You were just a warmling at the time. Too young to even be considered for mating. But as the years wore on, in his loneliness, he started to build up this ideal life with you. He'd watched you for so long, I believe he began to think he knew you. Perhaps even thought he loved you."

"And he grew to believe I loved him as well?" I guessed.

Gwen nodded sadly. "He may have."

"You have to understand how the clan put all our hopes into the idea of getting you back," Juniper added as she finished rubbing the salve on my wounded wrists. "Whenever a problem arose on the plateau, the council would promise that returning the moonlight dragon to us would solve it."

"You were the perfect counterpart to my imperfection," Amaya grumbled.

Juniper patted her adopted daughter's hand. "It isn't that you were imperfect, dear. It was that you were here. Celestina was the perfect answer to our troubles because she *wasn't* here. We couldn't see what she could do. We couldn't see that she has flaws just like the rest of us." Juniper met my eyes. "Because we didn't know you, Celestina, you became the savior that could lead the clan in restoring the dragon's fifth kingdom. More legend than real."

"And the perfect mate to bring more moonlight dragons into the world?" I added as the thought twisted in my belly.

"The promise of a fertile future," Juniper said with a frown. "Hearing that must make us sound like monsters."

"I understand why you'd feel that way toward me. And I understand Trace's mistaken infatuation with the idea of what I represent to the clan. What I can't understand is using those feelings to justify taking innocent lives."

Gwen and Juniper pressed their lips tightly together. Amaya sighed. "You upset the entire clan when you fled in the night like that. Many jumped to the conclusion that the vampires stole you from us. No dragon would willingly give herself over to our enemy, especially not a dragon who'd once been a vampire's slave."

"It wasn't like that with Soren, he never—" I tried to argue.

"The truth doesn't matter. Not in this case," Amaya cut in. "What matters is the story. You were a slave to a vampire. I freed you. The vampires steal you back in the middle of the night. War is going to follow. No other course of action makes sense. That's why I followed you. And I truly thought we had more time to get you back to the plateau."

"I wasn't going to return." My heart wept knowing I'd never see Soren again, never feel his hands on my body. "My life is with Soren. I'd hoped to stay with him forever."

"Then, in the eyes of the council, the attack was justified," Juniper announced.

I pressed my fingers to my eyes. "I learned my lesson. I won't run. For the sake of the innocent living in Fein, my life is here now. And I'd rather not live it as a captive."

Amaya pulled my hands from my face. "Stop being so dramatic, Moonglow. Trace had his tantrum. And we're here to fix you up." She dumped a pile of clothes on the bed. "I brought you warm sweaters, leggings, and skirts. Also, there are socks and underwear."

"And boots," Gwen added, holding out a pair of boots that looked to be just about the right size. "I sized them to Amaya's feet. If they don't fit, we can get you a different pair." The older woman set them on the floor and then cupped my hands in hers. "You don't have to fret about your life here, Celestina. I'm so pleased to welcome you into our family. I look forward to having another daughter to pamper." She smiled at me, but it was a sad sort of smile, one laced with years of sorrow.

I wanted to accept Gwen's kindness, but I slipped my hands from hers, clasping them tightly together behind my back. "After how Trace acted, I don't think I could ever accept him as a mate."

Her pretty brown eyebrows lowered as she frowned. "I can understand that. And I'll stand up for you in front of the council to make sure no one tries to force the two of you together. It isn't fair to my son or to you. But whether you choose him or not, I would like to call you my daughter…if you'll allow it."

When she put it that way, how could I not? "Thank you." My voice sounded husky.

Juniper leaned forward and unclasped my hands so she could wrap my wrists in gauze. After she'd finished, I dressed in a blue sweater and black leggings. I balled up the silver dress. It was ripped, stained with mud, and bloodied. And useless.

Still, I tucked it under the bed, not ready to throw it away, not ready to discard all reminders of my life with Soren. Even if keeping the ruined dress would hurt like poking at a bruise so it would never heal, I couldn't let it go.

"Sit." Juniper's gaze skated over where I'd shoved the dress before she patted the bed. "Let me get to work on your hair."

"I should cut it," I muttered after Juniper struggled for close to a half hour with the mess of knots tangling my long hair. "It would be simpler to care for it if it were shorter. Life on the plateau was going to be nothing like the court life I'd been raised to live."

"I have scissors back at my cottage," Gwen offered.

With that, we all headed downstairs and into the kitchen. Trace was standing at the stove cooking eggs. When he heard us enter, he turned around. His gaze met mine, and he froze.

"You set her loose." His hands tightened into fists.

"Son, we need to talk about how you treat the females of our kind," Gwen said.

Trace swallowed hard and then nodded. His gaze remained fixed on me. "How is your head this morning?" He pointed to his own head.

"It hurts." I saw no reason to lie.

"Your head is hurting? Why didn't you tell me? I have a powder." Juniper started digging around in the satchel she had slung over her shoulder. She found the powder and measured a small amount into my hand. "Swallow this. It'll help diminish the pain."

"What happened to make it hurt?" Amaya asked as she put herself between me and Trace.

"It hit the wall," I said after swallowing the bitter powder.

"She was struggling and—" Trace started to explain. Gwen cleared her throat, and he stopped. "How I acted…it was a mistake. I am sorry."

"That's a good start," Gwen said before I could even think of how to respond to that. A simple apology wasn't going to excuse the way he'd treated me yesterday. Or make me forget how he'd threatened to cut out my tongue. He would have done it, too, if I'd kept fighting him.

Gwen put her arm around my shoulder. "Celestina is going to stay with me until she decides otherwise."

Trace moved swiftly to block the door that led out to the back garden that Gwen had steered me toward. "But I need her close so I can guard her."

Gwen reached up and put a hand on her son's cheek. "Dear, I know this must be hard for you after so many years. You were so young when you left. Barely a man. But it's time for you to come home now. Come home, Trace. *Be* home. Your duty to protect Celestina is done. It's time for you to learn how to make a life for yourself in the village. A life *you* choose."

Trace lowered his head and stepped out of the way. As the four of us left his shop, I heard him mutter to himself, "I'm not sure I know how to stop watching over our moonlight dragon."

"Sounds like a *him* problem to me," Amaya grumbled as she walked beside me. "You're going to love Gwen's cottage. There's a colorful mural on every wall."

"And on the ceilings," Juniper added, with a chuckle. "My favorite is the ceiling in the kitchen with the flying sheep and vegetables."

"Don't forget the floors," Gwen said. "Be careful, though. The mural on the floor in the guest bathroom is still wet."

Her small cottage was as lovely as they had all promised with its sky-blue plaster walls and thatch roof. And there were paintings everywhere. Including several that were in progress sitting on easels in a sunroom at the back of the cottage that Gwen obviously used as a studio. I stood in front of one of the unfinished paintings. It was a portrait of Amaya and me as we stood at the edge of the plateau as the sun set in the west. I tilted my head to one side. Something about the painting was off.

"Hmm," Amaya said as she came over to gaze at the painting with me. "Your eye color is wrong. Gwen's usually better at noticing small details like that."

"Oh…right. That's what's wrong."

"Gwen! Moonglow's eyes are brown and green, not indigo," Amaya called out to my host who'd left the sunroom to show Juniper the new mural-in-progress in the guest bathroom.

Gwen poked her head into the sunroom and smiled at us. "I know that. But when I was painting Celestina standing there, my mind kept insisting I use that particular shade of indigo. It was the only color that felt right." She frowned as she studied me. "I'll fix it in the morning. Your eyes are lovely and unique, dear. Don't know why I didn't paint them correctly the first time."

Amaya squinted at me in much the same way Gwen had. "I like how your eyes are mismatched like that. Keeps you from looking too perfect."

"Thanks a lot," I grumbled. But I didn't feel upset by her insult. Instead, I laughed. And was surprised when Amaya laughed along with me.

"Come on, Moonglow. Let me show you the mural on Gwen's bedroom ceiling. It's absolutely scandalous!"

"When the two of you are done looking around," Gwen said as she headed toward the cottage's tidy kitchen, "join us for breakfast. I have fish pasties and crumb cakes baking in the oven."

My chest still ached from missing Soren and my friends in Fein. They were my hoard, my treasures, that I wasn't sure how I'd be able to live without. But for the first time since arriving at the plateau, I felt like I might be able to make a home here.

Chapter 43

Amaya

I walked as closely to Celestina as safely possible without touching her while strolling along the edge of the plateau. The cold spring breeze teased her considerably shorter hair. It'd been three weeks since our return to the village. Celestina moved silently. Occasionally, she'd pick up a sparkly stone and slip it into a pouch hanging from a loop on her leggings. She rarely talked, but she didn't appear unhappy. But she seemed to be listening for something, waiting.

She liked to cook. She'd make huge batches of delicious stew to deliver to families in the village, especially providing to families with young hatchlings. She'd even occasionally watch the youngsters to give the parents a break.

"She wants a family of her own," my mother had said more than once. I think she may have been right. But when it came to accepting the attention of any of the males in the village, she always politely declined. She wouldn't even speak with them.

Having her cut loose from Trace had nearly started a civil war in the village as the unattached males fought to win her favor. I stepped in and busted a few heads. Anther helped. So did Trace, even though he'd never let Celestina see it.

I still hadn't handed Cullen's book over to Gregory. I'd read it from the first page to the last several times. I didn't need it anymore. But Cullen's scent still clung to it. And keeping it close to me brought me nearly the same sense of calm that his voice had.

After connecting with him that one time, I'd continued to keep that pathway locked down. Sure, there were times I was tempted to reach out to him just so I could—

That kind of thinking would lead me to danger. I didn't want to end up like Celestina—in love with someone I couldn't have.

You already love your stupidly handsome prince, a voice (*my* voice) whispered. And dammit, my inner voice wasn't wrong.

"Why are you growling?" Celestina asked, startling me out of my tumbling thoughts.

"No good reason," I said. I never talked with her about Cullen or vampires or about anything that might remind her of the life she was clearly missing. "Ask my family. I growl all the time. Usually at them. But only because they deserve it."

"I hope you're not growling at something I did." She was so delicate in how she spoke. Her voice was like a soft, cozy blanket. It made me want to lean in closer to her. To rub the side of my face against hers. *It's a dragon thing.*

"Just growling at my own mind," I admitted, while *not* rubbing my body parts against hers. "It's a terror inside here, you know." I tapped my temple.

"You're too hard on yourself." She pressed her cheek against mine.

I froze. This was the first time she'd done anything that would suggest she was one of us.

I knew she wasn't totally averse to touch. I'd watched her with her vampires and had seen how she'd lean into them, how she'd accept comfort from them.

The clan could provide that for her if she could learn to trust us.

But her touching me could be disastrous. I pulled away before our magics exploded.

"We'd better not tempt fate," I said with a smile. "I haven't made anything explode in three weeks. I think that must be a record."

"We should figure out how to control it."

"We should," I agreed. "But not today. The weather's too nice. And I'm feeling too happy. Look at those fluffy white clouds. That one over there looks like a decapitated head."

"Have you heard news about the conflict between Earst and the Fein?" she asked without looking at me a little while later. The sun had reached its zenith in the time that we'd walked. Its rays felt warm on my face despite the cold wind whipping across the plateau.

"We're an insular society here. The affairs of the continent don't concern us." Even as I said it, I knew my words would wound her. She ached for news of her beloved.

She bit her lip and looked at me. "Should it be that way?"

"With your return to us, there are many who say we can now retake our position of power on the continent. It's what had been promised to us through the ages. The moonlight dragon would lead us to a future of prosperity and safety. And if that is the case, I suppose it would be wise to start keeping an eye on the other kingdoms."

"I don't feel qualified to lead anyone."

"Not yet, perhaps." I picked up our pace. "That's why we're going to see Gregory."

Every time I went to visit Gregory, I had *the book* tucked into my waistband with the intention of handing it over to him. And every time we left, it would still be tucked into my waistband.

I'd been teaching the other dragons how to do things that I'd learned in the book, like how to pull clothes and other items—such as weapons—to themselves when they shifted from dragon to human. Many of the dragons, mostly the males, scoffed.

"Why should I cover up all this handsomeness?" one of Anther's friends had demanded, waggling his cock at me like a dog would wag its tail.

Anther had punched him before I could do it.

The book held other important pieces of lost knowledge, like the names of past dragon leaders and recipes for healing serums that sped the restoration of our spent magic. When the council demanded to know where I was learning about these things, I'd lied and told them that it must be my ancient memories waking up, an explanation that seemed to satisfy almost everyone except for my mother.

Juniper watched me with an expression that made me wonder if she had somehow guessed the truth. That she knew how, like Celestina, I'd fallen for the enemy, and I'd let a vampire feed from me. Hell, I'd let him do much more than simply feed. Maybe my healer mother could smell that on my skin. Despite how vigorously I scrubbed every time I bathed, I could still smell his spicy musk, could still feel the imprint of his hands on my thighs.

"You're growling again." Celestina gently nudged me with her elbow. "You need to tell your mind to give yourself a break."

What I really needed was to open my connection with Cullen and let him use his wicked powers of seduction to relieve this tension that kept building within me. My longing for him had become a constant ache between my legs ever since I'd started denying myself his company—even when I was sleeping. *Stupid, sexy prince.* I should have stabbed him in the nuts the first time we'd met.

"Such a vicious dragon, you are, my beautiful menace." The familiar voice slipped into my mind like someone falling on to a comfortable sofa. *"I've sorely missed your threats, although I must admit picturing you stabbing me down there does have me wanting to lock myself in my library and hide."*

I hadn't meant to share that thought with Cullen. But broadcasting my vicious thoughts into his mind seemed to come as naturally as breathing. And hearing his voice made my shoulders relax. A smile crept its way to my lips. I should have slammed the barrier back down, but honestly, I didn't want to.

"Have you beaten back Queen Beatrice from your border?" I asked as a way of justifying why I kept the pathway with Cullen open. I was doing this for Celestina's sake, not my own.

His frustration pulsed through me like a molten wave of lava. *"Don't worry about us."*

"I'm not worried. Celestina is."

"How is my brother's princess faring?" He seemed a little too eager to know. And while he didn't deserve my answer, I gave him the truth—for Celestina's sake.

"She isn't trying to run back to Soren, if that's what you're asking. And she's protected and well cared for."

"But is she happy?"

"Of course she isn't!" Whoops. I guess I should have lied. Another blast of unhappy emotion hit me almost like a punch. *"Would you rather I told you that her feelings for your brother were so shallow that she could walk away from him and not suffer for it?"*

"I'd rather know that you were suffering for leaving me."

"What's going on?" Celestina demanded when I jerked for a second time after being hit by another wave of strong emotions. "Are you ill?"

"I accidentally opened my connection with that stupid Prince Cullen. And he's being overly dramatic like always."

"You have a connection with—? You can talk to him? You're talking to him *now*?" She grabbed my arm and squeezed it so tightly that I worried some of my bones might be cracked. "How are they? How is Soren?"

"Goodie. Now I have an overly dramatic vampire and an overly dramatic dragon asking endless questions. No, I'm not pining for you." I lied as I removed Celestina's hand from my arm before she accidentally blasted a hole in our universe. *"I hope I don't damage your ego too much by telling you that."*

"I'll take to my bed and stare at the ceiling for months."

I laughed aloud.

"What?" Celestina demanded.

"Prince Cullen is a—" I shook my head. *"Is Soren safe?"*

"He's throwing himself into harm's way, leading the fight at the front lines against Queen Beatrice's undead army. It'll be a miracle if he survives. I fear he doesn't wish to survive it."

"Soren is too busy handling Queen Beatrice's attacks to be missing you or anyone. Cullen says he's bravely leading his warriors," I told Celestina.

"That's not what I said," Cullen corrected.

We arrived at Ivy and Gregory's cottage. It was time to push Cullen out of my mind and out of my life. For. Good. I would hand Cullen's book to Gregory like I should have done weeks ago. And forget the prince existed.

"Is there anything else you'd like to know before I close the connection?" I asked Celestina.

Tears floated in her eyes. She opened and closed her mouth several times. "Can you have Cullen tell Soren that I love him? That I miss him so badly that I ache…here?" She touched her hand to the center of her chest. "My heart has been ripped apart. I-I don't know how I'm going to live without him, but I cannot lay down and die, because my life and Soren's are linked. I live for him. Can Cullen tell Soren that?"

Eww, no.

"I'm wounded that you're not wanting to lay down and die for missing me, Darkness," Cullen complained. I felt a bubble of laughter in my belly that I knew wasn't mine.

"That's enough." I slammed the connection closed.

"He'll tell Soren that you miss him." I rubbed at my aching arm from where Celestina had squeezed it. I'd need to shift to my dragon form to get rid of the bruise that had already bloomed into a pinkish-purple color. "And Soren misses you just as keenly. Now, a piece of advice. It'll be easier for both of you if you just stop it. Stop thinking about him. Stop missing him. Move on."

Before she could respond, I raised my hand and knocked on Gregory's door.

Celestina

If only I could stop loving...

The door in front of us swung open. Gregory greeted us with a smile that was nearly as large as he was. He gathered Amaya and me into his wide chest at the same time.

"My two favorite dragonlings," he boomed. "Ivy! Put the tea on. Amaya has brought Celestina around for a visit."

He pulled us inside, not letting go until he had the door shut behind us. Did he think I would run away if he let go of me before closing the door? Probably. My cheeks tinged red as I realized that I never made the effort to visit anyone in the village without Amaya or Gwen at my side. No matter how welcoming many in the clan acted, I felt like an outsider who would never know how to fit in with the village's various groups of tightly knit friends.

And none of them seemed to truly understand why I hadn't forgiven Trace and accepted him as my mate. In the eyes of the elder members of the village, our joining was inevitable. He'd dedicated his life to watching out for me, so I'd become his by default. I was thankful that neither Amaya nor Gwen felt like they needed to pressure me to accept him.

Gwen, in fact, seemed determined to keep Trace as far away from me as possible. After hearing how he'd threatened to cut out my tongue, she'd had a long talk with him. Afterwards, she'd told me that I wouldn't have to worry about him bothering me ever again. And he hadn't.

Gregory clapped his meaty hands together. "What part of dragon lore should I teach the two of you this lovely afternoon?" His eyes, the shade of wild violet flowers, glittered with pleasure.

Amaya cleared her throat nervously. I snapped my head in her direction. She lifted her sweater and withdrew a small, leatherbound book tucked in the waistband of her leggings. The scent of it immediately caught my attention.

I snatched the book from her and pressed the book to my nose, inhaling deeply.

It smelled spicy and smoky and exactly like Reinheart Palace.
Soren.

I rubbed the leather cover against my cheek when what I really wanted to do was strip down and rub it against my entire body. I wanted that scent all over me. I wanted to bathe in it, drown in it.

Gregory laughed. "I see you're a book lover, Celestina."

"I should have given you this book sooner, but…"

I could barely pay attention to whatever Amay was saying as I grew drunk on the scent that reminded me of the one place where I belonged. Where I felt loved.

Soren. He was my home.

Amaya twisted the book from my hands. "As I was saying, I retrieved this book from the Fein capital."

I cried out and tried to take it back from her. The dragon in me rose up in a way that I'd never experienced before and growled at Amaya. The teeth that snapped at her hand were as sharp as knives. I bit her hard enough that I broke the skin, and she started to bleed.

Gregory's eyebrows shot into his hairline. "Interesting."

Amaya shook her hand. It changed from human skin to dragon skin, her fingers to talons, then back to fingers with her human skin now completely unmarred. "Keeping this book will only hurt, Moonglow," she said as she slammed the book into Gregory's hands. After a stunned silence, she softly added, "I know."

No. No. No. I needed to get my hands on that book. It was a connection to Soren that I could hold. I couldn't let that go. I wrestled with Amaya. Her teeth grew to deadly points as she snapped at me. "We. Need. To. Let. It. Go. Moonglow."

Gregory whistled as he read the title.

"Is this real?" he asked.

"It is." Amaya bit me as I continued to fight her. I needed to smell that book again. "Dammit, we're going to have to get my mother to bandage you up. And she's going to tattle on me for harming you. My father won't be pleased."

Her words drained the fight out of me. I didn't want her family to lock her in her room for weeks to punish her for something that had been my fault. Not again.

I'd lived with the clan long enough to realize that they all lived in fear of Amaya and the powers her midnight dragon possessed. That *she* possessed. She was her dragon, and her dragon was her. Just two forms of the same soul. I still had trouble wrapping my mind around that concept since I still didn't feel like I could possibly be a dragon.

I hugged my arm, squeezing my hand over the torn skin. "I'm fine."

Ivy emerged from the kitchen with a tea tray that she hastily set down. "Amaya," she sighed. "Go fetch your mother."

"It's just a scratch," I said, even though the bites did look deep. I squeezed my arm harder, willing the bleeding to stop on its own. "I'd rather not bother Juniper about this." I didn't want Amaya to be punished. I'd bitten her first. And I'd fought her for the book.

Ivy peered at my bloody arm for a long moment before saying, "Let me get some rags. I suppose we can bind it up ourselves. But if it starts to look red and puffy, you'll have to promise me to go to Juniper for her salve."

"I'll bring some of that stinky stuff over to you in the morning," Amaya promised. She was standing so her back was to both Gregory and Ivy as she mouthed "thank you" to me.

Once my arm had been taken care of, and we were all seated in the comfortable chairs around the fire and sipping tea, Amaya explained how she'd found the book in Prince Cullen's private library and had stolen it.

Gregory hadn't touched his tea, or the large piece of cheese-berry cake Ivy had placed in front of him. He kept turning the pages of the book while shaking his head as he skimmed the passages. "This changes…" he kept muttering and "Do you know what this means…?" and "Ground shattering…"

"I'm sorry I kept the book for so long. I wanted—" Amaya glanced at me and blushed, which I found interesting. Almost as interesting as the wound Cullen had had on his neck the night of the ball that had made *him* blush when Gray had asked him about it. "I wanted time to absorb…well, everything."

"Of course. Of course," Gregory said, still immersed in what he was finding on the pages. "This was written by a midnight dragon. Of course you would want to learn all you could from it."

"Is this book where you learned how to pull clothes into your shift?" Ivy asked as she refilled my teacup. Today's blend was a mix of mint and dried cherries and exactly the calming flavor I needed.

"Page 102," Amaya answered. "And you'll see on page 108, Draco Falco talks about how midnight dragons can hold on to the dragon's third shape—air."

"The dragon history described in the beginning of this book seems to be radically different from the stories we'd been taught." Gregory sat back and shook his head again. "If this is true—"

"It must be," Amaya said. "That was why the vampires wanted to keep it from us. They didn't want us to know that the dragons once ruled the entire continent."

Ivy gasped.

I had to bite my tongue to keep myself from explaining that the vampires had stolen the histories of *all* the kingdoms because they wanted to guard their own secret—that they'd once been hunted and enslaved so their blood could be harvested. But that wasn't my secret to share.

"This." Gregory's voice trembled as he held the book. "I know the clan often discounts your worth and often complains how you're too impulsive. But this. This is the find of a lifetime. Thank you, Amaya. This book has the potential to change *everything* for us."

"I'm glad I snatched it then," she said as if his praise meant nothing. But tears glittered in her eyes as she said it.

"And you, Celestina." Gregory finally set the book aside and picked up his teacup. "You shifted forms today."

"No, I didn't."

"You did. In that fit of anger, you called up your dragon's teeth when you bit Amaya."

I blushed at the reminder.

"She also breathed fire in the Fein court when her prince angered her," Amaya added. "The binding spell had one hell of a kickback when it snapped back into place, though."

"Even more interesting." Gregory sat forward. "Maybe if we evoke enough strong emotions from you, we will completely break Queen Frieda's bonds."

"It's worth a try," Ivy said.

I cringed at the thought. Strong angry emotions made my stomach hurt. I'd been raised to remain level-headed, calm. As I'd gotten older, those lessons had served me well considering how my life had depended on never upsetting Queen Beatrice.

"Just be sure you're somewhere fireproof when you do it," Amaya said. "She destroyed a royal throne room when she lost her temper at the Fein palace."

"If we push, push, push, I bet the binding will eventually break," Ivy said. "Don't look so worried dear. This is wonderful news that we should immediately bring to the council."

Is it? To me, it sounded like torture.

"The binding spell didn't break when Trace was attacking me," I pointed out.

"That was Trace, dear," Ivy said gently. "Anyone would understand why you couldn't bring yourself to harm him."

Because we are fated for each other. Those are the words she'd left unsaid.

Gregory rubbed his bearded chin. "It's worth trying to see how far we can push it."

Maybe…maybe I didn't want to lose control like I had in the throne room again. Maybe I was fine with who I was. A powerless human.

Amaya tapped the arm of the chair next to my hand. "I won't let anyone harm you."

"No one knows more about managing anger issues than our Amaya," Ivy said with a laugh.

And that was how it had started. The council loved the idea. They hoped to use my anger to break the binding spell. A few days after we'd talked about it with Gregory and Ivy, the Council had me meet with them in a lovely parlor in Amaya's family's manor house to discuss the matter.

I tried to tell them that this wasn't a good idea. My magic rarely came to me when I needed it. And the kickback from the one time I'd conjured fire had harmed me. But none of the councilors listened. I was *their* moonlight dragon (a gift from the ancients), which meant they felt empowered to make decisions on my behalf without bothering to care about what I wanted.

Trace stood at the center of the room with his arms crossed, watching me in a way that made a shiver of fear work its way down my back.

"When she embraces her dragon, things will be different," I overheard Amaya's father say to Trace as he slapped his hand on Trace's shoulder after they'd decided to start my "anger sessions" first thing the next morning.

Saying things like that in front of me was enough to make me *want* to breathe fire. But I didn't feel the fire erupting from my throat like it had when I confronted Soren. And even then, I hadn't been close to transforming into this moonlight dragon that was supposedly hidden beneath my human skin.

The next morning Amaya stayed by my side as the Council led me out to the field that the dragons used as a landing pad.

"I don't want to do this," I told them.

"Gregory thinks this will cure you," Drix said.

"It'll hurt only for a short while," Anther said.

"If it works," I grumbled.

I had flashbacks of Trace dragging me up to that bedroom and tying me to the bed while threatening to cut out my tongue. My magic hadn't come to rescue me then. And the terror that came with that memory was enough to cause me to tremble all over again. These dragons were brutal. I didn't dare try to imagine what they had planned to do with me in the name of breaking my binding spell.

Nearly the entire clan had gathered on the field. Gregory stood at the front of the crowd with his arms crossed over his broad chest. Ivy matched his stance. Both looked worried.

Amaya hugged herself. "I don't think this is going to work."

"I don't think it will, either."

Drix spun me around to face him. He tied my hands together with a rough rope and then hammered the long end of the rope into the ground with a wooden stake. A lizard ran up and blinked at me several times before scurrying away.

"I never thought we'd see those lizards again," Ivy said. "They vanished nearly the same time you did, Celestina."

"Your Gregory ate them to extinction," Anther teased.

Gregory rubbed his belly. "Maybe I'll do it again."

Everyone laughed.

Except for me.

And Amaya.

"Pain isn't what triggered me in the past. It's anger," I reminded them.

"Oh, you'll be angry about this," Drix said as he pulled a long, curved dagger from a leather sheath. I hoped he realized that whatever horror he planned to inflict on me with that knife, I wouldn't be able to heal myself unless I managed to transform into a dragon. Which seemed like a long shot at this point.

"Make sure she's secure," Drix said to his son.

Anther tugged at the rope. It didn't budge.

If he couldn't move it with his dragon-enhanced strength, I certainly wouldn't be able to.

Drix showed me the knife. I wanted to be brave in front of Amaya. She was always so fierce and tough. But I wasn't. I'd never been like her.

"Amaya, dear, come closer." Drix waved to his daughter. "I need your assistance."

Amaya frowned as she closed the distance between us.

"Good," her father said. "Stand right there." He moved Amaya so she was standing directly in front of me. He stood off to the side with that huge dagger. "Perfect. Now we're ready to start."

He lifted the dagger. With a movement that was faster than my human eyesight could track, he sliced open Amaya's throat. Hot blood splattered my face and sweater.

"No!" I screamed! How could he do that? He'd raised her as his own blood. She was just as important to the future of the clan as I was. She was half of the gift from the ancients. And he'd tossed her life away? Because they thought my bound magic was somehow better, purer than Amaya's? "No! You're all monsters!" I growled as Amaya's body crumpled. "I'll never help you! You can all rot in this place for all I care!"

I thrashed, trying to free myself. I needed to get my hands on Amaya. I needed to use what magic I had available to force her to turn. If I could get her to change to air or to her midnight dragon, she could heal herself before drawing her last breath. I had to save her. I had to get her away from these horrid dragons. The rough rope dug into my wrists. But just as Anther had demonstrated, the rope held firm. And they'd positioned Amaya inches out of my reach.

I growled my frustration. Why wouldn't my magic come now? Why couldn't I slip out of these ropes like I had on the ship?

The ember of my flame stirred in my chest. If I could summon my fire, I could burn the ropes. There was no time to waste. Blood puddled around her head. A head that showed no life.

The clan stood in a circle around us, watching.

"Help her!" I screamed. "Let me touch her! Let me save her!"

Juniper moved toward me, but Anther grabbed his mother's shoulders and held her back. Gwen also tried to rush to our aid. She nearly made it to me, but Trace wrapped his hands around her middle, lifting her off the ground and pulling her back to the edge of the circle.

"Celestina has to do it," Drix spat. "She has to pull the dragon from inside herself if she's to save her midnight dragon."

Gregory pinched his lips together and hummed. Ivy shifted from foot to foot.

Despair flooded my chest, drowning the small flame that had tried to ignite there. Tears spilled on to my cheeks as I fell to my knees. "Amaya,"

I rasped, while pulling on the impossible rope, unable to get to her. "Don't die on me. Please. Don't. Die."

A spark stirred in my chest. It wasn't dragon fire, but it was something. I reached out my hand. It was glowing.

My magic.

It had answered me. For Amaya's sake, a spark of my magic had broken through the binding holding it back. I prayed it would be enough. I focused on my hand as I reached for Amaya. I knew the ropes wouldn't let me touch her. But perhaps my power could reach her when my hands could not. My hand glowed brighter. And that spark in my chest burned.

I could do this.

I could save her.

Suddenly, it all stopped.

Pain lanced through my middle. I screamed. It felt like a sword had slashed me open, spilling my insides onto the ground. Was I destined to die with Amaya? Were our lives linked like Soren's life had been linked to mine? Pain ripped through me.

Was this—?

Was this my *dragon?*

It felt as if a horde of invisible creatures were biting me. And then, before I could even draw another breath, everything went black.

Chapter 44

Amaya

"Daughter!" My mother's voice cut through the pain and blackness. I tried to cry out to her. But all that I could manage was a gurgling in my throat. "Get out of my way! I never would have agreed to this!"

"That's why we didn't tell you." My father's hard voice sounded distant. "The midnight dragon has always been a tool of the moonlight. It's the moonlight dragon that will bring us our golden future. It's the moonlight dragon that needs to be freed."

"That doesn't mean we should be careless with another life." I barely felt the press of my mother's warm touch on my cheek. "I can't save you, my sweet child." I wanted to tell her not to fret. But I was no longer able to draw a breath. My throat had almost instantly been flooded with blood. I was no longer able to see. I couldn't find my magic to shift.

This was death. And I welcomed it.

"But hopefully Celestina can save you," my mother whispered.

Celestina had screamed fiercely at the others for harming me. But then her voice had abruptly stopped. Had she shifted? Had she found her dragon?

Being so close to her, wouldn't I have felt the burst of power if she had?

"What can I do to help?" That was Gwen.

"Keep everyone back!" my mother shouted.

The wound in my neck screamed with pain as I was pushed across the grass.

"*Sorry. Sorry,*" my mother whispered over and over. "It's almost over."

An icy cold hand closed over my wrist. I felt the warmer fingers of a third hand pressing that cold hand against my skin. I wanted it to stop. I tried to pull away, but I couldn't muster the strength as my heart fluttered…and faltered.

"Pull her power to you, Celestina. Pull it and make her shift. Save her. Please." My mother's voice sounded garbled, like she could barely speak from sobbing so hard.

Don't worry about me, I wanted to tell her. I'd spent a lifetime making her worry. She deserved to be released from that burden.

"Hold on, my sweet child. Hold on a little longer," my mother begged.

Celestina grunted and there was a flash of burning pain as my power jerked and then was pulled, pulled from wherever it had gone in my body to die. It blasted up to the surface and exploded out toward Celestina.

And then I was nothing.

Nothing.

Is this death?

No.

No…

Not.

Dead.

I.

Am.

Air.

I tumbled in a shuddering breeze across the surface of the plateau. Light. Free. Happy.

I liked being air. I could stay this way forever. My father couldn't slit my throat when I didn't have a throat to cut.

But when I saw Celestina lying on the ground, I stopped.

She hadn't taken her dragon form. Neither the anger she'd felt from my father's betrayal nor the power she'd pulled from me had broken the binding spell.

She'd curled in on herself. Hugging her middle as if in great pain. That wasn't right.

I shifted to my midnight dragon and dropped to the ground to stand over Celestina, hissing at the others, warning them to stay away from her.

My mother rolled away from me when I snapped my sharp teeth in her direction. I didn't want anyone near my moonlight dragon. Not even her.

Celestina was *mine* to protect.

"*Mine.*"

"Yes, dear," my mother said as she held up her hands. "She *is* yours to protect. But something is wrong with her. The binding spell must have hurt her when she tried to shift. You need to let me get close to see if I can help her."

"*Mine*," the feral part of me roared. I didn't want to let anyone near Celestina, especially not after they'd harmed us both. The clan didn't deserve her. I bent to gather her up into my taloned claws and take her away from here. I knew of a cave...

"She's hurt," my mother repeated as if she realized my intent.

"Please," Gwen stood next to my mother. Her hands clasped to her throat. "Please, Amaya, let us see what we can do to help her."

I glanced over at my father and the other males. They were keeping their distance. Smart move on their part. I'd fight them if they came at me. It didn't matter that I was a female or that my dragon was smaller than theirs. I was the midnight dragon, a nightmare made into flesh. I could destroy them all without feeling an ounce of remorse. They'd wanted to anger a dragon. Well, they got their wish.

I.

Was.

Seething.

But these two females had helped Celestina and me. They had loved on me when others had kept their distance. Even within the fog of my wildness, I knew I could trust them.

I shifted back to my human form and dropped to my knees next to Celestina. The cool breeze chilled all my parts. I glanced down and realized that in my haste I'd shifted without pulling clothes to me. I quickly turned back to air, and then a heartbeat later shifted back to my human form, pulling a clean black sweater and fresh leather leggings onto my body as it became solid again.

"What's wrong with you?" I demanded of Celestina. "What happened, Moonglow?"

Celestina rolled and whimpered.

"There's no visible injury," my mother said as she placed her hand on Celestina's forehead. "But something is definitely wrong." She carefully placed her other hand on Celestina's abdomen. As soon as my mother's hand touched the area, Celestina cried out as if she'd been struck.

This felt familiar.

My mother jerked back. "I have no idea what this could mean. Do you remember having ever seen anything like this, Gwen?"

Too familiar.

"No. Maybe the kickback from the binding spell caused some kind of internal damage?" Gwen asked.

"If that were the case, there should be signs of bruising." My mother lifted Celestina's sweater, ever so slowly, ever so carefully, to peer at the perfect milky skin below.

But what I was thinking couldn't be true.

It would be…impossible.

"Cullen?" I tossed open the pathway, hoping he hadn't blocked me. *"What's going on where you are? What has happened to Soren? Is he hurt?"*

"Yes, dammit! He went in with a group of warriors to save a troop who were surrounded by Queen Beatrice's undead army. When he and his men reached the troop, another wave of undead closed in around them. Soren was stabbed and bitten. And the undead carried him off. Wait a minute. Why are you asking about him?"

"Celestina collapsed just now."

"That's impossible. The bond—"

"Must have completed itself because she looks like she's dying."

Cullen swore. *"We're fighting back. We're trying to rescue Soren. But their fucking army keeps coming back to life."*

"Don't you dare let him die." I pushed that thought as hard as I knew how.

"We're trying to save him, Amaya." His thoughts hit me like a blistering windstorm.

I bundled Celestina into my arms. There was no way I was going to let anyone else carry her.

"Soren has been injured and captured by Queen Beatrice's undead army. Celestina's life is in danger because of his injuries," I announced to the clan.

"That's impossible," Trace snapped.

I turned Celestina away from him. "They are bonded partners. If one falls, the other falls. It's a horrid system, but that's vampires for you."

"But the bond only goes one way!" Trace shouted. "I was there. I watched the ceremony. She didn't take the oath."

Gwen shook her head. "Look at her, son."

"She's faking." Trace gestured with a dismissive wave. "She's upset that we harmed you, Amaya. And she's trying to trick us. She's trying to punish us by pretending her precious vampire prince is injured."

"He is injured! I just communicated with his brother and confirmed it."

"You're communicating with vampires?" my father screeched. After what he'd done to me, I didn't owe him any explanations.

"If Soren dies, she dies," I said. I held up my hand when Trace tried to object again. "I don't care what you saw at the palace. Something has happened between them. Maybe the words don't have to be spoken. Maybe the oath can be a whisper of a feeling, a promise in a kiss, a vow spoken with the body." I thought about the well-worn pathway that I'd accidentally created between Cullen and me. "It's not the words that matter. Only the emotions behind them." I softened my voice. "I know this is hard for you to hear, Trace. But Celestina loves that vampire warrior of hers. It's not a mind trick they played on her. She's not confused. And if the clan doesn't help the Fein defeat Queen Beatrice, we're going to lose the last moonlight dragon. Forever."

"If he's this injured," my mother said, "it may already be too late."

No, it couldn't be too late. I didn't want to carry the burden of being the clan's last hope alone. I needed Celestina to be in the world with me, to be part of this story, to be the strong one where I was the constant failure.

"You're not a failure." Cullen pushed that thought so forcefully into my mind, I stumbled. *"You're clever and brave and you leave my mind in a muddled mess because I'm obsessively thinking of you when I'm sure you're too busy to spare me a second of your thoughts."*

I didn't dare admit that I'd been obsessively thinking of him as well. Not even to myself. Not when he might hear me thinking it.

"Do you really believe taking her to this vampire prince would save her?" my mother asked.

"I think if we can get them together, they can save each other." I hoped that was true.

"We can't lose the moonlight dragon," my father said. I think he meant it as in "we can't let her leave the plateau." But I was still in no mood to argue with a man who'd coldly slit his own daughter's throat.

"You should go, Amaya." Trace blinked up at the sky. "Take her to him."

"Come with us, Trace. The vampires need help. They need our help."

He shook his head. "They're our enemy."

"I don't think we need to be enemies," my mother said quietly as she brushed away a small lizard that had crawled up her leg. "We've not interacted with anything outside of the clan for so many generations, we've disappeared from the continent's memories. We've become nothing more than myths and fairytales to them. And humans and vampires have become the monsters that lurk in the shadows of our nightmares. But is this the truth?"

"I don't know what to believe anymore," Trace said. "The humans…they are our enemies. They mistreated Celestina for twenty-three years. Queen Beatrice chased us away from the valley, away from Celestina. She's threatened to kill us. And she nearly succeeded in killing Celestina. There is no question in my mind that she'd happily kill us all."

"Then help them fight her," I hugged Celestina tightly to my chest, hoping I could provide her with some comfort for the pain she clearly was suffering.

"No," my father said. "No one from the clan will leave here."

"You will let Amaya go," my mother spun on her heels to confront my father. "You will let her take Celestina with her."

Gwen stood shoulder to shoulder with my mother. "She will go. You will allow it."

Ivy stepped forward with Gregory holding her arm. "Let them go. Amaya knows what she's doing. And the moonlight dragon is too important to risk losing this way."

"Come with us," I implored. "Help me save her prince. Help me stop Queen Beatrice from overrunning the Kingdom of Fein."

"We don't need to save a kingdom, only one man. You're more than capable of accomplishing that task, Amaya," Gregory said. "You go. Save him. Then bring them both back here."

My father nodded. "We'll keep the vampire safe from the queen."

Others in the crowd were nodding. And I realized that this was going to be the best I could expect. With a resigned sigh, I kissed my mother's cheek. "Think of me, and I'll be able to reach you."

"Always, my daughter. I'll always keep you in my mind and my heart. Fly with the gods." She cupped my cheek in her warm hand. "And come back to us."

I nodded. "I will try," was the best I could promise.

Keeping a tight holding on Celestina, I shifted to my dragon form and shot up into the sky. I turned into the headwinds, flying directly toward the Fein border, following the tug in my chest that I'd felt ever since I'd left Prince Cullen. I prayed I'd reach the battle in time to save Celestina.

"Don't you dare die on me now, Moonglow."

Chapter 45

Amaya

"Guide me to your brother," I sent to Cullen through our telepathic pathway. I'd placed Celestina in a nearby cave in the mountains on the Fein side of the border and well clear of the undead army. Before leaving her there, I'd used my magic to pull several woolen blankets from the manor house that I piled on top of her. Once I was sure she was comfortable—as comfortable as she could be while feeling the injuries of her bonded partner—I took to the sky.

"How many are with you?" he immediately answered.

"I have me."

"You're going to get yourself—"

"I'm going to get your damned *prince. Guide me to him."* I sent Cullen an image of the rocky peaks below me where a line of warriors were walking in an unnatural manner down a narrow mountain trail.

"I'm also a damned prince. And you're going to listen to me and let me help—"

"Where is he? Soren and Celestina don't have time for this argument. An argument I'm going to win in the end anyway. So, shut up and tell me where I can find your brother."

Cullen swore colorfully before he sent me a fuzzy image of a heavily guarded tent. *"My spies tell me that he's in there."*

"I'll get him out." I shifted to air. No reason to let those creepy undead warriors see me.

It didn't take long to follow the trail Cullen had crafted and to find the tent within Queen Beatrice's camp. It was the one with the most armed warriors milling around outside it—living, alert warriors dressed in purple leathers with purple cloaks slung over one shoulder. The number of warriors didn't bother me. I was, after all, air.

I entered the tent through a vent flap at the top. The interior was dark. Celestina's prince was laid out on a palette. His brow was covered in sweat while blood oozed from a gaping wound across his stomach.

"I thought vampires could survive nearly anything." I pressed the words into Cullen's mind. *"This wound doesn't look that serious."*

"You found him?" Cullen's excitement felt like my own. *"How is he? Is he awake?"*

"He's not awake. There's a belly wound that's actively bleeding. Not gushing. Just slowly leaking out. I think he should be awake. And from what I've heard about vampires, shouldn't he be healing by now? Or was that a lie? Are vampires weaker than you want us to believe?" That would explain why my little love bite had hurt Cullen so badly.

"That's not why I had such trouble with your bite. Dragons can injure vampires in a way that makes it difficult for us to heal ourselves." Cullen shot a burst of spiky worry into my mind. *"Blood loss is our main weakness. If my brother has lost too much blood, he'll be weakened to the point where his body can't even begin to heal. And there could be internal damage."*

"I suppose those are parts of his intestine hanging out there."

"Gods. How are you going to get him out? Are you safe? Has anyone spotted you?"

"I'm air. Of course no one can see me."

"I can."

"Don't remind me. I don't… You shouldn't be able to do that."

"You're not flustered, are you, Darkness?"

"I'm…I'm not…"

"There are too many soldiers around the tent you're in. You're going to need a diversion to get you and my brother out safely."

Too many—? Did that mean Cullen could see the tent?

"You're here?" I demanded. At the same time, I heard a shout in the camp. And then the heavy thuds as several guards ran past. One of the guards who'd been standing outside, a big burly warrior with a face filled with scars, stepped into the tent.

Well hell. Having company inside the tent complicated matters. I didn't want to blow him up. That would make too big of a mess and alert more guards.

But I needed to get rid of him.

He walked over to the palette and kicked Soren where his intestines were leaking out. Soren cried out, but never opened his eyes. I hated to think how that kick had affected Celestina.

"Not so tough now, are you, Beast?" the warrior growled. He pulled back his boot to kick Soren again.

I shifted to my human form and grabbed the bastard's boot before it could do any more damage to my Celestina.

The man gasped and spun around to see who was holding him. I let his booted foot drop and straightened.

His eyes widened when he saw me. I hadn't bothered to pull on any clothes with the shift. For one, there hadn't been time. And for another, this reaction was the one I wanted.

"Hello there." He gave a lewd grin that made my stomach sour. "How did you get in here?"

I smiled at him and hoped my expression didn't give him any hints about the monster I was about to become.

"That anxious to get to me, are you?" He licked his lips. "I suppose I could see to your needs, my pretty whore." He grabbed my arms and tugged until I was flush against his battle leathers. I could smell the dried meat he must have eaten for lunch on his breath.

"I would love to eat you," I whispered and then slammed my wickedly sharp dragon teeth into his neck, severing his head from his body. "But I don't eat rotten food." I spit out the pieces of flesh that had gotten stuck to my teeth.

I needed to get out of there before any more stinky humans barged in on us. I knelt next to Soren, pulling him off the cot.

A heartbeat later, I shifted. The transformation ripped a hole through the top of the canvas tent as my dragon outgrew the space. I clutched

Soren to my chest and took to the air. The warriors still standing watch outside started to shout and throw spears.

"Got your brother," I told Cullen.

"Thank the gods. Head back to the cave."

My dragon-keen eyes, which could pinpoint the smallest forms of prey—a mouse, a mole, a lizard—even when flying far above the treetops, zeroed in on Cullen almost immediately. The diversion he'd created was to expose himself in the worst possible way.

The foolish vampire was darting around tents while pursued by several dozens of Queen Beatrice's warriors. He was going to get himself killed.

I pulled my wings back and sent myself into a nosedive. I tipped Soren to the side, so I could hold him with one taloned claw, while I snatched up Cullen with my other.

"Ooof!" he grunted from the impact.

It nearly broke my wings to flap hard enough to stall my descent and then climb back into the air again.

It would have been a perfect escape if not for the archers.

They started firing, filling the sky with their steel-tipped arrows. My scales were tough enough to repel them. But the vampires in my arms were fragile things. They could be injured by one of those arrows. And I wasn't going to risk Celestina's life any more than I already had.

I spun so my back took the brunt of the arrows, my scales easily protecting me from feeling anything more than several dull thumps. My leathery wings, however, didn't fare so well. Several arrows tore through my right wing. I winced at the pain, hoping Cullen wouldn't notice.

I didn't want to worry him about something that wasn't going to cause us that much trouble. I simply needed to get away from the camp first. And gain some altitude.

"You're hurt!" Cullen shouted in my mind.

"Shh…I'm flying here." It wasn't the steadiest path as air poured through one wing like water from a leaky bucket.

"Dammit! I can feel your pain. It's excruciating!"

"Thanks for reminding me. Still trying to get us away from the enemy while pretending it doesn't hurt."

"Sorry."

The wind whipped through the holes in my injured wing, ripping the leathery membrane and causing the gashes to widen. It took all I had in me not to scream aloud.

I hadn't managed to get high enough. And there was a mountain coming at us that I was about to smash into. But on the plus side, we were out of range of those horrible archers.

There was only one thing I could do to save us.

I shifted to air.

Both Soren and Cullen started to freefall.

I shifted back to my dragon form. The shifting from one form to the other healed my torn wing. I immediately threw my wings back and dove after the falling men. There was still several hundred yards of space between them and the ground when I swooped them into my taloned claws.

"*Holy Goddess Perth! What the hell, Amaya? We-we nearly—*"

"*So dramatic, my brave prince. You weren't even close to being smashed against the rocks.*"

"*You dropped us!*"

"*I couldn't fly with a torn wing.*"

"*You. Dropped. Us.*"

"*And I caught you. I couldn't fly with a torn wing.*" How could he not understand that? "*We would have all crashed to our deaths on the side of that mountain if I hadn't shifted forms.*"

"*Could you—could you give me a warning next time?*"

"*Let's hope there's not a next time.*"

"*But if there is—?*"

"*I'll totally warn you.*"

"*That's all I ask.*"

His voice went silent in my mind. I missed it. "*How is your brother faring?*"

"*He's no worse than he was when you first added me to your escape plan.*"

Which I took to mean that he was half-dead. "*We're nearly to the cave.*"

Cullen didn't answer me, but I felt his relief ripple through my body.

A few minutes later, I set down at the entrance to the cave nestled high in the neighboring mountain. I placed Cullen on his feet, but kept Soren pressed to my chest. Cullen reached out his hand like he was going to pet me. But he stopped himself before he touched my scales.

"Beautiful," he breathed the word.

I tried to ignore his praise. Why would I care what some silly vampire thought of me? Goddess, I didn't want to feel all warm and gooey inside because someone had said one kind word to me. But I couldn't seem to stop the feelings from coming.

"Well, here's a few more kind words you deserve to hear. You, Amaya, are amazing. And I'll be forever in your debt for saving my brother. We wouldn't have been able to get him out of the camp. We could use compulsion on the living warriors. But our powers don't work on the undead, and Queen Beatrice has the undead guarding the camp's perimeter."

"Let's save him before you go and make dramatic vows." I carried Soren toward the back of the cave where I'd put Celestina in the makeshift nest of blankets.

I laid the vampire prince down next to Celestina, pressing his body to hers.

"He's going to need to feed. If you're not comfortable with letting him feed from Celestina, I could have him take my blood."

I shifted back to my human form, pulling my sweater and leather pants on at the same time so I wouldn't be naked in front of Cullen. "What would it be like for her? Would she feel the same way I did when you fed on me?"

Cullen's brown eyes darkened. "It should be the same."

"Will she be strong enough to handle the blood loss?"

"Because of their bond, her blood will be more powerful than mine for him. He'll heal faster, which in turn, will bring Celestina back to health faster."

I nodded. Celestina would want to be the one to help him. "Why isn't he feeding already?"

"He's too weak. I'll have to open a vein for him."

"No." I pressed my hand on Cullen's chest to stop him. "I'll do it." I doubted I could handle watching anyone else injure my Celestina. I knelt next to her, tilting her head to one side. And bending down like I was going to kiss her neck, I pierced her skin with one of my dragon's teeth. She jerked from the pain but remained unconscious.

Cullen helped his brother press his lips to where Celestina's blood was flowing. Soren immediately started feeding.

Celestina gasped. Her body rose to press against Soren's. Her eyes opened slightly as she threaded her fingers with his.

"Let's give them some privacy." Cullen tugged at my hand.

I let him lead us back to the mouth of the cave. He'd kept hold of my hand as we walked. I wasn't sure why he'd want to touch me like this. But I guess I didn't mind it. We stood side-by-side at the cave's entrance, looking out in the direction of the mountain where Queen Beatrice and her army had made camp. I tightened my grip on his hand when he started to release mine. I wasn't sure why I craved his touch. He wasn't another dragon. I shouldn't want him like this.

From this side of the mountain, I couldn't see any evidence of the fighting and deaths that was happening even now. It appeared peaceful here.

"Her army of the dead is relentless," he said as if he could hear my thoughts. He likely could. "They don't stop to sleep or eat. They attack night and day. Our warriors are tired."

"What are you going to do?" I asked.

He sighed. "There's nothing we can do, Amaya, other than keep fighting."

Chapter 46

Celestina

I sucked in a quick breath as Soren pressed his mouth to my neck. His hot tongue licked a jagged wound there. He was healing me the same way he'd heal his own puncture wounds closed after he'd fed. I squirmed against his hard length. I needed...needed...

But this couldn't be real. I was living with the dragons now.

"Celestina," Soren rasped. "You came back for me."

"I did? I don't remember... Where are we?" I lifted my head. "We're in a cave. Why are we in a cave?"

He cupped my cheek and nibbled on my lips. Suddenly, all the questions demanding my attention vanished.

This. I wanted this. And I didn't care how it was happening. Or why.

I reached between us. There was a huge rip in his battle leathers. I used it to gain access to his smooth skin covering tightly corded muscles.

"Let me make love to you," he begged between drugging kisses. "I need to feel you, Sky Girl. I need to fill you up to convince myself that you're really here. Is that...? Will that be...? Will you allow that?"

I nodded. "I need you more."

With his fangs, he ripped open a vein in his wrist and offered me his blood. I drank in the metallic liquid, loving how it heated my body. Still, I needed more. I couldn't get my leggings off fast enough. He worked my sweater up off over my head and immediately sank his fangs into my breast's tender flesh. I gasped as the sudden flash of pain was replaced by a pulling that traveled all the way down to my already overheated core.

Goddess. I bucked against his leg, chasing the release my body craved.

He reached between us and pressed a finger inside me while swirling my throbbing clit with his thumb. Teasing. Knowing exactly how to get my body to respond to his touch.

He lifted his head. His pupils were blown wide. "That's it, Sky Girl. Come for me."

My body obeyed. The entire world seemed to explode with flashes of light as my body convulsed on his hand.

And here we were. Together. I didn't know how. And part of me didn't want to know the specifics. All I wanted was to hold on to the now, to enjoy what his touch, his mouth, his feeding on me did to me. How his body shattered me only to pull me back together.

"That was only the first one," he murmured.

His large, calloused hands pressed my legs wide apart as he slid down my body to nestle between them. He gently sucked my clit into his mouth, licking and teasing until I was squirming beneath him. He pulled back so he could blow his hot breath against my sensitive bits.

"Celestina, you taste like honey cakes. I could eat you forever." His fangs flashed in the cave's dim light before he struck again. Down. There. In that most sensitive place.

He'd bitten me there once before, but, even so, the shock of the pain had me wiggling away. Soren clamped his hands on my hips, to keep me in place. The pain swiftly became something different, something hot and *nuhnnn...*

I threw my head back and buried my hands in his hair as he proved just how much he enjoyed eating me out. I didn't think I could come harder than I just had, but his wicked teeth and tongue proved me wrong as my body splintered into a flash of bright light.

When I finally managed to catch my breath, Soren looked up at me and smiled. I smiled back. I so loved it when he played with me like this. And I could tell by the hungry look in his eyes, that he wasn't nearly done.

He crawled back up my body, pressing his lips to mine, letting me taste myself on him as he deepened the kiss, pressing his tongue in my mouth, as he pushed two fingers into my pussy and then worked his thick thumb into my puckered hole. I reveled in the feeling of absolute fullness as he pumped his fingers in and out of both slick holes. I came hard and fast, holding him tightly as my body pulsed on his hand. I loved the roughness of his battle leathers against my naked skin. And yet…

"I need…I need more…" I panted as I fumbled with the buttons on his leather pants. "I need all of you."

He withdrew from my body and, after wiping his hands on the blanket, took over the task. As he shed his pants, I bared his chest. There was a long, jagged red line marking a barely healed wound on his belly that made me frown. But it didn't seem to bother him when I ran my hand over it. Still, I didn't like seeing any injury on his perfect body. I kissed it, wishing I could stop him from ever going to battle again, from ever getting harmed even in the slightest way.

My vampire prince was *mine*. He was the most important part of my beloved hoard. He deserved to be cherished. Protected. The part of me that I still hadn't really accepted raged inside me. *Mine. I protect what is mine.*

"You are well?" I asked him, unable to stop worrying about that mark on his body.

"I am now." It was a strange answer. But I guess I understood what he'd meant. For the past several weeks, I'd been walking around with a gaping hole in my chest from having to live without him.

But that didn't explain the jagged red line. It still worried me. I traced it. "What happened?" I asked between kisses as we wrapped our bodies around each other and sank back into the nest of blankets.

His hand closed over mine. "What's important right now is you. I—I can't think when I need you so fiercely, Sky Girl. You're the reason I'm still here in this world. You're the light in all the darkness that surrounds me. I don't know how you got here to me or why. All I know is that I'm not going to fucking waste a second of this."

He flipped me over and, wrapped his arm around my middle, positioning me so my ass was in the air. I balanced myself with my hands on the blankets. "Brace yourself, darling, because I'm going to fucking show you how much my cock missed you." With his knee, he spread my legs wider and then with one fluid movement pushed inside me. Oh, how my body had missed him…missed this. Even at the awkward angle, with him holding me up while my head was hanging toward the cave floor and my fingertips barely touching the blankets to balance me, his cock hit places inside me that more than approved of his actions. I arched my back as he pounded relentlessly, my body tightening, tightening around the flood of sensations. His strong fingers dug into my hips as he continued to move at a frenetic pace.

"Come for me again, Sky Girl," he growled.

Everything went black for a moment as my body obeyed and tipped over the edge yet again. He followed me, filling me. Breathing hard, we tumbled back into the nest of blankets. He spun us to the side, so his body would take the brunt of the fall. And once we were half-buried in the nest of warm wool, I turned in his arms and gently brushed my lips over his.

"Hello," I said as soon as I lifted my lips.

"Hello," he replied. A smile crinkled the corners of his eyes. He brushed the side of my face with the back of his hand. "How?" He shook his head. "How did you get to me?"

"I don't know. I woke up with you here." I touched the place on my neck where the wound he'd healed had been. "Where are we?"

"I don't know." He sat up slightly so he could take a better look around. "A cave."

I gave his chest a playful shove. "Thank you. I would have never figured that out on my own." He captured my hand and lifted it to his mouth. He sucked my forefinger into the hot cavern of his mouth. I sighed. "How do you suppose we both ended up in this cave together?"

He pulled my finger from his mouth and gave the tip a tender kiss before taking a moment to ponder that question.

"Well"—he slapped my bare ass as he jumped to his feet—"we should get dressed and find out."

I groaned, not wanting to leave our nest. But I managed to crawl my way to my feet and gather my discarded clothes. I tugged on my leggings, but paused when I felt the tingly sting of where he'd bitten my clit. My body shuddered with delight at the reminder of what we'd just done.

Other than the first bite that he'd healed with his tongue, he'd left all the others. I ran the tip of my finger over where he'd bitten my breast, enjoying how pain and pleasure blended together. My lower lip felt bruised from where he'd kissed me too enthusiastically. I pressed my tongue against the sting and smiled.

This. This is what I love. Soren always gives me exactly what my body craves.

I pulled my sweater over my head and tightened the ties on my leggings.

"Are we ready to find out where the hell we are?" he asked as he buttoned his ripped and bloodied leather coat.

I hesitated. I didn't want to leave this place when leaving meant I'd have to deal with reality. And my last memory was of Drix killing Amaya in hopes that my anger would awaken my dragon.

Oh goddess, my last memory is of Amaya's throat being cut!

I couldn't—I couldn't—I couldn't—

"Shhh…breathe, Celestina. Breathe. We'll figure this out together. I promise." He rubbed my back vigorously until I was able to catch my breath. With a look of panic, he threaded his fingers with mine. "I'll fight the entire continent to keep you by my side. Fuck the prophecies and kingdoms and responsibilities. I'm not going to let you go, not ever again."

While I believed his words, I doubted even Soren could turn the impossible into a reality. And falling apart about everything I'd already lost wasn't going to help anything. I pulled myself together, straightening my spine, lifting my chin.

Neither of us knew what waited for us at the mouth of this cave, but we'd face it—woefully unarmed—together.

The sun was starting to travel toward the horizon, sending sharp beams of light directly into the cave's mouth. I had to squint in the sudden brightness to make out the silhouette of two figures sitting side-by-side a few hundred steps away. Both Soren and I stopped. Were they friends or foes? I cupped my hand over my eyes to block out the glare. I recognized the outline of the woman sitting to the right of the taller, lankier figure.

"It can't be." My voice must have carried in the cave. The woman stood and turned toward us. My eyes had adjusted to the bright light enough that I could make out the sharp features of her face and the inky blackness of her hair.

"Amaya!" I screamed. I fell to my knees as my legs gave out on me. "How? You're alive! How?"

Maybe it was time I started believing in the impossible.

Chapter 47

Celestina

After many, many hugs and a few tears on my part, Amaya explained how Juniper had defied Drix. Juniper had made sure I put my hands on Amaya, and even though I wasn't conscious of any of this happening, my magic had been able to pull on Amaya's, forcing her to shift to her air form. It had saved her life. Prince Cullen then explained how Amaya had bravely rescued Soren and had brought us both to this cave so we could heal each other.

"His intestines were hanging out?" I whirled to Soren. "You were injured so badly that your intestines were hanging out?"

"It wouldn't have been a fatal blow if those creepy undead soldiers hadn't bitten me so many times. Blood loss makes it nearly impossible to heal ourselves. And then I was captured, so I couldn't feed to regain my strength."

"You nearly died." Icy dread overtook me as I imagined what it would be like if I lost Soren forever. As miserable as life had been when we were forced to part, at least I woke every day knowing that Soren was in my world and living the life he was fated to live. To lose the hope that one day we would be reunited would have destroyed me.

"You're missing the main point of what we're telling you, Moonglow," Amaya said with an irritated huff.

"The bonding didn't just go one way," Prince Cullen said. "When you were injured, Soren, Princess Celestina felt it. When you were dying, she was dying along with you."

"What?" Soren backed up a step.

"Your lives are entangled with each other's, brother. Which means if you don't want to kill your princess, you must stop going on those suicide missions while leaving Gray and Raya behind."

"No. That's impossible. I was the only one who made the vows," Soren said at the same time as I growled-shouted, *"You've been doing what!?"*

Soren had enough sense to look remorseful.

Even so, smoke curled from my nose, and I felt my teeth sharpen. *"You will not needlessly endanger yourself ever again,"* said with my growly voice that carried the strongest push of compulsion I could conjure. I knew doing that to him was crossing all kinds of boundaries, boundaries he'd never allowed himself to cross when I was wearing that slave collar. But I didn't care. Keeping him safe—even from himself—was more important than keeping his trust or fostering a healthy relationship. It wasn't as if we'd be allowed to stay together anyhow. And dammit, I needed to know he would take care of himself. I needed him safe.

"You didn't need to do that," Soren muttered as he dredged a hand through his hair. "Knowing your life is linked to mine is incentive enough to keep me from recklessly charging the front lines." He flashed an irritated look in his brother's direction. "And I haven't been going on suicide missions. The siege never stops. My warriors are exhausted. I've been helping where I can, leading from the front. And, yes, I leave Gray and Raya behind, because I need them to take charge in my absence—making decisions, issuing orders, and answering questions." He closed his eyes and drew several deep breaths before speaking again. "We're on the verge of losing, Sky Girl. Our warriors stay dead after they've been struck down while Queen Beatrice's pop back up to fight again."

"I'm sorry I used compulsion on you." I slipped my arms around him and pressed as tightly against his chest as I could manage. I was grateful that he didn't push me away. Instead, his arms tightened around me. "I panicked at the thought of losing you."

Soren touched his forehead to mine. "My heart has shattered, completely shattered, every time you've been hurt. And it felt like someone ripped that organ from my body when you were taken from me. I wanted to burn down the world to get you back."

"You believe dragon fire will kill Queen Beatrice's undead army?" Amaya demanded irritably as if she'd heard enough of us proclaiming our love for each other.

"That's our working theory," Prince Cullen answered. "She's using a combination of blood magic and her own magic. It's powerful and awfully corrosive."

"Then I'm going to go make sure the queen's warriors stay dead," Amaya said right before shifting to her dragon form and flying out of the cave.

Amaya

I learned something I never knew about dragons that day. Our fires were not infinite. Did Gregory know this? Or was it yet another piece of knowledge that had been lost when our kingdom fell?

After I'd gone off to kill the undead army, Cullen called me back. He needed me to deliver Soren, Celestina, and himself to the vampire's main camp at the border. He didn't ask me to carry them, but when they'd started the long hike toward the camp, I huffed an impatient breath, scooped them up into my talons, and carried them the rest of the way.

Without waiting for a thank you, I flew back toward the battlefields to take on the undead army. I was able to roast several hundred of the creepy already-dead humans, shifting to air whenever an arrow managed to pierce a wing or puncture my more vulnerable underside. Unfortunately, the undead army weren't the mindless killers I'd hoped they would be. They'd quickly shifted tactics in the face of a new enemy, shielding themselves in the crevasses and caves that peppered the Northern Mountains.

That's when I realized I couldn't singlehandedly defeat Queen Beatrice's army. But I kept fighting, determined to give the Fein warriors a break from fighting an unbeatable foe. The creepy corpses did seem to stay dead when I burned them.

"Return to camp!", Cullen shouted in my head. *"You shouldn't run off by yourself with no plan other than 'bring death.' That's how warriors get themselves killed."*

Aww, vampire boy was worried for my safety, which I should have found that sweet. But I couldn't enjoy his concern when his emotions tightened like a vice around mine, making me jumpy and overly cautious when decisive actions were clearly needed here. So, I blocked him.

Despite the wall between our thoughts, I could still feel him reaching for me. A muted version of his prickling concern curled like ropes around my emotions. *Foolish vampire.* I was a dragon. A dreaded midnight dragon at that. Destruction was what I was born to do.

I cornered a troop of undead in a cave and began to roast them as if they were in muffins in an oven when the first wave of dizziness hit. I nearly fell from the sky before I managed to shake it off. I shot another burst of fire at the cave's opening only to get hit with dizziness again. The world spun. I couldn't tell up from down. I slammed into the rocky ground, breaking bones in both my wings.

Damn. That hurt.

The undead flooded out of the cave with spears ready to finish me off. Their bodies looked seared around the edges. Some were missing limbs and others had deformed faces thanks to my fire. But the creepy warriors were still in fighting form. Apparently, the only way to truly stop them was to reduce their bodies to ashes.

I wouldn't be able to do that while the world was spinning around me faster than a child's toy top. In a panic, I found a tiny spark of magic hidden deep inside my chest and used it to shift to air.

Thankful to still be alive, I raced back to the Fein's camp and into the tent where Soren, Cullen, Celestina, Gray, and Raya were discussing strategy. By that time, I didn't have enough magic left in me to turn into anything.

Despite my formless shape, Cullen spotted me.

"Amaya?"

"Yep." I didn't want to talk about it.

"What are you doing?"

"What does it look like I'm doing?"

"Nothing. You're literally nothing right now."

"Very perceptive of you, Vampire."

He adjusted his glasses. *"Ah. I see."*

He moved over to where Celestina was standing near a map that had been unrolled on to a broad wooden table and whispered in her ear.

Her gaze shot to the ceiling, missing where I was floating by yards.

Cullen wrapped his fingers around her wrist.

"What are you doing?" Soren growled.

Both Gray and Raya moved swiftly to separate Cullen from Celestina.

Cullen's hands flew into the air. "I'm trying to help Amaya."

"That's what you said when 'helping Amaya' meant attacking us, drugging Sky Girl, and stuffing her into a dungeon," Raya said. She looked two breaths away from stabbing Cullen in the eyeball. *Oh, how I like her!*

"Amaya is stuck in her air form. Prince Cullen asked me to help her," Celestina explained in that soft voice of hers.

Soren bumped his chest against his brother's. "And helping Amaya involves you touching my mate?"

Celestina pressed her hand to Soren's chest and brushed a kiss against his willing lips. They kissed a bit longer than I thought was necessary, but the two were like that whenever they were together—touching, kissing, groping. "I can't see Amaya when she's air. Cullen can."

Soren grumbled. But after Celestina pressed another kiss to his lips, he nodded to Gray and Raya for them to step out of the way.

Cullen once again took Celestina's wrist in his hand and lifted it so her fingers brushed through me. Her fingertips sparked.

That little bit of magic did the trick. I dropped naked from the ceiling.

Cullen whipped off his cape and wrapped it around me as I lay in a helpless heap on the tent floor.

Celestina dropped to her knees on the floor next to me. "What happened?"

"Dragon fire eventually runs out," I rasped. My eyes didn't want to stay open. It took every ounce of energy to fight the darkness tugging at me. "I fought. But many of the undead hid from me. Too many."

Celestina rubbed my arm. "You must rest."

"You have given my warriors time to regroup," Soren said as he paced.

"Time we desperately needed."

"Delaying the inevitable," Cullen murmured. "Despite our superior strength, speed, and ability to heal ourselves, we'll never be able to win against an enemy we cannot kill. What we need are more dragons."

"The clan won't come!" My voice cracked with emotion. "They hate you!" I didn't know why admitting that brought tears to my eyes. I hated Cullen, too.

No, you don't, my pesky inner voice corrected.

My feelings didn't matter here though. Celestina was safe. The clan had tasked me to save her life and bring Soren back with me so the dragons could protect him. They had no desire to meddle in outside affairs. Except, that was wrong. Many in the clan *did* want to involve themselves. They saw Celestina's return as the opportunity for the dragons to rebuild the fifth kingdom. And to do that, they needed to leave the plateau.

Celestina seemed to sense my turmoil. She seemed to understand that I needed to get away from the glaring eyes, that I needed some time alone to regain my strength and my emotional balance. She hooked her hands under my arms and helped me to my feet. "Let's get you somewhere comfortable to rest. Raya, would you mind sharing your tent?"

"I'd be honored." Raya rushed over and helped Celestina support me. The room spun in and out of focus. I'd never pulled this much magic. I'd never pushed myself so close to exhaustion. It was…disconcerting.

I…didn't…like…how…everything…was…getting…gray…and… fuzzy…

Cullen swept me off my feet and hugged me tightly against his warm chest. Having him hold me like this shouldn't have made me feel so safe or so protected. "I'm taking her to my tent."

Soren blocked the exit. "Are you sure that's wise?"

Content to let Cullen take over my care, I snuggled into his arms, closed my eyes, and let my thoughts slide into the gray nothingness waiting for me on the flipside of consciousness. As the last remnants of my awareness faded, I heard Cullen tell his brother, "Protecting Amaya is the only thing I'm sure of."

I didn't hate that.

Chapter 48

Celestina

After I'd made sure Amaya was resting comfortably—which is to say Cullen shoved me out of his tent—Soren and I made the rounds of the camp. It felt like old times. Everyone in his army still loved him. Everyone still looked to him for advice and leadership. But none of the captains and the warriors we encountered cracked jokes or smiled as they had before.

Soren was right. His warriors were exhausted and beaten down. It felt as if they had already accepted the inevitable. They were going to lose— and likely die—in these mountains.

"Queen Beatrice has started to reanimate *our* dead," Driscoll reported after one of Soren's captains had provided a brutal description of troop losses. "One of my men discovered that three of our mass gravesites are empty. And when he followed the tracks from the last gravesite, he recognized the dead men from our camp regrouping under Earst's battle banner and wearing the queen's purple uniform."

I pressed my hand to my mouth.

Soren pinched his lips together. After a stunned moment, he thanked Driscoll for the information and dismissed Cullen's favorite spy.

"What are you going to do?" I whispered once we'd started walking again.

"Burn our dead."

"Are you worried about what will happen with morale when your warriors start recognizing the warriors they're fighting against?"

"Honestly, I don't believe morale can get any worse than it is already."

"He's wrong," a voice whispered in my mind. A foreign voice...but also a familiar one. *"Today will be remembered as a happy day for his army when compared to what I'm going to do to Soren and his precious kingdom. And you're going to be the one tearing his world apart from the inside."*

No. I would never help Queen Beatrice, for that was clearly the voice I was hearing. Was this real? Or was the stress of the battle making me hear threatening voices that weren't there?

"Oh, you'll help me. You have no choice but to do what I say."

Even if she still had some level of control over me, I wouldn't let her win. "Soren." I gripped his arm so hard, he stopped midstride. "Soren, Queen Beatrice—"

Soren raised his eyebrows when I didn't finish. "Talk to me. What's wrong?"

A smile that wasn't of my own making curled my lips. Words that weren't mine were spoken by my mouth. "Nothing's wrong. I simply wanted to say that Queen Beatrice isn't all bad. She has always been a fair ruler. The Fein will like living under her power."

"I...see..." he said slowly, carefully.

Relief washed over me. He did *see.* And now he knew I couldn't be trusted.

What would he do about it? Would he lock me in shackles? If she were to force me to take my dragon form, shackles wouldn't hold me. Would he knock me out? If she were in control of my body, leaving me unconscious wouldn't stop her from using my muscles.

"I should—" *leave.*

Soren kissed me before I could get that last part out. His fingers twined with mine while his lips made me feel all the deep feelings that I didn't want to feel for him right now. Not when I needed to get away from him, away from this camp.

"I know what's happening," Soren said when our lips finally parted.

"I've known for quite some time that Queen Beatrice could use one of Queen Freida's binding spells to control you. Cullen saw all the various bindings when he first met you. That's one of his talents. He sees threats when others can't. That's why he can see Amaya when she's in her air form."

"You should have…you should have… I need to get away from here." I tried to put space between us.

His fingers tightened. "Don't run from this."

"We have a plan to help her, don't we?" Gray asked as he walked up to join us. Gray and Raya had been attending to other matters in the camp while Soren had taken reports.

"Of course, Soren has a plan, Nimrod." Raya nudged Gray's arm as she joined us as well. "He came up with a way to handle the binding spell weeks ago."

I appreciated Raya's attempts to calm me. But this was yet another vital piece of information that Soren had kept from me. "I thought we were going to trust each other!"

"We are! At first, I didn't tell you because it didn't matter. The slave collar held essentially the same amount of power over you. And then after the collar came off, we really haven't had much time together to discuss everything, have we? It's been one disaster after another." The steady way he looked at me helped slow my racing heart. "And we don't have a solid plan, yet. But Cullen is researching ways to break the bindings. Not just him. He has all the librarians at the Palladian Library looking for answers."

"You still should have told me. I don't feel comfortable putting you or anyone at risk."

"Even if giving you up would help, I'm not going to do it, Sky Girl. Not again. The continent wouldn't survive my losing you a third time. I wouldn't survive it." He drew a long breath. "And besides, running from here won't solve anything. If Queen Beatrice can control you, she can always force you to return."

He was right. I suddenly had trouble catching my breath.

When was this horror ever going to end?

My life had never been my own to live. And after Queen Beatrice completed her goal of destroying the Fein, which kingdom would she use me to attack next? I wasn't a warrior. I didn't have the heart of a killer. I didn't want to be a tool to bring any of the kingdoms to their knees.

"Do you need to borrow my spoon?" Mary, the wizened old cook, held out her oversized spoon for me to take. She might have been small, but she used her oversized spoon to keep the Fein's highly trained warriors in line. Even Gray and Raya took several steps back as she approached.

"Mary!" I threw my arms around her. When I'd first been brought to Soren's camp as a slave, she'd taken me under her wing, taught me how to help prepare the meals, and had treated me like I was part of her family.

"Ugh! Don't get all mushy on me." She pushed me off her. But I could tell by the way the corners of her eyes crinkled that she didn't mind that I was hugging her. "Are you here to work?"

"I would love that! Is Patty here to help as well?"

Mary shook her head. "I sent Patty home a few days ago. Things aren't—" She shook her head again. "It's too dangerous for her to stay."

The dragon fires in my chest stirred at the thought of Queen Beatrice's undead army harming someone like Mary.

"I told you to leave as well," Soren said to the old woman, his voice a gentle rebuke. "We can cook our own meals."

"Your warriors are coming back to camp with barely enough energy to clean themselves up, and that's if they manage to come back at all," Mary growled. "If they can keep going out there to defend our border against a terrible foe, I can damn well stay here and make sure they have a hot meal ready for when they return."

Soren cleared his throat, but even so, his voice sounded rusty when he said, "Thank you, Mary. You are a treasure."

The dragon fires in me started to burn even hotter at the thought of Mary sacrificing herself. None of this would be happening if Queen Beatrice hadn't used me to gain inside information about the Fein. If not for me, she wouldn't have known that the Fein were vampires. She wouldn't have learned about the Tiburnian's use of blood magic. All of what she was doing here was because she had been able to see things through my eyes.

"This. Should. Not. Be. Happening." Anger flooded my heart.

"Sky Girl," Raya moved toward me, but Gray grabbed her shoulder and hauled her back.

"What are you doing?" Soren asked. He, too, stepped away from me.

"I'm furious," I told him.

"Your eyes and skin…they're glowing." He pushed Mary behind him. "That can't be good. Take some deep breaths."

"No." I glanced down at my arms. They shimmered. My entire body vibrated with energy. I felt powerful. Nothing could stop me from protecting my hoard, my family. Not even a bitch of a queen who relished bloody spectacles. I shined brighter and brighter as I pulled magic from the ground and let it fill me and fill me. "You want a bloody spectacle!" I raised my arms and shouted to the sky. "I'll give you a bloody spectacle!"

The magic exploded.

It knocked Soren, Raya, Gray, Mary, and everyone in the camp who were within sight of me flat on their backs. The magic surged across the landscape in a circular wave pattern that grew wider and weaker as it pressed out its borders.

My arms dropped to my side. They were no longer glowing. No part of me glowed anymore. Nor could I feel the stirring of my dragon fire. My power was gone, spent on an empty display of fireworks. I felt like a human again—weak and rather helpless.

"You foolish girl," Queen Beatrice hissed in my mind. Even her voice sounded faint. Faint enough to easily ignore.

"I didn't hurt anyone, did I?"

Soren picked himself up off the ground and brushed the dust from his battle leathers. He helped Mary to her feet. She had a cut above her eyebrow that was slowly oozing blood.

"Sky Girl, that was—" Mary grumbled.

"I'm sorry!" I said in a rush. I wanted to help her, but at the same time, I was afraid to touch anyone. "I didn't mean to—"

"If that's what you do when you're not even trying, I can't wait to see what you do when you go up against Queen Beatrice," Mary said with an approving nod.

"I agree," Gray said. He was clutching his right arm, but he was smiling. "That was…wow."

Raya nudged his uninjured side. "I've been telling you from the beginning that she's amazing."

"And you're right," Gray agreed.

"I don't think I can do that again." I felt dizzy, like maybe I needed to sit down. As soon as that thought hit me, my legs collapsed, and my bottom hit the ground hard.

"Any time you use magic, it takes time to recover," Soren said. "And the binding spells pack kickbacks that will hurt you whenever your magic tries to break through them." He started to lift me into his arms. But I didn't want to be carried.

I wiggled to keep him from sweeping my feet out from under me. "I can walk."

He kept his arm across my shoulder to make sure I didn't collapse again. "Whatever you want, Princess," he said, "I'll make sure it happens."

"I want to help Mary with the dinner prep."

Soren frowned. "That wasn't what I was expecting."

"That's my girl." Mary slapped her wrinkly hands together. "She's always been my best helper. Only slightly better than my Patty, and both are heads over heels more disciplined than your lazy louts, General Kitmun."

And that was how I came to be standing at the worktable, peeling and dicing carrots and chopping onions. I missed Patty's excited chattering. She'd often talk so much that I wouldn't have a chance to utter a sound for hours. But today, I stood at the table alone. Still, the monotony of my chopping movements calmed me.

The only irritation was that the invasive green lizards seemed to be taking extra interest in my work. I kept having to stop to brush them off the table. Maybe they were hungry. I doubted they'd find much to eat this high in the snowy mountains.

Soren remained nearby. He was talking with Gray and Raya and a few of his captains. Every so often he'd glance at me. And smile.

I could live for those smiles.

So, as I worked, I pretended we had a lifetime in front of us to enjoy little pleasures like seeing the charming smiles he saved just for me, an expression where Soren lifted one corner of his mouth lifted a bit higher than the other in a look of pure delight. And for a beautiful moment, I managed to trick myself into believing it.

Amaya

I sat up with a start, shoving aside the silky blankets that had been wrapped tightly around my body. Cullen spun toward me, clearly surprised I'd wake up so suddenly after suffering such a strong power drain. But he must have felt the jolt of magic that had surged through the camp. He must have understood that not even the dead could have slept through a magical burst that strong.

I recognized the sharp sting of the power. That was Celestina's magic.

Cullen adjusted his glasses as he leaned toward me. "Amaya? What's happening?"

I felt energized, like I could burn twice as many undead warriors before collapsing again. And I felt clearheaded. Puzzle pieces I hadn't realized existed suddenly fell into place.

Of course. Of course, I said to myself as I sucked in a quick breath when I realized exactly what needed to be done.

In my excitement, I grabbed Cullen's arm and pulled his mouth to mine to kiss. "I know how to free Celestina from her binding," I said once our lips parted.

"Bindings," Cullen corrected as he chased after me through the camp. "There's more than one. At least two."

"Two." I nodded as I hurried toward the epicenter of the power burst. "Two makes sense." I needed to get to Celestina. If I slowed down to think things through, or if I discussed what I planned to do with someone else, I wouldn't do it. I'd lose my nerve.

I was a force of destruction. This was why the ancients had paired me with Celestina. Because I could destroy. And sometimes destruction was the only way to blaze a path for something new to bloom. That was how gardens were created. I knew that from working in my mother's garden. The weeds had to be torn away, and the ground churned up, before something beautiful could take root.

At the far end of the camp, I found Celestina preparing a meal for the vampires. Was this how the vampires treated her? Like a servant? We were dragons. We were superior. The vampires should be serving us.

But that was beside the point. I had a binding to break. I grabbed Celestina's arm and spun her around to face me.

"I am sorry," I uttered, allowing a tiny slice of remorse to slip loose before I shut down all my useless, squishy emotions. *I'm sorry that I'm going to hurt you—sister of my heart.*

I called forth my dragon claws—and with a quick swipe of my hand, dug my razor-sharp talons into Celestina's perfect face, gouging out both her eyes and tearing apart her face in the process.

She screamed.

Blood sprayed everywhere.

Mary took one look at Celestina's ruined face and started screaming as well. And I remained standing in front of her, staring. Waiting.

Cullen wrapped his arms around my chest, yanking me away from Celestina.

"What the hell—?" Soren thundered as he ran to catch his precious princess as she collapsed into his embrace. Gray and Raya followed closely behind him. Gray already had his swords drawn. What was he thinking he'd do? Strike me down? *I'd like to see him try.*

Everyone started shouting at once. So many voices. Too many voices, I couldn't make sense of any of them.

"Was this your plan?" Cullen's calm voice, spoken directly inside my head, cut through the shouting and the accusations. He didn't sound upset, only curious. *"Is this going to free Princess Celestina? Or does something else need to happen?"*

"It should be all that's needed." I hoped. If not, Celestina would end up permanently blinded.

"Shift," I whispered aloud. "You need to shift."

Shifting forms would heal her ruined face and replace her eyes.

"It was her eyes," I told Cullen. *"Her mismatched eyes. A member of the clan had painted our portraits. Gwen is a stickler for details. She remembers the smallest ones. And she had painted Celestina's eyes in the portrait indigo. Not brown and green. Indigo. She said she thought the blueish-purple color was what the painting wanted. But canvases are simply cloth pulled over a wooden frame. They don't have color preferences. Was Gwen remembering details from a long time ago? She knew Celestina when we were both babies. If Celestina hadn't been stolen, Gwen would have become her adoptive mother.*

"When I returned Celestina to the clan, it must have triggered Gwen's memory of Celestina's vibrant eye color. Which would explain why she painted Celestina's eyes a bright indigo instead of the mismatched eyes Celestina has now. And here's the important question. What would make eyes drastically change their coloring? A spell cast upon them, perhaps?"

"That's brilliant."

"Only if I'm right. Otherwise, I'm the monster here."

His arms holding me tightened, but not in a threatening way. *"You're not a monster, my beautiful Amaya. Your heart is too big, and you care too much for others to ever allow you to become the villain of this story."*

I hoped he was right. I'd spent my entire life being feared, being told that I needed to curb my impulses, to ignore my instincts.

Turn.

I held my breath.

Turn.

Celestina had sunk in on herself as Soren held her. She was silently weeping.

Turn.

Gray and Raya had positioned themselves between Celestina and me.

Turn.

The air around us felt wrong. Had I…had I…made a mistake?

"She needs to take her dragon"

"Does she know how?" Cullen asked. *"Is it instinct? Or is shifting forms something that needs to be taught?"*

"It should be instinct, but she's been separated from her dragon for so long that she might not know how to call it. She should have shifted by now. A serious injury should have triggered her to shift to heal it." What if this was a mistake? What would the clan do to me when they discovered that I'd ripped out the moonlight

dragon's eyes?

Soren tore open a vein in his wrist. He was about to press the bloody wound to Celestina's lips. Vampire blood could heal many things, but I didn't think vampire blood could bring back lost eyes.

"Stop!" Cullen shouted, reaching out a hand. "Don't give her your blood."

"I need to help her. And you need to keep Amaya away from me or I will kill her. Get her out of here. Now!"

"You need to listen to me. Amaya knows what she's doing. You must let her help Celestina." Cullen moved me closer.

Raya brandished her sword. "I don't think so," she said.

"If you care for Amaya's life, get her out of here, Cull," Gray said softly. Dangerously.

"Amaya?" Celestina's voice cracked. She lifted her head from Soren's shoulder and turned her sightless face toward me. "Why?"

"Can you feel your dragon?"

She sobbed as she shook her head.

I growled in frustration. *Dammit, she needs to shift.*

With a burst of magic, I broke out of Cullen's arms and pushed through Gray and Raya, blowing them out of my way. I hissed at Soren and grabbed Celestina's hand.

"Don't fall apart, Moonglow. Pull my magic." I held up my other hand, blocking a sword from striking me with the flat of my palm. I could feel my magic stir, but it wasn't enough. I needed her to force me to shift. If she did, I could pull her dragon out with me.

"Focus!" I barked at her.

Soren was yanking Celestina away from me. The others were shouting. And fighting Cullen, who'd slid through Soren's warriors to stand beside me.

Time was running out. I needed to pull Celestina's magic like she did with mine. But the midnight dragon was a tool for the moonlight dragon to use. I didn't have the same powers that Celestina had. My importance came from the link I shared with Celestina.

"Didn't you read the book I gave you?" Cullen demanded. *"That's not what the text says. Midnight dragons are powerful all on their own. Stop telling yourself what you can't do and help her."*

"I am powerful." I scrunched my eyes closed and focused on tearing Celestina's magic through her. Her magic hit me so hard, I fell to my knees.

Celestina threw her head back and screamed as her body vanished. Air was the transition point of our shift. And as the air shimmered all around us, the ground rumbled beneath our feet.

Then in a blink-and-you'll-miss-it moment, a shimmering moonlight dragon appeared. She was the largest dragon I'd ever seen. Her scales were translucent. She spread her massive wings and held them out, so they'd fill with wind. The wings glittered with all the colors of the rainbow. She looked down at me and blinked her large indigo eyes.

"Goddess, you are beautiful," Soren gasped as Celestina flapped her massive leathery wings. Slowly, gracefully, she rose from the ground.

"Thank you." Celestina's words echoed in my mind.

Tears filled my eyes. *Dammit. Stupid Cullen.* My vampire wrapped his arms around me and kissed my cheek. "You did it, my beautiful menace."

"Did I? Hmm…I did. I guess I really did."

Chapter 49

Celestina

The world suddenly felt smaller. And for the first time in my life, I could take a full breath. *This.* This was who I was meant to be. I soared above the mountain peaks, above the birds, above the clouds. The sun sinking below the horizon colored the sky in vivid streaks of reds and oranges. I could spend a lifetime up here and never tire of this feeling of freedom.

Another dragon shot like a bolt of black lightning in front of me. Startled, I drew my wings back against my body and immediately started to tumble from the sky.

"Oh, for fuck's sake," Amaya's voice cut through my mind. *"Don't be so dramatic."*

As if my body knew what to do better than my mind, my wings stretched back out and stopped my rapid descent. With a chuffing laugh, I spiraled back up, up, up until I was flying alongside the midnight dragon, matching her height and speed. She looked over at me and nodded her approval.

We were meant to be in the skies together like this, Amaya and me. We were creatures of the air. Graceful, lithe, and beautiful. As night descended on the land, I was amazed to discover that while Amaya disappeared into the darkness, I glowed softly. It reminded me of the phosphorescent diatoms floating on the Faraday Sea. When I'd watched them from Cullen's ship, they'd felt familiar. Was this why?

I spun in lazy circles and flew large loops, delighting at the patterns of lights I formed in the sky. The midnight dragon stayed with me like a shadow, echoing my movements, occasionally suggesting her own.

Then I plunged through a cloud and emerged to find...

Flames.

Not dragon fires. These were the flames of war.

All my joy dissolved as I remembered Queen Beatrice and what she was doing, how she was twisting nature, how she was targeting the vampires.

My hoard.

They were in danger. I needed to get back to them.

I turned away from the fighting taking place on the side of the mountain to retrace a path back to the Fein camp. Amaya nipped my shoulder. She turned her massive head down to the soldiers below us.

"We can help." She pushed the thought into my mind.

The vampire warriors were swinging their swords, fighting off a troop of unkillable soldiers. I might not be able to blast my fire to kill the undead army already battling the Fein without harming the vampires, but I could keep Soren's warriors from being overrun by this new wave of undead marching toward them. I followed the midnight dragon, swooping low. We both released our fires, burning everything in our paths.

The midnight dragon looped in the air behind me, repeating the process of burning the army I'd already scorched, reducing their bodies to ashes.

"They will rise again if you don't burn them into nothingness," Amaya explained. *"Let's go attack Queen Beatrice's camp. Cut off the head of the snake before she can bite us."*

That sounded like a splendid idea. I followed Amaya as she led the way to a collection of tan tents arranged on the side of a nearby mountain. I was about to open my mouth and blast the area with my fire when Queen Beatrice stepped out of the largest tent. Her hand rested on a tiny, bony shoulder.

Robert.

Goddess, no. Queen Beatrice had brought her youngest son to a war camp. Three more boys emerged from the tent. *She brought all her babies to the battlefield?* The oldest was only seven and the youngest was three. And the two twins in the middle had only recently turned five.

Queen Beatrice looked up at me and smiled. I could no longer hear her voice in my head, but I could imagine the words she'd say if she could— she was using those tiny, innocent babies of hers as a shield. If I wanted to kill her, I'd have to kill them first.

No, I can't do that.

"I can do it." Amaya's voice flitted through my mind a moment before she began to dive toward the queen and her children.

"No!" I dove after her. My massive snout slammed against the side of her head, sending the burst of fire she'd aimed at the queen veering off course. Her fire burned several of the tents that surrounded the monarch's tent. Men came running out. Some of them were on fire.

"I won't allow you to burn innocent children!"

Queen Beatrice's smile grew wider as she stood behind her four boys. They kept their heads down. This wasn't right. Those imps should have been jumping with excitement to witness live dragons flying so close to them, but instead, they stood as still as statues. I wanted nothing more than to swoop down and gather the poor little boys into my arms and protect them.

"I will protect them," I vowed.

"How?" Amaya demanded. *"And why? They come from the bloodline of a killer."*

"They're babies. And we're not villains." And that was all the reason I needed.

Amaya chuffed unhappily but spread her wings wide, catching the wind, letting it lift her away from the enemy encampment.

"We need more dragons," she said. *"If we're going to fight the undead army by ourselves instead of killing their queen bitch, we need more dragons. And the clan won't come. Not for me. I've already tried to bring them with me to save you and Soren. And the council denied me."*

I snorted at that. The Council had made such bold speeches about how

I was supposed to lead them into a new age of the dragon. Well, if they wanted that to happen, they'd have to leave the plateau and join the fighting that was happening here.

"Hey, Moonglow," Amaya transmitted. *"Doesn't the moonlight dragon have the power to call the other dragons? Isn't it a call they won't be able to resist? You could connect to them through me."*

I closed my eyes and concentrated on sending out a message to all the dragons by channeling Amaya's magic. I wasn't going to send a growly compulsion, like Amaya was suggesting. Just an invitation. *"Come, dragon clan. Come, all who can hear me. Fight with me. Retake the continent. Breathe new life into the fifth kingdom."*

"Mountainside straight ahead!" Amaya warned.

I opened my eyes in time to see the jagged peaks rushing toward me. With a flick of my wings that came naturally—thank goodness—I shot up into the night sky. My body blasted through a fluffy cloud, coating my scales in glistening dew. Once I was above even the highest of the mountain peaks, I leveled off and flew straight again. I shut my eyes and repeated the call to my fellow dragons.

"Come."

The clan could meet at the Fein camp to strategize. The boys would have to be spirited away to safety before we could launch a full-on attack of Queen Beatrice's unnatural forces.

"Come, my dragon kin."

Working as a team, we would unleash our dragon fire on the undead.

"Our new homeland awaits."

We would free the slaves in Earst and rule over the land. It would be a kingdom that would welcome both dragons and humans. One, where the citizens didn't live in fear of their leader.

"Fight with me. Let's take our rightful place as this land's original magic."

I could picture it now. I'd be giving the dragons their dream of rebuilding their kingdom while creating a future where Soren and I could rule together. In the same place. Loving each other.

"Wow, just wow. That was inspiring." Amaya's wry voice echoed in my mind. *"But they won't come. You'll have to compel them."*

"I—I won't do that." I knew what it was like to be forced to do something against my will. And I'd hated every moment of it. I wouldn't

do that to the dragons. I wouldn't endanger them without their permission. *"Maybe they'll recognize that this is the opportunity that they've been waiting for, that this is the reason our eggs finally hatched, and they'll come."*

"They don't trust you, Moonglow. They'll fear that you're trying to lure them into a trap."

I growled.

Amaya chuffed. *"We'll figure something out. But for now, let's go find your vampire prince. I'm sure he's anxious to see for himself that your human form is still as perfect as ever."*

Yes, I could feel the tug pulling me back to the one who owned my heart.

Trace and the rest of the clan had been wrong. Even in my dragon form, I wanted Soren.

I spiraled through another cloud as I sped toward the Fein's military camp. My heart soared with happiness. I was loved. And I was free.

Following Amaya's lead, I landed in a clearing yards outside the camp's boundary. Being an oversized creature, I didn't want to accidentally squish something or someone.

Soren, Cullen, Raya, Gray, and Mary all charged out of a tent and ran toward us.

"Celestina!" Soren called up to me as he skidded to a stop directly in front of me. "Celestina! You are magnificent, my love. You're truly my Sky Girl."

Raya and Gray remained several yards behind Soren. Neither had pulled a weapon. I was surprised that Gray hadn't drawn his swords. He didn't even look as if he wanted to. He crossed his arms over his chest and smiled as if he were happy for me. I supposed I shouldn't have been surprised. Even though he'd often worried that I was a security threat, he'd also tried to fight for what he thought was best for me.

The smile Raya was wearing couldn't have been wider. She stared up at me, nodding in approval as if she'd known all along that I would break free from the muting spells and take my dragon form.

More and more of the vampires emerged from the camp to see Amaya and me as we stood on our hind legs with our necks stretched high. It felt like we were nearly as tall as mountains as we held out our impressive wings that were as powerful as a blizzard. And even though I was enjoying the attention, I ached to wrap my arms around Soren, laugh with Raya, tease Gray, and cook stew with Mary.

But I didn't know how to shift. Amaya had used her magic to pull my dragon out of me. Would I need her to use her magic for me to transform again?

I started to ask her when I heard a gasp. In a blink, I was no longer gazing down at my friends who were far beneath me. I was staring at my own toes. My human toes. My naked, human toes.

Wasn't I wearing shoes?

Oh.

Goddess.

Here I stood, in front of my friends and half of Fein's army, completely and embarrassingly naked because I'd not used my magic to pull my clothes from the plateau.

"Whoops," Amaya said as she shifted back to her human form, with perfectly combed hair, and wearing black pants and a matching black sweater. "I need to teach you how to bring clothes into your shifts back to your human form."

"*Please*, do that," Soren begged as he whipped off his tunic and pulled it over my head. I hadn't even had a chance to push my hands through the tunic's armholes when Soren hugged me.

"You are the most beautiful dragon to have ever flown the skies," he breathed against my neck as I snuggled against his broad chest. "I'm so happy for you. You broke the muting spell."

"Amaya did," I corrected. "She broke both the spells Queen Frieda had cast on me. There was a muting one and another one Queen Beatrice was planning to use to control me."

He held my shoulders and pulled back so he could look at me. "She destroyed your eyes."

"When I shifted, the damage was healed."

"But your eyes are different. They're indigo now."

"Are they?" I blinked. "They feel the same."

"They're the same eyes," Cullen clarified as he linked his fingers with Amaya's.

Interesting.

"The spells Queen Frieda cast were placed in her eyes, changing their color in the process. There was only one sure way to break the spells. And that was to tear the cursed eyes out of her body. Isn't that correct, Amaya?"

Amaya shifted from booted foot to booted foot before answering. "I did what had to be done. I knew that once you shifted between forms, your eyes would be restored to how they were before you'd been infected with those spells. But you couldn't shift with the muting spell in place. That's why I had to get rid of the spell by relieving your body of your eyes."

"And it worked," Culled was quick to remind us. He tightened his hold on Amaya's hand. And Amaya leaned closer to him. "While it was violent, it worked. Princess Celestina is free from the two spells that had been put on her as a baby. Thanks to Amaya."

Soren growled low in his throat.

I kissed the tip of his nose. "Amaya freed me when no one else could."

Though Soren still didn't look happy, some of the tension slipped from his shoulders.

"That was reckless," he grumbled. "But...thank you. Thank you for doing what no one else could figure out."

Cullen kissed the side of Amaya's head.

"Not here." Amaya smacked his shoulder.

Cullen smiled as if he'd been handed the rarest book in existence. But not even that smile could erase the lines of fatigue that had been etched deeply into his features. All my friends looked defeated. Even Soren.

"We are going to stop the undead army," I told them. "And remove Queen Beatrice from power." I needed the dragons to help us. But I wasn't going to force the clan to come. I could only hope they'd answer my call to broaden their world. "We need to plan how to best do that. And it's past dinnertime. I'd still like to help you with preparing the meals, Mary, if you think you can use me."

"I'd be honored to have your assistance, Dragon Princess," Mary said with a curtsy.

"Then it's settled." After I dressed in my Fein battle uniform, I went to work, handing out bowls of stew to exhausted and wounded warriors. Amaya joined me, though I suspected she was there because she felt like I needed a bodyguard. She snarled at the warriors she handed the stew to.

Once we were done, Mary, Amaya, and I returned to the main tent where Soren and Cullen were reviewing the maps marking where Queen Beatrice's undead armies were fighting his warriors.

"Have you heard from the dragons?" I asked Amaya. "Do you think they'll come?"

Amaya closed her eyes and grimaced as she listened. "I'm sorry, Moonglow. They're as stubborn as ever, unable to see a world past the plateau."

Three lizards ran across a map. "Doesn't it seem like there are more of them now?" Soren wondered aloud as he brushed them away.

He was right. The lizards were popping up from every nook and cranny in the rocks and in the tent. Mary yelped and held up her spoon as two crawled over her boot.

"They appear to be yours, Sky Girl," Cullen said as he adjusted his glasses.

They are mine. I held out my hand and watched the little green creatures crawl over each other in their rush to reach me. "The old stories often get the specifics wrong," I said as an ancient instinct stirred to life. The dragons weren't the only creatures the moonlight dragon could call on for battle. These lizards were mine. The storytellers had forgotten or had changed the tales, but I could feel the truth of it as surely as I could feel the press of Soren's hand on my hip.

These lizards are mine to call.

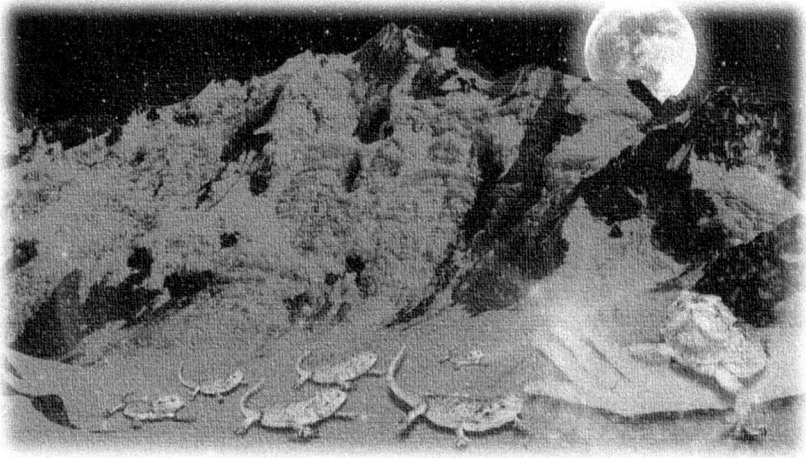

Chapter 50

Amaya

"The lizards do seem to be gathering around you, Sky Girl," Soren said, sounding worried. He reached down and pulled a dagger from his boot. "They aren't going to attack, are they?"

Celestina frowned at the lizards but didn't say a word. After several moments, she turned on her heel and walked out of the tent with the green lizards rushing to catch up to her. We all followed her back to the clearing outside of the camp.

She held up her hands and the green lizards, hundreds of them, scurried to surround us. As she drew in a long breath, her indigo eyes started to glow white.

"Become!" she growled.

The air around the lizards shimmered. One by one, the lizards lifted from the ground as they shifted. Their bodies grew larger and longer. Their green color turned metallic. Their tiny front legs transformed into beautiful wings that shimmered like a sky filled with rainbows. And deep red flames licked the ends of their long, spiky tails.

"Our new army," Celestina said as one of the winged beasts took to the air and coated the nearest cloud with fire.

Soren paled. "We've been eating the lizards."

"So have we," I admitted as I clenched my teeth. Had we been unwittingly eating our own kind? I felt like I might throw up. No, I was definitely going to throw up.

"Those are wyverns." Cullen adjusted his glasses. He moved closer to me and started to rub my lower back as if he could sense my stomach's turmoil.

"They are mine to call," Celestina said with that strange light still shining from her eyes.

"If my research is correct, they're not dragons," Cullen explained. "They don't have the same reasoning abilities. They can't talk or transform into people. They're more like dogs of war." He adjusted his glasses again. "I never knew they could transform at all—certainly not into lizards. But then again, the books I've studied all considered the stories of wyverns to be fables the storytellers had created."

"They are *mine*," Celestina repeated as more and more of the iridescent wyverns took to the sky. "They will rescue the young princes first and then destroy the rest. I will lead them."

Celestina started to transform, but Soren caught her wrist.

By whatever bond those two had forged, he had the power to stop the transformation. Or, more likely, Celestina stopped it out of respect for that bond. She was, after all, the superior creature.

"Lead them? You're not a trained fighter or a tactician. Sweetness, you can't rush into battle without a plan."

She snapped her teeth. "I'm going to save you and stop Queen Beatrice from harming anyone else."

As much as I hated to say this, I couldn't hold the words in. "I agree with your overgrown warrior. We need a plan. The bulk of Queen Beatrice's army might be undead, but they're not brainless. They quickly adapted to my attack. While having more fire-breathing creatures to fight with us will help our side, I don't want to risk giving Queen Beatrice an opening she could use to escape. The last thing we need is for her to rush off and use her magic to attack our clan."

"And if you want to save the children," Raya added, "we need to use stealth."

Celestina blinked several times before her eyes stopped glowing. The wyverns gracefully returned to the ground and shifted back into lizards. "You're right. The boys must be protected." She rubbed the back of her neck. "Calling the wyverns made me feel powerful, invincible. I was ready to rush into the enemy camp and rain fire on everyone there."

"You are powerful," Soren said, hugging her to his side. He kissed the top of her head. "And fearless. But I'm glad you're willing to let us mere vampires and humans help."

We all returned to the central tent where Soren kept his maps. Seeing on paper the location of the two armies drove home how outnumbered the Fein were.

"Her numbers keep growing, especially now that they're harvesting our dead." Soren sounded tired as he leaned over the map and pointed to a mountain pass. "Here." He pointed to another mountain pass. "And here. Those are the places Queen Beatrice would use if she wanted to escape back to Earst."

"I hadn't realized how far she'd pushed into Fein territory," Celestina said as she ran her fingers over the map.

Mary carried in dinner for us. The flavorful stew was nearly identical to the venison stew Celestina liked to cook for the families at the plateau. We ate as we strategized.

I was impressed with Soren's intelligence. He recounted how Queen Beatrice's army had responded to their attacks and proposed what we could do to take advantage of the undead warriors' relentless battle tactics. He suggested that his warriors attack in a way Queen Beatrice would expect. That would be the diversion. The wyverns would then circle around and take the camp, the queen, and her generals by surprise. It was a sound plan.

"No." Celestina whirled on Soren. "Your strategy puts too many of your warriors at risk. And unlike Queen Beatrice, we can't simply bring those who fall by the sword back from the dead. There must be another way."

"There is," I said, and laid out my plan to destroy Queen Beatrice and her unnatural army.

"I don't like it," Cullen transmitted into my mind. *"Your plan puts you in the middle of the enemy camp."*

I smiled at him with my sharp dragon's teeth. *"That's where I do best."*

Cullen took off his glasses and growled at me.

"What's going on between the two of you?" Soren asked.

"Lovers' spat," Cullen answered as he bared his fangs at me.

"A disagreement," I corrected, wishing we were alone so I could show him just how much I liked seeing those pearly white fangs of his.

Gray shook his head. "An argument? You two are just staring at each other."

"Clearly, they've formed some kind of telepathic connection," Raya said. "And by the looks they're giving each other, I'm putting my coins on lovers' spat."

I snarled at Raya.

"Oh!" Raya purred. "Are you going to include me in your sex games? I do like a three—"

"No." Cullen cut her off. He kept his gaze locked with mine. "I don't share."

My silly heart pounded faster. The selfish monster inside me liked that he wanted exclusive access, especially considering how I'd bite off the fingers of anyone who dared touch him.

"The brats are a priority," I said.

"The children," Celestina immediately corrected. "We need to free Queen Beatrice's sons before we can do anything else."

After many back-and-forth arguments and disagreements about how we should proceed, the others eventually agreed that I was uniquely qualified to rescue the little human brats…children. I had, after all, already rescued Soren from Queen Beatrice's camp by turning to air and whisking him and his reckless brother out of the camp while soldiers had fired arrows at us. I was sure I could do it again. As soon as the boys were a safe distance away, I would let Celestina know that it was safe for the wyverns to go in and lay waste to everything and everyone in the camp.

"The commotion I make by taking the boys away from their evil mother will cause any nearby troops to rush back toward the camp."

"And to follow after you," Cullen pointed out.

I bowed my head in agreement.

"If that happens, Amaya will need to fly in the direction of our largest number of waiting wyverns," Soren said. He went on to describe how his warriors would set up a perimeter around the camp to stop anyone from escaping.

"Queen Beatrice doesn't survive to see morning," he concluded.

No one inside the tent disagreed. Not even Celestina, who was the least bloodthirsty of us. "I would feel safer knowing she's gone," she murmured after a long silence.

It was close to midnight once we'd all agreed on our roles and the perfect time to set the plan into action. "No need to wait for something awful to happen. Let's go," I said. I started for the tent's exit so I could transform into the midnight dragon. Since my dragon form flew faster than I could in my air form, I planned to remain a dragon until I reached a point where Queen Beatrice's forces might spot me. That was the benefit of being a midnight dragon. My scales disappeared into the darkness.

But before I made it more than a step outside the tent, and before I could transform, Cullen pulled me into a tight embrace and kissed me until I was panting with lust.

"We're not finished here," he grumbled into my mouth.

"No," I agreed. "There's much I still want to do with your body."

He nipped my lower lip. "I'm still waiting for you to eat me, Darkness. And if you do a good job, I'll return the favor and eat you until you're screaming my name."

He said that loud enough that everyone in the tent heard him. My cheeks flamed hot. Not from embarrassment, but from wanting to do that now. I didn't care if the entire world heard how much we ached for each other. Dragons had a long history of lusting after anything with a heartbeat. It would be odd if I exclusively mated with my own kind.

"Keep your wits about you and return to us whole, Amaya," Cullen transmitted. The calm of his words created a tingly warmth in my chest that I liked too much to be able to dismiss as heartburn.

Dammit. I had feelings for my stupid vampire prince.

And those feelings weren't hate or anger or any of the other emotions that powered my naturally grumpy personality.

"You're the one who needs to act with care. If you die, I will use Queen Beatrice's blood magic to bring you back just so I can kill you myself, you understand me, fang boy?"

"No dying. Got it." He kissed me one more desperate time before we parted to take down a kingdom.

Chapter 51

Celestina

Leaving the princes' safety in Amaya's hands grated. Not that I didn't trust her. While the clan often portrayed the midnight dragon as being unstable and dangerous, from what I'd seen she always acted with a single-minded focus and displayed unwavering loyalty to those she cared about. If she promised to get the princes to safety, I knew she'd do everything in her power to do it.

Still, I wanted to be the one putting my arms around the little princes. I wanted to be the one to reassure those precious imps that they didn't need to fear dragons or vampires.

Those babies were *mine* to protect.

I growled.

"What is it?" Soren asked as I watched Amaya's midnight black scales disappear into the night sky.

I glanced over to where Soren was standing beside me. He tangled his fingers with mine. "How do you do it?" I demanded.

"Do what?" he asked.

"Stay calm while sending those you love to fight in your stead?"

"I'm not calm." He tightened his grip on my hand. "I'm dying with the thought that anyone I love will be out there fighting without me by their side."

"I-I can't do this. I can't stand here and watch Amaya and Gray and Raya leave." My voice cracked.

"It's not like we don't also have important roles to play in this plan, Sky Girl. You're going to be the one confronting Queen Beatrice. *I* should be doing that. And I want to scream at the thought that you'll be leading the wyverns into battle without me. This is my battle, and I'm letting the one person I love most in the world put herself at the greatest risk. We don't know what powers Queen Beatrice is concealing. We don't know what she might do when you go after her."

"This is my battle, too," I reminded him.

"I know. That's why I'm not trying to stop you from fighting in it." He shook his head. "The Fein have known for a while that this conflict was coming. We'd hoped to delay it by making an alliance with Queen Beatrice. But she proved too capricious of a ruler.

"When she'd enslaved you, I could barely keep myself from beginning the war with Earst right then and there. And once I discovered that you were the legendary moonlight dragon, with the power to call the other dragons, I had thought the Fein had found the perfect weapon to use against Queen Beatrice. But, Princess, now that I have you, now that I *love* you, I would rather chop off my sword arm than watch you fly into battle. And the thought of sending Amaya or any of the other dragons into harm's way digs at my soul.

"The vampires and dragons have never been allies. Yet, when I look in your eyes, the only future I see is one where we're together. As equals. Creating a country that's safe for both our kind. Making decisions that protect the vampires from humans and allows the dragons to step out of hiding." He heaved a deep breath. "And providing a place where our children and their children can thrive."

I opened and closed my mouth several times before I could trust myself to speak. "I wanted to hate you for trying to use me, but I never have been able to."

He framed my face with his hands. "I don't know how I got so lucky to find someone as forgiving as you. Goddess knows I don't deserve you, not after how I've acted."

I pressed a kiss to his lips. "Your honor would have never let you hurt me."

"But I have hurt you," he countered.

"Not on purpose. And neither of us are ever going to be perfect. I'm sure I'm going to get cranky with you and burn down more throne rooms."

He chuckled. "Just…don't melt my parents' thrones again. They're still upset about that."

"Gah! Your parents are never going to like me."

"They're going to love you after we save their kingdom." He kissed me so hard I felt the tingling all the way to my toes. "Stay safe, my heart. And be ruthless."

"I have the boys in the cave. They're safe," Amaya said. *"Are they always this squirmy?"*

I slumped in relief. My wyverns were hovering all around me on the far side of the mountain waiting to be commanded. *"They have always been a handful. You are going to stay with them?"* We hadn't discussed who was going to watch the boys after they'd been lifted to safety. I simply assumed she would.

"Nope. I'm coming back to fight alongside you."

"What?" The boys were too young and too curious for their own good. They couldn't be left alone, especially not high up in a cliffside cave.

"Don't worry, Moonglow. Juniper and Gwen have arrived and have agreed to take over babysitting duties."

"They're here?"

"Apparently, they weren't able to ignore your invitation to come and fight. Even though you didn't magically compel them, they said their love for you was all the pull they needed."

I was sure their love for Amaya also played a role in that decision.

"Are any other dragons joining us?" I asked.

"The others are too stubborn to leave the plateau." Amaya's answer came coated with frustration.

I shared her disappointment. I would have felt better knowing we had a larger aerial army with me as I entered my first battle. I didn't know how well the wyverns could fight or how long their fires would last. Amaya had collapsed with exhaustion after pushing herself too hard on the battlefield. I hoped I would know when to pull back.

But now wasn't the time for doubts or second guesses. I directed the wyverns to follow me to Queen Beatrice's camp.

"Time for the queen's final bloody spectacle to begin."

The wyverns called out to each other as they flew. It was a high-pitched keening that sounded like the whistling cry of a windstorm.

We crested the mountain peak to find Queen Beatrice's camp alight with torches. Soldiers were running around, preparing to defend themselves. Warning shouts echoed through the valley as they spotted me. A glowing, moonlight dragon wasn't the best creature for stealth attacks. Archers started firing almost immediately. A few of my wyverns were hit in that first wave. I cried out in rage and fear as they spiraled out of the sky.

The remaining wyverns moved as a unit. They descended on the camp, burning everything in their path. While they destroyed the camp, I flew toward a wide ledge where a line of archers was targeting my wyverns. They needed to be stopped. I sent my dragon fire out across the ledge as I streaked like a comet over the archers' heads. The side of the mountain lit up from my blaze.

Panting from the effort, I hovered near the steep mountain ledge, gazing down at the destruction I'd caused.

I'd never killed before. I didn't like the sick feeling twisting in my belly at the sight of my handiwork. I didn't know those archers. But certainly, some were honorable men born to a capricious leader. They didn't deserve the death I'd given them. Not one of the two dozen men had survived the heat of my flame.

I kept hovering there, staring down at the dead.

"Moonglow! What are you doing?" Amaya transmitted as she swooped down from somewhere off to my right. She bumped me in the air with her massive head.

"I-I can't—" How did I explain to her that I couldn't do this? The prophecies had been wrong. I wasn't a creature built for war.

"*Save the panic attack for after the battle, Moonglow.*" She'd circled around and was flying toward me again. "*Your friends will die if you don't pull it together.*" She bumped into me a second time. "*Come on. The undead army should be rushing to the queen's rescue any moment now.*"

That had been the key to our plan. We needed the undead to return from their battlelines to the camp so we could trap the queen's entire force in the valley and roast them.

The Fein troops guarding the exit routes out of the valley had been instructed to allow runners to escape so word could get out to the undead, warning them that the fighting had shifted to the camp.

I tore my gaze away from the ledge and back toward my wyverns. Heavy smoke had filled the air. The quick-flying wyverns had set fire to all the tents below us. I followed Amaya as she flew low in the valley surveying what little was left of the large encampment.

Still, the undead weren't rushing back to the valley.

Where were they?

"'Kill the conjurer of the spell, and the undead will fall...at least that's how it should work,'" Cullen had told us at one point during our planning session. Did the absence of the undead mean Queen Beatrice had been caught in the wyverns' firestorm? Was she already dead? I hoped she was. The thought of confronting her, of killing her no longer sounded like a task I could stomach. Hopefully, the undead had returned to their dead state as Cullen had promised they would.

Amaya was flying through the camp, roasting what had already been burned to keep the dead from rising again.

I followed her lead, burning the already dead soldiers, reducing their bodies to ash, while searching for Queen Beatrice.

Where was she?

Had victory really been this easy?

"*Cullen says the undead are holding their lines!*" Amaya shouted in my head. "*They're attacking the Fein with renewed strength. The Fein are being overrun. He says we need to cut off the snake's head. Now.*

"*Cullen? Talk to me. What does cutting off the snake's head even mean? Oh! He says we need to find and kill Queen Beatrice. Sheesh, why didn't you say that in the first place? We're looking for her."*

"But where is she?" I asked.

Had she somehow slipped out of the camp and past the forces Raya and Gray were leading? Or perhaps Soren had overlooked another escape route.

"Are Raya and Gray still in place?" I started to fly toward the narrow pass where Raya should have stationed her warriors.

Amaya flew in the opposite direction. *"I'm going to kick undead butts."*

"Take some of the wyverns with you." I sent an order to most of the wyverns to follow Amaya out of the now silent valley while I concentrated on searching the destroyed encampment more closely. *How did the queen evade us?* The escape routes had been sealed off before Amaya had gone in to rescue the boys. I scanned the steep mountains that surrounded the valley. The rocky cliffsides were intimidating. But they were also pitted with deep crevasses and caves. The queen could be hiding anywhere within them.

I discovered I could see further in my dragon form, focus easier on small details. And the longer I looked at the mountains, the more I saw. It was as if I could focus on all the small details within my entire range of vision at once.

There! A flash in the darkness. Like a piece of metal reflecting a bit of moonlight. It had been visible for less than a heartbeat. Just long enough to notice and long enough to start to question whether it had been a figment of my imagination.

It's probably nothing, I told myself as I shifted the position of my wings. Like sails on a ship, my leathery wings altered my course, and I flew directly for that little flicker of light.

If there's someone hiding in there, it's not going to be her, I told myself as I landed on the ledge in front of the small cave's opening. But still, I needed to see for myself that Queen Beatrice hadn't sought shelter inside the small space.

The cave was too tight for my dragon form. I had to shift into my human body before I could enter. Unfortunately, I still didn't know how to use my magic to conjure clothing during my transformation, which meant I had to enter the cave naked, cold, and relatively defenseless. Well, I could still breathe fire in case any thrones needed destroying.

I stepped softly, straining my ears as I listened to the muted drip, drip,

drip of water at the back of the dark cave.

"Finally." Queen Beatrice stepped out from behind a large rock. She was dressed in black trousers with a purple surcoat with Earst's coat of arms stitched in gold. An elaborate golden circlet adorned her blonde head. She walked toward me as if greeting an old friend. She held a fist-sized black box in front of her like it was a shield.

"Queen Beatrice is here in a cave!" I shouted through my connection with Amaya.

Queen Beatrice didn't look at all like the young queen who had damned me to be a slave to the most fearsome general on the continent. Her cheeks were sunken. Dark bags hung under her eyes. And her skin was as wrinkled as a silk gown that had been balled up and discarded in the bottom of a wardrobe. I sucked in a quiet gasp at the sight of her.

"Does this shock you?" She ran the tips of her fingers across her wrinkly face. "I've not fed from a vampire today. I'd hoped to feast on your prince. But he escaped before I could taste his sweet blood and restore my beauty. Blood magic comes with a cost. I have to drain several vampires dry every week just to keep going.

"But it's worth it. And if not for you, I wouldn't have been able to create my undefeatable blood army. I learned of the healing powers in vampire blood through your eyes, my little spy. Such a delicious secret, isn't it? An entire continent living in fear of vampires and their hunger for blood, when in fact, their blood holds the cure for us. And how convenient that they live in one kingdom instead of in nests scattered throughout the continent. It'll make enslaving them that much easier."

"I won't allow it," I said.

"Once I defeat their little uprising, I plan to take your vampire prince and keep him for myself as my special pet," she continued as if I hadn't spoken. "I watched what he did to you. How he touched you. How he rode you like a whore. I can give him what you never could. Beauty, talent, refinement. And his cock will give me daughters with powers beyond our imaginings. Natural blood magic that doesn't corrode."

I growled. The rumbling sound caused small stones to fall from the ceiling.

"Growl all you want, dragon. You're no threat to me." She tilted her head to one side as she appraised me. "I was beginning to doubt you were even smart enough to find me. Felt like I'd been waving that polished coin in the moonlight for ages."

"Amaya?" She should have answered me by now.

I stretched out my consciousness, searching for her. All I found was silence. It felt as if someone had stuffed cotton into my head. My thoughts were sluggish.

"Amaya!"

"Oh, dear. Are you just now realizing no one will be coming to rescue you?" her soft voice belied the violence she was capable of. "That must be a horrible feeling, to find yourself alone and friendless. But then again, you never were able to attract more than a small handful of fair-weather friends. My mother had to pay your parents to put up with you."

"I don't need friends to end you!" In my rage, I opened my mouth to scorch her with my dragon fire. All that emerged was a frustrated scream.

Queen Beatrice laughed. The demented sound echoed off the damp stone walls. "You could never do anything right. You couldn't even die when I needed you to." Two burly warriors wearing Earst's purple leathers emerged from the deep shadows at the back of the cave.

"I won't let you use me ever again," I swore in a panicked rush as one of the men roughly grabbed my arm. I tried to swipe at him with my dragon talons like Amaya would often do, but my hands remained frustratingly human. The second man grabbed my other arm. They dragged me, as I kicked and struggled, deeper into the dark cave. "You're a monster who killed your own mother."

The queen stumbled back a step as if my words had physically struck her. "That was...I didn't..." She straightened. Her chin rose as she drew in a steadying breath. "You were her weakness," she said, her voice sharper than before. "My mother had started to *care* about you. I had no choice but to cut the rot from my family line. Soft sentiments from a leader could destroy a kingdom. Certainly, even you can see that. This is a handy box, is it not?" She rubbed the small black wooden container she'd been holding in front of her against my cheek. The magic coating it stung. "This ancient relic dates to the War of the Magics. A secret weapon my family has been keeping, waiting for the perfect opportunity to use it. It's the magic the vampires used during the Great War to best the dragons. You see, this box gives me power over your abilities. And I think the first thing I'll do is take control of those pesky wyverns you used to destroy my camp. What do you think? Should I have them kill all the Fein warriors blocking the two trails leaving the valley?"

I struggled against the men holding my arm. "No! I'll never allow you to do that!"

But without my consent, I could feel my magic already flowing through me as an order went out to the wyverns. I could feel the queen's commands blooming in the wyverns' minds, telling them to kill Soren's army. I could sense them shifting their flight patterns, feel them targeting Soren's warriors. *Raya! Gray!*

No! I struggled against the men holding me.

I could feel the attack happening through my connection with the wyverns, and there was nothing I could do to stop it.

Chapter 52

Soren

I rubbed my chest with my fist hoping to soothe the knot of panic that had settled there as I crouched on the side of the mountain overlooking the queen's encampment. "Something is wrong."

For one thing, I never panicked during a battle.

But then again, I'd never watched the love of my life fly into danger while I remained behind the lines to coordinate our defenses. Fuck, she'd looked magnificent as she'd claimed her power.

But now, panic clawed at my chest. "Something is definitely wrong."

"No shit." My brother pointed to the sky. "The wyverns are turning on us."

On the opposite side of the peak, the small dragonesque creatures moved like a well-organized flock of birds. They'd been following Amaya's lead, heading toward the undead army slaughtering my warriors. But before any of the wyverns had breathed their first burst of fire in that direction, they'd shifted like the wind. And sent a wall of fire to blast the troop of warriors Raya had been leading.

"Where's Celestina?" I demanded, burying the worry I felt for Raya.

There wasn't anything I could do from here to help her. I was perched too high on this mountainside to be of any use to any of my friends.

I'd last seen Celestina flying like a glowing apparition into the smoke-filled valley below me. But when she'd dipped lower, she'd disappeared into the thickest part of the smoke and had yet to emerge.

Cullen closed his eyes as he communicated with Amaya. Almost immediately, he started shaking his head.

"Dammit." I stood and made my way down the steep slope, heading toward where I'd last seen Celestina.

"Something is blocking Amaya's connection with your princess. She says it feels like blood magic," Cullen called out as he started to follow me.

"Stay here. We still need someone with eyes on the three fronts to direct our troops."

"She's not hurt," Cullen shouted. "You'd already know through your bond if she was hurt."

His reassurance didn't slow my pace. Celestina might not have been physically injured, but that didn't mean she was safe. Queen Beatrice's violent character was known throughout the continent. And while I'd given Celestina a few self-defense lessons, she still had plenty to learn before she'd be skilled enough to protect herself.

My gaze skirted across the valley. Where was she? I could barely see anything thanks to the smokey fires still burning down in the encampment.

Celestina. If only I could communicate with her like Cullen could with Amaya.

Rocks tumbled down the steep side of the mountain as I slid and ran toward the valley. I'd made it halfway down when I felt a tugging in my chest. I was going in the wrong direction.

I wasn't sure why I knew that. But I could feel the wrongness of my path as sure as I could feel my heart as it slammed against my ribs. Maybe I sensed I was going the wrong way because Celestina was my fucking heart.

And she wasn't down there in that valley. She was over...*there*. My gaze zeroed in on a dark spot on the side of the mountain not that far below me.

"If you feel your life is in peril, Celestina, you have my permission to run from me.

I'll fetch you," I'd once told her. It was a promise I intended to keep for the rest of my life. I'd lost my mind when I'd tried to let her go.

"You need to pull your shit together before you get yourself killed!" Gray had screamed at me over a week ago after a close call in a skirmish that had nearly left us both dead. He'd then punched me in the side of my head so hard that my neck still ached from the whiplash I'd suffered from the blow.

He hadn't been wrong. I had been reckless.

Honestly, I hadn't wanted to survive this war.

Not without Celestina.

I punched the side of the mountain, cracking stone and splitting open my knuckles. I squeezed my hand over my bloodied knuckles as I continued to pick my way across the rocky terrain, blindly trusting that my instincts could find her when my eyes could not. Soon, I reached the opening of a dark cave.

I stood outside, listening to the echoing sound of voices coming from within.

"Stop," came an angry growl. I felt frozen in place even though the command hadn't been meant for me. I'd never been happier to be struck by a compulsion. It meant Celestina had found a way to fight whoever was holding her. No muting spell had ever been able to block her from using her power to compel other magical creatures. *"Stop the wyverns from attacking the Fein. Make them follow Amaya's lead and attack your undead army."*

"I..." a soft voice whined. Queen Beatrice's voice. "I don't want to."

"But you already have," Celestina said as if bored by the interaction. "I can feel the pull of my magic move through me as the wyverns are being redirected."

I broke free from Celestina's compulsion and peeked into the cave's opening. Two burly warriors from Earst were holding Celestina's arms pinned to her side. To her naked side.

I bared my fangs.

Those two men touching what belonged to me were dead.

They might be breathing now, but their lives had ended the moment they put their hands on my Sky Girl. I'd personally make sure of it.

Silently, I pulled my sword from my sheath.

Celestina started to command Queen Beatrice to do something else, but barely got the first growly word out of her mouth before the queen slapped her hand over Celestina's mouth. The sound of the blow reverberated through the cave.

No. Fuck, no. No one hits my mate.

Spurred by an ancient instinct to protect what was mine, I spun into the dark, damp cave. With an elegant arc, the sharp edge of my sword sliced through the queen's neck. She was dead—her head on the ground—before her mind registered the sting of my blade, before her eyes could register a look of shock, before her mouth could form a scream.

But I wasn't done. I kept moving, letting my sword sing through the air as it sliced through the arms that had dared touch Celestina. Two more swings and the Queen's guards were on the ground. Dead.

Well, hell. I'd been planning on tearing their throats open with my own teeth. More personal that way. But…dead was dead.

Celestina's startled, indigo gaze met mine. (The color change still surprised me.) Her eyes widened as she looked down at the three dead bodies lying at her feet. She slid her foot away from the queen's severed head. "She's really dead," she said as if the reality of what I'd done was just now taking hold. "Just like that, it's over. I'd pictured her end would come with a great struggle, and that when we finally succeeded it would feel…more momentous." She shook her head. "This happened all so fast."

"A life taken in violence is never momentous. I've taken more than my fair share and know this from experience. Battles are messy and violent. There's no glory in it—just one life ending while another survives to fight another day. It's up to the storytellers to compose a tale with weight and meaning. But for the warriors on the ground, the story is simply about who gets to live."

Our gazes held. And my breath froze in my throat. My princess, my better half, my mate was strong and brave and glorious. How the fuck did I get so lucky to find her?

The gods must have had a hand in this. Or fate.

Celestina reached out to me. "Momentous or not, what you did just now was impressive."

I stepped over a dead warrior to pull my beautiful dragon into my arms. Her body molded to mine as I grabbed her shapely ass and pressed her snug against my already rampant cock. "You were impressive."

I loved that she didn't have a stitch of clothing to keep me from touching her everywhere.

"I killed," she whispered as she dropped her head to my chest.

"I know, sweetheart. You had no choice. They would have killed your wyverns if you hadn't. That is the trouble with war—the need to kill warriors who are merely following orders that fulfill the whims of their leaders."

She shuddered, and I tightened my grip on her. She turned her head and nudged a wooden black box with her toe. Magic sparked as she pushed it away from us. "That's what the vampires used to defeat the dragons during the War of the Magics. It mutes a dragon's powers, rendering us helpless."

"Not completely helpless." I kissed the top of her head. "I heard how you used your compulsion to stop the wyverns from attacking my warriors. You could have ordered the queen to free you, but you traded your one opportunity to save yourself to rescue my warriors." Even after being dragged into the musty cave and pushed around, Celestina still smelled like berries. I could get drunk off her sweet scent.

"It's still muting me." She nudged the box with her toe again. "Do you know how to turn it off?"

I (reluctantly) let go of Celestina's ass to reach down and pick up the box. As soon as it was in my hand, I could feel the hum of old magic. "This isn't a vampire invention. It's fueled by blood magic, a power anyone can use to tear the earth's magic from the core of life itself. If a vampire had made this, I'd be sensing a darker magic. It doesn't even feel like the same magic that had been wrapped around you from those binding spells. This is clearly something else."

"Queen Beatrice told me that it's been in her family for generations. Do you think she lied?"

"Maybe. This feels like a Tiburnian invention, which would make sense. Queen Beatrice was a capricious and impulsive ruler. And everything that has led up to this invasion—the war with the Tiburnians, building an undead army, using you to gain insight on the Fein, using you as a potential weapon and a means of sparking a war between the Fein and the dragons—feels carefully planned."

Celestina shook her head. "That's not something Queen Beatrice would be capable of."

"I agree." I dropped the box and used the flat side of my sword to smash the vile thing. It exploded in a blinding flash of red.

"Better?" I asked, blinking rapidly to get my sight back.

I felt rather than saw Celestina nod. "I can hear Amaya shouting in my mind. As Cullen suspected, the undead army has collapsed. I bet it fell at the same time you removed Queen Beatrice's head from her body. The wyverns are burning the dead to ashes now so there's no chance of them coming back."

"Hmm, it sounds like everything is under control then, and that we're not needed out there. Which means I can do this." I spun my princess around, so her backside was pressed against my front. I lowered my mouth to the nape of her neck and savored the honey-sweet flavor of her skin.

Celestina

I stood frozen by lust. Goddess, this vampire knew how to drive me wild. He'd turned me so I was staring at Queen Beatrice, lying dead at our feet. Her body to the right of us, her head directly in front of us. Her cold, blue eyes staring sightlessly at me.

It should have disgusted me, but I'd spent enough time around such gore in Queen Beatrice's court that I saw the blood and felt nothing.

"Thank you for coming for me," I said as he nuzzled my neck.

"I will always come for you," he murmured against my skin.

"Queen Beatrice would have won if you hadn't struck when you did. I—I'd been rendered helpless."

He nuzzled my neck a little longer before answering. "You would have figured out a way to defeat her. I merely hurried things along." He nipped my neck's soft skin. "I had to. I was getting impatient for this." He sank his fangs into my neck.

I hissed a breath at the sudden sting. But my blood sang as he drank it warm from my body.

"I'm going to make you come next to the body of your dead queen. I'm going to make you scream my name so loudly that your lovely cry of pleasure will be all the queen hears as she rots in the Great Beyond," he lifted his head long enough to promise.

As he drank some more, he eased his hand between my legs and teased me with his talented fingers while the ridge of his arousal pressed against me from behind. I rubbed up and down over his leather pants, stretching my back, loving the heat his hands and mouth were igniting in my core.

Still kissing me, he moved to stand in front of me. His beautiful green eyes seemed to glow in the darkness. His gaze remained locked on my face as he knelt in front of me. He had me widen my stance before pressing his lips against my throbbing heat. He licked and sucked until my legs were trembling. I dug my fingers into his thick black hair, holding on as if my life depended on keeping his head there while I struggled to take a steady breath.

"Look at her," he whispered against my heat. "She and her mother tried to keep you controlled and powerless. But look at you now. You have something she coveted. You have a continent on its knees for you, my beautiful Celestina." He swirled his tongue against my center. And that was enough. While staring at the dead queen who had terrorized a kingdom, I screamed Soren's name as I came apart.

"Queen Beatrice's kingdom is now yours." He rose to his feet just in time to catch me. My limbs had turned boneless, and I collapsed into his embrace. "As am I, my queen. I'm yours to command."

Goddess. Is this happening? Is it true? Earst has truly fallen. And its fall has paved the way for the return of the dragons.

Chapter 53

Celestina

Soren and I made it back to Fein's camp at the border on foot. We'd gone straight to Soren's tent so I could change out of the tunic he'd given me from off his own back and into my clothes. When we finally emerged, we found Amaya outside the central tent, squaring off with Anther and Trace. She stood with her hands on her hips. With a snarl, she leaned slightly forward toward the male dragons. "How dare you come here?"

"We came to help," a naked Anther answered, spreading his arms wide.

"Help?" She snorted. Smoke swirled out of her nostrils. Everyone in the camp, except for Prince Cullen, backed up. I didn't blame them. I didn't want to be around arguing dragons, and I was one. Prince Cullen remained within the line of fire, standing directly behind Amaya. And grinning. "You came to help?" Amaya demanded. "The fighting ended hours ago. Celestina and I destroyed the enemy by ourselves."

Well, not exactly by ourselves. The wyverns helped. Those beautiful creatures had happily gone back to pretending they were common lizards. And the Fein warriors had served a large role in keeping the undead army at bay, too. But I didn't think Amaya would appreciate it if I corrected her. Besides, I wasn't feeling too pleased with the clan myself. I'd been told that they were mine to call, mine to lead into battle. But instead of doing the right thing, they'd decided to refuse me.

With Soren sticking by my side, I walked up to them "Anther. Trace."

The two dragons immediately took notice of how my hand was twined with Soren's. And I was sure their superior dragon senses could detect the scent of sex on us. That was no doubt why Trace's gaze narrowed, and his shoulders tensed.

"While we no longer need assistance from the dragon clan, you are welcome for as long as you wish to stay," Soren offered while tightening his grip on my hand. It had to be difficult for Soren to welcome the dragon the clan had decided to become my mate.

"See, you can be a diplomat," I joked.

"I will do anything, become anything you need me to be, Princess." Soren's low rumbly voice made the air catch in my throat.

"My father sends his regrets," Anther quickly stepped forward to take over the situation before Trace said something that triggered a battle none of us wanted to fight. "He kept the others from answering your call, Celestina. He was worried about what would happen to our society if we lost even one of our kind to a war that wasn't ours. If we all came, there could have been a chance that we'd lose many."

I tilted my head to the side, trying to come up with something to say that wasn't argumentative. The battle was done. The war was won. Fighting with the clan about their behavior wouldn't change anything.

"That's bullshit, Anther. You can tell Daddy that I said that," Amaya snapped. "The clan placed Moonglow on a pedestal. You forced her to return to the plateau because she was the dragon mentioned in some vague, ancient prophecy. You told her that the clan needed her to lead them as the fifth kingdom rose again. But when it came time to act, time to rise, you hid behind excuses instead of fighting for our future. If you'd planned to let Moonglow fight this battle alone, you should have allowed her to stay with her vampire prince. He, at least, has the balls to fight. You…you all disgust me."

"It's not—" Anther tried to explain.

"You're here now," I said, because I wasn't in the mood to listen to excuses or to fight another battle. "As Soren has already said, you're welcome to stay—as long as you put on proper clothes." Soren nodded to a couple of his captains. They smiled and tossed their capes at the naked dragons. "And you're welcome to offer advice as the Fein take control of the Kingdom of Earst."

"The kingdom belongs to—" Soren started to say but was interrupted as two large dragons shot out of the sky and landed next to us with enough force that the ground trembled. Four tiny boys leaped out of the pair of dragons' taloned claws.

With a loud squeal, they ran over to us.

"Lady Celestina! Lady Celestina!" Ronald, the eldest brother, yelled as he jumped up and down in front of me. His twin brothers Rupert and Ryan trailed close on his heels. And little Robert toddled toward me behind them. The four boys' eyes were sparkling from the excitement of the rescue. I wondered if they'd been told their mother was dead. She'd never been very kind to them or attentive. But she was their mother, and they would miss her. And because of that, I hurt for them.

I crouched down so they could run into my open arms, surprised at how much I'd missed the troublesome imps.

"Lady Celestina!" Ronald shouted again after I'd smothered each one of them with hugs and kisses. "Did you hear what happened? We were abducted by a dragon! But she turned out to be a kind dragon. She took us away from the fighting and these two other dragons fed us sweets and told us stories, like you used to tell us."

Robert tugged on my tunic. "I can see now why you prefer the dragon stories to the vampire stories," he said with a lisp. "Dragons are the most awesome magical creatures in all the lands. Far cooler than nasty old vampires."

"Hey, now!" Soren objected as he gave Robert a stern look.

I wrapped my arms around my grouchy prince and pressed a chaste kiss to his lips. "Don't worry. I still like vampires, especially a certain bossy one."

"I've developed quite a fondness for dragons as well," Soren said with a smile. "Particularly for a certain moonlight dragon." He kissed me back in a decidedly less chaste manner. "I love you, Celestina."

"You're not going to order us all to clear out of the camp so you can have sexy times with your princess, are you?" Raya complained as she shoved Soren away from me.

"Raya!" I shouted and threw myself into her arms. She was safe. I hadn't seen her since before the battle. And I'd nearly died when, through the bond I shared with my wyverns, I knew they were attacking first her troops and then Gray's. I'd been so worried that they hadn't survived.

"Not a scratch on you," Soren said as he looked her over from head to toe. "You always have been the luckiest fighter of us all."

"I think you mean the one with the most skill?" Raya sassed back with a hand on her hip.

"Both." He hugged Raya. "You had me worried there for a moment when the wyverns started blasting their fires. Don't do that again."

Raya wiggled until he stopped squeezing her. She brushed herself off as if our hugs had been covered with mud. But she was smiling as she did it. "I managed to get everyone to take shelter under rock overhangs and small caves. Only a few of us suffered burns. But nothing that required a healer's attention."

"And we won!" Gray cheered as he charged into the camp and hugged everyone he could get near. "Earst is ours!"

"Excuse me?" Amaya said. "The dragons took down the army, not some puny vampires."

"From what I heard, it was Soren's sword that put an end to the queen's existence," Gray countered.

Before Gray and Amaya started yet another battle, the two dragons who'd flown the boys into the camp shifted back into their human forms. They'd mastered Amaya's skill in pulling on clothes during the transformation. Gwen was dressed in a purple sweater, black trousers, and boots. Juniper, Amaya's mother, had donned a homespun flowered dress with a matching fur-lined cape and sturdy boots. Gwen shot Trace a worried look before coming over to stand next to me.

"I'm glad to see you safe," she said, while Gray and Amaya continued to argue. She put her hand on my cheek. "Your mate has done a good job protecting you."

"He has," I agreed.

"Not that she ever needs protecting," Soren leaned forward to add. "She's amazingly powerful."

"The muting spells have been broken?" Trace surged forward, grabbed my arms, and spun me toward him. "How?"

Soren growled and violently shoved Trace away from me. Trace was lucky he still had his arms, seeing how the arms had been the first things to go on those royal guards who had attacked me in the cave.

"How did you break the spells?" Trace repeated as he rubbed the spot on his chest where Soren had pushed him.

"And your eyes, dear," Gwen added softly. "They're exactly as I'd imagined them."

"What happened?" Trace frowned as he looked at me again, but this time kept his hands clasped behind his back. "Your eyes are no longer mismatched. What's going on?"

"I broke the spells," Amaya proudly announced.

"That's right. Amaya did it," I agreed. "It was brilliant. She figured it out and got rid of both spells for me at the same time. And good thing she did, too, since I needed access to my magic and my dragon form to keep from getting killed by Queen Beatrice and her army of the undead."

"This wasn't our battle," Anther said as he, too, moved closer. He squinted as he peered at my indigo eyes. "You should have never interfered in the affairs of the outer—"

"Queen Beatrice still had the means to control me with those spells. If I hadn't acted, I would have been fighting the battle for her side and under her control. Not only that, she also had a magical weapon that she'd planned to use to gain control over the rest of the clan. This was our battle, Anther, and I'm grateful for the Fein who helped Amaya and me win it."

Anther pressed his lips together.

"I'm ashamed the clan didn't come to your aid," Juniper said. "And I'll make sure that the clan never denies you again. It has always been written that when the last moonlight dragon returns, we would accept that dragon as our leader."

"Unfortunately, you and I were females," Amaya added. "The council has long been ruled by angry old males."

"Celestina was stolen from us and raised by humans," Trace added. "She doesn't understand our ways. How can we expect her to lead us?"

"Regardless of her past, by her birthright, we are hers to call," Juniper said as she crossed her arms over her chest. "When our moonlight dragon needed us, we failed her."

Everyone fell silent. They seemed to be looking to me for direction.

But what could I say? It felt like everyone had already chosen their sides.

"A queen is dead." I cleared my throat. "She was a threat to both the Fein and the dragon clan. She'd shown in her actions that she wouldn't stop until she'd destroyed our societies. And she'd already taken countless lives during her reign. She'd abused her power and tormented the innocent. Still, I don't celebrate her death. Whether we're talking about the life of a human, or a dragon, or even the life of a vampire, it should be celebrated and held sacred."

"What do we do now?" Gwen asked. "Who will take Queen Beatrice's place?"

The argument Amaya and Gray were having over whether the Fein or the dragons deserved to rule Earst erupted again. This time it seemed everyone joined in to loudly voice their opinion on the matter. Even Queen Beatrice's sons joined in. Although, they seemed to be shouting simply for the joy of shouting.

Soren held up his hand, calling for silence. Surprisingly, the dragons obeyed as quickly as Soren's own warriors. Was he using his compulsion powers? I didn't feel the prickle of magic on my arms, nor did I feel compelled to keep my silence, but that didn't mean he hadn't snuck some power into his gesture. It awed me to think that he could command a room with the strength of his charm alone.

"Princess Celestina was raised in Earst," Soren said once everyone was listening. "She has a vision of what this kingdom could become and how to achieve it. Her ability to call the wyverns is the reason we defeated Queen Beatrice."

"Wyverns?" Trace and Anther both muttered.

"She's the bravest warrior I know," Soren continued. "Hands down, Princess Celestina is the best choice—the only choice—to rule Earst. Or perhaps I should say Queen Celestina?"

No one objected.

Not even Trace.

"A dragon kingdom," I said with awe. My gaze softened as I focused on Soren. The corners of his eyes creased as he took note of the smile that tugged on my lips. "A kingdom for both of us to lead," I corrected. "I will be the queen only if you stand by me as my king."

"I will always stand by you, Your Majesty."

My mind raced with the possibilities. "We'll free the slaves. We'll stop punishing the citizens for speaking out against injustice. We'll—we'll make the kingdom better, safer, and more welcoming than before and…" I glanced over at the queen's sons. Gwen was hugging them. "Goddess, they don't know." I swallowed. "Earst is their birthright."

"No," Soren said. "Royal sons never inherited leadership roles in Earst. And the kingdom needs a leader with the vision to right the wrongs and fix its problems. That leader is you." He brushed a kiss against my lips. "Let's all go inside the tent and hammer out the details."

"But the boys, I should take care of them." I started to move toward where the smallest boy had latched on to Gwen's legs.

"Go," she said as she gave Robert a tight squeeze. "I'll care for them as if they were my own."

And so, we headed into the central tent. Dragon, vampire, and human—we all worked together to develop a vision for the future, a vision of a kingdom where all could live free. A future where Soren and I would get to live together and love each other.

Goddess, how did I get so lucky?

Amaya

"Well." I stretched my neck left and right when I left the camp's central tent after several hours of peace talks. I still felt more than a little feral after the battle. While we were fighting and even after it had ended, whenever my powers had started to flag, Celestina had fed me some of her own. I doubted she knew she was doing it. But because of it, I now felt more alert and on edge than before we'd taken on Queen Beatrice and her gruesome ghouls.

Prince Cullen walked beside me like an idiot, smiling at me while doing nothing to fill in the awkward gap of silence that followed my one-word utterance.

"Aren't you going to say something?" I demanded.

"You're stunning."

I snorted. "And you're covered in blood and soot."

He looked down at himself and then back at me, seemingly unperturbed by his untidiness. "As always, you are correct, Princess."

"I'm not a princess."

"You could be," he murmured.

"What?"

"What?" he repeated as the corners of his eyes crinkled with pleasure. "Amaya, I—"

"I'm heading back to the clan," I blurted. Whenever I was near him, I wanted things, impossible things. And I didn't think I could resist another offer to go live with him at his palace. "So..." I shifted my neck around again. "Have a good life."

He took a hasty step toward me before I had a chance to shift forms. "Wait. That's it? You're running back to your clan? Never to see me again?"

"It's my home."

"Amaya," he said as if he'd caught me in a lie.

"What?"

"You could stay with me for a while."

"And do what? Return with you to Reinheart Palace?" I snorted.

"I'd let you take some more of my books."

"You can't be serious. You think I'd fit in living in your posh palace, pretending to be a lady?" Smoke curled from my nose. "I'm not Celestina. I'm neither gentle nor tame."

"I don't want gentle or tame." He took my hand in his. "*We have a connection*," he added, putting his calming voice directly into my mind as his thumb traced tingly circles on the back of my hand.

"An accidental connection."

He lifted one dark eyebrow. "Amaya."

"*That man* abducted me." I freed my hand from Cullen's. "And then I met you and my world was turned upside down. It wasn't planned. None of this was planned." I gestured wildly to the mountains all around us.

"But it happened. *We* happened, Amaya. If you won't run away with me, let me run away with you," he said, speaking quickly as if afraid I'd disappear at any moment. "Let me come with you to the plateau. I could study dragon society firsthand. Maybe write a textbook or two on the subject."

"What about your place in Fein? With Soren planning to forge a new kingdom with Celestina in Earst, doesn't that make you the new crown prince?"

"My sister will make a better ruler than I ever could. I already plan to abdicate the position to her."

"And your spy craft?"

He bit his bottom lip and hummed. "Now, that would be hard to give up. But you'd make an excellent partner. A beautiful siren who can transfer to air? It's as if you were created for the work."

"A partner?" *Not a tool he can use?*

"A partner," he emphasized. "You do only what you feel comfortable doing. And if you disagree with me, I'll listen. We'll discuss the matter and come to an agreement. Together. That's how partnerships work. In love. In work. In life. I'm greedy, Amaya. I want it all from you."

What the hell was wrong with me? Why had I suddenly forgotten how to breathe? I opened and closed my mouth like a land-locked fish.

"We can start by hunting down Captain Proctor and giving him the death he deserves," Cullen suggested. "I remember you have some wickedly creative ways we could go about putting an end to his existence."

"*That man* does need to suffer." But falling into a relationship with Cullen? Agreeing to hunt alongside a vampire? That couldn't be wise. I skated out of his reach. "I don't think I can—"

"I don't know if it's because of the pathway we've forged between our minds or fate, Amaya. You say meeting me turned your life upside down. For me, being with you makes my life feel buoyed. Like I can stop searching for something I never knew I needed. When I'm around you, I feel like I've found a place where I truly belong. Wherever you go, that's where I want to be. And I think...I *hope*...you feel the same way." His voice softened. "I love you, Amaya."

My shoulders dropped. My heart melted. I turned swiftly away from him in case he could read on my face the tingly—and totally inappropriate—emotions that were surging inside me.

"I suppose I find you tolerable," I grumbled around the lump of emotion blocking my throat.

"Tolerable works for me." He wrapped his arms around me like a farrow monkey, a creature that hunted by squeezing the life out of its prey. His embrace felt tight and warm and exactly what I wanted.

"I'll permit you to hunt *the man* with me, and then I suppose you can come with me to the plateau, fang boy, if that's what you want to do," I said, hoping I sounded as if I honestly didn't care. But I suspect the goofy smile I couldn't hold back totally gave me away.

This was what a stupidly handsome—and stupidly wonderful—vampire had reduced me to. I was acting like a silly maiden with this ridiculous grin.

He traced the shape of my smile with the tip of his finger, a finger that trembled slightly as if touching something rare and precious.

"Your smiles *are* rare and precious," he said and then kissed me. "Princess."

"I'm not a princess," I corrected…again.

"You will be."

Epilogue

Five Years Later

Soren

"Keep your tips up," I instructed the four boys as they practiced their sword work. Robert had recently turned eight and was surprisingly the best swordsman in the group. Ronald, at twelve, had recently experienced a growth spurt that left him tripping over his feet whenever he tried to make a decent swing with his sword. I mussed his blond hair and told him to keep working at it. He might never make it as a warrior, and that was fine. But I still wanted him to learn how to protect himself and his siblings.

He could return to his studies in the library only after he spent an hour in the bailey yard going through the lessons with his brothers.

Celestina fiercely loved the boys and considered them part of her hoard, so shortly after taking our places as rulers of the kingdom I'd suggested we adopt them. In time, I'd grown to love the scamps as if they were my own sons.

Besides, there'd never been a recorded mating between a dragon and a vampire, so we didn't know if children of our own were even possible.

Celestina's and my magic came from different and seemingly incompatible sources. For all we knew, these boys would be the only children we'd be given. And if that turned out to be our reality, I would be content. The boys were growing into fine young men who were fiercely protective of my beautiful Celestina. Not that she needed protection.

She was a powerful force that no ruler on the continent dared challenge. Not even the Tiburnians.

Celestina and I had lived together (*always* together) in Earst for five peaceful years. Our first act when taking the throne had been to free the slaves and dismiss the nobility that had allowed Queen Beatrice to thrive.

Some vampires from Fein had moved into the kingdom to help the local humans build their businesses and villages. The small village surrounding the castle had grown into a bustling city with a multistory library and university at the center.

Celestina arranged for a historian from the dragon clan to fly to the castle several times a month to tutor the boys. Ronald, who aspires to teach history at the university one day, has been begging to spend the next summer studying dragon lore with the historian and with my brother who has been writing his third book on the subject.

Celestina has proved to be a just and capable queen, and I serve gladly as her helpmate.

"Soren," Raya called as she came running into the bailey yard. "It's time."

"It's time?" Gray, who'd been helping with the training, tossed his practice sword to the ground and took off running toward the castle. "I promised to let Patty know!"

"Go on." Raya smiled as she nudged my arm. "Sky Girl is asking for you."

I felt faint. The boys all stopped their training to watch me.

"It's been five years." My voice cracked.

"Five *wonderful* years," Raya corrected.

"We'd given up hope that this was possible." And we'd been happy with the life we had. "Had we been greedy to ask for more?"

"Accepting a miracle is not greed."

"What if something goes wrong?" We shouldn't have tried for a child. It'd been reckless. And—

"You have paid and bribed and bullied the best mages and healers and midwives on the continent to attend her. You're not going to lose her."

"We shouldn't have done this." I began pacing. "This…this was a mistake."

"Breathe, my friend." Raya put her hand on my shoulder. "Go, be strong for your mate."

I gently lifted a lizard that had been perched on my shoulder and placed it on the snowy ground before jogging toward the castle. My heart thudded in my throat.

The boys tried to follow me, but Raya deftly intercepted them and started playing a game of tag.

It seems to take forever to reach the tower room. Celestina had reclaimed the room in the tower that had once been her punishment. She'd turned the space into our royal chambers. We'd installed windows and lavish furniture, which made it comfortable. But despite its luxuries, it was still at the top of a long, winding staircase. Celestina cried out before I could reach the door. Her shriek echoed down the tower's stairs. And I charged up those last steps like a raging bull.

Dragons laid eggs only when they mated with another dragon while both were in their dragon form. Otherwise, the dragon had to endure giving birth just like the humans which, from what I'd heard, was bloody and messy and dangerous.

Hence the need to hire mages, healers, and midwives. The room was crowded with them. I had to shimmy between the crush of bodies to get to the bed where my love lay on top of the covers dressed in a white cotton gown. Sweat coated her forehead. Gwen, Petunia, and Amaya were all at the head of the bed. Gwen wiped Celestina's face with a soft wool cloth.

"You should have sent for me sooner," I scolded and offered Celestina my hand to hold as I knelt beside the bed. She took my hand and squeezed as if trying to crush all my bones.

"I didn't want to interrupt the boys' training. They so love their time with you." Her voice was breathy. Weak. It frightened me. My gaze shot to my sister who was standing at the foot of the bed with the midwife she'd brought with her. The older woman with her gray hair wrapped up into a bun looked so serious as she shifted Celestina's bent legs, spreading them a bit wider.

"The boys might forgive you for pulling me away from their training considering the work you're putting into giving them a new sibling," I told Celestina. "Raya had to fight them off with her sword to keep them from following me up here."

Celestina tried to smile at that, but her face tightened with pain and her back arched off the bed.

Fuck.

She squeezed my sword hand so hard, I feared I'd never be able to swing a sword again. But I gritted my teeth and let her use me to relieve a small portion of her burden.

"The baby is coming," the midwife announced. I'd noticed that the older woman had pushed the mages and healers and other midwives to the side. "A few more pushes, and you'll be done."

Celestina, breathing hard, nodded. Gwen continued to wipe the cloth over Celestina's sweaty face.

"Moonglow, why don't you just turn to air and leave the baby behind on the bed?" Amaya, who looked a little green, asked.

"The baby would transform into air with her," the midwife answered without even looking up at us. "She must stay corporal and push…now."

Celestina cried out. Her beautiful round belly spasmed so hard I could see the muscles moving below her white gown. She arched her back again and squeezed my hand with the strength of a god. I groaned but didn't pull away from her. I'd never pull away from her.

"Annnnd…" the midwife said, drawing out that one little word, "your baby is here."

The room exploded with cheers. Though, when I looked over my shoulder, I saw Amaya tip over backward and hit the floor. Passed out. Juniper crouched beside her daughter, patting her forehead with the damp cloth Gwen had been using.

I couldn't explain the relief I felt when I gazed into Celestina's beautiful indigo eyes. She looked exhausted. But she was breathing. And alive.

I kissed the side of her head. Her hair was damp with sweat.

"You are the most beautiful creature in this world," I whispered. "And when you're stronger, I'm going to need to take some of that lovely blood of yours to heal the hand you've just demolished."

"Sorry about that."

"I'm not."

The midwife came over to us. She held the baby, now wrapped up in a tight bundle, as if she were carrying the most precious treasure in the world.

She was.

"Here is your daughter," the midwife said as I helped Celestina sit up so she could hold our baby.

"Our daughter," Celestina repeated in wonder as if she couldn't believe what she was seeing. The round little face was almost a mirror image of Celestina's. And she had a shock of curly brown hair on the top of her head that resembled Celestina's silky mane. But the babe had my eyes— green with golden flecks.

The beautiful little creature wiggled a bit in Celestina's arms before she opened her mouth and showed off a perfect pair of tiny fangs.

"Look, Sky Girl. It's just like you predicted. She's a vampire," Raya whispered from over my shoulder.

I hadn't noticed until that moment that the mages and healers and midwives, save for the one still attending to Celestina, had all left the room. I imagined Raya had something to do with that.

"She's just like her father." Celestina's smile lit up the room. "What a charming little vampire."

It was hard to remember the time when we'd first met, and Celestina had been afraid of vampires and their ability to trick and charm. *Look at her now—loving me, loving our daughter, and working hard within our kingdom to protect vampires from those who might want to enslave us for our blood.*

The tiny baby wiggled some more, stronger this time like she wanted out of the bundle the midwife had made. And when she opened her mouth again, she screamed. It was a high-pitched screech that had me jumping to my feet. As I moved closer to her, a rush of heat seared the side of my face.

What the hell?

"Look! She's also a dragon," Gwen said with a laugh. She quickly grabbed a blanket and used it to smother the flames devouring the nearest wall tapestry. "A strong dragon at that. Warmlings don't usually manifest the ability to breathe fire until they are about a year old. Juniper and I will help you baby-proof the castle."

"Thank you," I said, my heart pounding. "A vampire with dragon powers. Or perhaps a dragon with vampiric traits. Either way, she's perfect." I touched the baby's velvety soft cheek, and the little infant wrapped her tiny hand around one of my fingers.

My heart exploded.

"She is perfect," my beautiful Celestina repeated as she gazed up at me. "I used to look out that window over there, dreaming of my future, wishing for the dragons in that valley to come and rescue me. I never—not even in my wildest imaginings—could have ever foreseen finding the life you have given me, Soren. Look at us. We're together. And we have *her*. Who would have ever believed this could be possible? You took me into your camp when I was nothing more than a slave but treated me like my life mattered. You saw my magic when I called myself ordinary. You loved me when I felt unlovable. And now, thanks to you, I have a kingdom, a mate who loves me, and a beautiful girl who looks like her handsome father." She placed her hand on my arm. "I love you, Soren."

Careful not to jostle our new bundle of joy, I kissed Celestina. "I love you, my dearest Sky Girl," I whispered against her honey-sweet lips. "I thank the fates for giving me to you."

"Goddess help us, they're starting to kiss again," Amaya scoffed from where she was still sitting on the floor.

Celestina laughed as she pulled me close, tugging at my sore hand until I was on the bed with her nestled between my legs and her back pressed to my front so I could hold both Celestina and our new baby.

"What should we name her?" I asked, surprised we hadn't talked much about names before now.

"That's an easy one." She caressed the baby's forehead making our daughter sigh with pleasure as her sparkling little eyes slipped closed. "She represents everything we've dreamed about, everything we've wished for. She's our Hope."

"Hope," I repeated, testing the feel of the name. It felt…right. "Princess Hope," I amended. "You're going to have an exciting life here with me to train you in combat, your four older brothers to tease you but also watch over you, and a mother who will teach you wondrous things like how to fly into rainbows. Welcome to your kingdom, Princess."

Thank you for reading
Curse of the Midnight Dragon

Thank you so much for joining me on the journey through my Moonlight Dragon series. I wrote the first book while my mother was in the hospital and then in hospice. I poured my frustrations of not being able to help her heal into the story. Sorry Celestina. I wrote *Curse of the Midnight Dragon* after my mother had passed away. It's a story that carries the burden of my grief. I would like to say that, in writing the book, I have exorcised the pain of losing a parent. But that would be a lie. Pain and loss dig their claws deep into your soul and show up at the most inconvenient moments. Through the writing of this book, though, I've learned how to better deal with my negative emotions that burble up to the surface to wash away my happiness.

While this is the end of the series, it's not the end of the magic. Sign up for my e-newsletter for updates on when new romantic fantasies will be published at www.dorothymcfalls.com

If you enjoyed this book, I would appreciate it if you'd help other readers enjoy it, too. After all, most books are sold by word of mouth. What can you do?

Recommend it. Please help other readers find this book by recommending it to friends, readers' groups, social media, and discussion boards.

Review it. Please tell other readers why you liked this book by reviewing it.

I owe a debt of thanks to my readers who have supported me throughout my writing journey. These romantic fantasies aren't the kinds of books many of you expected from me. Thank you to the readers who followed me from cozy mysteries into a new genre. Also, thank you to the new readers who have discovered my writing through this series. You are all gifts. I especially would like to thank Melissa Widener for beta reading an early draft of *Curse of the Midnight Dragon* and Sara Brodt who is working on bringing the books alive with audiobooks.

About the Author

Dorothy McFalls was born in New York but raised in South Carolina. She makes her home in South Carolina. Though writing has always been a passion, she pursued an undergraduate degree in Wildlife Biology and a graduate degree in Public Administration and Urban Planning. She put her educational experience to use, having worked in all branches and all levels of government including local, regional, state, and federal. She even spent time during college working for a non-profit environmental watchdog organization.

Switching from government service and community planning to fiction writing wasn't as big of a change as some might think. Her government work was all about the stories of the people and the places where they live. As an urban planner, Dorothy loved telling the stories of the people she met. And from that, her desire to tell the tales that were so alive in her heart grew until she could not ignore it any longer. In 2001, she took a leap of faith and pursued her dream of writing fiction full-time. * *Dorothy also writes mysteries as Dorothy St. James*

Visit Dorothy McFalls at:
http://www.dorothymcfalls.com
http://www.dorothystjames.com

Books by Dorothy McFalls

Romantic Fantasy
The Moonlight Dragon Duology
The Last Moonlight Dragon
Curse of the Moonlight Dragon

Regency Romances
The Marriage List
Lady Iona's Rebellion
The Nude

Paranormal Romances
Taken by Moonlight

The Protectors Series
A Wizard for Christmas
Neptune's Lair
Mystical Seduction

Romantic Suspense
The Huntress

Books by Dorothy St. James
Read all of Dorothy's delicious Southern mysteries.

Ms. Starr's Most Inconvenient Change of Heart
(A Raven's Run Mystery)

The Beloved Bookroom Mystery Series
Book 1: The Broken Spine
Protecting the printed word can be deadly.
Book 2: A Perfect Bind
Secrets in a library comes at a cost.
Book 3: A Book Club to Die For
Getting into this book club is murder.

Southern Chocolate Shop Mystery Series
Book 1: Asking for Truffle
Death in a chocolate shop.
Book 2: Playing with Bonbon Fire
Beach music, spicy chocolates, and murder.
Book 3: In Cold Chocolate
Sea turtles, chocolate turtles, and a shot in the dark.
Book 4: Bonbon with the Wind
A hurricane, pirate's treasure, and a new batch of chocolates.

The White House Gardener Mysteries
Flowerbed of State
The Scarlet Pepper
Oak and Dagger

Birds of Paradise
(An Aloha Pete Short Story

Milton Keynes UK
Ingram Content Group UK Ltd.
UKHW020156291024
450401UK00022B/277/J